Fealty to the King

Children of Cain

BASED ON THE 927-YEAR HISTORY
OF THE SNARSHYIM EMPIRE

FEALTY TO THE KING © copyright 2014 by Milo Swanton. All rights reserved. No part of this book may be reproduced in any form whatsoever, by photography or xerography or by any other means, by broadcast or transmission, by translation into any kind of language, nor by recording electronically or otherwise, without permission in writing from the author, except by a reviewer, who may quote brief passages in critical articles or reviews.

ISBN 13: 978-1-940014-27-2

Library of Congress Catalog Number: 2014945659

Printed in the United States of America
First Printing: 2014
18 17 16 15 14   5 4 3 2 1

Cover and interior design by James Monroe Design, LLC.

This book is also available in an electronic version.

Wise Ink, Inc.
Minneapolis, Minnesota

www.wiseinkpub.com
To order, visit www.itascabooks.com or call 1-800-901-3480.
Reseller discounts available.

Fealty to the King

Children of Cain

Milo Swanton

WISE Ink
CREATIVE • PUBLISHING

My thanks to all my family and friends who played roles in my world throughout the years I imagined it.

Thanks to Kevin and Dave for encouraging me to pursue my dream of publishing my writing, and also to Ryan for his encouragement and listening to the chapters as I wrote them. I thank my first readers, David, Phil, and Katie, and the real Nelber and Kulm for inspiring memorable characters. More thanks go to the professionals who helped prepare my book: Amy and the others at Wise Ink Creative Publishing; my editor Connie who urged me to use what I call "long hyphens"; my proofreader Molly; Shawn, who drew the graphics; and Jay for interior design.

Contents

Destiny
Recorded Year 860

To Benefit the Clan | 3
Back He Must Go | 13
The Parchment Contains Words | 20
Loyal Companion | 26
Live or Die | 37
What's Left of It | 43
Clanlord of the Herkt | 50
Deal | 65
To Me He's Ugly | 72
Secrets | 80
Just His Head | 93
Conflagration Waiting to Happen | 105
I Prefer Green | 109

Vision
Recorded Year 861

Citadels | 119
Best News | 130
Reunions | 138

Her Pies are Delicious | 142
His Name Is Thoiren | 157
Rash | 173
Thoughts of a Maiden | 180
The Chizdekyim Way | 185
Prodigy of Banshim's Anvil | 200
Amends | 213
It's Your Color | 225
A Strong Man | 237
General Conflagration | 251
Sudden Family | 261
What I Have for You Better Stab your Heart | 265
The Tribemaster Likes His Banners | 270

Knowledge
Recorded Year 863

Mark of Cain | 279
Consummated in Blood | 288
Kill Grebnar | 297
Consummated in Tears | 302
The Biggest | 314
Consummated in Love | 317
Hojyim Colors | 323
Written in the Snarshyim Language | 334
Name Change | 339
Downfall of the Empire | 347

Greatness
Recorded Year 868

Done by High Summer | *359*
All Our Forces | *368*
To Taubueth | *374*
Battle Pennants | *378*
Lord of the Snarshyimt | *390*
A Snarshyim Kingdom | *403*

Epilogue | *423*
Characters | *425*
Snarshyim Language Primer | *430*
Glossary | *433*

The opening chapter from the next novel | *435*

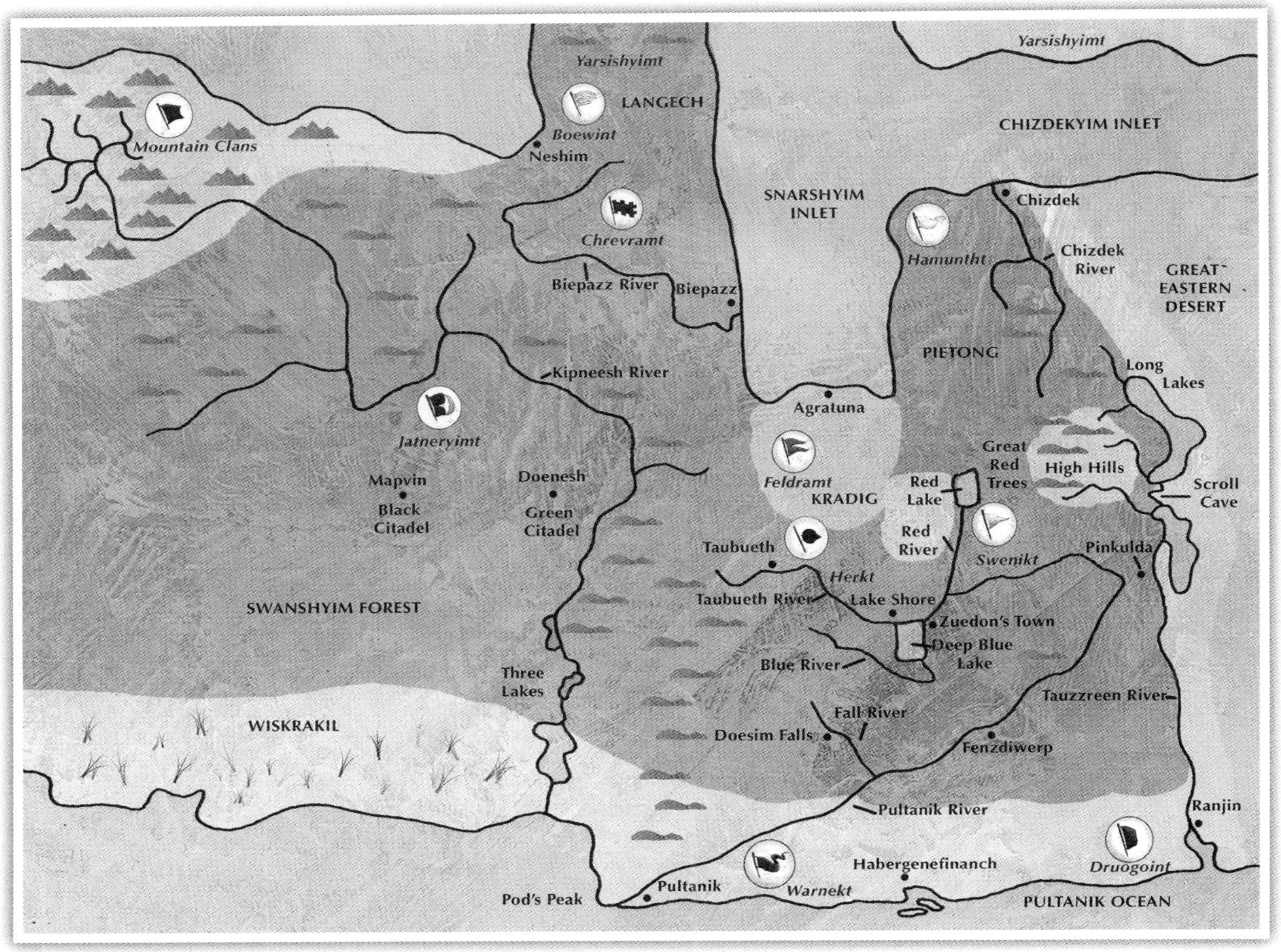
Yarsishyimt
LANGECH
Boewint
Neshim
Mountain Clans
Yarsishyimt
CHIZDEKYIM INLET
SNARSHYIM INLET
Chizdek
Chrevramt
Hamuntht
Chizdek River
GREAT EASTERN DESERT
Biepazz River
Biepazz
PIETONG
Long Lakes
Kipneesh River
Agratuna
Jatneryimt
Great Red Trees
High Hills
Feldramt
Mapvin
Doenesh
Red Lake
Scroll Cave
KRADIG
Black Citadel
Green Citadel
Red River
Taubueth
Swenikt
Pinkulda
Herkt
Taubueth River
Lake Shore
SWANSHYIM FOREST
Zuedon's Town
Deep Blue Lake
Blue River
Three Lakes
Tauzzreen River
Fall River
WISKRAKIL
Doesim Falls
Fenzdiwerp
Ranjin
Pultanik River
Habergenefinanch
Druogoint
Pultanik
Warnekt
Pod's Peak
PULTANIK OCEAN

Destiny

Recorded Year 860

To Benefit the Clan

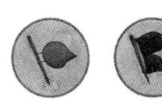

Herkt, Jatneryimt

BRUTEZ   **SWANSHYIM FOREST**

Brutez from the clan of the Herkt crept as close as he dared to the nearest of many campfires blazing in the forest on a chilly autumn night. He crouched within the undergrowth, watching a blinking ember from the fire settle on the boot of one of five men huddled around the flames, and strained to hear their conversation.

"Grebnar should return from the coast soon," the owner of the boot told his four companions as he snuffed the ember under a thumb.

Brutez recognized the voice of Sir Rendif, Lord of the Jatneryimt.

Rendif continued, "We'll raid Agratuna if he reports he found no Herkt."

One of the others nudged closer to the blaze and puffed through clenched teeth, "Do we have enough men?"

Rendif stroked his graying hair. "Puutnam reports Matkulk's force has reached Doenesh. Together we'll have several hundred warriors."

As Brutez watched the man sitting opposite the fire gaze in his direction, he crouched lower, taking care not to rustle the foliage.

Rendif kept talking, "If Grebnar doesn't return tomorrow, we'll move toward Agratuna to meet him."

The gazing man raised a finger in Brutez's direction, shouting, "Something's breathing there!"

Brutez crashed into the forest, no longer concerned about making noise. He heard Rendif yelling orders, and the shouts of men as they chased him. The way ahead was dark, so he navigated by the silhouettes of the trees in the glimmer of a quarter moon. He ran as fast as he dared without charging into a tree. Boughs of needles stung him in the face. Stumbling from the branches, he leaped to avoid tumbling over a log.

He kept running, and the shouts faded into the forest behind him. The crisp air was invigorating and heightened his senses. He heard himself breathing, and the crackle of twigs underfoot echoing in the hollows.

The echo bothered him. When he held his breath, breathing sounds persisted, and when he cut through a thicket, the brush rustled after him. Somebody *followed*. Brutez clutched his war hammer and ran with it swinging alongside his hip.

A sword ripped through his frock. He whirled, landing a hammering blow into his assailant's shoulder. A shield slammed his head, loosening his helmet. He put a knee into his opponent's groin and clubbed him to the ground with the war hammer.

Others approached, so he scrambled up a hill to his right. Labored breathing followed him, and a hatchet whizzed past his ear. He wanted to run faster, but the moon was behind a cloud, and he couldn't see well enough.

The hill was a long and steep incline, and his pursuers were unable to stay close. At the crest, he no longer heard them. Plunging down the shorter but steeper decline on the other side, he lost his footing. He dropped the war hammer and dodged trees, trying to regain his balance, but slipped on the stony streambed at the bottom. His loosened helmet fell off while he clambered from the water. The first step revealed he twisted his ankle, but the prospect of capture motivated him to keep going.

He faltered for several hundred more cubits before stopping to listen. Hearing nothing but wind in the treetops, he rested on the leafy ground. He wriggled off his boot and tied a makeshift splint to the swelling ankle. Cutting off the top of the boot, he tied the lower half around his foot.

Deciding against a probably fruitless and certainly dangerous search for his mount, he sought a clearing. He found a gap in the forest and sat on a fallen trunk to wait for a break in the clouds so he could look at the stars.

Brutez asked himself what he was doing in the forest with a twisted ankle. The answer came. *Following orders for the good of my clan*. He wondered what he would do if he gave the orders.

The upper winds opened a hole in the clouds. Brutez obtained a fix from the stars and hobbled in an easterly direction toward camp. He had three horizons to go on the shaky ankle, but the words he overheard by the fire urged him onward.

Klinteg   Swanshyim Forest

Klinteg spoke, "Uncle Vulrath, we should break camp."

Clanlord Vulrath chewed on a piece of bread. He had a flattened nose between narrow gray eyes. His wide face was framed by a sweeping bearded chin around a set of curled lips. Between bites, he asked, "Why, Klinteg?"

"We should find the Jatneryimt before they find us."

Both warriors squatted on the turf beneath a stag-hide canopy next to the brook running through their forest camp. Wind rustled in the treetops, dispersing early morning sunbeams into patterns of light over the camp's cluster of tents full of sleeping warriors. Sentries roamed the perimeter, and some mounts stood roped together, snorting and shuffling their hooves among the first fallen leaves of the season.

Vulrath talked with his mouth full. "Let them find us, so I know where they are."

"We should send a scout." Klinteg scrubbed his hands in the brook. The water gurgled over a bed of stones and pebbles, banked by a row of spears stabbing into the soft ground. Red pennants, shaped like drops of blood, flapped from the ends of the shafts.

"I sent Brutez last night, but he hasn't returned," said Vulrath.

"Perhaps something happened to him." Klinteg watched bushtails carry nuts up the trees. Some of the curious rodents scampered in front of the tents, sniffing the bony remains of last night's feast lying in the ashes of spent fires.

"Nonsense, Brutez is our best scout. He's stealthier than a feline beast and runs like a stag through the forest." Vulrath devoured the last bite of bread.

Klinteg dunked his head into the brook's bubbling cool water. When he emerged, a voice called, "Clanlord, I found some Jatneryimt!"

Vulrath snorted. "Heptor, I ordered you to remain in camp."

Heptor stood across the brook. "I couldn't sleep, so I explored the river and saw the Jatneryimt, about ten of them." He was a sturdy young man with a squarish head, small ears, thick cheeks, and curly brown hair. A war hammer was tucked into a leather belt cinched around his loose-fitting tunic.

"Maybe they'll lead us to the rest," said Klinteg.

Vulrath stepped from beneath the canopy, planting a foot in the center of the brook, and cupped his hands around his mouth. "Slumbering Herkt, prepare for battle!" He waited for the fifty warriors in the camp to assemble in a half cirlce around him. "Heptor spotted Jatneryimt at the river. We'll kill all except one."

Vulrath   **Kipneesh River**

Vulrath observed nine mounted men following the rushing Kipneesh River southward on the near bank. The lead rider's cape was the Jatneryim colors of green and black. The clanlord ordered his warriors to attack.

The Herkt swarmed from the woods along the river. One Jatneryim mount threw its rider into the turbulent water. A well-timed club dismounted another rider before he had wielded his sword. Both fallen Jatneryimt were slain. The two trailing riders attempted to flee upriver, but their mounts stumbled, and they ended up lying among the rocks with chopped-off heads. Another tried to escape to the opposite bank but was washed down the rapids and likely drowned.

The leader fought with a sword but had no chance after his three remaining men fell. His attackers pummeled his mount's legs until the poor beast collapsed. He was disarmed and pinned to the ground by several spears aimed at his throat.

Stepping from the trees, Vulrath commanded his burly nephew to bring the captive to his feet. Klinteg held the Jatneryim upright, arms pinned behind his cape. The prisoner glared at the clanlord with brown eyes.

Vulrath motioned to the slain Jatneryim warriors. "Where were you going with these others?" He placed a dagger's edge along the prisoner's throat, digging the tip beneath the cape's drawstring.

The man didn't flinch.

Vulrath cut the drawstring. "We left a brave one alive. He must die."

A shout came from across river. Brutez waved his arms less than a stone's throw away. The young man stood in a sandy area on the opposite bank where the rapids calmed to a shallow flow around some rocks. His narrow-shaved beard glinted red in the brightening sun, redder than his ruffled hair. He had a bruise on the left side of his head, scratches across his nose and cheeks, a torn frock, and the remnant of a boot on one foot, which he tried to keep from touching the ground.

"He's hurt," said Vulrath. "Larboelm, get a rope to help him cross."

The husky Larboelm disappeared into the forest. Heptor joined several other Herkt plucking anything valuable from the Jatneryim bodies. Other warriors recovered four mounts, including one with a shimmering ebony mane. Grebnar's mount was too badly wounded and had to be killed, which Vulrath regretted because he would have retained the magnificent animal for himself.

Larboelm returned with the rope. He tied one end around a tree and slung the remaining coil to Brutez. The scout came across, declining offers of assistance while emerging from the water. He stumbled along the riverbank around several fallen Jatneryimt, looking at each body as he passed. Reaching Vulrath standing by the surviving Jatneryim, Brutez knelt, dripping at his clanlord's feet.

"Swift Brutez, why do you limp?"

Brutez looked up. "Twisted ankle, Clanlord."

"Look at our prisoner."

Brutez rose, again favoring his good ankle, and looked into the man's face. "This is Sir Grebnar the Bold, Sir Rendif's most trusted companion."

Heptor asked, "How do you know that, Brother?"

"I've spied on him many times."

"You'll never spy on him again." Vulrath shoved Heptor aside. "I've decided how he's going to die." He grinned at Klinteg, who held Grebnar tight, and took the prisoner's sword from the ground. "I'm going to slice his throat with his own blade."

"Don't!"

Vulrath glared at Brutez.

"Pardon, Clanlord. I only mean to benefit the clan. I expect Rendif will pay a large ransom for this man."

"He defies me." Vulrath studied Grebnar staring at him. "He must die unless he answers my questions."

"*I'll* answer your questions," said Brutez.

What? The bold remark surprised Vulrath, but then he recalled Brutez's scouting mission. "Of course, what did you discover last night?"

The circle of warriors tightened around the scout as he spoke.

"I overheard Sir Rendif talk about Grebnar coming to report whether Agratuna is vulnerable to attack."

Vulrath snapped a look at Grebnar, but the Jatneryim remained stoic. "Brutez, what will Rendif do when Grebnar doesn't return?"

"He'll join another Jatneryim force from Doenesh and move toward the coast, intending to meet Grebnar."

"That's it!" Vulrath waved Grebnar's sword. "We'll gather our forces and go north to meet them." The noisy Kipneesh River engulfed the cheers of his men. He commanded, "Brutez, go with two men and take Grebnar to Taubueth, using these mounts we captured."

Klinteg flattened Grebnar with a nasty blow across the chin. The prisoner's cape dropped, cut free earlier by Vulrath. Klinteg retrieved the green and black garment and tucked it under his arm to keep. "You live, Jatneryim, but you'll wish you hadn't."

Klinteg   Swanshyim Forest

A fogbank ahead on the left wasn't silent like the others. Klinteg heard sputtering mounts and rankling armor within the misty vapor. He rode with his uncle, the clanlord, through a burned-out section of the forest at the head of a large force of the Herkt during their search for the Jatneryimt. Ashen, leafless trees spindled to the heights like gargantuan bones picked clean by the wind and bleached by the sun. An occluded sky added a dreary backdrop to the lifeless monoliths, threatening rain. White wisps coiled within a green belt of vegetation growing around the scorched trees in the blotches of fog.

Vulrath signaled a halt for better listening and waited while the Jatneryimt moved farther left within the fog, but Heptor caused a disturbance by losing control of his mount. The clanlord growled, and he clenched a gauntlet, one with a Herkyim blooddrop embroidered in beads. He swung his arm as if to strike Heptor with the beaded gauntlet, but instead waved it to signal the attack.

The fifty Herkt from the clanlord's camp were joined by two hundred more from other patrols. Most were on foot. They charged through gaps in the foliage, shouting. Although some had spears, most carried axes, war hammers, and cudgels. Red blooddrop pennants flapped from the shafts and handles of the weapons, on the reins of the mounts, and alongside the men's hips.

Sir Rendif's warriors surged from the fog, carrying two different banners on poles. Green semi-circles billowed like sails. The other banners were upright black rectangles with triangular notches on the outer edges. A greater number of Jatneryimt wore helmets and brandished incisive armaments, wielding more spears and swords than the Herkt did with their battering implements.

Klinteg watched Heptor ride into the fight behind a screen of footmen, attacking a line of Jatneryimt along a patch of mushy ground. One Herk flipped his adversary into the slop behind the line. Heptor's mount, struggling for footing, trampled the fallen warrior's chest. Another Jatneryim dropped like deadweight when a monstrous club busted his skull. Swinging his war hammer, Heptor followed his clansmen through a hole into the Jatneryim ranks.

Vulrath prompted his mount forward into the skirmish, flanked by his bodyguard, Larboelm. Klinteg followed, using his great axe to deflect a Jatneryim hatchet. He struck a downward blow into the enemy's neck. Blood gushed from the wound, and Klinteg finished the dazed Jatneryim with a slash across the throat.

Larboelm wielded a spiked mace. Dismounting to swing it in a wider arc, he embedded the spikes into a Jatneryim's shield. He yanked the mace, tearing the shield from his opponent's grasp, and he hammered the defenseless warrior with his own shield. The blows splintered the shield as pieces broke from the whirling spiked ball.

Still mounted, Klinteg joined Vulrath, and both looked down at Larboelm as the bodyguard stood by the body of the Jatneryim he had battered to the ground.

"You're a brute," said Vulrath.

Larboelm raised his mace in a crude salute. A piece of shield hung from it.

Vulrath pointed. "Heptor's in trouble. Save him."

On foot, Larboelm crossed a patch of waterlogged brush toward Heptor.

Klinteg stayed with his uncle while the battle raged around them, watching Heptor and Larboelm. Heptor fought with his war hammer from atop his mount against three other riders surrounding him. Larboelm dropped his mace and rolled below an enemy mount, tugging a foreleg until beast and rider tumbled, allowing Heptor to escape through the opening. The dismounted Jatneryim and the two mounted ones surrounded Larboelm. Heptor charged the two riders, shouting and swinging his war hammer. Larboelm tackled the dismounted Jatneryim, killing him with a dagger. He retrieved his mace and joined Heptor fighting against the riders.

The fog enveloped them, so Klinteg gazed elsewhere. He saw Sir Rendif, whom he recognized from the time he was exchanged as a hostage, and followed the Jatneryim leader into a fogbank. Emerging from the mist without finding Rendif, he sighted Larboelm charging into a line of enemy warriors.

The clanlord was *in trouble*. Klinteg rode through the damp forest brush and saw his uncle fall from his mount within a circle of Jatneryimt. Larboelm was enraged, assaulting the enemy warriors with his spiked mace. Klinteg charged, hefting his axe in rabid fury. The Jatneryimt offered token resistance before breaking away.

Larboelm knelt beside the fallen leader. Klinteg dismounted to join him, leaving his axe in a long holster on his mount. Vulrath was pierced through the torso, pinned to a deathbed of squishy moss by the sword he took from Grebnar. Klinteg pressed an ear close to his uncle's moving lips.

"Fight!" the clanlord forced a last word and expired.

Klinteg extracted the sword from the body. Heptor and other Herkt gathered at the spot. Klinteg regained his mount and organized the men for a renewed attack against the Jatneryimt. The enemy warriors had disappeared into the fog, and their victorious shouts resounded in the sepulchral forest. Klinteg urged Larboelm to follow, but the disconsolate bodyguard refused to move.

The battle couldn't continue if Larboelm lost heart to fight. Klinteg dismounted, thinking of another means for vengeance. "We're done here. We have a Jatneryim to kill at Taubueth."

Back He Must Go

Herkt, Jatneryimt

Brutez   **Taubueth**

A misty rain dripped from the treetops over Brutez riding his new mount, the one with a shimmering ebony mane. Three other riders followed. The captured Sir Grebnar had two nooses tied around his neck and attached to the mounts of Rankeb and Konrash, two young Herkyim warriors who were Heptor's friends.

Brutez led them through soppy branches and past a row of dilapidated sheds to the base of a wall standing in the forest thirty horizons east of the Kipneesh River. Rankeb and Konrash paced their mounts sideways in opposite directions, choking Grebnar with the nooses between them. The Jatneryim let out a pained grunt each time the movements of the equines tugged the ropes.

Brutez gazed up the wall and studied the weathered rock. The stronghold at Taubueth hardly could be called a castle because it consisted of nothing more than a wall surrounding an oblong courtyard and a donjon with no towers. It lacked a moat and gate.

An old man with a mass of snow-white frazzled hair and beard appeared with guards on the rampart overhead. He was Zamtoth, the father of Brutez and Heptor. "My son, where are Vulrath and the other warriors?"

"Fighting Jatneryimt, Father." Brutez passed a hand through his damp, matted hair, careful to avoid the healing bruise on the side of his head. "I couldn't join the battle because I twisted my ankle on a patrol."

Zamtoth ordered the guards to lower the only means of entry to Taubueth, a crooked ladder made from branches and lashed together with leather thongs. If not for the solid construction by Taubueth's builders, the stronghold long would have crumbled to rubble from lack of care. The forest advanced to the base of the wall, and a thick mass of trees invaded one end of the courtyard. The Herkt occupied Taubueth for centuries only because it was there, for they never constructed much.

Konrash asked Brutez if he wanted Grebnar put on the rack.

"No, chain him in my quarters."

Rankeb and Konrash untied Grebnar's ropes from their mounts. The Jatneryim fell to the ground, gasping for air through his strangled throat. Heptor's friends ascended the ladder with the ends of the ropes, dragging the prisoner by the neck after them. Grebnar lost whatever remained of his consciousness.

Two guards descended to take the mounts to a stable outside the wall. Brutez made a painful ascent on his tender ankle, wincing as he stepped off to the rampart. Zamtoth accompanied him down a stairs to the ground inside Taubueth.

Brutez told his father about the Jatneryim prisoner, and how he thought Sir Rendif would pay ransom for his release. He described his patrol, about overhearing Sir Rendif's plan to raid Agratuna, and then twisting his ankle while he ran away.

"You mentioned a battle, Son."

"I have no news of it, Father. The clanlord sent me here with Sir Grebnar before pursuing the Jatneryimt."

Brutez joined Rankeb and Konrash at a crackling fire by

the donjon doorway. Some women fed the three famished warriors with cheese and smoked sausage on toasted bread, washed down with brew.

Brutez retired to his chamber inside the donjon after supper, carrying a link of sausage for the prisoner there. He sighed upon entering the dimly lit room. Grebnar was chained face into the wall so his limbs stretched in four directions. Brutez set the sausage next to a flickering candle in a recess over his bed. He unchained the prisoner's arms and one leg, leaving him on the floor, and lay upon the bed on the side of his face without the bruise to fall asleep in the glow of the candle.

The prisoner's coughs wakened him. Grebnar leaned against the wall. His dark hair was cropped across his brow, and his lighter colored mustache was trimmed in a straight line along his upper lip. Brutez reached for the sausage next to the waxen remains of the candle and tossed it to the Jatneryim.

Grebnar spoke for the first time since his capture. "Thanks." His voice rasped from yesterday's torture.

"You're called the Bold."

"I've killed many Herkt."

"I've spied on many Jatneryimt. You failed to kill me many times."

"I remember your father," said Grebnar. "He used to lead your clan." The Jatneryim bit from the sausage.

"He aged."

Grebnar talked between bites. "Why aren't you clanlord? Can't your father choose his successor?"

Brutez shrugged. "The strongest becomes clanlord. Vulrath killed my three older brothers in fair combat. Heptor and I were too young to fight."

"Why don't you challenge him now?"

Brutez jumped from the bed to pace before Grebnar. "You *would* like to see the Herkt quarrel among ourselves."

Grebnar declined to reply, instead eating more sausage.

"I'll fetch some brew." Brutez stepped toward the door.

"I'll try to have you treated well, but I can't guarantee that will happen."

Zamtoth   Taubueth

Zamtoth joined his son as shouts in the night from outside the stronghold sent them scurrying to the rampart.

"The warriors must be back," said Brutez.

Klinteg called from beyond the wall, "Where's the Jatneryim prisoner? Bring Sir Grebnar out here."

The ladder already was lowered to the outside. Thick clouds obscured the moon, so Zamtoth grabbed a torch to see better into the darkness below. Klinteg stood at the foot of the ladder, staring upward with beady eyes into the light of the flame. Several dozen warriors surrounded him, standing in more torchlight among the trees.

Brutez asked, "Klinteg, what do you want with Grebnar?"

"His kinsmen killed the clanlord. He'll pay with his life."

Brutez descended the ladder. "You'll throw away the ransom."

Zamtoth saw his son keeping most of his weight on his better foot.

Brutez reached the ground. "That's a high price for revenge."

Klinteg shouted into his face, "I'm clanlord! I'll do as I please."

Brutez shouted back, "What makes you clanlord?"

"Nobody has challenged me." Klinteg stepped backward to cross his arms.

Brutez stepped forward. "*I do.*"

The warriors murmured. Zamtoth cringed as Klinteg slammed Brutez against the wall and drew a sword.

Klinteg yelled, "Insolent! I'll slash you with this same sword that killed Vulrath, and that will be the end of your challenge."

Zamtoth shouted in his commanding former clanlord's voice, "Stop!"

Klinteg withheld the sword. All eyes fixed on Zamtoth atop the wall. "This dispute must be resolved in tournament."

Klinteg lunged with the sword, but again Zamtoth commanded him to stop.

The former clanlord continued, "Klinteg, I gave three sons to your uncle so our clan wouldn't tear itself apart. My fourth son has the right to tournament." He appealed to the gathered warriors. "Valiant Herkt, many of you and your fathers served me faithfully. Brutez deserves a fair fight."

The sound of drawn weapons emanated from among the trees. The arrival of Rankeb and Konrash with Sir Grebnar saved Klinteg from immediate reply. They had hobbled the prisoner's feet and shackled an arm's-span length of chain to his wrists. They slung the chain around a parapet and shoved Grebnar over the side so he slammed face-first into the wall with a grunt.

Klinteg turned a full circle, scanning the warriors, and returned to face Zamtoth. "Brutez will have tournament midday tomorrow." He sheathed the sword. "His death merely is postponed."

Zamtoth objected, "The tournament must be a fair fight. Brutez injured his ankle serving the clan and needs time to heal."

Klinteg's mouth curled into a snarl, but hearing murmurs of agreement from the warriors behind him, he conceded. "Is a week enough?"

"Double that, a fortnight."

Klinteg shook his head, opening his mouth to speak.

Zamtoth intervened before his counteroffer was rejected. "You must present the relic swords. I hope you know where Vulrath stashed them."

"I'll bring them." Klinteg wrinkled his nose in a sneer. He shouted to Rankeb and Konrash, indicating Grebnar slung from the parapet. "Drop him."

Brutez straightened from leaning against the wall to countermand the order. "No, he stays! Clanlord Vulrath placed Sir Grebnar under my charge, and so he remains until we have a new clanlord." He called to Rankeb and Konrash, "Haul him up."

The pair hesitated until Klinteg turned away without objection. They pulled Grebnar's limp form to the rampart while Brutez climbed the ladder to get there.

"Return him to my quarters," Brutez commanded. "Leave him chained by one ankle as I had him."

Zamtoth watched the torchlight recede into forest darkness as the warriors left with Klinteg. He wasn't surprised they weren't stopping at Taubueth for the rest of the night because he knew well the restless nature of the deceased clanlord's nephew, much like his son, Heptor. Klinteg and his warriors would travel without rest until reaching home in a river valley fifteen horizons southeastward.

When Grebnar was gone Zamtoth asked, "Brutez, is that Jatneryim worth putting your life against Klinteg?"

"Grebnar is married to Sir Rendif's sister, so he and Rendif are wedlock brothers. Rendif depends on him to tip the Jatneryim balance of power against Matkulk."

"That's the true reason for returning him, not ransom." Zamtoth understood his son's bold challenge to lead the clan.

"Our clan benefits from Sir Rendif leading the Jatneryimt, which is more likely to continue if Sir Grebnar goes back to him."

Zamtoth agreed. No threat of reprisal would deter Matkulk from ravaging Herkyim lands. Rendif preferred striking places that didn't retaliate. "Then back he must go," the old man told his son. He liked how Brutez thought through matters before acting, more than any of his sons, of whom Heptor was the only other survivor.

"We must assume the Jatneryimt raided Agratuna, Father."

Zamtoth worried about his daughter, Majdel, the firstborn

of his children. She was given in marriage many years ago to the man who became Lord Chieftain Feldram living at Agratuna, and now the Herkt failed to protect the coastal settlement.

"I'll ask Shemjib to go there for news about your sister, Brutez. I want him to leave at daybreak before Heptor gets here."

Zamtoth expected Heptor and the other Taubueth warriors to arrive tomorrow, having stopped for the night while Klinteg's band continued in the dark. Heptor would want to go along to Agratuna, but Zamtoth's younger brother Shemjib, the uncle of Brutez and Heptor, had no patience for young Heptor's reckless nature.

"I'll send Rankeb and Konrash with him," said Brutez.

Zamtoth agreed Heptor's two friends should go before their beatings killed Grebnar.

The Parchment Contains Words

Swenikt

JORGIS　　　　　　　　**LONG LAKES**

A baleful western sky made Jorgis a concerned traveler.

"Hurry, Pokyer," he called to his lagging servant. "We must find shelter."

"I'm comin'." The stubby Pokyer struggled with a heavy pack over a large rock in his path.

Jorgis waited for him atop a low ridge, overlooking two long lakes near the great eastern desert. Pokyer caught up, and both men scrambled behind the ridge into a gully.

Jorgis pointed across the gulch. "See the crevice there? It might be a cave."

He scaled the rocky crags toward the spot. Looking back, he saw his servant wiping strands of blond hair from his eyes before starting to climb. Although no more than a few years older than Jorgis, Pokyer moved as slow as a man twice his age. He shifted his pack higher on his shoulder and clambered after Jorgis.

Thunderclouds rolled overhead. The wind blew against them at haphazard velocities. Light rain speckled the rocks and tickled the men's noses.

Jorgis reached the crevice and ducked inside as torrential rain pelted down. Pokyer labored the last slippery distance and almost fell into the cave. He tossed the pack down the hole before dropping inside to escape the furious weather.

"An unfortunate delay," said Jorgis. His voice's echo indicated the cave's considerable length, although its height allowed him only to crouch. "I didn't expect a storm, considering the fair weather when we started this morning."

The place was so bereft of light he couldn't see his hands. He reached into the darkness around his feet for Pokyer's sopping pack and rummaged through its contents.

Pokyer asked, "Whatcha lookin' fer?"

"The firerock." Jorgis dug around a flask and below a bedroll before locating the object he wanted. It was a hard lump, smooth to his touch. *"I have it!"* He extracted the firerock and placed it outside the cave's dripping entrance. The thing glowed when brought inside, a feeble luminosity but enough for Jorgis to see the black shape of his hand. He called into the depth, "Pokyer, where are you?"

"Here," Pokyer answered from the darkness. "I found somethin'."

"Not darkwings, I hope."

"No. This." Pokyer gave Jorgis a cylindrical object. It had knobby ends.

Jorgis lifted the firerock for a closer look. "A scroll. Is anything else back there?"

"Yup, more scrolls."

Thoiren   near Pinkulda

Chief Thoiren of the Swenikt sat with his wife, Befdaul, at the head of a jovial assembly in the easternmost room of their tribal longhouse. Sounds of feasting, games, laughter, and other lighthearted revelry filled the air. Although an aged couple, they radiated as much life as their granddaughters running among the people in the room. The chief winked to his wife as if to say, *Isn't this fun?*

The longhouse was a grand hall built on the western bank of the Tauzzreen River, a waterway flowing near the edge of the great eastern desert, across which neither invaders nor anybody ever came. Immense logs, once tall, straight pines in the forest, formed the northern and southern walls of the building. Woodwork lattices connected the walls in five places to divide the interior into four rooms. A thatch roof, supported by wooden beams, covered the structure.

The Swenikt lived eastward the Herkt. More peaceable than their warring neighbors, they paid an annual tribute of grain and livestock to the Herkt to be left alone. Instead of fighting, they concentrated on extracting good yield from the soil, so on the autumn day when the amount of daylight equaled the length of night, they gathered to celebrate a bumper crop.

A sandy-haired youth stood on a table and waved the crowd silent. He leaped a half turn on the wood surface to address his leader. "Chief Thoiren, tell us a story."

The others responded with cheers of agreement.

"Mercy." Thoiren shook his thinly white-haired head. "I've burdened you with my stories countless times." He became distracted by his granddaughter crawling on him. Befdaul stole the child's attention with an invitation into her waiting lap.

"You tell the best stories," said the young man, whereby he led the merry throng in a repetitive shout, "We want a story! We want a story!"

Thoiren waved his arms in capitulation and stood to the delight of his tribe. The young man jumped off the table, and the chief began his tale.

"When I was a young man, I possessed the ability to speak with inanimate objects. Befdaul taught me." He winked again at the sparkly-eyed woman holding their granddaughter. "I picked up a nut one day in the forest." He held forth a thumb and forefinger as if holding the nut and brought the imaginary seed to his nose. "I asked, 'Nut, what makes you grow?'"

Someone taunted, "He's talking to a nut!"

Thoiren grinned, moving his hand to his ear. "The nut answered, 'It's not my business to know what makes me grow. The knowledge to grow is inside me. I only know I'm supposed to become a tree.' I shouted at the nut, 'A tree!'" The chief waved the invisible seed above his head. "'I'll chop you down to build a house!'"

His audience shouted for more.

Thoiren obliged. "After my conversation with the nut, I shouted to the sky." He looked at the rafters. "'Sky, I know you drop rain to help stupid nuts become trees, but where do you get the water?'"

Someone yelled, "What did the sky say?"

"The sky in its infinite wisdom replied, 'I get rain from the same place I get snow!'"

Amid the laughter, Jorgis and Pokyer stepped into the hall. They were travelworn with unkempt hair, unshaved faces, and dirt-crusted cloaks. Pokyer stooped under the burden of his pack, but even standing straight, he would have been a head shorter than Jorgis.

Thoiren invited the newcomers to approach. "Jorgis, you arrive in time for our harvest feast. Did all go well at Chizdek?"

Jorgis knelt before him, showing the small bald spot on the back of his brown-haired head. "I won the hand of Chief Hamunth's daughter. She's coming in spring with her kin for the wedding."

"That's wonderful," said Befdaul with a smile. She released

her granddaughter who became restless with the apparent end to Thoiren's stories.

Jorgis stood. "I have another great prize." He poked the inattentive Pokyer in the ribs. The servant dropped his pack and produced a strange pale object from inside.

Thoiren asked, "What is it?"

"A scroll." Jorgis took the roll from Pokyer and unraveled a section on Thoiren's table. "It's one of twenty-seven we found in a cave three days upriver."

Thoiren, Befdaul, and anyone else close enough admired the pictures on the parchment. One drawing depicted a serpent in a tree. Another dramatized a majestic winged being with a brilliant sword guarding a hedgerow gate, and one more showed a man standing over the bleeding body of another.

Thoiren pointed at markings surrounding the pictures. "What's this, Jorgis?"

"Writing."

Thoiren was puzzled.

Jorgis explained, "The parchment contains words."

Of course. Thoiren remembered Jorgis telling him about such a thing, and how he learned to speak written words. "What does it say?"

"I don't know. The writing speaks an unknown language."

"A shame," said Befdaul. "The words must be as interesting as these pictures."

Jorgis breathed deep and stared into Thoiren's face. "Chief, I can learn the strange language of the scrolls by crossing the desert."

The people in the room murmured, and Thoiren waved them silent. "Jorgis, how would you cross?"

Jorgis prompted Pokyer to produce another scroll from his pack and took it from him to unroll. "Look at this map." He moved a finger along some curvy blue lines between a green area and a red one. "Here's the Tauzzreen River flowing between the forest and the desert. You can see the long lakes."

Thoiren pointed at a bended blue line within the green

area. "Is this the Pultanik River?"

Jorgis tapped the narrow space between the two rivers. "Yes, here's Pinkulda."

Pinkulda was located one horizon downriver on the ridge that prevented the Pultanik River from joining the Tauzzreen River from the west. Seeing where they were on the map, Thoiren scanned eastward. "Looks like mountains across the desert."

"Then many unknown lands beyond them," said Jorgis. "I wish to go there without delay. Do I have your permission, Chief?"

"Seems like a long way. Will you return before your bride arrives?"

"Although my heart yearns for a woman's love, I *do* desire to learn the secret of the scrolls."

Thoiren paused before responding, "Do as you wish."

"I thank you, my chief."

"You need not thank me. I'm curious, too."

"I'll return to the cave with adequate means to bring the other scrolls here for safekeeping. Then I hope to start my journey before the winter becomes too cold."

"A good plan." Thoiren stroked his thinning beard. He consulted the map. "How about going southward to this place on the coast? The trip's longer to your ultimate destination, but the desert crossing is shorter and should be warmer that way."

"Good suggestion. I can travel down the Tauzzreen River before crossing the desert."

Thoiren warned Jorgis about the tribe downriver. "Don't stray too far into Druogoinyim territory."

Befdaul leaned over the map. "Who will go with you to these far lands?"

"Pokyer will go." Jorgis patted his servant's back.

Pokyer forced a smile.

Thoiren rolled the map scroll together. "Listen people, I have another story."

Loyal Companion

Warnekt

Vinlon **Pultanik**

Vinlon, Tribemaster of the Warnekt, stood on a rooftop overlooking the Pultanik Ocean. The ocean's namesake river passed through rolling farmland south of the great Swanshyim Forest before flowing into the sea one hundred horizons southwest of Pinkulda. Surf pounded a low and rocky coastline. The smell of dead fish filled the salty air because a violent squall recently littered the seashore with rotting carcasses.

The tribemaster cradled a white feline. The creature raised its head, hoping for scratches under the chin. Footsteps on the stairs startled the furriness, but Vinlon calmed it by scratching the desired spot. A balding head with a tuft of white hair on top appeared in the stairwell.

"Thought I'd find you here," said the newcomer.

"Come up, Radzig," Vinlon invited him. "Look at the latest construction."

Radzig ascended the remaining steps, bringing the rest of his lean and muscular body into view, and joined Vinlon overlooking the worksite. A keep stood on a promontory at the mouth of the Pultanik River, splashed by the surf on one side and bathed in waning sunlight on the other. A long black-ribbon pennant flew from the top, stretched to its full length in a steady warm wind blowing from the south off the ocean. A large permanent camp of wooden shacks arranged in rectangular blocks covered the rest of the triangular piece of land between the river and ocean. The inhabitants labored to construct a wall around the keep. They hauled granite blocks on barges across the river to docks next to the camp. Husky bovines pulled the blocks to the fledgling wall where stonecutters shaped the rock to fit into the structure.

"Good progress today," said Radzig. "I watched a stone larger than any other being set into the wall."

Vinlon stroked his hair, fingering the thinning silver-streaked strands behind his neck. "I know it's nothing like the structures we saw in Richee, but this will be the greatest fortification in our land. Someday the Herkt and Jatneryimt will stop fighting one another and attack us. Then we'll need this stony monolith."

"The Herkt will never join the Jatneryimt."

Vinlon supposed Radzig couldn't imagine a scenario involving cooperation between their northward neighbors, bitter enemies that they were, but he had a prediction he expected him to accept. "We'll be more secure here in Pultanik than anywhere."

"Especially Habergenefinanch," said Radzig. "One torch could turn the place to a pile of ashes."

Vinlon shuddered over the vulnerability of his ancestral town located forty horizons eastward on the coast, although the Druogoint, a hostile neighboring tribe, never attacked there in his lifetime.

Radzig continued, "I'm here to invite you to supper, a feast before my son leaves."

Radzig was a friend Vinlon inherited from his father, but spending time with the man's family filled the tribemaster with sadness for what he had lost.

Vinlon declined. "Don't expect me." The feline in his arms, sensing his agitation, jumped to the floor and prowled about his feet, licking itself around the mouth.

"Spear wants morsels from our table," said Radzig.

"He's free to follow you home."

Radzig wrinkled his nose in disappointment. "I'll save a chair for you if you change your mind." He descended the stairs.

Vinlon looked at Spear by his feet, gazing into the beast's green eyes to offer a challenge. "Aren't you going with him?"

Spear blinked, seeming to feign disinterest, and then showed it by walking away, not to follow Radzig, but to find one last patch of light from the setting sun in which to curl into a furry white ball and take a nap.

Adjusting the sheathed sword at his side, Vinlon took a seat at a table under the last bit of daylight to study a pile of small wood blocks. Rolling up his tunic's sleeves to keep the floppy tan fabric from interfering, he stacked the rectangular blocks into two parallel columns and arranged the wedge-shaped ones to span across the top. *Simple to build a miniature Richeeyim arch*, he mused, but his builders continued to have no success constructing the real thing from massive blocks of stone. Radzig's son, Jaspich, and the other men going with the Richeeyimt to their homeland—the Kingdom of Richee they called it as translated from their language—were directed to learn the craft of building the arches. Only then could the Warnekt hope to construct lofty and spacious edifices like those Vinlon and Radzig admired during their journey to Richee in their younger days.

Vinlon knocked over the model arch and departed downstairs with his cloak. Spear scurried through his feet on the steps, almost tripping him. *Cursed creature*, he fumed. It always did that. The feline accompanied him to the docks by the river. The evening was too warm for the cloak, so he draped it on one arm over his rolled-up sleeve.

The Richeeyim vessel was moored at the riverbank, riding

a rising tide. The flat-bottomed craft was an unwieldy mode of transport on the ocean, but none better existed, so the Richeeyimt reduced the danger by never choosing to venture out of sight from the coast. The vessel was forty cubits long with a cabin in the stern of an otherwise open deck. It had a single mast for a square sail, and slots for oars along both sides belowdecks.

The bad weather before yesterday delayed departure to a worrisome time of the season. Vinlon figured the voyage would skip stopping at Habergenefinanch. He knew the route from experience, going farther east past unfriendly Druogoinyim lands and their settlement at Ranjin in the mouth of the Tauzzreen River, and continuing around thirty horizons of barren coastland before reaching the fertile lands of the Richeeyimt.

He passed by a group of his tribesmen around a cookfire. They were the ones traveling to Richee, some half dozen of varying ages, but Jaspich wasn't with them. Vinlon left his cloak, saying he would return for food. Spear sauntered away, fading into gathering darkness.

The Richeeyim captain welcomed Vinlon aboard the vessel. The tribemaster didn't remember his language and struggled to communicate with him, especially since he spoke in a growl and whistled through gaps in his teeth. He wore the same sun-bleached attire as his shipmates, although not as tattered as the others. The singular garment with arms and legs was tied snug around his neck, wrists, and ankles.

Vinlon inspected the cargo: swords, spears, bows, and arrows of the finest Warnekyim craftsmanship. His trading partners used the armaments to repel the Kendulyimt and other invaders from lands farther east.

He joined the men at the fire ashore. They offered him fish. The smell of rancid fish wafted to him all day from the coast, so he had no desire for it, even unspoiled. Spear jumped into his lap and rubbed whiskers into his face with a purr. *Cursed creature!* He shoved it away. The thing had fish breath.

Apparently not all the fish scattered like driftwood by the storm was rotten.

The feline leaned against his leg watching the fire while the men asked him about Richee. He described elaborate buildings, and his good memories of the food. Although he forgot the language, he recalled Habergenefinanch meant *far coastal land*, and how the Richeeyimt pronounced it differently.

A man named Dekloes wondered why the ancestral Warnekyim town had a foreign name. He appeared to be the oldest traveler. His graying beard obscured a scar on his cheek he received from a Druogoinyim dagger.

Vinlon answered, "The Richeeyimt claim they lived in this Pultanik region before we Warnekt took it from them."

"They lie," said Dekloes. "We always have lived here. My family talisman has carvings going back ten generations."

"What about before that? The Richeeyimt say they lived here centuries ago."

Dekloes tossed a fish head into the fire. "How can they know what happened so long ago?"

Vinlon waved to the nearby Richeeyim vessel. "Have you seen them looking at and marking parchments?" His arm motion distracted Spear from watching the fire.

"Yes, they're always doing it."

Vinlon explained, "They record words in symbols to remember everything."

A younger man about Jaspich's age asked, "Why don't we do that?"

"The symbols work only in their language."

Vinlon pondered again how to record words in the Snarshyim language of his people. Spear interrupted, mewing for him to follow. Vinlon left the group around the fire, remembering to take along his cloak, and followed his furry guide along the riverfront. Spear's whiteness made the feline easier to spot in the warm moonless night, as did a sentinel tail standing as tall as any Warnekyim standard on the march.

They passed by boats that came downriver with harvest

produce from as far away as Fenzdiwerp near Swenikyim lands. Vinlon thought about his upcoming annual harvest tour during which he visited as many farms and settlements he could before winter, for the Warnekt welcomed visits from their tribemaster.

Spear entered the stoneworker district and stopped, mewing by a flatsnout that roasted on a spit. Vinlon smirked in amusement. The little carnivore's affinity for pork was unsurpassed by any other of its cravings, and the beast possessed the sense to detect it from an amazing distance.

Vinlon asked the man basting the carcass, "Is it done?"

"Getting there, Tribemaster." The cook wiped a hand on his grease-streaked tunic.

Spear's mewing became louder and more insistent.

"He doesn't care how well it's cooked." Vinlon poked a thumb in the feline's direction. "Cut him a chunk, so he shuts up."

The cook obeyed, and Vinlon motioned for him to toss the morsel far away. Spear rushed after it in eager haste.

The tribemaster roamed around the tables where the stoneworkers primed for their meal with brew, joined by their families. Vinlon received a report from the foreman, a sinewy fellow covered in stone dust, about the challenge of installing the large stone into the wall that day. Rolls in baskets arrived, and Vinlon grabbed one to dull his hunger.

Spear returned, looking plump and licking himself around the whiskers. Vinlon no longer could wait for the roasted flatsnout and left to search for a quicker meal. Spear came along, not moving as fast. They passed two stoneworker boys practicing with wooden swords. Vinlon shouted words of encouragement. He favored young men in his tribe who wanted to become warriors.

The moon was up but presented only a sliver in its current phase. The moonstar shone as brightly as ever, forever the moon's companion and the third most-luminous object in the sky. The warmth of the recent day persisted, reinforced by the stiff humid breeze blowing from the ocean.

Vinlon went to the foundry, not only to check the progress on a new sword but hoping to find the men sitting there at supper. *How wonderful*, the odor of grilled bovine greeted him at the door. Banshim, the master forger, may have been reluctant to share his steak but didn't show it, or perhaps he took from the portions of his three apprentices who were present. His older daughter, a comely brownish-blond maiden with deep brown eyes, served them. The younger daughter, a girl who couldn't walk, sat at the table, done eating. Vinlon wondered why Banshim never remarried after his wife was caught in a fishnet and drowned in the river. He asked once but received an unintelligible mutter in response. Vinlon would marry another woman if he could.

The place was stifling hot from the heat of the foundry coals, although the wind blew through an open window facing the ocean. Vinlon was glad he hadn't rolled down his tunic's sleeves. On the contrary, he untucked the garment from his trousers and stowed his cloak on the bench away from his body.

After the meal, Banshim presented his work in progress. The blade already was fired many times, giving the metal a blue tinge, and the forger promised his new alloy would make the lightest and strongest weapon Vinlon ever wielded. The tribemaster surmised it also would be the shiniest.

Banshim described his design for the hilt, intending to make the most elegant sword anywhere. Vinlon kept his skepticism to himself. He remembered tales of the Herkt possessing an exquisite set of broadswords, and the accounts mentioned jewels and gold. His old sword at his side was plain, as adequate for killing as any fancy blade, although he conceded Banshim's new alloy would be better.

Banshim droned on, engrossed in talking about his craft. His teeth appeared incredibly white because his face was so blackened with soot, and his straggly hair, although gray, looked dark as coal.

Spear brought a small rodent, held limp by the neck in his jaws.

"Good for your furry ferocity," said Banshim. "I'm glad to be rid of that pest."

The hunter dropped his prey at Vinlon's feet, seeking praise. The beast responded to a vigorous scratching behind the ears with a loud purr.

Banshim told Vinlon to see Leenarth, saying the master archer developed a new bowstring that could fire arrows an extra twenty cubits. Although innovations delighted Vinlon, who encouraged the Warnekt to pursue them, he decided not to visit Leenarth until morning. He was fed and now desired female companionship.

He could find some women where the off-duty warriors spent their time. The keep's garrison lived in barracks outside the incomplete wall, but the same women went there lately, and Vinlon was bored with them. He went to the triangular camp's eastern fringe where sentries guarded the side not protected by water. Spear followed, hauling along his catch. The night felt cold compared to the foundry heat. Vinlon wrapped his cloak around his shoulders but removed it as he sweated from walking.

The outskirt had scattered shacks, not clustered like deeper within the camp. Vinlon entered one, leaving Spear outside. A pretty young blonde showed interest, but the tribemaster declined. He avoided women his daughter's age, although he never thought of his girl, age ten the last time he saw her, as an adult. No other choice appealed to him except for a shapely redhead, but that hair color reminded him of his wife.

Spear followed him to another shack with the carcass, now gutted. The rodent's head was left behind atop a stack of entrails. Vinlon found his companion for the night, older but attractive, with long raven hair and experienced in the pleasures. She didn't recognize him as tribemaster, so he hoped for a more authentic time with her, as if such a thing were possible for a single encounter.

Not that Vinlon preferred one-time dalliances. Showing each new companion what he enjoyed and determining what she liked *was a hassle*. He wouldn't spend too many times with the same woman, even after learning those things, because then feelings could develop and lead to pain of the heart. Battle wounds healed, but he never recovered from the gouge in his soul after his wife returned to her father, Warlord Druogoin, taking their son and daughter with her.

Assuaging his manly passions invariably left him unsatisfied. He envied his happily married friend, Radzig. Crossing outside between shacks with a lady companion, whose name he forgot, he didn't see Spear anywhere and wondered if the feline also went looking for a female.

The raven-haired woman didn't talk much but knew what to do, at least for him. She wasn't so good letting him know what to do for her. Her moans and groans didn't sound genuine, and she insisted on putting out the lamp. He thought, *What use is getting an attractive wench if I can't see her?* He lay back afterward, disappointed. She didn't even snuggle against him in her sleep. He missed the times years ago with his wife. They knew the bodies of one another and talked about things. He drifted to sleep, reminiscing about her flaming red hair and lithe form.

Daylight wakened him lying on his back. The woman was gone, as typically happened, but a pulsing white furry ball warmed his feet. He lamented the sad state of his affairs. His most loyal companion was a creature *that licked itself.*

Vinlon rose to dress. Spear mewed, complaining about being disturbed. The morning was cool enough for Vinlon to put on his cloak before stepping outside. The day promised to be as fair as the previous one except less windy. A Warnekyim black-ribbon pennant wafted limp from the top of a nearby observation tower. He walked to the base of the wooden structure, holding the hilt of his sheathed sword, and called to a watchman, "Look at the docks. Is the Richeeyim vessel still there?"

It was, so Vinlon had time to say farewell to Jaspich. He planned to go to the docks, then see Leenarth's improved bowstring, and hopefully find breakfast somewhere.

The camp wakened as he passed through, trailed by Spear. Children ran. Older boys carried firewood, stoked fires, and hauled water. Older girls and women cooked, mended clothes, and cared for infants and weanlings. Craftsmen worked. Stoneworkers walked by, leaving for the fortress under construction with any iron tools they had sharpened overnight.

Vinlon and Spear joined a procession going to do a day's work at the docks or on the boats. They saw raft loads of raw granite arriving at the water's edge, transported from the other bank. Before reaching the Pultanik River's wide mouth, the rock was hauled along the ocean on a well-worn path eight horizons from the west. The quarry was located at a crumbling rocky crag called Pod's Peak where a myriad of boulders was strewn along the shore.

Vinlon reached the Richeeyim vessel as it was poled away from the riverbank on its way to ride the lowering tide to sea. He spotted Radzig waving to Jaspich, who stood at the rail onboard the departing vessel. The son was a copy of the father—tall, lean, and muscular. Only his brownish hair, and the greater volume of it, was different. Vinlon stepped beside Radzig so Jaspich would see him and return his wave.

He looked into his friend's bloodshot eyes. "You had a late night?"

"You missed a sumptuous feast, Tribemaster," said Radzig. "Plenty is left for you to help finish tonight. You must come with Spear. Our feline went into heat and howled all night."

Vinlon thought this was Radzig's feeblest appeal to get him to visit his place. "Let the thing outside. Plenty of males are out there."

Radzig looked down to Spear circling their feet and purring. "You know our feline wants only Spear."

Vinlon thought again about his sad state of affairs. His beast received more devotion from a female than he ever did.

He picked up the living furriness and stared into its blinking emerald eyes. "You have a job, Spear, a chance to live up to your name."

Live or Die

Herkt, Jatneryimt

BRUTEZ   **TAUBUETH**

The crack of wood and clang of metal resounded from the gateless walls of Taubueth. Brutez exchanged blows with Heptor under a canopy of the courtyard trees that were turning more orange, red, and yellow with each passing day. Although his younger brother was stockier and stronger, Brutez anticipated his moves; a feint with his war hammer, blocked, now his other arm swinging with a dagger, saw that coming, *duck*! Brutez passed on a chance to counter with a war hammer blow against Heptor's exposed chest. He didn't want to keep beating his brother because then he wouldn't quit, and although his ankle felt better after a week, the stress from sparring made it sore again. He allowed Heptor's next strike to knock the war hammer from his hand.

Heptor was triumphant. "I have you now, Brother!" He wound his weapon over his curly-haired head as if to deliver a deathblow. "You must yield!"

"I surrender." Brutez knelt, more to take the weight off his hurting ankle than anything else.

Heptor flung aside his war hammer and looked at Zamtoth, seated nearby. "You see, Father? I should fight Klinteg to lead the clan."

The old man watched his youngest son put away his dagger. "You can challenge him next if Brutez loses."

Brutez knew his father didn't have much regard for Heptor's boast. He recovered his discarded war hammer now lying on the ground within his reach. "I'm going to Aunt Yeemzal." His uncle's wife, the clan's expert with herbs and healing, would remedy his sore ankle.

Zamtoth went with him.

"Don't worry, Father. I'll be fully recovered by next week." Brutez tapped the fading bruise on his left face. "This will be better, too."

He was thankful his father negotiated the extra week from Klinteg, but even fully fit, he didn't think his chance in tournament was good, especially if he fell into his opponent's grasp. Klinteg inherited the brawny strength of his uncle, who killed the three older brothers. Brutez didn't have the advantage of knowing Klinteg's style like he did against his last remaining brother, having pummeled him since they were small boys.

His father's words matched the thinking. "You need more challenge than Heptor."

Brutez determined to find some, although he didn't know how. None of the Taubueth warriors were much competition, especially since Rankeb and Konrash were gone. "Father, I'll think of something." They reached the entrance to Yeemzal's hovel, a dilapidated wood structure leaning against the wall of the donjon.

Zamtoth patted his son's back. "You're good at that."

Brutez stepped inside, leaving his father behind. The aroma of plants, wood, bark, and dirt filled the one-room cabin, mixed into an olfactory soup. The scents came from jars and bowls that packed shelves and counters and were stacked on the floor and into corners. Brutez ducked below strips of animal hide and clusters of leaves, branches, and ferns hanging from the room's low ceiling.

Seeing nobody, he called down a set of steps dug into the ground by the donjon wall, "Aunt Yeemzal? Are you there?"

An older woman's voice responded, shrill but strong. "Come, Brutez."

He descended the stairs and pushed through a thick screen of skins into a room looking like a cave, although a well-illuminated one. A fire blazed in a hearth on the near side, pumping smoke out a chimney at ground level behind the hovel, and a series of torches lined the irregular stony walls. Skins covered the floor except in the corner with a low, bed-sized table.

Yeemzal blocked his view of the room's other side. She retained much of her ravaging beauty for a woman almost twice the years of her nephew. Although gray, her hair was loose and long, thick, and shiny with luster. Her eyes were pools of blue on an unwrinkled face. Brutez supposed her youthful complexion had much to do with the mud pastes she put on herself. She was tall, reaching his eye level, and slender, but no longer as wispy slim as she once was.

"Let me guess, Brutez, you ignored my warning about exerting yourself."

"My ankle, dear aunt."

"Of course." Yeemzal shook her head in more disapproval. "Sit there and remove your boot." She indicated the low table in the corner.

Brutez obeyed. His aunt disappeared up to the hovel and returned with a leather strap. Kneeling beside him, she squeezed and pinched his bared ankle. The soreness dissipated under her expert touch.

"What do you think?"

Brutez thought she asked about his ankle until she said more. "Do you suppose Shemjib has reached Agratuna?"

No doubt she thought much about her husband. Brutez wondered what news Uncle Shemjib would bring back from

Agratuna. *Did the Jatneryimt raid there? Was his sister Majdel harmed?*

"He might have," he answered his aunt's question, not wanting her to worry if Shemjib tarried. "I can't say how long he'll stay."

Yeemzal had wanted to go with her husband to see where she had lived as a girl and to visit her brother, who became Lord Chieftain Feldram. Shemjib took her captive on a raid when she first flowed and married her after winning her love. Feldram came to the wedding as a youth with his father, who considered it a means to stop the Herkyim raids into Kradig, the Feldramyim territory. Only then was the older Feldram convinced his daughter consented by free will to marry the Herk who captured her. During that festive time many summers ago at Taubueth, the younger Feldram, who was now chieftain, fancied a girl named Majdel. They were betrothed, and Majdel left for Agratuna to wed Feldram when she came of age. Brutez barely remembered his sister, not even recalling the color of her hair.

Yeemzal finished massaging his ankle and wrapped it tightly within the leather strap. "Now *don't strain* it."

Brutez swung his legs down from the table, but Yeemzal's hand on his knee prevented him from standing.

His aunt looked at him with sadness in her deep blue eyes. "You're like a son to me, Brutez. I don't want anything to happen to you."

He was like a son to her indeed, for he spent more time as a maturing child with Uncle Shemjib than his father, who had older sons to heed. Brutez's older cousins, the twin sons of Shemjib and Yeemzal, had been butchered by the Jatneryimt. Born on the same day, they also died on the same day.

She also was like a mother to him, for he had none since Heptor was a weanling and soon after his sister left for Agratuna. Although Yeemzal's talents with herbs and healing were great, she couldn't overcome every ailment. Brutez cringed at the memory of listening to his mother's anguish, begging his father to kill her. He finally did, if Brutez could believe what his oldest brother told him.

Brutez assured Yeemzal he would listen to her this time about resting his ankle, although in his mind he made no such commitment, and he left, grateful he didn't have to drink one of her awful potions. Although he could have gone through the bedchamber and upstairs inside the donjon, he went outside through the odiferous hovel and returned to the structure through its main entrance. A stairs led to his quarters, where Sir Grebnar the Bold sat chained by one ankle to the wall.

"I forgot your breakfast," he told the Jatneryim.

Grebnar shrugged. "I've had worse treatment."

Not since Rankeb and Konrash left, Brutez thought. The prisoner looked better, although a purple band ringed his throat. Brutez had convinced Aunt Yeemzal to give him treatment, although she considered him personally responsible for the deaths of her sons. Considering that, Brutez advised Grebnar not to drink the potion she gave him because he couldn't guarantee it wasn't poison.

"How was your practice?"

Brutez frowned at the Jatneryim's question.

Grebnar persisted. "Why shouldn't I ask? My life is in your hands, isn't it?"

Yes, it is. Brutez thought about it. If he beat Klinteg, Grebnar would be freed on ransom, otherwise the truth of the matter, Klinteg had a fortnight to contemplate which method of killing the Jatneryim would entertain him the most.

"I'll be ready."

Grebnar was dubious. "Is that so? Are you training against any worthy opponents?" His chain rankled as he rose to his feet. Standing tall in better health, he was the same height as Brutez. He looked powerful, solid with muscle.

Brutez realized his father's expectation he would think of something had come true. He dodged Grebnar's question. "The day I brought you here, you told me you killed many Herkt."

"Twenty-nine."

"What? You remember the precise number?"

"Only those I slew in combat. I recalled each one while sitting here these days. Some I killed bare-handed."

"That's why you're called the Bold?"

Grebnar snorted. "What's bold about killing somebody who's at your mercy?"

"Then what makes you bold, Grebnar?"

"I don't care if I live or die."

"Then you don't care who wins our tournament for clanlord."

"Not true. Given a chance to live, I'll live."

"Here's your chance."

Grebnar assumed a defensive stance. "Come at me with your dagger."

Brutez drew his blade, unsure of his meaning.

"Come. Don't hold back."

The Herk lunged, resolving to stab the Jatneryim in the heart. A foot kicked Brutez in the kneecap, a hand grabbed his wrist coming with the dagger, an arm wrapped around his neck, and before he knew what happened, he was pinned within his prisoner's grasp with his own dagger on his throat.

Grebnar's breath blew hot into his ear. "Call somebody to unshackle my chain, or you're number thirty."

"Your thirtieth will be your last."

Grebnar leaned around and stared Brutez in the face. "You have no fear in your eyes, Herk Brutez."

"I don't care if I live or die."

Grebnar shoved Brutez away and tossed the dagger to his feet. "I'll train with you."

Brutez kicked the dagger to Grebnar's feet. "You can start by teaching me that move you used against me."

What's Left of It

Feldramt

Shemjib **Agratuna**

Nervous atop his mount, Shemjib scanned the open space around him in all directions. The barren landscape of Kradig was flat except for rocks and whitish clumps of salt, providing his traveling party no cover from a potential Jatneryim raiding force.

He had ridden northward with Rankeb and Konrash across more than twenty horizons of the white-splotched wasteland since leaving the forest at a clifftop ten horizons north of Taubueth. They huddled within their great cloaks against a chilly headwind, although a shining sun and azure sky promised a warmer day ahead.

Shemjib, an aging man, felt sore from too much time on the mount. He planned to dismount and walk as soon as he spotted a telltale change he expected in the landscape. A vulpine-skin cap protected his scalp from the sun's burning rays. His baldness contrasted his older brother, Zamtoth, whose face was surrounded by a mass of white hair like a lupine's fluffy winter fur. Shemjib kept his beard and remnant of ashen gray hair shaved, although he allowed stubble to grow during the trip. He wouldn't shave until returning home, where his wife would do it for him *all over his body*. He anticipated what would happen next, rubbing fragrances over one another from her store of remedies in the hovel, and rolling in the furs before a roaring fire in their subterranean chamber. Yeemzal was a marvel in her various positions.

A scrubby bush appeared ahead, the telltale sign of the journey coming to an end. Shemjib dropped to the ground. His feet crunched in the salty crust while he led his mount by the reins. White crystals caked the equine's hooves.

Rankeb and Konrash dismounted, too. Before this ride together, Shemjib didn't know they were brothers, but only as friends of his troublesome nephew, Heptor, who invited them to live at Taubueth a year ago. They came from the same place as Vulrath's bodyguard Larboelm, a town on the shore of a deep blue lake across from Swenikyim territory.

Other than youthfulness and dull wit, they had no outward appearance of being related. Rankeb stood a head taller, but the stouter Konrash weighed more. Rankeb had straight dark hair and a well-shaped face that could be considered handsome if he ever washed it and groomed his beard. Konrash was fair-haired and ugly. A wart hung on the side of his crooked nose, and a pockmarked scab covered his right cheek.

The trio passed the bush and more waist-high shrubs, and the ground changed to sand. A long blue ribbon stretched across the land one horizon ahead; the sea. More coastal signs appeared as they walked. Snowy-white seabirds were gliding over and diving into the water. The incessant surf thumped the sandy beach. The Feldramt once told Shemjib how a north wind caused the roughest sea. The waves swelled from a far northern ocean and propagated down a wide sea passage a hundred and fifty horizons in length before hammering this coast, twenty-five horizons wide at the southern end. The passage was called the Snarshyim Inlet.

Shemjib mounted his equine to scan both eastward and

westward along the coast for a clue telling him which way to go. He saw nothing, but being unfamiliar with the terrain, he never expected to reach the coast at Agratuna's exact location after crossing Kradig, and since they missed their destination, he had to choose the best way. Having seen no sign, either tracks or refuse, of a large raiding force, he concluded no raid happened, or this was farther east than one would have gone, so he assumed the latter and led his companions westward.

The coast became rockier after a stop for a meal at noon. More vegetation appeared inland, even trees, assuring Shemjib that Agratuna was ahead rather than behind. The travelers coaxed their mounts up an escarpment, sprayed by the turbulent sea pounding the rock. They ventured inland to avoid the shower.

A dozen or so armed men emerged from behind higher outcroppings of rock. They wore hooded drab-brown wide-sleeved cloaks that reached their ankles. Some wielded hand axes. Others held spears. Shemjib relaxed when he saw brown dual-triangle banners flapping from the speartips. He signaled Rankeb and Konrash to put away their weapons. The newcomers were Feldramt, not bandits or Jatneryimt.

One spoke another language in a commanding tone that sounded like a challenge.

Shemjib dismounted and directed Rankeb and Konrash to do likewise. Confused, he responded in his own Snarshyim language, "Who do you think we are?"

The Feldram's thick black beard and a craggy nose showed inside his hood. He switched to the same language. "You're not Chizdekyimt?"

Shemjib wanted to berate the man for thinking he was a vagabond. He pointed to a blooddrop-shaped brand on his mount's flank. "We're Herkt from Taubueth. I'm married to your lord chieftain's sister. Are Feldram and his wife, my niece, well?"

The Feldram wasn't forthcoming with an answer, filling Shemjib with dread. "Come with us to our captain. You may keep your arms, sir, but your men must relinquish theirs."

A good compromise, Shemjib decided, reflecting a mix of respect and suspicion. He ordered Rankeb and Konrash to drop their axes and daggers. Some of the Feldramt, who were not holding bannered spears, took the weapons. The craggy-nosed Feldram led them to a camp with a bonfire blazing from a hole in the ground, billowing coal-black smoke away from the sea.

One tall young man wore a cloak like the others, but with his hood down. He had blue eyes on a narrow face, a patchy beard, and thick, raven hair waving in the sea breeze. The Feldram leading the Herkt identified him as the captain and told the patchy-bearded young man who Shemjib claimed to be.

The captain smiled. "Welcome, Shemjib. I'm Sangern, one of Lord Chieftain Feldram's sons."

"Then I'm your uncle by marriage," said Shemjib. "Are your parents well?"

Sangern shrugged. "Depends on how you think about it. We suffered the worst Jatneryim raid in years."

Shemjib lamented the regrettable but expected news. "We feared that."

"My father recovers from a spear wound, and my mother is unharmed, but they grieve for our tribe and my younger brother's awful burn."

Good news about my niece, Majdel, Shemjib thought, but enough bad tidings to keep from celebrating it. "Are they at Agratuna?"

"What's left of it," said Sangern. "I'll take you there now."

The young man told his men to care for the Herkyim mounts and invited Rankeb and Konrash to a fish fry at the camp. He gave Shemjib a fresh mount and took him farther west along the coast on a trail wide and firm enough to travel at a gallop's pace. They went through several towns untouched by the raid before reaching a high mound, the outermost berm surrounding Agratuna.

They crossed a gap, guarded by warriors under Feldramyim brown dual-pointed banners. A moat, filling with tidewater from the Snarshyim Inlet, separated the outer berm from the next one within. A rocky isthmus, gapped by channels for allowing the tide through, was topped with wood planks for crossing the ditch. The riders went through three more berms and over the two moats between them in order to enter Agratuna.

Much of the town was burned to the ground. Shemjib smelled it before he saw, the stench of burnt wood mingled with scorched flesh and hair. A grid pattern of shops and houses spread before him. A few buildings remained, but the rest were reduced to stone foundations littered with ashes, cinders, and charred timber.

The ruins no longer smoldered, meaning the raid happened days ago. The burning came from a huge bonfire nearby. Broken handles and carts burned in the flames, and so did arms and legs. Two men in sooty, tattered clothes, with rags covering their mouths and noses, tossed a mangled girl's body into the fire.

Shemjib followed Sangern shoreward into the grid. Some survivors removed combusted refuse from the waist-high rectangles of leftover stone. Others sat against the low walls with blank stares, and more wandered without purpose around the grid.

A stone quay marked the shore. The water was calmer because a rocky cape and some islands blocked the great south-coming waves of the Snarshyim Inlet. A few spindly trees grew on the cape and more plush ones on the islands, changing color and dropping leaves for the season.

Gutted boats lined the quay, covered with the charred debris of fallen masts, sails, and rope. Sangern led Shemjib to one of the few usable buildings in Agratuna, a rectangular structure with high stone walls and a patched timber roof. Leaving their mounts outside, they entered the single room inside.

The place was packed with so many people Sangern and Shemjib barely fit inside the door. Most were wounded. Shemjib saw bandaged limbs, gashes, and bruised faces. Sangern announced Shemjib to the lead couple.

Lord Chieftain Feldram was raven-haired like his son. His eyes and the furs on his body were brown, the color of the Feldramyim banner. He had stubble for a beard, no doubt not shaving since the raid, and judging from his leg propped with a splint, he hadn't walked either.

Shemjib wouldn't have recognized his niece if she wasn't sitting by her lord husband. Majdel still had blue eyes, a trait passed to her son, but the plump woman before him with chopped silver hair wasn't the thin platinum blond girl he remembered from two decades ago.

"Lord Chieftain, I regret our clan didn't stop the Jatneryimt," said Shemjib. "We attacked them, but they escaped."

"They came by hundreds, the biggest force I've ever seen," said Feldram. "We had no chance, and they were cruel."

Matkulk. Shemjib considered the brutal Jatneryim to be the type who would boil babies and eat them for breakfast. Brutez had told him he was one of the raiders.

Feldram continued, "They took our winter provisions, the whole stockpile of salted fish and crustaceans. We have fewer people to feed because the Jatneryimt killed so many, but more stragglers come every day."

"I have two men with me," said Shemjib. "We can take some of your people with us to Taubueth for the winter. Yeemzal will care for the wounded who can get there."

Feldram's grim look brightened with a question. "How's my sister?"

A moan preempted Shemjib's answer. Majdel leaned over some furs beside her, wakening a boy of about ten years. "Mother's here, Chrenlon." She stroked his sweating brow.

Feldram spoke over his wife's voice as she gave the boy more assurance, "A hot beam landed on our son's chest. The burn is severe."

"Yeemzal does wonders for burns." Shemjib now wished he had brought along his wife for another reason than enjoying her presence. "Her ointments and dressings stink worse than anything, but they heal."

Feldram asked his wife, "What do you think, Majdel? Should we send Chrenlon to Taubueth with your uncle?"

"It's his best chance. I fear the burn will fester."

Shemjib wondered. "Should he travel?"

"He'll suffer, but he suffers now."

"We'll rig a means to carry him. Your father will be glad to see you after all these years."

Majdel frowned. "My regrets I can't go to Taubueth. Give my father, your brother, my greetings, but I must go to Biepazz to meet Lord Chrevram on my husband's behalf."

The Chrevramt were a neighboring tribe. Their fort at Biepazz was located on the western coast of the Snarshyim Inlet.

Feldram tapped his wounded leg. "I won't be going anywhere." He told his son, "Sangern, you're going with your brother to Taubueth."

Clanlord of the Herkt

Herkt, Jatneryimt

BRUTEZ   **TAUBUETH**

Air! Brutez desperately wanted some as Grebnar's forearm dug into his throat. His fingers clawed at the limb choking the life out of him. They scratched and dug into the flesh, working on their own volition to get his assailant to relent, but Brutez knew he wouldn't. He forced his air-starved mind to think. *Relax*, he told himself. *Don't waste the energy you have left.* He dropped his arms to his sides. *Think! What can you do? So difficult*, he was drifting into a daze. *No, concentrate!* He thought about the position of his body relative to Grebnar. His feet were pinned between his opponent's ankles. The rest of Grebnar was behind him. His arms hung limp.

He slung back an arm, bent at the elbow, and jabbed his strangler in the ribs. The impact didn't hurt him, but Brutez detected a looser grip from Grebnar's legs and freed a foot. He stomped on the Jatneryim's foot. Grebnar spread his feet to steady his stance, and Brutez snapped his foot back and upward, heel first.

Grebnar howled. Brutez dropped to his knees as Grebnar's forearm was released from his throat, and he heaved to breathe, hands clutching at leaves on the ground. Grebnar's howl changed to groans beside him. Brutez heard his brother howl, not from pain but laughter, and his father's voice.

"Heptor, control yourself. Get in there before he recovers."

The laughter changed to a shout. Brutez only wanted more air, but he willed himself to his feet to face his oncoming brother. By reflex he deflected an arm swinging with a war hammer and kicked the dagger from Heptor's other hand. He allowed his arm that blocked the hammer to slide down the arm holding the weapon, finding leverage in the armpit, and turned his body to push against his brother's opposite shoulder with his other hand.

Heptor stumbled over Grebnar and landed on his back. Brutez scurried to acquire the dropped dagger. Retrieving a shield he had when the fight started, he took a defensive stance to catch his breath.

Zamtoth shouted, "No rest! Finish it!"

Heptor regained his feet, still holding the war hammer. Grebnar lay prone between Brutez and Heptor. The brothers dodged one another, circling the Jatneryim.

"Enough prancing," shouted Zamtoth. "Brutez, what are you waiting for?"

Brutez gasped for breath and lunged, planting a foot on Grebnar's hip to gain elevation. His shield met Heptor's hammer as he descended, and he struck his brother with enough force to knock him off his feet. Then he made a roundhouse turn with the shield while Heptor tried to stand. He slammed the side of his brother's head, putting him face to the ground and groaning.

Brutez dropped his shield and dagger, no longer caring if his father wanted him to keep fighting. He considered the fight done and leaned over to catch his breath at last. He looked at Heptor with some concern, but his brother's wearing a helmet gave him hope he didn't hurt him any worse than knocking him senseless.

A cordon of warriors surrounded them to keep Grebnar from attempting an escape, although the prisoner didn't seem capable at the moment. Two warriors came to assist Heptor, each gripping him below an arm and helping him walk toward Yeemzal's hovel across the yard for treatment. Brutez smirked, noticing how nobody moved to help Grebnar.

Zamtoth approached, wearing a broad smile. "Well done, Son! You're ready to meet Klinteg tomorrow."

Brutez agreed. His ankle, more than two weeks after the sprain, felt good even after being wrenched between Grebnar's feet. He helped the Jatneryim to his feet.

Grebnar winced, favoring his groin. "I owe you a good beating," he said with a menacing brown-eyed stare.

Not today, Brutez knew. He waved for Jonerch and Gordib from the remaining warriors to take Grebnar to his chamber.

Jonerch was a long-time friend. Brutez spent countless days with him when they were boys, practicing scouting skills in the forest. Jonerch had ruby-blond hair and no longer tried to grow a meaningful beard. Although not as brawny as most Herkt, he ran faster than any of them, even Brutez, and possessed deadly skill with a dagger. He could skin a stag faster than anyone.

Gordib was a friend Brutez inherited from his deceased next older brother. Brutez liked him because nobody played better pranks against Heptor. Gordib's brown hair had retreated up his head, leaving him bald in front, so he compensated by letting it grow down his back. A pointy beard grew long from his chin. A branding of the Herkyim blooddrop on one cheek added to his crazy appearance.

Jonerch attached the hobble around Grebnar's ankles. Brutez bade his father farewell until supper and went with his friends taking Grebnar to the donjon and upstairs to his room. Jonerch reattached one end of Grebnar's hobble to the wall and followed Gordib out the door.

Grebnar sat on a three-legged stool Brutez provided him.

The Jatneryim also had a straw mattress. A slant of sunlight from a slit in the wall crossed his shoulders, being the only means of illumination in a chamber without candle or fire.

"You surprised me, Brutez. You're the most nimble opponent I've ever faced, but I didn't think you limber enough to place a kick behind yourself like that."

"I hope what you taught me surprises Klinteg."

"Remember your greatest strength."

Brutez knew what Grebnar meant. *He didn't care if he lived or died. Was that true?* He never considered the meaning of death and wondered what Grebnar thought about it. "Grebnar, why don't you care about dying?"

"What do you remember before you were born?"

The answer was obvious to Brutez. "Nothing."

"Did you care about not being born?"

"Of course not, how could I? I didn't exist."

"How's being dead any different?"

Brutez tried to follow Grebnar's reasoning. The dead didn't remember and didn't care because they didn't exist. The thought of no longer existing unsettled him.

He challenged Grebnar. "How can you be sure we stop existing when we die?" He considered the beliefs of the vagabonds who lived in the high hills and other rugged places and spoke their own language. "The Chizdekyimt claim to talk with their deceased ancestors."

Grebnar shrugged. "They only think so."

"Who would they be speaking to, their lord of the dead? What's his name?"

"Pod. It's nonsense. What good are their superstitions? They live worse and die easier than we do."

"I suppose their beliefs comfort them."

Grebnar laughed. "I don't know about that. Let's consider some other superstitious people. What do you know about the tribes living west of the Jatneryimt?"

Brutez didn't want to admit to not knowing much, so he responded with what he knew. "They speak another language."

"Not only another language but many dialects of that language, so they barely understand one another, and they have as many beliefs as ways of saying their words," said Grebnar. "Everything is a deity to them; in the sky, the sun, the moon, the stars, the moonstar, clouds; down here, the trees, the rivers, the rocks, the soil, animals. Do these things comfort them?"

Brutez shrugged.

Grebnar continued, "No, they live in fear of angering this thing or that, and they burn sacrifices hoping to gain favor, wasting perfectly good food and wood, and what good does it bring them? Their crops still fail, and they still die."

Brutez asked, "What good are their deities?"

"No good!" Grebnar snapped his fingers. "What's the sun other than a great ball of fire?" He motioned to the chamber's cold hearth. "Fires go out. How can something that doesn't last be a deity?"

"It can't."

"Consider us who speak the Snarshyim language. We don't believe this nonsense."

Brutez pondered Grebnar's claim, tallying the clans and tribes in his mind: *the Herkt, the Jatneryimt, the Swenikt, the Warnekt, the Druogoint, the Hamuntht, the Feldramt, the Chrevramt, and the tribe living north of the Chrevramt whose name he didn't remember.*

"At least most of us don't," Grebnar hedged. "Some Snarshyim clans living among the superstitious folk, such as the Kaligt and the Nitzent, believe likewise, and the mountain clans at the headwaters of the Kipneesh River have their own strange beliefs."

Brutez had forgotten about the mountain clans, fierce warriors with long pikes the Herkt liked to hear about because every time they did, they were killing Jatneryimt. He had heard that the vicious Jatneryim Matkulk was born in a mountain clan.

"What strange things, Grebnar?"

"Mosik's clan has a rite for boys passing to manhood. The birthmarksigns are flayed from their chests as if to purify them, but all they're left with is worse scars. Other clans have rituals involving incantations and spells. I've heard stories about apparitions, but I don't believe them."

Although Brutez shared Grebnar's skepticism, he thought he must believe in something, and after some contemplation, he had a notion. "I'm not sure I stop existing after I'm dead."

"Then how do you not care whether you live or die?"

Brutez sighed. He never talked with anyone who made him think as much as Grebnar did, even his father or uncle, especially on matters of the unknown, matters the people of the Snarshyim clans and tribes generally didn't contemplate.

"I like living, although I rather would do so without suffering," he finally said. "Perhaps dying is better, so maybe that's why I don't care."

BRUTEZ   **TAUBUETH**

Food was something Brutez thought best about living. Looking between a woman's breasts was another. He had both before him at his place near the end of the long supper table in the donjon's main chamber. The food steamed from serving platters on the tabletop, wafting delectable aromas to his nostrils and teasing his tongue to expect plenty of tasty stimulation. A stack of stag cuts, doused with gravy and ringed with onions and peppers, was set at the head of the table before his father. A roast wedgewing and the dark meat of a marshbill were placed by Brutez. More dishes sat in front of Jonerch seated next to him: buttered greens, bread, berry jams, and starch roots.

The breasts belonged to Heptor's latest consort, Nazzel, who inclined against her man across the table, leaning forward so the lobes threatened to spill from her bodice. Brutez saw her entire birthmarksign. She caught him staring and smirked to let him know she enjoyed his notice. He averted his gaze to a tray of longears arranged side-by-side in a fungus sauce. *Too late*, his brother also noticed, so he was doomed to endure taunts.

"Brutez, this could be your last night to frolic." One side of Heptor's face was a bruise where Brutez slammed him with the shield. "Nazzel has a friend wanting to explore your hard, bulging muscles, especially the one you haven't used lately."

Laughter exploded among the several dozen diners along the table, causing Jonerch to spill brew on Brutez. *Curses*, Brutez fumed. His father was laughing, and even more irksome, so was Aunt Yeemzal at the far end. He would vex his brother.

He spoke as loudly as Heptor, for all to hear, "Bring her to me after the meal."

The smile faded from Heptor's squarish face, and Brutez curled his mouth in a snigger. His brother hadn't expected him to accept the offer but now must honor it.

Zamtoth stood at the head of the table. "Herkt of Taubueth, we'll declare fealty to a new clanlord by this time tomorrow but we'll mourn losing a great warrior from the clan, so we celebrate tonight before the tournament takes its heavy toll." The old man raised his mug. "Hail the Herkyim warriors! Hail my son, the warrior Brutez!"

Brutez watched everyone else stand, mugs raised.

They shouted, "Brutez! Hail the warrior Brutez!"

The feast began. Brutez devoured juicy wedgewing meat, fare from the migratory fowl brought by the Herkt living by the eastward lakes. Although he enjoyed watching the birds fly in their wedge formations, they looked better cooked on the table. He thought about Klinteg feasting with his kin in a camp outside the walls of Taubueth. Hundreds of Herkt were come to witness the tournament.

Heptor called for a refill of brew, and a mug was passed down the table from Gordib's direction. Brutez knew his brother wouldn't suspect. Sure enough, Heptor guzzled from the mug and spewed the contents all over Rankeb, who was sitting on the other side of him from Nazzel.

Heptor shouted over raucous laughter, "Curses, what was in that?"

Gordib pounded a fist on the table in delight. "I don't know. Ask Yeemzal."

Yeemzal spoke from the far end, "Don't fret, Nephew. My additive will cleanse you sometime the middle of tonight."

Brutez gorged and drank, hoping to remain alive to have more the next evening.

Afterward he took a flask of brew and a tasty portion to Grebnar in his quarters, including the remains of the wedgewing from his corner of the table. A fire burned in the hearth, warming the cold, stony walls. He set the platter on Grebnar's stool and the flask next to it. "Eat hearty. This could be your last chance."

The Jatneryim sat up from lying on his mattress. "Nonsense. I have every confidence you'll fare better than your brothers."

"I should fare better," said Brutez while Grebnar took a swig from the flask. "My oldest brother was undone by thinking he was invincible. My second brother didn't bother to think and went into the fight without a strategy, and my third never should have tried. He was weak and only made the challenge because it was his turn." He laughed with a wry smile, thinking of his rash younger brother. "I must win, if only to save Heptor from making his own challenge."

As if called by mention of his name, Heptor arrived, and he brought a woman. Brutez didn't recall seeing her around Taubueth. He surmised his brother found her in the visiting camp. She had mangy black hair that tumbled about her shoulders, and a thick nose to go with her wide face; otherwise, she looked pretty. Although large-bodied, Brutez didn't consider her pudgy. Her waist, even without a pleasing female curvature, still appeared trim compared to what he saw higher.

"I think you'll like Vel, Brother." Heptor gestured with open hands, presenting the woman as the gift he intended her to be. "I saw you admiring what my Nazzel has, so I got you the biggest I could find."

"You're a good brother, Heptor." Brutez looked into the woman's blue eyes. "I'm glad you're here."

She returned his smile.

"You're not getting my leftover." Heptor winked. "I just met her."

"You *are* a good brother."

"Go on," Heptor urged Vel. "Show my brother."

She lowered her bodice, and Brutez gazed down from watching her eyes and smile, not passing on the chance. He thought, *too bad the ugly scab of her birthmarksign mars the sight.* Then he remembered to step from Grebnar's view.

Heptor teased, "I don't want to know what you've been doing in here with the Jatneryim, but this will be better." He exited but quickly returned. "I almost forgot. Aunt Yeemzal won't be using her quarters tonight." He winked again and pointed at Grebnar. "Unless you plan to share with him." Then he was gone for good.

Brutez motioned for the woman to cover herself. He looked into her eyes again. "Where do you live, Vel?"

He expected her to speak in a husky voice, but it came like a song. "On the ridge."

Good, from the southwest, so she didn't come with Klinteg's faction, Brutez figured. He turned to Grebnar, who was picking clean the wedgewing carcass. "My brother thought he jested, but this woman's here for you, Grebnar. Consider her another last chance."

Grebnar smacked on a bone. "Nonsense again, I told you I have every confidence in you, so I plan on returning to my wife. Brutez, if you think this is a last chance, you should take it."

Brutez took Vel's hands into his and looked into her face while speaking to Grebnar. "I've had chances, enough to know I want to keep the rest for my wife someday." He watched her eyes moisten. "Sorry, dear Vel. You're a certain delight for a man, but I'm not that man. Let me return you to your camp."

She bowed her head.

Grebnar called, "Wait! I haven't conversed with a woman for weeks except the healer, but she hated me. Will you stay, Vel, talk and laugh with me? I could listen to your sweet voice all night."

She looked up with a smile and glistening blue eyes. "I would like that."

BRUTEZ   TAUBUETH

Brutez thought this part of the tournament perhaps was worse than dying, standing naked before his nude opponent while Zamtoth inspected Klinteg's body and Larboelm inspected his. At least they stood in the privacy of the donjon with nobody else present.

Klinteg was a mass of chiseled muscle, thick and strong, although he carried some flab around his midriff. Brutez scanned him no longer than needed to see he had no bruise or malady to exploit. The only blemish was his birthmarksign, a scab on the left side of his chest like a scar over his heart.

Brutez endured Larboelm's hands fingering through his hair searching for hidden poison darts. The bodyguard found a burr that must have come from one of the furs in Aunt Yeemzal's residence where Brutez slept. Brutez had returned to his chamber at dawn, finding Vel asleep on the bed and Grebnar sleeping on his mattress without any sign either had removed any clothes. Grebnar asked to witness the tournament, but Brutez thought best Klinteg not see him.

Larboelm brought trousers, a tunic, boots, and a leather jerkin. Zamtoth gave the same to Klinteg. The rules of the tournament, requiring each combatant to be dressed and armed by the other side, assured no use of poison or other unfair advantage. Then came gloves made from a stiff hide, attached to metal vambraces going to the elbows, and coifs for their heads that draped chainmail over their necks and shoulders.

Each received a dagger and another weapon of choice. Zamtoth handed Klinteg a hefty double-bladed axe. The former clanlord's nephew gripped the long and thick shaft and wielded the weapon over his head, in front of himself, to each side, and both one-and-two-handed, testing its weight and balance. He grunted in satisfaction. Brutez thought the war hammer Larboelm gave him was too light, so he exchanged it for a cudgel with a twice-weightier chunk of iron on the end.

The shields were constructed from the hardest wood in the forest, reinforced with metal ribs, two cubits square, and studded with metal spikes. Zamtoth and Larboelm kept them in their possession to carry outside with the helmets. Brutez and Klinteg carried their weapons.

The midday was bright, although overcast. The two contestants and their attendants shuffled through fallen leaves to the middle of Taubueth's crowded courtyard. The people, men and women, boys and girls, young and old, filled the entire space within the walls except for an open spot in the center, and lined the ramparts and the stairs leading up to them. Their only sound was coughing and wheezing. A soft breeze rustled through the tree foliage inside and outside Taubueth.

Reaching the open spot, Brutez saw the relic swords for the first time since Vulrath killed his third brother. Each great broadsword was three cubits long, wide as a hand's span. The points of the twenty-four blades stabbed the leafy ground, six to each side of a square. The handguards and pommels gleamed dull gold in the clouded daylight, adorned with intricate patterns of jewels. The gems varied, but each sword had only one type, and diamonds prevailed.

Brutez and Klinteg took turns calling loyal companions to come forward and take a sword. Brutez's selections included Heptor, Jonerch, Gordib, and Herkyim warriors who faithfully served Zamtoth when he was clanlord. The twenty-four swordsmen formed a larger square to keep back the crowd from the combat area, six to each side standing five cubits apart from one another. They gripped the handles in both hands at their waists, holding the blades upright before their faces.

A pole stood five cubits tall in the center of the square, topped by an iron casting of the blooddrop Herkyim standard. At Zamtoth's signal, Brutez took position by it and faced Klinteg. He held his cudgel at his side and shouted, "Hail the Herkyim warrior Klinteg! If I fall, do you pledge fealty to him as clanlord?"

The twenty-four swordsmen shouted in response, "Hail the Herkyim warrior Klinteg! If you fall, we pledge fealty to him as clanlord!"

The hundreds of people on the grounds, and lining the ramparts and stairs, shouted in a mighty voice, "Hail the Herkyim warrior Klinteg! If you fall, we pledge fealty to him as clanlord!"

Brutez stepped away to one side by the crowd, and Klinteg took the place by the iron blooddrop, facing him. He held his axe upright with one arm extended from his body, setting the butt of its shaft on the ground. "Hail the Herkyim warrior Brutez! If I fall, do you pledge fealty to him as clanlord?"

"Hail the Herkyim warrior Brutez! If you fall, we pledge fealty to him as clanlord!" the swordsmen shouted.

"Hail the Herkyim warrior Brutez! If you fall, we pledge fealty to him as clanlord!" the people repeated.

Klinteg carried his axe to the opposite side of the fighting area from Brutez. Zamtoth went to him with his shield and helmet. Larboelm gave Brutez his shield, placed the helmet on his head, and disappeared into the crowd with Zamtoth. Brutez and Klinteg faced one another fully armed with nothing between them but the iron blooddrop standard.

Klinteg dropped his shield and came with his axe in both hands. Brutez moved forward with his cudgel in one hand, shield on his other arm, and dagger tucked by his side. Leaves scraped underfoot, mixing into the jostle of the breezy branches overhead, for the crowd remained silent. Even the coughing and wheezing ceased.

Klinteg's axe swooped through the air. The weapon came toward Brutez in a slow arch, which he easily evaded. It arched back with the same swooping sound as Klinteg swung with all his might. Brutez rolled below it, feeling the breath of its passing, while deftly keeping his own shield and weapon from impairing his movement. The axe swung low, slow enough for Brutez to regain his feet and jump over it. *So far, so good*, he thought. His opponent was slower than Heptor, and he was expending his strength.

A few passes of the axe later, Brutez pretended to fall, bringing a gasp from the crowd. He released his hold on the cudgel, so he could reverse the direction of the dagger in his belt to point outward from his hip, using his body to screen Klinteg from seeing what he was doing. The axe swung down, but he grabbed the cudgel and rolled away with it in time.

The axe embedded in the ground, and Brutez charged from behind with his cudgel and shield. Klinteg released his immobilized weapon and turned around, drawing his dagger. Brutez would have slammed him with his shield and clubbed him with the cudgel, but Klinteg stopped his advance by sticking his dagger into the shield, and used his other hand to grab hold of Brutez's arm swinging the cudgel. Klinteg's superior strength overpowered Brutez. His shield was yanked from his arm and tossed aside, embedded by the dagger. The cudgel was forced from his grasp and that arm wrenched under his chin.

Brutez knew he had precious little time. Although his arm blocked Klinteg from choking him, his shoulder would pop out of socket, and Klinteg would use his free arm to strike him or get him into a hold he couldn't escape. He thought about the position of his body relative to Klinteg, as Grebnar taught him. His dagger stuck from his hip on the same side as his wrenched arm, and he had a free hand. He pushed hard with the heel of that hand against Klinteg's side to leverage twisting his hip, and then he jabbed his opponent with the dagger.

The effect couldn't have been more than a prick, but the sense of a sharp tip in the side surprised Klinteg enough to loosen his hold on Brutez's arm. Brutez yanked the limb down from his throat, freeing himself from his opponent's grasp, and ducked below a swing from Klinteg's free arm. By stooping, Brutez found his cudgel within reach on the ground. He took it in both hands and spun around, swinging with all his might. The dense iron mass crashed into Klinteg's knee with a loud crack.

The former clanlord's nephew fell on his back with a scream of agony. Brutez pressed his advantage by smashing the other knee. Klinteg screamed more. Brutez dropped the cudgel and drew his inverted dagger to stab his rival's stomach several times. Blood pooled on the ground, turning the nearby leaves red and seeping around the discarded cudgel.

Leaving the blade in place, Brutez stood over his fallen opponent. Klinteg no longer screamed, but his tortured breathing made a horrible rasping sound. Brutez removed his helmet and let it drop. *What a waste for the clan to lose such a mighty warrior*, he thought. Not heeding a rising murmur from the crowd, he knelt by Klinteg's head to extract his helmet. The dying man's reddish-brown hair and beard were matted with sweat.

Brutez looked into his gray eyes and saw fear. "I promise never again will a Herk kill another Herk to lead the clan."

He scanned the crowd, turning within the square of twenty-four swordsmen standing at attention with their long blades. The people pressed forward, chattering and gesturing, until Brutez's stern expression returned them to silence. He took the iron blooddrop and stove its shaftpoint into Klinteg's heart. The defeated warrior expired with a gasp. Brutez stood by, solemn, leaving the Herkyim standard staked through the body.

One by one, Klinteg's men first, the swordsmen came to present their blades at Brutez's feet, each saying, "I declare fealty to you, Brutez, Clanlord of the Herkt."

Except the last one, Heptor said, "I declare fealty to you, Brother, Clanlord of the Herkt."

Brutez saw his father standing in front of the crowd. The old man displayed no expression indicating how he felt about a son finally winning the tournament.

Brutez stepped in front of the stack of gold-handled broadswords and shouted so loud his throat hurt, "Hail the Herkyim warriors! All hail the Herkt!"

The people packing the stronghold of Taubueth responded, "Hail Brutez, Clanlord of the Herkt!"

Deal

Feldramt

Majdel **Biepazz**

Majdel traveled on a sorrel mount, escorted by armed men. A contingent of Chrevramyim warriors joined her group of Feldramt last night, riding in the vanguard with cutlasses, bows, and quivers full of arrows. All but the youngest one wore hauberks of clinking metal. The boy carried the Chrevramyim banner, a purple rectangle notched with square cutouts around its three outer edges. Majdel's Feldramyim warriors rode behind, armed with hand axes, swords, and spears adorned by brown dual-triangle banners.

More mounted Feldramt rode in a group together, not warriors but men who worked on boats. Some herdsmen and two well-trained canines guided fifty head of livestock along the path. The rest of the people—several dozen men, women, and children—were refugees from Agratuna or one of the towns the Jatneryimt raided farther west. Some were mounted, but most rode in carts pulled by bovines.

Although screened by trees, the Snarshyim Inlet made its presence known with its unending din of water roiling against the unseen shore to the right. A chill sea breeze, smelling of salt, swirled through the branches overhead and winnowed down showers of leaves, which scuffled along the ground.

The coast had guided the entire journey. The Feldramt first traveled ten horizons westward from Agratuna, passing through ravaged towns. Choppy seawater stretched to the sky on the right, and the Kradig wasteland filled the landscape to the left. Then they entered the forest, turning northward around the southwestern corner of the Snarshyim Inlet, and followed the coast for ten more horizons.

Placid water, rippled instead of wavy, appeared between the tree trunks ahead. The Chrevramt led the way past some log buildings to a pier lined with boats and rafts. Majdel saw a rectangular lake, gray under a cloudy sky, and realized it was a bay, for a gap in the trees lining the eastern shore marked a passage to the Snarshyim Inlet. The northern side barely was visible a horizon away. A river flowed into the tree-lined bay from the west.

A meal waited, but Majdel wouldn't dine here with the others. A man named Steebnaf took her to a rowboat. The oarsmen propelled them over the rippling water toward a large structure beyond the river on the western shore.

Wedgewings flew overhead, honking in a wedge formation. Seabirds floated across the passage to the Snarshyim Inlet. The Swanshyim Forest stood guard around the bay, dropping pieces of a once-green canopy from every limb.

The serene scene belied the violence Majdel witnessed two weeks ago. The Jatneryimt poured in waves over Agratuna's berms and across its moats at low tide. They plundered, burned, killed, and violated women. She escaped the worst because her husband sent her to one of the offshore islands with a boatload of women and children, but Chrenlon couldn't be found and suffered the grievous burn. Sangern remained safe in an eastward town that wasn't sacked. For once Majdel didn't begrudge her older son for carousing with Chizdekyim wenches.

The big structure on the western shore was a palisade of

upright logs cut to points on top. Each alternating trunk stood taller than the ones in between, acting as parapets for the defenders keeping watch. The forest was cleared outside the walls to just beyond the range of an archer's bow.

Leaving the rowboat behind, Majdel followed Steebnaf to a gate. The vertical row of logs, pointed at the bottom and armored with iron plates, opened outward and upward. They walked below the heavy mass and some Chrevramyim purple, notched-rectangle banners hanging from the lintel. Passing through a log wall maze, they entered the wider end of the Chrevramyim fort at Biepazz. The outer walls narrowed to the third point of a triangle going deeper into the forest.

A gigantic rock sprouted thirty cubits high in the center of the compound, twice higher than the palisade. The big rock's backside was cut to fit one end of a longhouse built against the stone. Majdel marveled at the structure, not constructed from logs like everything else at Biepazz but squared stone blocks. A stone roof arched over the narrow space between the lateral walls. Not even Taubueth's donjon had a stone roof.

A pair of large metal-studded doors, curved on top like the roof, stood open at the far end. Majdel heard utensils clatter on platters and the merriment of the diners within the hall. She stepped inside behind Steebnaf and gazed at the ceiling, fearing that the massive rock could fall on her head. She wondered, *How does it stay up there?*

The supper table ran the whole length of the place, thirty cubits long and laden with bread, vegetables, fish, and meat. The diners sat in regimented positions, males on one side and females on the other, and youngest to oldest. Children sat at the near end and the elderly at the far end.

Steebnaf took Majdel along the female side of the table toward the older end. Pausing between two other gray-haired women, he addressed a man across the table, "Lord Chrevram, I present Lady Feldram, newly arrived from Agratuna." He left Majdel standing there.

Chrevram had ruddy cheeks and a bushy gray mustache,

but not much other hair. His big ears were redder than his face. He smiled and invited Majdel to join the meal. At least they were about the same age, she thought, so she could sit across the table from him. She barely took her place when a server handed her a brew.

Chrevram waved for a refill. His happiness was enhanced, for he cheerily introduced his wife sitting on Majdel's right side. Then he slapped the back of the hairy and burly man to his right, who forced a frown into a reluctant grin. "This is Tribelord Boewin, visiting us from Neshim."

The stout woman on Majdel's left side introduced herself as Boewin's wife, and Majdel fretted over sitting between the two wives and interposing their conversation.

Boewin had his own concern. The forced grin was gone. "Lady Feldram, *why* isn't your lord husband *with you?*"

Majdel hoped he would ask for a refill so he could become happier. She took a long draught from her mug and set it down before answering. "Lord Chieftain Feldram was speared by the Jatneryimt and couldn't come. I bring you his regret."

Boewin lifted his mug. "You have my wishes for the chieftain's full recovery."

Majdel doubted he meant it. She felt his wife's sympathetic hand on her left hip and reached over her lap with her right to give it an appreciative squeeze. Lady Chrevram invited her to take a selection from the platter of barn fowl and starch roots before them. The women conversed among themselves for the remainder of the meal.

Majdel spoke on her husband's behalf after the main dishes were cleared. She described her tribe's plight after the Jatneryim raid, considering Tribelord Boewin to be an unwelcome listener and speaking to Lord Chrevram. The Feldramt were desperate for winter provisions, so sending any of their people elsewhere for the season meant fewer they must feed. Some went to Taubueth, including both her sons. Majdel brought others with her to Biepazz, ones with useful skills such as cooks, forgers, and herdsmen. She brought livestock and intended to leave behind the mounts so the Feldramt wouldn't have to feed them, hoping to trade the animals for boats full of provisions. The boats would stay at Agratuna to replace ones that were sunk. She had boatmen to man the craft.

Boewin interrupted, "What about your warriors? You have an escort, don't you?"

"I have seventeen warriors," she said. "I won't need them if I return by boat."

"I could use them, Cousin," Boewin told Chrevram. "Mosik's mountain clan is pillaging my lands, and I worry about the Jatneryimt and Yarsishyimt, too. I'm threatened from every direction."

Chrevram's frown resonated with Majdel's annoyance. The warriors were hers, and she wanted to deal with Chrevram not Boewin.

"Every direction except yours," Boewin told his cousin.

Chrevram's frown vanished, but Majdel still was annoyed. At least Chrevram returned his attention to her. "Your animals are good to pay for boats. I'm not so sure about provisions, but I have a proposal."

Majdel's mood brightened. *Certainly a deal could be made.*

Chrevram pointed to the younger end of the table. "Do you see the girl down there in an amber gown?"

The female diners on Majdel's side blocked her view, although Chrevram's wife leaned out of the way. No matter, she remembered the girl, a copper-skinned beauty with honey-blond hair to match her dress, so she nodded.

"My daughter," said Chrevram. "Our daughter." He included his wife. "She's a lovely girl."

"A sweet girl," said Lady Chrevram.

"And vivacious," said the father. "Her name is Zabfrul, and Boewin here has no son to give her in marriage."

"I have only daughters." Boewin glared at his wife across the table. "They're surrounding Zabfrul down there."

Majdel realized where this was going.

Chrevram confirmed her premonition with a question.

"How old is your son?"

She had two sons, but she knew which one he meant. "Sangern is nineteen, but Zabfrul's a bit young."

Lady Chrevram whispered into Majdel's ear, "She's starting to flow."

Her husband offered his proposal. "If Sangern can wait I'll pay an advance dowry by loading your boats with provisions."

Trust me, Majdel thought. *Sangern could wait if Zabfrul didn't mind him wiling away the time with wenches.* "He'll wait," she promised. She would use the time to convince her son of his duty, as if taking such a beauty could be called that. After all, she married out of duty and learned to love her husband.

Chrevram slapped the table. "Done, we have a deal!"

He yelled for his drink to be reloaded. Majdel presented a wan smile and took a hearty embrace from Lady Chrevram, who beamed with smiles.

Tribelord Boewin spoke to Lord Chrevram, "While we're arranging marriages let's talk about unloading one of my daughters to your son. Where is the boy?"

"He's north with the Yarsishyimt."

"They captured him?"

Chrevram shook his head. "I sent him there to learn stonecraft."

Majdel felt Lady Chrevram's touch on her shoulder and leaned to listen.

"Our son's name is Wikston. He's sixteen."

Chrevram kept talking, "Do you know my grandfather hired Yarsishyimt to build this place? I want Wikston to learn the skill."

"I want the Yarsishyimt forced out of Langech." Boewin pounded the table with a fist. "It's my peninsula. They don't even speak our language. Let them join the rest of their kind across the inlet."

"Cousin, you know I disagree," said Chrevram. "The Yarsishyimt are peaceful, and we don't need more enemies."

"Make sure your boy doesn't take a Yarsishyim girl for a

wife. He's to have one of my daughters!"

"On that we agree."

Dessert finally arrived. The pie was orange, *gourd pie*.

Majdel decided to deal with the other visiting leader. "Tribelord Boewin, let's talk about my seventeen warriors."

To Me He's Ugly

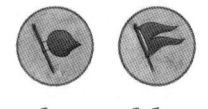

Herkt, Feldramt

YEEMZAL   **TAUBUETH**

Jewels sparkled and the gold gleamed brilliant in firelight. Yeemzal set the last of the relic broadswords on iron pegs in the back wall of her main room. She stood back to admire the entire row of twenty-four, arranged at shoulder height in a line between the low bed-sized table at one end and another table with chairs at the other. The wall was empty for thirteen years while Vulrath held the swords as clanlord. Now the swords were returned to the quarters of Shemjib and Yeemzal, to rooms that had belonged to Zamtoth when he was clanlord. The blades were spaced a cubit's distance from one another, pointing upward at a common angle in the direction of the table with chairs.

    Yeemzal heard footsteps and Heptor's voice descending the stairs from the hovel, and she stood by the wall beside the entrance for amusement. Her nephew came through the curtain of skins with the buxom brunette wench who had become his companion. They gazed across to the swords on the opposite wall, not noticing Yeemzal next to them.

"Look at them, Nazzel," said Heptor. "How they shine in the firelight."

Precious stones were embedded in the golden handguards and pommels of the swords. Each handle was bejeweled with a unique pattern of amethyst, diamond, emerald, jacinth, moonstone, onyx, pearl, ruby, sapphire, or topaz.

Yeemzal never received a clear answer from the Herkt about the exquisite weapons. They didn't remember a time before they owned them, and they certainly didn't possess the craftsmanship to create them. No Snarshyim clan or tribe did, not even the Warnekt. Yeemzal surmised they were forged by the same people who built Taubueth centuries ago.

She spoke in a forceful voice meant to startle Heptor, "Stop drooling."

Nazzel shrieked. Heptor flinched, a lesser reaction than Yeemzal hoped to get, and took hold of his woman's hand to calm her. "An impressive display, Aunt Yeemzal." He leaned around Nazzel to speak. "Why shouldn't I admire it?"

Yeemzal pinched her lips together, suppressing a snort. Her nephew was no less likely to leer at jewels and gold than to ogle women. "Why are you here, Heptor?" *Why did you bring your wench?*

Heptor answered both questions, "Nazzel's missed a flow. Is she with child?"

Yeemzal asked the woman, "Do you ever miss them?"

"Never."

Arms crossed, Yeemzal asked, "If you're with child, do you want me to kill it?" She wouldn't, thinking the world endured enough death without bringing it to the womb.

"Curses, no!"

Her nephew's emphatic response pleased her, and Nazzel smiled.

"I'll mix a testing powder. Come back tomorrow."

Zamtoth arrived, passing by Heptor and Nazzel on their way out.

"That's a sight I missed," he told Yeemzal, regarding the mounted broadswords. "A good sight waits for you outside, Wedlock Sister, although to me he's ugly."

Yeemzal shouted, emotion soaring, "Shemjib!"

She rushed upstairs and out the hovel past her aromatic stock of herbs, potions, and ointments into the night. Her husband descended the rampart steps across the yard with Rankeb, Konrash, and others she didn't recognize. They ran toward one another.

"Yeemzal!" her husband called.

She saw in the torchlight he had grown an ashen beard and what little remained of his hair. He opened his arms to receive her embrace. The last remaining tension of the past couple weeks ebbed from her body. Her nephew, Brutez, survived his ordeal, and her man returned safely to her. She refrained from kissing him and pulled away before he tried. Strangers approached, and she wanted his beard gone before they kissed.

He reported, "The Jatneryimt sacked Agratuna. Your lord chieftain brother and Majdel are well, although his leg needs mending. I brought others for your care."

She saw them among the strangers, walking wounded except for a boy carried by Jonerch and Gordib on a litter. Their bloodstained wrappings covered heads, hands, arms, and torsos. Some were missing hands or whole arms.

Yeemzal asked, "How many?"

"Majdel told me twenty-seven Feldramt went with us, including eight unwounded riders in the escort. How many wounded would that be?"

"Nineteen," said Yeemzal. Her husband never was adept with numbers. "Your delay worried me." She expected him to return before the tournament.

"Thirty people travel slower than three."

No problem with his numbers there, Yeemzal figured.

"The storm was the worst," he continued. "It caught us unprotected in Kradig."

Yeemzal was grateful for Taubueth's stone walls during the tempest a week ago.

Her husband noticed the iron blooddrop standard stabbing the ground nearby. "Some clansfolk going home from the tournament told us Brutez won."

The leading stranger reached them. A tall and lanky young man without a wound, he was raven-haired and blue-eyed in a manner familiar to Yeemzal.

Shemjib presented him. "This is Sangern, your brother's heir and our nephew."

Sangern looked gorgeous with his wide smile, reminding Yeemzal of her deceased sons before they shaved their heads. "My lady aunt, I see you're even more comely than my uncle described."

Blessed boy, Yeemzal embraced him. He smelled good, too, like fresh pines, even after many days traveling, unlike her husband and a more putrid stench close by.

"Rouse the kitchen to feed our guests," she told Rankeb, the source of the bad odor, and hoped the ugly dimwit Konrash, who also stank, left with Rankeb.

The boy arrived on the litter carried by Jonerch and Gordib. He was a younger likeness to Sangern, a few years shy of his maturation, but was in a stupor.

"Shemjib told my mother you can help my brother Chrenlon," said Sangern.

Sure enough, she thought, *another nephew*. He emanated a more ominous smell. Peeling a soggy rag from below his neck, she saw the reddened, welted, and blistered burn on his chest and shoulder, gristly black in spots and oozing in others.

"When did this happen, Sangern?"

"Two weeks ago."

Yeemzal became more hopeful. The boy had a chance, since the rotting had taken that long to start. "I'll help him, Nephew. You made the right choice bringing him to me." She commanded Jonerch and Gordib to take Chrenlon to her quarters.

"I'll show the Feldramt to the dining hall," Shemjib offered. He patted Sangern's shoulder. "Come, Nephew."

"Send me any others needing immediate treatment," Yeemzal told him.

She went to the hovel and collected a potion, an ointment, and pond leaves from her wealth of remedies. Going below, she saw how Jonerch and Gordib moved the low table away from the corner and placed an ursine skin, one without a head, under the boy. Giving approval, she dismissed them.

She poured the potion sip by sip into Chrenlon's mouth. Even while delirious, he helped by moving his lips. She applied a preliminary poultice of leaves swathed in ointment.

Shemjib appeared with Sangern from the inner chamber and the donjon interior. The Feldramyim heir gaped at the row of bejeweled and golden-hilted swords.

"The other wounded can wait until tomorrow," said Shemjib.

Yeemzal was skeptical, but the sooner she was alone with her husband the better, so she withheld comment. She explained her treatment, telling Sangern nothing more could be done for now, so she urged him to join the meal upstairs by returning the way he had come. He was about to leave when Zamtoth, Larboelm, and Brutez emerged from the inner chamber.

Shemjib was jubilant. "Brutez, Clanlord Nephew, I declare fealty to you!"

Brutez smiled. "It's strange hearing that from the uncle who disciplined me in my youth. I'm pleased by your return and your news that Majdel is unharmed." He looked at Chrenlon on the low table. "Although I regret not all is well."

Annoyed by the intrusion, Yeemzal glared at the big oaf Larboelm. His floppy mop of sandy hair belonged more in a scrub pail than on the head of a man, and the hairs of his beard were stiff enough to be used for a brush. *Why was he here?*

Brutez must have noticed her frown. "Larboelm has been the clanlord's bodyguard since he grew to this monstrous size. He insists on serving me, Aunt Yeemzal, and I've accepted him."

Yeemzal nodded grudging approval. Having the allegiance of the former clanlord's bodyguard only could promote unity within the clan. Even so, the oaf's dimwitted grin irritated her, and before he made matters worse by speaking, she grabbed Sangern's arm and introduced him to Brutez. "This nephew of mine and his brother there who I'm healing, sons of my brother, are also your nephews, Nephew, as sons of your sister."

Shemjib added, "You're their uncle as I am and yours."

Yeemzal released Sangern's arm. "Sangern, you speak on your lord father's behalf as his heir. This is Clanlord Brutez to whom all Herkt have declared fealty."

"The honor is mine." Sangern looked Brutez in the eyes.

Good, Yeemzal thought. *The young man considers himself an equal.*

"Mine, too," said Brutez. "I invite you to join your kin at the meal. I'll come soon with plenty of questions about your mother, my sister."

If Sangern realized he was being told to leave for the Herkt to converse in private, as indeed he was, he had the tact not to show it and left through the inner chamber. Brutez motioned for his father and uncle to join him at the table. Yeemzal sat with them. Larboelm took a menacing stance behind Brutez, at least seeming that way to Yeemzal.

"We must discuss the prisoner, Sir Grebnar the Bold," said the clanlord.

Shemjib asked, "Where is he?"

"Brutez keeps him chained in his chamber," said Yeemzal. She thought they spent too much time together but left the opinion unspoken.

Shemjib glared at her, a signal to let the clanlord answer the questions. He asked Brutez, "Now that you won the right to preserve his life, what will you ask for ransom?"

Yeemzal watched Larboelm for any reaction to the

reminder that Klinteg was killed to save the Jatneryim, and she was relieved to see none.

"I haven't thought much about it," said Brutez.

"Ransom never was the purpose," said Zamtoth.

"True, Father. I only mentioned it to keep Vulrath from killing him. All that matters is returning him to the Jatneryimt."

"What's so important about that?"

Yeemzal was thankful her husband asked the question, so she wouldn't raise his ire by asking it herself.

Brutez and his father, the current and former clanlords, answered together, "Matkulk."

Yeemzal frowned. She could talk about herbs, and no matter how many words she used, men would look at her as bewildered as she felt now, but they could communicate with one another in a few code words.

She dared to speak, "Matkulk?"

"He's the Jatneryim brute responsible for that burned boy." Her husband pointed to their sedated nephew. "Clanlord, I understand Grebnar and Rendif are lesser menaces, so you're releasing Grebnar without ransom?"

"I can't. I traded Klinteg's life for his. The whole clan has sworn fealty to me but not all agree with my decision. We must get something in return."

"I know what we should demand." Shemjib clenched his fists. "Sir Rendif must restore the plunder he took from the Feldramt, acknowledge our protection over them, and vow to make no more raids, although I admit his promise wouldn't mean much."

"I like your words, Uncle. I want you to take them to Rendif."

No! Yeemzal screamed in her mind. She willed herself not to protest in voice.

Shemjib did. "Why me, Clanlord? I'm worn from travel."

"You witnessed the carnage at Agratuna. You'll speak with conviction on the matter, and you can get Rendif to agree to our terms for releasing his wedlock brother."

Shemjib surrendered to the logic. "When do I leave?"

"The unrest in the clan will worsen. You must go tomorrow."

"Yes, Clanlord Nephew."

No, dear husband, Yeemzal thought. *You shouldn't have declared fealty so soon.*

Shemjib continued, "I need something to prove we have him."

"Larboelm, what happened to Klinteg's clothes after we dressed for combat?"

"I kept them, Clanlord."

"He wore Grebnar's green and black cape. Do you have it?"

"I do, Clanlord, and Grebnar's sword."

"Take both and go with my uncle."

Brutez turned to Shemjib with a look saying, *Anything else?*

Shemjib responded, "I'll leave with Larboelm at daybreak."

Having settled the matter, Brutez retired from the firelit chamber with his father and Larboelm.

"I'm sorry, Yeemzal," said Shemjib. "I have my duty."

She embraced him before he saw her crying. *Only one night together.*

He asked, "Will the boy be senseless for a time?"

She fingered his beard. "Time enough." Except for Chrenlon they were alone. "Let me shave you. *All over.*"

Secrets

Warnekt, Swenikt

Vinlon **Fenzdiwerp**

Vinlon emerged from the deck cabin, shivering on a colder morning. He saw his breath on this crisp and clear daybreak but anticipated a warmer day. The rising sun's rays filtered through tree branches on the riverbank. The limbs were bereft of leaves, although some browned cusps lingered waiting for a windier day to fall.

A dull roar upriver, rumbling within a mist across the Pultanik River, enticed the tribemaster to the raft's forward rail. The waterfall soon would appear, a cascading liquid wall more than twenty cubits high, marking the end of Vinlon's journey sixty horizons upriver and the border of his lands. The Swenikt claimed the territory on the left bank above the falls, and the Druogoint claimed the right. Both banks below the waterfall belonged to the Warnekt.

The river's straight and lazy course allowed an easy sojourn against the current for the four previous weeks of the annual harvest tour. Some river craft moved upstream, but most floated downriver filled with harvest bounty going to the construction site at the river's mouth.

Most evenings Vinlon's raft reached a settlement for spending the night. The tribemaster enjoyed sharing tidings and feasting with the people, although he regretted his expanding midriff. He envied Radzig, who remained lean no matter how much he ate or aged.

A terrible storm during the first week caught Vinlon away from any town. He huddled in his tiny cabin on the raft with cold rations and worried how the storm affected his men traveling with the Richeeyimt on the ocean.

He strayed from the Pultanik River once, going up a tributary called the Fall River, so named because the water tumbled down rapids and waterfalls. He rode to Doesim Falls, a thunderous mass of water next to a town with the same name, where he spent a couple nights with a miller's daughter he knew long enough to produce three offspring, so she claimed. Last year he saw two little girls with no end to snot running from their noses, and this year he was introduced to a baby, his supposed son. He kept returning to the woman because she was more fun to please than others.

The roar of the upcoming waterfall now thundered rather than rumbled, returning his mind to the present. He realized his fingers tapped the rail and stopped them. A torrent of greenish-brown water curled over the crest of the falls, visible over the mist. Both riverbanks had docks and buildings, but mostly on the right.

Fenzdiwerp was the largest town on the tour, in fact the largest settlement Vinlon ever saw outside of Richee. The buildings on the right bank filled the low rolling land to the limit of his sight. He considered it to be a Warnekyim town, although the residents included significant numbers of Swenikt and Druogoint, which was fine because their presence kept those neighboring tribes from raiding the place. It had no stronghold nor fence or wall surrounding it. The three tribes came there not to fight but for commerce and communication. Vinlon received notice Chief Thoiren of the Swenikt arrived above the falls several days ago and waited to meet him, promising news of great interest.

Vinlon determined not to keep the chief waiting. His crew had moved the raft upriver all night while he slept, so they reached Fenzdiwerp this morning. Radzig met him upon his arrival with a mount to ride. The balding man rode ahead on land during the tour to announce the tribemaster's pending visit to each town.

He waved to the cloudless sky. "A fair day, Tribemaster."

Finally warmer, too, Vinlon thought, who no longer saw his breath or shivered under his cloak.

Radzig asked, "Are you fed and drinking yet?"

"Only watered." Vinlon had started the day by relieving himself into the river.

Radzig's confused look amused him. "From the river?"

Vinlon smiled. "Into it."

Radzig gave a chagrined look of understanding. "We'll skip stopping at the streamer." He proposed going to the inn for breakfast and led the way into town on their mounts along a street going closer to the waterfall. "Tribemaster, Chief Thoiren will meet you on his raft above the falls as soon as you get there."

Vinlon was pleased. He preferred going to his counterpart's place and observing whatever he wasn't meant to see, rather than worrying about what a visitor saw when coming to him.

Radzig continued, "You should visit the mill near the inn. The miller has devised an ingenious way for the waterfall to turn his grindstone."

"I'll do that," said Vinlon, trying to sound more enthusiastic than he felt. He wanted Radzig to keep informing him about innovations, but he saw a waterwheel at Doesim Falls.

A feline scurried across the street. Another hurried after.

"Spear could have fun here with his friends," said Radzig.

"He has fun anywhere he kills something," said Vinlon.

He left Spear behind because the feline wouldn't board the raft. The creature would find him when he returned to the construction project in spring, mewing in anger for being abandoned. Vinlon would stroke his fur to make him happy.

The harvest tour was going overland after Fenzdiwerp. Vinlon hoped to reach winter quarters at Habergenefinanch before much snow fell. He would be scolded by a black female feline named Birdbane he had left there last spring.

After breakfast fulfilled its tasty promise, Vinlon and Radzig rode from the lower town upslope around the waterfall. A back view from the crest showed much of the land around Fenzdiwerp was cleared for cultivation.

Druogoinyim orange trapezoid banners in the upper town angered Vinlon. "Radzig, tell the rascals to tear those down some night." He would order his Warnekyim officials to fly more black ribbons around Fenzdiwerp. *It was a Warnekyim town.*

They left their mounts at a riverside stable. Thoiren's raft, a floating longhouse, was moored on the Swenikyim side of the river.

"Radzig, how will they drag that monster back upriver?"

"They won't."

"It can't stay." Vinlon wouldn't allow the Swenikt to stake a greater claim in the Fenzdiwerp area. *It was a Warnekyim town.* "Have the rascals cut it loose some night after Thoiren leaves so it drops over the falls." He hoped it didn't break loose by itself while he was onboard.

Radzig smiled. "Too bad Jaspich isn't here. He enjoys that sort of thing."

And you? Vinlon wondered. Radzig lived in Fenzdiwerp as a youth and must have been a rascal.

They boarded a small boat. Although the current flowed slow and smooth, Vinlon cringed. *The waterfall was too close.* He rather would have crossed the river below it and ascended the other side.

Thoiren's raft loomed larger. *The thing was huge.* Swenikyim standards were raised over both ends on poles. The cobalt blue triangles with concave sides were cut from boards, Vinlon figured, because flags wouldn't be flying so straight on a windless day. He was relieved when his boat's crew steered the flimsy craft to the upcurrent end of the floating house as far from the waterfall as possible. The cascading water roared fainter but still unnerved him. He wished to reconsider meeting at his counterpart's place. *Curses on observing.* He didn't like what he heard.

A three-cubits-wide walkway without railings surrounded the longhouse on the raft. The Swenikt didn't object when Vinlon stepped aboard with his sword and Radzig with his hatchet. The hosts had plenty of armed men present, and the visitors wouldn't surrender weapons anyhow.

A door swung inward from the spot they boarded at the upriver end. Radzig stooped to fit under a low plank ceiling. The raft's logs were the floor, chopped flatter on top by axes. Vinlon was careful not to twist an ankle in a crevice. The walls were trunks from white bark trees, unchocked in the gaps between them. Straw mattresses were stacked against the near wall on both sides of the door, interspersed with bedding and piled on top with feather pillows.

Some men and two women clustered at the far end of the room, which was as wide as the raft but not as long. Vinlon saw an opening to another room in the left corner behind them. Square openings in the walls vented daylight on both sides.

Skin-covered pedestals scattered the room for sitting. Two were occupied by the right wall on the same side as the shore. Vinlon recognized Chief Thoiren, a man with a cheerful disposition and wispy white hair sprouting from more places on his head and face than Radzig's tufts did from his. The other man appeared to be Thoiren's son. He had the same round face and flabby cheeks, although his steely eyes and lack of a smile weren't so amiable. His beard was trimmed except for long sideburns. Thinning dark brown hair covered his head.

"Chief Thoiren," said Vinlon, not waiting for an introduction.

Thoiren raised both hands, palms open. "Welcome Vinlon, Tribemaster of the Warnekt." His smile showed plenty of toothy gaps. "I was told to expect you in Fenzdiwerp. Please sit."

Vinlon introduced Radzig before squatting on a pedestal in the center, facing Thoiren. He kicked back with his heel against the brown and white pelt draping to the floor from his pedestal to feel what it covered and determined he sat on a log stump. Radzig sat on a pedestal somewhat behind and to the side. Usually he stood, but Vinlon supposed he wearied of stooping below the ceiling.

Thoiren introduced his cohort. "This is Kevyar, my son and heir."

Kevyar acknowledged himself with a nod, hand on a sheathed sword and still offering no smile. He snapped his fingers. The two women came forward carrying four tankards of brew, giving one to each sitting man.

"The day is young, but I'm old and ready to drink," said Thoiren with a chuckle. "We'll eat after we talk."

Vinlon patted his stomach, digesting breakfast. He supposed Thoiren would think the gesture meant he was hungry. In truth he didn't want for much food the last four weeks and had expanding girth to show for it. He accepted his tankard and drank, relying on the brew to help him forget he sat atop a waterfall.

"I teased you with prospect of news concerning you." Thoiren waved to the group across the room, and a gray-bearded man stepped forth.

"Dekloes!" Radzig jumped to his feet, bumping his forehead on the ceiling. He dropped his tankard, and spilled brew leaked between the logs of the floor into the river. One of the women approached to retrieve the tankard, but Thoiren waved her away.

Vinlon's thoughts stumbled over themselves. *Dekloes should* be reaching Richee. His news couldn't be good. *Considering the furious storm and its howling wind and slashing rain, what happened to the other Warnekt on the Richeeyim vessel? What about Radzig's son?*

Radzig looked wide-eyed at Dekloes, rubbing a white tuft of hair where he struck his forehead. His voice sounded desperate. "What happened to Jaspich, Dekloes?"

"He's fine. Everyone's fine."

Radzig slumped on his pedestal, holding his head in both hands. Vinlon beckoned Dekloes to sit so he didn't need to crane his neck during their conversation. The man took a stump on Vinlon's left, Thoiren's right, and faced the space between the two leaders.

Vinlon prompted him, "The storm got you three weeks ago? What happened?" He drank as he listened.

"I never was more frightened in my life, Tribemaster, more than I experienced in any battle, even the one *I got this*." Dekloes pointed to the scar on his cheek within his beard. "The sea was like hills, going up and down. The vessel cracked, almost broke in half. We were lucky to limp into a bay."

Vinlon's stomach tightened. "Which bay?"

The answer Vinlon feared came from Dekloes. "Ranjin."

"Druogoint."

"Yes, Tribemaster. I was so seasick when I reached the shore I thought I would vomit out my guts. My shipmates did no better, even the Richeeyimt. The Druogoint had no trouble taking us under their power."

Radzig lifted his head from his hands. "Jaspich, he's fine?"

"He's fine," Dekloes repeated his earlier report. "For now."

Radzig snarled. "What do you mean, *for now?*"

Vinlon realized fear for his son didn't have him thinking straight. He knew what Dekloes meant. "Warlord Druogoin wants ransom." He drank more from his tankard.

"He wants weapons like the Richeeyimt had," said Dekloes.

Radzig scoffed. "The man's a curse."

He's also my dear wedlock father, Vinlon bemoaned the fact. "Will that ransom all our men?"

"Only Jaspich."

Vinlon jumped to his feet. His bushy hair, not pulled behind his head for weeks, brushed the ceiling. His tankard didn't spill anything only because it almost was empty. "He's deranged. What does he demand for the others?"

"Nothing," said Dekloes with a smirk. "He never knew about them. Our other men passed for Richeeyimt by not speaking, but Hoj recognized Jaspich."

My dear son, Vinlon thought, not mocking because Hoj *was dear* to him, but his mother taught the boy to hate him. *Not a boy*, he reminded himself. Hoj became a grown man since he saw him. "Did he recognize you, too?"

"No, I was foolish enough to be caught speaking Snarshyim words."

"So we must ransom only Jaspich. Aren't the weapons we were sending to Richee enough? How many were lost in the storm?"

"Only some spears went overboard. Warlord Druogoin wants to develop a trading partnership with the Richeeyimt like we have, so he let them keep the weapons and gave them whatever they needed to repair their vessel. He offered men to help."

"Not good. Our other men could have been discovered and captured."

"That's why the offer was declined. The Richeeyimt did the repair themselves and are sailing home as we speak."

Vinlon smiled at the good news that most of his men and the trade goods were going to reach Richee, and the knowledge to build Richeeyim arches still would come back. The big problem remained ransoming Jaspich. He resumed his seat. "I hope Druogoin realizes we need time to produce more armaments."

Only then he realized Thoiren and his son listened to the whole conversation, keeping silent so they would be ignored. *Curses! He came to the Swenikt hoping to glean information from them, and in his haste to hear what Dekloes had to say, what did he* reveal? *Not much*, he mocked himself, *only our whole trading relationship with the Richeeyimt. Curses!*

"We'll determine the ransom details later, Dekloes. Why do you return to me here on Chief Thoiren's floating hall?"

Surprising Vinlon, the chief spoke, "I also had two men captured by Warlord Druogoin, although I warned them not to venture too far down the Tauzzreen River. My man Jorgis, who is like a son to me, joined with this Hoj who recognized your man Jaspich and is your son in wedlock, Tribemaster Warnek, if my old man's memory isn't failing me."

"He is," said Vinlon, *although he hates me*. "For what purpose did your man join my son?" *Your man, who is like a son to you, and my son who acts like he isn't mine.*

"They're going to Richee."

Vinlon looked for smugness in Thoiren's gap-toothed smile, *but how could he tell? The man always was cheerful. Weren't old men supposed to be grumpy because their bodies ached? That's what Radzig claimed as an excuse for being grouchy.*

The tribemaster considered why the sly chief who eavesdropped while he talked with Dekloes offered information. *Thoiren is telling me about the Swenikt contacting the Richeeyimt*, he surmised, *and speaks of better relations with the Druogoint.*

The chief waited. *The old man uses silence to his advantage*, Vinlon told himself. *Thoiren's cursed cunning flustered him.* He recovered enough wits to ask a decent question. "What about your other man the Druogoint captured?"

"The servant Pokyer," said Thoiren, seeming to newly remember, although Vinlon suspected he didn't forget anything. "He's a dimwit but reliable. He returned to me near Pinkulda with your man Dekloes. I suppose the warlord decided you would get his ransom demand quicker if Dekloes followed the rivers instead of taking the supposed shorter route through the forest. Or, perhaps he didn't trust your man to deliver the message, since he told it only to Pokyer, who told me, and then I told Dekloes."

He relapsed to silence, having unnerved Vinlon with more

talk about the Swenikt cooperating with the Druogoint. The tribemaster wondered what Thoiren planned next. *Would he resort to the old man's trick of pretending to sleep as he listened to everything around him?* Vinlon considered what to say, something Thoiren couldn't turn against him, but only could think how he wanted to join the rascals some night soon and crash this cursed houseboat over the waterfall into a pile of broken lumber.

The chief resumed talking. "Your wedlock father Druogoin is a reasonable man."

My wedlock father, Vinlon fumed. *Curses! He isn't reasonable.*

Thoiren continued, "He doesn't expect Dekloes to take your response to him and risk becoming a hostage again. That's why I'll give your reply to the freckled redhead Druogoinyim woman he sent with Pokyer."

Freckled redhead? Vinlon knew he shouldn't take the bait but couldn't resist. "This woman, is she young, about twenty years?"

"I forget her name, my old man's memory," said Thoiren. "Help me, Kevyar."

He picked up his tankard, which he set beside his pedestal right after he received it, and drank. Vinlon doubted he had memory trouble.

Kevyar emptied his tankard into his mouth and set it down. He hadn't spoken yet, but his first word mentally slammed the tribemaster. "Thigrel."

Vinlon's daughter, whom he hadn't heard anything about in years.

Kevyar continued, "She's not the prettiest redhead, although I would have her if I had no other choice. Somewhat pudgy for my taste but she likes Pokyer, and he'll return with her to Ranjin to keep her satisfied."

Vinlon fumed, thinking about his daughter being satisfied by a servant, and he wanted to choke Kevyar. *Not the prettiest redhead and pudgy,* the man said. Vinlon wanted to punch him in the face and *then* choke him.

Kevyar

Fenzdiwerp

"Do you see what happened by keeping silent and listening?"

Yes, Father, Kevyar thought.

He sat across a small table from Thoiren in the raft's other room, leaning against a wall so a shaft of light from one of the small square openings in the riverside wall didn't shine into his face. The room had barely enough other space for storage. The place was packed with foodstuffs, fishnets, bows and arrows, axes for fighting and others for chopping wood, cloaks, spare boots, rope, and candles. Unknown to everybody but the chief and his son, it also had a stash of gold and silver.

Kevyar didn't think he should have to respond to his father's question, but did. "They told us some things we didn't know."

"Better, Son. They told us things they didn't want us to know." Thoiren drank from his refilled tankard.

Too bad we did the same, Father, Kevyar thought. *Why didn't you heed your own advice?* He used less confrontational words to ask the question. "Why did you mention Jorgis and Pokyer?"

Thoiren set his tankard on the table. "I didn't tell them anything Dekloes didn't already know. Did I mention the scrolls?"

No, Kevyar answered by shaking his head. He wasn't sure how important keeping the scrolls a secret from the Warnekt was, since the Druogoint knew about them. If only they were written with Chizdekyim symbols, which Jorgis could read, he and Pokyer wouldn't have traveled for a translation and been captured.

"Everything I said had a purpose, Son. You saw how I unsettled Warnek, but you insulted his daughter before I could pry more secrets from him."

Kevyar considered claiming he didn't know Thigrel was the tribemaster's daughter, but to what purpose? His father still would be displeased, and if he thought he didn't know who Thigrel was, he would consider him to be more of a dolt. His best recourse was to be a son eager to learn. "What else did you hope for him to talk about, Father?"

"I don't know. Before Pokyer returned from Ranjin, we were unaware the Warnekt visited the coastland where I suggested Jorgis to go. We didn't even know it was called Richee. None of us could read the writing on the map. Everybody has secrets, and Warnek was getting careless, so I was willing to listen."

Kevyar willed himself to keep a smirk off his face. *Father, you have your own secret*, he thought. *Jorgis is like your son, you say. More than true!* He once went to his half brother's Chizdekyim mother, who lived with his supposed-Swenikyim father among the great red trees at the headwater of a tributary to the Pultanik River. There he extracted the truth from her by the point of a sword.

"We must join our guests on the bank." Thoiren stood from the table. "Remember to listen, like you were doing before you told Warnek his daughter was no beauty, and we might hear more interesting things."

Kevyar now allowed himself a smirk, and he spoke words meant to irritate the scolding old man. "I'll listen in town tonight."

Thoiren paused while passing to the other room, wagging a finger. "I know what you do in town. Stay away from wenches and take your wife with you. I didn't bring her along only to serve brew. I *want* a grandson."

Thoiren left suitably irritated. Kevyar heard his tense footsteps in the other room. *A grandson*, he mused. Why did his father assume Jankwel, the homely fisherman's daughter from the town by the deep blue lake at the headwater of the Pultanik River, and the wife he was arranged to marry, wouldn't produce for him another granddaughter? Kevyar had secrets, too. Jankwel's flow was late, so another child could be coming. Moreover, Thoiren didn't know about a grandson here in Fenzdiwerp. Kevyar would see the boy when he visited his mother later.

Not that he cared if his father knew. The secret he didn't want the chief to discover concerned the tribute he *wouldn't* be collecting for the Herkt. The news reached his wife's town from across the deep blue lake that the Jatneryimt killed the Herkyim clanlord, and a duel would determine his successor. Kevyar concluded the Herkt would be too busy to bother collecting their annual indemnity from the Swenikt, and he thought best not to ask for his father's opinion. *Dear Father, I listen better than you think I do.*

Just His Head

Herkt, Jatneryimt

BRUTEZ   **TAUBUETH**

"A few more links. His arms are still loose."

Brutez turned the wheel below Chrenlon's feet. *Click! Click! Click!* The chain pulled the boy's ankles.

Sangern stood by his brother's hands. "That's good."

Brutez moved alongside the rack to make sure his nephew's body wasn't suspended from the surface. Sangern checked the wooden bit between his brother's teeth. The boy was set for another round of torment now at the end of the third week.

At first Yeemzal lanced and cut away poisoned flesh from the burned chest and shoulder. She poured boiling liquids and burned Chrenlon with a hot iron. Taubueth's strongest residents took turns restraining him, but even a sedated boy of ten years could thrash free from their grips while writhing in agony. Brutez, Sangern, Heptor, Rankeb, Konrash, Jonerch, Gordib, and various Feldramyim warriors all had bruises and scratches to show for it. Heptor jested about using the rack to restrain the patient, but nobody laughed. They patted him on the back for a brilliant idea.

The rotten stench left the wound during the first week, requiring no more scalding and burning. Another awful process followed, keeping the burned flesh clean as it healed. Chrenlon was put on the rack for peeling away dead skin, scraping off scabs, breaking blisters, and squeezing out pus. He screamed himself hoarse.

The boy was stripped to the waist, exposing the ugly charred wound. Raw flesh ran from his shoulder by the armpit downward over his birthmarksign and left nipple, which were burned away. Blistering red skin surrounded the raw area, coalesced with scabs and dried skin, and pinkish gnarled skin ringed that. The blistering and scabby ring shrank day by day, reducing the area of the open wound and leaving more of the boy's chest healed.

Brutez and Sangern broke blisters. They picked away scabs and dead skin. Chrenlon came out of his stupor in screams, gnawing on the bit gag and flopping against his constraints. Blood and fatty pus oozed around Brutez's fingers. The screaming became a shrill pitch hurtful to the ears. Then the boy passed out.

"Blessed mercy," Brutez muttered.

"Agreed, Uncle," said Sangern. "I'm glad my mother doesn't hear it as she waits for news of his recovery."

Brutez pinched behind a large scab to rip it away, a good time to do that one when Chrenlon wasn't feeling it. "Aunt Yeemzal is confident he's out of danger."

"I should return to Agratuna while the weather remains decent for traveling," said Sangern. "I don't want Mother fretting all winter."

Brutez pulled a strip of dry skin. "You should leave tomorrow." *The trees are barren and any day snow would fly*, he figured. "I'll send as many provisions your escort can carry to help feed your people at Agratuna this winter."

"You're most generous, Clanlord Uncle. I don't know how to thank you."

Brutez squeezed the juice from a blister. "Bring along your

mother when you return in spring for your brother. I haven't seen my sister since I was a little boy."

Sangern smiled. "She won't need convincing, and my father will want to see *his* sister."

That sister, Yeemzal, arrived from her quarters on the other side of the bowels of Taubueth's donjon, bringing the latest poultice. Its stench overpowered any smell of burned or oozing flesh coming from Chrenlon. Approving of how well Brutez and Sangern did their work, Yeemzal dismissed her two nephews.

The rack was located behind a steep wooden stairs leading to the main hall. Brutez followed Sangern, leaning an elbow on the handrail because his hands were bloody and slimy. They found Heptor, with his friends Rankeb and Konrash, at one end of the long dining table, lingering over remnants of that night's meal.

Sangern ambushed Brutez's brother, smearing his back with blood and ooze. "Uncle Heptor, I'm going home tomorrow."

"You need a proper farewell. Let's pour brew with some wenches."

Rankeb and Konrash hooted approval. Sangern showed his support with a smile and a pat on Heptor's back.

Then Heptor stood before Brutez, so close the clanlord smelled cured cheese on his breath. "Clanlord Brother, are you joining us?"

Brutez wiped the blood, pus, and ooze from his hands on his brother's tunic. "You'll have more fun without me."

Heptor laughed. "I'm sure of that." He waved to the others. "Let's go."

Rankeb and Konrash followed him outside. Sangern went, too, sharing in the mirth of the others like another one of Heptor's friends, which in fact he had become.

Brutez selected a sausage from the leftover food and, taking a chair by the fire, worried. *Where's Uncle Shemjib? He's been gone for three weeks.*

A youth arrived, reporting Larboelm's return. "He's at the

far stable."

Brutez dropped the sausage, feeling dread. *Why only Larboelm? Where's my uncle, and why must I go to the stable?* He told the boy to stay and hurried from the donjon into the night, crossing the yard. Drunken shouts and laughter came from Heptor and the others in the distance.

Climbing the rampart, Brutez thought, *Why in all the centuries the Herkt lived in Taubueth didn't they put a gate in the wall or dig a tunnel under it?* He would order it done so the rickety ladder could be retired, but any project must wait until spring.

Seeing his breath, he realized how much the warmth of that sunny day had turned to cold in the cloudless night. He shivered without a cloak.

The moon's sliver shined in a clearing over the outward stable, the farthest building from the stronghold. The moonstar was its most brilliant this time of the month when the moon was out of phase. Brutez wondered, *Why doesn't the moonstar phase?*

A darkened figure appeared, coming from the stable. Brutez couldn't see his face, but he had the same height, bulk, and tangled hair as Larboelm. The dreadful feeling returned. *Why did Larboelm ask me to come here?*

"Where's Shemjib?"

Saying nothing, the man beckoned him to follow behind the stable and showed him a stagskin bag on the ground next to the timber building. The foreboding within Brutez sickened him. He didn't want to look inside the bag but knew he must, although he knew what it contained.

The bag weighed what he expected, and the rotting stench from within was no surprise. The head didn't have enough hair to grab, so he extracted it by the ears and looked into the twisted face of his uncle. The gray eyes stared with a hollow gaze, the sunken cheeks were covered with stubby beard, the yellowed teeth grimaced from an open mouth, and fleshy tubes hung from inside the neck.

Brutez wanted to return it to the bag and never look at it

again, but the hide fell to the ground, and he had no hands free. "Hold that open, Larboelm." He kicked the bag.

He needed time to think and rebagging the head gave him a moment. *How will I tell Aunt Yeemzal?* He forced himself to think of questions for Larboelm. The first question was answered. The Jatneryimt weren't interested in ransoming Sir Grebnar the Bold. The puzzling question was, *why?*

Larboelm told him what happened. "We met Jatneryimt at the Kipneesh River and surrendered our weapons, but they meant to kill us until we showed them Grebnar's cape and sword. They took those things, kept beating us, and put us in the Doenesh dungeon for two weeks before a brute with a strange mustache axed your uncle's head."

"That's it? You had no chance to negotiate?"

"We never saw Rendif. I was released with the head and my mount."

Brutez needed to know more. He had one option. "Larboelm, provision two mounts and wait here behind the stable, and pack extra for colder travel."

"Yes, Clanlord."

Brutez took along the bag with Shemjib's head, stuffing it into a bush by the stronghold wall. He scaled the ladder, thinking again about digging a tunnel. The drunken revelry across the yard now included women. He told the youth waiting in the donjon to retire for the night without returning to the stable.

He still kept Grebnar in his chamber, since he never decided what else to do with him. The Jatneryim sat in the chair, head on the table, and snored. The dying embers in the hearth provided barely enough light to see without bumping into anything.

"Wake up!" Brutez jolted Grebnar with a kick into his buttocks.

The Jatneryim woke with a menacing glare. "Curses, Brutez. I was dreaming about my wife."

Brutez ignored him, moving across the room for the

key. He unlocked the Grebnar's shackle from the wall. The Jatneryim cooperated, turning aside in his chair while Brutez locked the shackle around the opposite ankle from the one already chained.

Brutez put on a cloak, slipping the key into an inside pocket, and tossed another cloak to Grebnar. "Come."

"Why?"

"You've been here a month. Don't you want to leave?"

Grebnar was more precise. "Thirty-seven days."

He donned the cloak and followed Brutez with a rattle, taking the largest steps his hobble allowed. They descended the stairs and left the donjon. Brutez slowed for Grebnar to keep pace, although he wanted to hurry before they were seen.

The sentries on the rampart saw them, but they didn't concern Brutez. He helped Grebnar get on the ladder. The Jatneryim hopped down the rungs, clanging all the way.

"Your people's reply to my offer for ransom is in there." Brutez pointed into a certain bush by the wall and turned his back, so he wouldn't have to see. He heard rustling foliage and a squishing sound.

"This is the work of Matkulk," said Grebnar.

"Agreed. Return it to the bag and give it to me." Brutez turned around when the squishing stopped and took the bag from Grebnar. "Sir Rendif would ransom you."

"He's my wedlock brother."

"Not everyone loves his wedlock brother."

"He depends on his."

"Come with me."

Larboelm wasn't waiting behind the stable, but Brutez figured he needed more time to equip two mounts than it took to retrieve Grebnar.

"Whose head is that?"

"My uncle's," said Brutez.

Grebnar had the sense to say no more.

Larboelm came, holding the reins of two mounts in one hand and a torch in the other. Brutez saw his face for the first time in the torchlight, battered with bruises. His lips were bloated purple, his nose smashed, and one eye swelled shut. The mounts were packed with winter bedding, drinking skins, and bags of provisions. Brutez recognized one of them as the same mount with a shimmering ebony mane he rode while bringing Grebnar to Taubueth. He checked through the baggage on that mount, finding sausage and cured cheese, fur-lined boots, and furry gloves.

Satisfied he had what was needed, he told Larboelm to take Grebnar with the mounts to the shack by the Taubueth River and to wait for him there. He held forth the grisly bag. "This, too."

Larboelm looked at his hands, filled with reins and the torch.

"Give him the torch." Brutez pointed at Grebnar. "No, better, let him have the mounts." Larboelm needed the torch to lead the way.

Brutez returned to the stronghold, wanting to consult his father. Sangern's farewell celebration now involved a large group in the donjon hall. Heptor's friends and their wenches were joined in a drinking game by Jonerch, Gordib, and Taubueth's Feldramyim guests. Aunt Yeemzal sat at the table close by Sangern and Zamtoth. *Doubly bad*, Brutez fretted. Not only was his father with his aunt, he might not be sober enough to give good counsel.

Heptor called over the din of laughter, shouts, and pounding on the table, "Brutez, join the game."

Nazzel distracted Heptor by wrapping a hand behind his head and stuffing his face into her ample bosom. While the drunken revelers hooted and hollered, Brutez slipped behind Zamtoth and grabbed his father's shoulder.

The old man looked, and Brutez was relieved he seemed alert. "Come, Father."

Zamtoth didn't hear, so Brutez tugged his arm to get him to follow upstairs.

Brutez stopped outside his chamber. "Father, Larboelm

returned."

"Is Shemjib back?"

Brutez knew no easy answer. "Just his head."

His father closed his eyes, breathing deeply, and opened them, wistfully wet. "Where is it?"

"Larboelm took it away."

"Good, best Yeemzal doesn't see."

Brutez cringed. *How will I tell her?*

His father continued, "It doesn't make sense. Sir Rendif would ransom Grebnar. He's in great peril without him."

"I fear we're too late making the offer."

"Matkulk killed my brother."

Brutez had expected that conclusion from his father but wasn't so sure about the rest. "We must release Grebnar."

Zamtoth grabbed his shoulders, looking him in the eyes. "He must go back more than ever. Get him out of here. Our people will want his head, especially Yeemzal."

Brutez withdrew from his father's grasp and nudged open his chamber's door, showing Grebnar was gone. "I'm going with him."

Zamtoth's eyes squinted in puzzlement, so Brutez knew he must explain. "The clan won't accept releasing him without getting anything in return."

Zamtoth's confused look disappeared. "They would think you're intimidated. Going with Grebnar indicates you're working a plan. Do you have one?"

"No, Father."

"I didn't think so."

Zamtoth stepped into the chamber. "How many men are you taking with you?"

Brutez followed him inside and closed the door. "None."

"Is that wise?"

"Grebnar won't betray me."

"What if Matkulk leads the Jatneryimt?"

"Then I'd need so many men we would be considered invaders."

"Matkulk's forces should be in the west."

"Whatever Matkulk is doing, Father, I must get Grebnar out of here tonight. You'll be clanlord while I'm gone."

"I know something about being one."

"Larboelm will be at your command. He may have been loyal to Vulrath and Klinteg, but he's proved faithful to me."

Zamtoth agreed. "He's unquestionably loyal."

"Sangern is leaving for Agratuna tomorrow," Brutez told him, but of course his father knew that. *He's been celebrating*, he recalled. "I promised to give him all the provisions he could carry, and the other Feldramt are welcome to stay until spring." That left one matter unsettled, the most difficult one. "I must tell Yeemzal."

Zamtoth offered, "I'll tell her tomorrow when she's sober."

"I'm clanlord, and I sent him to his death. I must tell her even if she's spirited." *Maybe better to tell her that way*, he mused.

His father put a hand on his shoulder. "Even so, I'll go with you."

Brutez gratefully accepted that offer.

When they returned to the raucous hall downstairs, Heptor was falling on his face because somebody tied his boots together. *One of Gordib's pranks*, Brutez figured.

Yeemzal no longer was there, so Brutez and his father descended the steeper wooden steps to the lower level, thinking she went to her quarters. Under torchlight they saw Chrenlon resting on the rack. *Why not?* Brutez contemplated his aunt's decision to leave him there. *Then he wouldn't roll over on his wound.*

The door to Yeemzal's inner room, the bedchamber, was partly open. Brutez peered inside, seeing nothing but darkness. "Aunt Yeemzal, are you there?"

Somebody within mumbled. Zamtoth arrived with one of the torches. The light showed Yeemzal sprawled on the bed in her day clothes. Her long gray hair was tangled over the side of her face.

Zamtoth shook her with his hand not holding the torch.

"Yeemzal."

She rolled over, eyes opening but not seeing. "Shemjib?" She reached and grabbed Zamtoth's beard. "No, Zamtoth. Where's Shemjib?"

Brutez wanted her to become coherent before he told her. "Aunt Yeemzal, I sent him to the Jatneryimt, remember?"

She sat up and rubbed her eyes. "The drinking game. I lost."

Brutez sat on the bed by her, taking one of her hands in both of his. "Aunt Yeemzal, are you hearing me?"

"Brutez, yes. You sent Shemjib to the Jatneryimt. Have you heard from him?"

Brutez decided she was as alert as she would get. He took a deep breath, swallowed hard, and spoke the words that would devastate her, "They killed him."

She shrieked, "No!" yanking her hand from his grip and shoving him away. "Why did you send him? Why didn't you send somebody else?" She pressed her face into the bed and wailed.

Brutez agonized about what to say next. *What could he say? Her questions accused him. Why did I send him? Why didn't I send somebody else?*

Zamtoth gave him the torch. "You must go. I'll stay with her."

Brutez wanted to abandon his plan, but no, he decided, if he did that, Shemjib would have died for nothing. "Farewell, Father. I don't know when I'll see you again."

He left through Yeemzal's other room so he didn't have to pass through the drunken revelry in the donjon's main hall. By the light of his torch, he glanced at the twenty-four broadswords lined on the wall and wondered if they ever were used in battle. He climbed the stairs to his aunt's hovel full of cures and went outside.

The night was colder. This was no autumn chill. The air had the bite of winter, but he had the torch for warmth. He crossed the yard to a guardhouse by the wall to get a war hammer and a bow with a quiver of arrows. A bloodstained cudgel was there, swathed in *Klinteg's blood*. Brutez took his tournament weapon with him, leaving Taubueth.

A path curved southward around the forest trunks on level ground. The torchlight touched only the nearest pillars of bark. The shadows of others stood in the gloom beyond, the vanguard of a silent and immobile host standing in ranks for many horizons.

The path sloped downhill a horizon later, switching back on itself several times before reaching the Taubueth River. The river wasn't much, bubbling over a rocky valley bottom like the Kipneesh River did, but on a smaller scale on its course to the deep blue lake twenty horizons eastward. Brutez remembered years without much rain when the river stopped flowing. Even this season with regular rainfall, it needed a spring thaw to be rejuvenated. Now at the onset of winter, it could be walked across almost anywhere.

Brutez reached the shack where Larboelm and Grebnar waited. "Larboelm, discard that where nobody will find it." He pointed to the bag holding Shemjib's head. "Then return to Taubueth."

"I'm not taking Sir Grebnar to the Jatneryimt?"

"I am."

"Clanlord, I'm your sworn bodyguard. I should go with you."

"You can't always be with me. You went with my uncle, leaving me at Taubueth, didn't you?"

Larboelm frowned.

Brutez continued, "While I'm gone, follow my father's commands."

"Yes, Clanlord."

Unquestionably loyal, Brutez recalled his father's words. Larboelm took the bag, grabbed his torch, and disappeared on the path into the night.

Brutez set the bloodstained cudgel from the guardhouse next to Grebnar, mallet down and handle upright. "You need a weapon."

Grebnar's brown eyes glinted in the torchlight. "I prefer a sword, but I'll take it. You Herkt most adore your weapons when you can bludgeon somebody with them. We Jatneryimt think armaments that cut and slice are more efficient."

Brutez took the key from his cloak's inner pocket and knelt to unshackle Grebnar's ankles.

The Jatneryim asked, "Are you sure you want to do that?"

"How else will you ride your mount?"

"Why don't you think I'll kill you in your sleep?"

"The same reason I didn't let you be killed."

"I admit I prefer you to lead the Herkt, but why do you suppose I won't leave you sleeping and return to my people without you?"

"Sir Rendif could be dead." Brutez finished removing the chain between Grebnar's ankles. "You might need a new ally."

Conflagration Waiting to Happen

Warnekt

VINLON   **HABERGENEFINANCH**

One torch, Vinlon thought as he rode outside a large wood palisade by a bay. *Habergenefinanch would be easy to burn.* The weathered logs appeared old and dry, combustible.

Radzig, Dekloes, and an escort rode with him. They traveled the twenty-five horizons from Fenzdiwerp in less than four days, fast enough to finish the trip in favorable weather. Vinlon regretted each sunny day that passed without being used for travel, but lingered in Fenzdiwerp against his better judgment, wanting to see the rascals do their work. Finally on a clear night after Chief Thoiren returned home upriver, he sat on the roof of his inn by the falls and watched the floating house tumble over the waterfall on the far side of the river. The dark form wasn't easy to see under a crescent moon, but hearing it smash on rocks gratified him.

When the sky clouded over on the first day riding south

to Habergenefinanch, Vinlon feared getting bad weather for the journey, but then another sunny warm day followed. The Swanshyim Forest reasserted itself beyond the cultivated land around Fenzdiwerp, but the path through it was well worn and easily traveled. The trees thinned as the days of riding passed, and the landscape of rolling hills became flatter. A cloudy sky returned, and with it, a sharper cold. *Cold enough to snow*, Vinlon predicted when he saw his breath puffing. A morning frost didn't melt. A chilling northwest wind blew through bared treetops and swirled to the ground in icy blasts, tormenting the travelers until the wall of Habergenefinanch blocked the breezy onslaught.

A spongy swath bordered the bay up to a width of a hundred cubits, which was overgrown with a tangled mass of shrubs and twisted trees elsewhere but cleared here and spanned by piers to the water's edge. Many of the piers would be smashed by ice and need repairs in spring. Any boats had been hauled inland for winter.

The bay's leaden gray surface rippled away from the shore under the outblowing wind. Bristled trees lined the far sides, separating the sight of the water from a clouded sky of like color. The southside trees were gapped by passages to the sea between the barrier islands.

The travelers passed several small doors in the palisade before reaching a gate large enough to admit their mounts. Two Warnekyim black-ribbon pennants flapped from a watchtower, blowing stiff in the wind toward the bay. A narrow street ran into the town between thatch-roofed wooden buildings one or two levels high. Straw was present everywhere, stacked in bales along walls and spread on the ground. *One torch*, Vinlon fretted. The place was a conflagration waiting to happen.

The street was crowded with people, barn fowl, and livestock, so the travelers dismounted and led their mounts by the reins. Vinlon enjoyed passing by the warmth of a foundry. The next building smelled of fresh-baked bread. The way widened to a commons. A stone well stood in the center of the open space, a rare inflammable object in Habergenefinanch. The water in it was too muddy for drinking, at least by people, but a man offered a bucketful to his canine.

Radzig and Dekloes followed Vinlon along another street, going parallel to the bayside wall, while the men who escorted them from Fenzdiwerp went another way. The trio passed a butcher's shop and left their mounts at a stable facing the end of an intersecting street.

Radzig continued along the street parallel to the wall toward his house, a place overlooking the wall with a scenic view of the bay. He was eager to see his family, who had traveled to Habergenefinanch along the coast with a group from Pultanik.

Vinlon went with Dekloes up the intersecting street deeper into town. They came to a commons, larger than the previous one and bordered by the long meeting house built by Vinlon's ancestors. The tribemaster's residence stood on a knoll next to the longhouse, flying a black ribbon from its roof.

Vinlon entered his favorite inn with Dekloes, looking for a meal and news. When he saw Leenarth, the master archer from Pultanik, he knew the man had news. The newcomers took seats and were served brew. Leenarth's plateload of woolstock chops, starch roots, and gravy smelled delicious.

"I've loitered here waiting for you, Tribemaster," said the archer. "I bring dire news from Pultanik."

Vinlon dreaded but had to ask. "What happened there?"

"Nothing there, but news came from the three lakes. The Jatneryimt came down the Kipneesh River to sack our towns."

Vinlon clenched his teeth and fists, and he wanted to draw his sword, although the gesture would be useless. *He must retaliate!* That couldn't be done until spring, which made him angrier. Leenarth described the flow of refugees coming to Pultanik and their stories of destruction, and Vinlon seethed. His meal arrived and grew cold.

"I'll call the warriors to gather at Pultanik after the spring thaw," he told Leenarth at the end of the report. He interlocked his fingers to steady the angered shaking of his arms. "The Jatneryimt will regret attacking us."

Vinlon's cold food was replaced by a hot serving, and the tribemaster ate. His news was bad, too. "We must ransom Radzig's son Jaspich." He told the master archer he would spend the winter making bows and arrows for the Druogoint while Banshim made swords and spears. The armaments were to be exchanged for Jaspich at Fenzdiwerp in the spring, according to an arrangement proposed by Chief Thoiren.

"Banshim stayed at Pultanik," said Leenarth, referring to the master forger.

Vinlon motioned to the third man at the table. "Dekloes is going there when the weather improves. He'll tell Banshim what's needed."

A horrific mewing outside had the sound of a feline maimed by a cleaver. Vinlon knew before looking. Birdbane didn't take long to find he had returned for the winter to Habergenefinanch, and she was upset he was gone all summer. He went out to make amends, stooping to stroke the creature's soft black fur. It purred but mewed some more before abandoning its anger. Vinlon supposed he owed the beast some gratitude, for he expected the tribemaster's residence to be cleared of vermin. He would do the same for his tribe, ridding them of Jatneryim vermin.

I Prefer Green

Herkt, Jatneryimt

BRUTEZ   **KIPNEESH RIVER**

The fire crackled as Brutez added another log to the flame. Sparks and snowflakes swirled in the night, melting over the blaze where heat met cold in the air. Grebnar sat with Brutez, chewing the last bits of meat from a longear carcass.

The Kipneesh River gurgled over rocks before them. They had crossed the largest ford between Taubueth and Doenesh before making camp. The firelight glinted on the dark rushing water and illuminated the nearest trees on both sides of the river within the flurry of snow.

Brutez had misgiving over his decision to travel alone with Grebnar. This fire was the most visible one of the journey, giving away their position up and down the river valley, but Grebnar insisted he would hold sway over any Jatneryimt they encountered.

He tossed his gleaned carcass into the river. "I must ask you, Brutez, why didn't you kill me to avenge your uncle?"

Finally he spoke about it, Brutez thought. "You're no more to blame for his death than I am for Chakstim and Rendif."

Grebnar frowned.

"I recognized their bodies when you were captured." *Captured on this same river,* Brutez thought, *although a few horizons upriver.*

Grebnar waved his hands. "How did you recognize my sons and know their names?"

"I spied on you many times." Brutez fixed his gaze on Grebnar to observe the Jatneryim's reaction to his next words. "Sometimes I was under your nose."

What? Grebnar's surprise was written on his face. "You infiltrated my camp? I would have noticed somebody the size of you."

"I was smaller."

"You spied on me as a youth. Why don't your people call *you* the Bold?"

Brutez shrugged. "Doesn't matter. Now they call me clanlord."

Grebnar asked him troubling questions. "How long will you be their clanlord? Will they call you that after running away with your enemy?"

Brutez looked at the Jatneryim sitting across the fire under increasing snowfall. "I don't consider you an enemy."

Grebnar challenged him. "What if I still consider you mine? I lost more than my sons the day your clansmen ambushed us."

"I saw Tharkwip's body," said Brutez, referring to Grebnar's friend.

Grebnar snorted. "You're right. I don't blame you for the deaths of my sons and friend, but I'll tell you something that should surprise you." His face became distorted behind the fumes of the fire as he leaned forward. "Your aunt blamed me for the death of her twin sons, your cousins, only because I'm a Jatneryim."

"I'm not surprised," said Brutez, although he suspected Grebnar had more to say.

He did. "During my captivity, I thought about your

twenty-nine clansmen I killed."

"You threatened to make me the thirtieth, using my own dagger."

"I didn't tell you how much one pair looked like twins."

Anger surged within Brutez. He wondered, *Did Grebnar kill my cousins?*

The Jatneryim continued, "They looked alike except for different colored eyes. I fought both years ago when your Clanlord Vulrath was foolish enough to attack the Green Citadel. They fancied themselves honorable by fighting me one at a time. They died as they were born, moments apart."

Brutez lived among the Jatneryimt long enough to know they called the stronghold at Doenesh the Green Citadel, in like manner they referred to the lava rock fortress at Mapvin as the Black Citadel. He also knew his cousins were killed while attacking Doenesh. *Grebnar killed his cousins.* He didn't want to believe it.

"These *twins*... were their heads shaved?"

"Stubble, like your uncle's head, who was their father, I suppose. You see, Brutez, I *am* to blame for killing your cousins. Don't you consider me your enemy?"

Brutez seethed and wondered why he was so angry. He knew Grebnar killed twenty-nine clansmen, each somebody's relative. Why did his relations matter more than the others? He calmed himself, unclenching a hand from his war hammer. "I don't. We must stop killing one another."

"Why?"

Grebnar's question left Brutez without immediate answer. The Herk brushed snow from his shoulders before he had one. "It's a waste."

"I agree. Our peoples would make better lives for themselves if they cooperated rather than plundering and butchering one another."

Something about the Grebnar's words bothered Brutez. "Who do you mean by saying *peoples*?"

Grebnar brushed snow from his shoulders. "The Jatneryimt

and Herkt, who else?"

"You misspeak when you say *peoples*. You ought to say *people*."

"People?"

"Yes, people and not only Herkt and Jatneryimt. I mean all the clans and tribes who speak the Snarshyim language. We're *one* people."

Grebnar stood to shake more snow from his clothes and hair. "The other clans and tribes don't think that way. *Ours* don't."

"Only we do, my friend," said Brutez. "We must convince our own people and then the rest of the Snarshyimt."

"I regret that's for another day. This one's done, and all we have left for us is sleeping on cold ground. I'll take the first watch."

"Cold ground tonight but perhaps tomorrow night you'll share Sejel's warm bed."

Grebnar put more wood on the fire. "That would be more appealing if we didn't have to talk about our sons being dead."

Brutez noticed how Grebnar showed no reaction to him knowing his wife's name, although the Jatneryim never spoke it, referring to her as *my wife*. "She'll be glad you returned."

Grebnar laughed. "She'll consider me back from the dead."

Brutez stepped across stony ground, now covered by enough snow for footprints, to retrieve the bedding from his mount. Clearing the snow and leaves from a spot near the fire, he unrolled his bedding and removed his cloak and boots. He took his war hammer and dagger in hand and climbed into the furs, covering his head in them. The steady sound of water rushing over the stones and rocks in the Kipneesh River soothed him.

> *Reflections of the high summer sun sparkled from the trickling water of the Taubueth River. His mother sat beside him on the grassy bank, feeding his baby brother. He remembered she looked pretty with ruby red hair and*

sapphire blue eyes. His older brothers frolicked in the river, splashing one another and shouting in boyish voices.

She asked him, "Brutez, why don't you play with your brothers?"

He didn't answer. I'm not like them, he thought.

"You're a thoughtful boy in the manner of your father," she answered for him. "You won't only be clanlord like him but more."

His side exploded in a surge of pain.

A gruff voice shouted, "Wake up!"

Brutez was smothered in fur and disoriented. *What's happening? Who's yelling at me?* He remembered he was with Grebnar.

"Wake up! Who's in there?"

Another hard blow hammered him in the side. *Why is Grebnar kicking me? Why is he asking me who I am?* It was somebody else. Brutez no longer held his weapons, so he reached to pull the bedding from over his head before he received another kick. Snow spilled cold on his face. He couldn't see who tormented him.

"Get up so we can see you!" Another kick assailed him.

He heard Grebnar's voice. "Stop kicking my prisoner."

Prisoner? Brutez's thoughts came, although his side pained him. *What game is Grebnar playing? Is this a betrayal?*

He flailed at the furs to escape them. Unfriendly hands grabbed him below the armpits to haul him to his feet. The snow on his face melted and dripped from his beard-trimmed chin. He saw a man with a withered face, looking like tree bark, with a huge wart on one cheek above his gristly beard. Two other men held him by the arms and another stooped to unravel the furs from his feet.

The fire still blazed, sizzling as snow fell into it. Grebnar stood by it, holding the cudgel Brutez gave him, the one stained with Klinteg's blood. Two men flanked him and a third stood behind him. More men took charge of the mounts by the campside and searched the baggage within the circle of firelight.

The man at Brutez's feet found his war hammer and dagger and showed them to the one with the wart.

The warted-one spoke in the gruff voice Brutez heard when he was kicked. "Why is your prisoner armed, Boldness?"

"So careless of me," said Grebnar. "I owe you my thanks for discovering his treachery."

"Carelessness has become your habit, Boldness. We saw your fire from halfway to Doenesh. Tell me. Were you so careless when you disappeared?"

Grebnar didn't respond. He simply stared with that grim look of determination Brutez knew too well.

The warted-one paced before Grebnar. "This is mysterious like when you left your boys rotting in the river. Since your wife and daughter also disappeared, why do we find you with this armed prisoner instead of them?" He pointed to Brutez. "Who is this, Boldness? He looks like a Herk."

"I'm not answering your questions." Grebnar tightened his grip on the cudgel.

Brutez assessed the situation. This new Jatneryim was suspicious, and Grebnar wasn't bragging about capturing the clanlord of the Herkt. Not a betrayal, but the Boldness was playing some game. *Were these Matkulk's men this far eastward?*

"You're right, Boldness. Now isn't the time for questions. Pack your things. We're taking your prisoner."

Grebnar countered with a suggestion. "How about getting a night's sleep? The fire's hot here."

"The fire's a problem. It attracts too much attention."

Brutez winced as his arms were yanked behind his back, straining his shoulder joints. His wrists were lashed with rope.

"Now you look more like a prisoner." One man elbowed Brutez's jaw.

Grebnar lurched forward, surprising the three men around him and getting away from them. He elbowed the jaw of the man who struck Brutez. "I'll do the same to anyone who harms *my* prisoner. Whatever you do to him, I do to you."

None of the Jatneryimt challenged Grebnar, instead making preparations to leave. One man kicked snow over the fire.

"Leave that," the warted-one told him. "It's a good diversion."

Brutez wondered, jaw aching. *Who out there is the man concerned about?*

The Jatneryimt allowed him to put on his cloak and boots before placing him on his mount. They unbound his wrists to tie his arms around the equine's neck, so the shimmering ebony mane rubbed into his face, and they tied his feet with a rope passing from one ankle to the other under the belly.

A man took the mount by the reins, and another led Grebnar's. Grebnar climbed the Kipneesh River's western bank on foot with the other Jatneryimt. Snow kept falling, although diminished, while Brutez enjoyed his mount's pleasant warmth.

This time he didn't dream in his sleep. Come daylight, snow covered the forest floor and coated the tree trunks and branches, but no more fell.

Grebnar talked, "This isn't the way to Doenesh."

"We're going to the Black Citadel, Boldness," said the warted-one.

Both men were behind Brutez where he couldn't see them.

"I prefer green," said Grebnar. "I'll take my mount and go."

"The mount stays with us and so should you."

"I'm going. I insist."

Brutez heard a scuffle, the dull thud of a solid mass hitting flesh and a cry of pain, and then more fleshy thuds and the crunch of bodies landing on snow. He heard a mount whinny and the sound of hooves gallop away.

A face with a wart and gnarled like bark appeared in front of his. "How careless of Sir Grebnar. He left you with us."

Vision

Recorded Year 861

Citadels

Herkt, Jatneryimt

Brutez **Black Citadel, Mapvin**

The cell was dark except for a dull red hue glowing from its rocky walls. The floor was warm, almost hot. It was rough, covered with pits and bumps, and laced with rocky edges sharp as knives. The smell of sulfur and the fumes were barely detectable at first, but irritated eyes, nose, and throat. A frigid wind blew through, passing from one iron portcullis to another. Perhaps it helped by dissipating the toxic sulfur or made it worse by fanning the hot rock.

Days in the cell blurred for Brutez, much as they did when he traveled westward roped to his mount. The bouncing ride, rubbed by the animal's bony back all day, was an agony. Nights were no better, long and each colder than the last, and without Grebnar to restrain his captors, he endured beatings. The threadbare blanket they gave him wasn't the warm fur bedding he slept in before his capture and left him shivering. Some nights he was fed and the others not. None of his food was tasty. They gave him only the stale bread and fatty pieces of meat nobody else wanted.

The terrain remained the same, hilly and covered with trees and snow. He wondered if the Swanshyim Forest ever ended in the west. A black blotch in the tree cover across a valley became a wall facing east, black as coal and standing high in the shade of a setting sun. *The Black Citadel?* If so, it was the home of Matkulk, the Lord of Mapvin.

Brutez didn't sleep much on the cell's pitted and bumpy surface. Although he spread his cloak beneath him whenever lying on the floor or leaning against a wall, the radiant heat from the rock threatened to bake him, and if he wasn't careful, his arm strayed past the cloak's edge, so he burned a hand or cut it on the sharp rock.

If he stood, he froze. His nose, ears, and fingers numbed, and then his face and arms. He had to choose between hot or cold, only finding relief during the transition between lying and standing. Sometimes he sat in middle of the cell, away from the walls, and experienced both temperatures at once, baking hot below his waist and freezing in the wind above it.

> *The scales were rock hard, each the size of a hand and razor sharp on the edges, but he held tight because the fall was great. A vast forest passed by far below. Immense tracts of barren treetops undulated over hills and filled valleys, shimmering pale under moonlight. The glimmering water of rivers twisted through the distant valleys, and lakes spotted the landscape with gleaming reflections of scattered clouds.*
>
> *He felt fire within the great leviathan. Redness glowed between its scales. Heat emanated from its body as if coming from a bed of coals, scalding him and blistering his skin, but he held tight because the fall was great.*
>
> *The beast swooped and floated upwind on great webbed wings. He sensed its emotions as he held tighter, feelings of pure hatred and unquenchable rage. With insatiable hunger, it flew to and fro over the land, searching for something.*
>
> *He sensed its thoughts.*

Kill! Destroy! Death!

Its long skeletal tail whipped against cold air. The wind froze his back while the beast's inner fire seared him in front. It sensed movement and weakness on the ground and dove, making a terrible shriek. The long neck stretched forth, and a blue and crimson plume of flame shot from its mouth and nostrils, burning like sulfur. Horizons of trees became engulfed in an inferno of fire. The beast glided low, tail lashing, with stretched-forth talons. It caught something and flipped it into its fiery maw to devour.

Kill! Destroy! Death!

It swept upward, soaring higher than before in its futile search for satisfaction. Mountains rose to the northwest, snowy white on the peaks and swathed in pines on their slopes. Seawater shone to the northern and southern limits of the sky, and eastward was empty space.

A scarlet line appeared beyond the desert. A new sensation smoldered within the beast, a feeling always there with the abject hatred and anger but previously hidden—fear. The leviathan shrieked, no longer to terrorize but now in terror. The eastern sky brightened, turning orange and yellow. The beast dove into a valley to escape the advancing daylight but to no avail. The sun was rising and impossible to stop. Its relentless light probed the valley, exposing the leviathan. It shrieked for a last time before bursting into flame and sprinkling to the ground in a shower of cinders and ash.

The floor was warm, almost hot, and Brutez burned his hand again. He was served meals at indeterminate intervals but never enough to satisfy his hunger. The food was raw, but no matter because placing it into one of the dips in the floor cooked it well enough and made for a good serving bowl, too. An even worse deprivation was thirst. His throat was raw from the sulfuric fumes, and he developed a severe cough. He welcomed times when gale winds drifted snow into his cell for him to scoop into his mouth before it melted on the warm floor.

> The beings were creatures of light, beautiful to behold. They glared so brightly he couldn't see the features of their faces or surmise what they were wearing. He saw only heads, arms, legs, and wings.
>
> They were beautiful to behold, but spoke only lies.
>
> "You killed your uncle."
>
> "You have failed."
>
> "You will die here."
>
> "You will never matter."
>
> "The Snarshyimt are ours. Their destiny is destruction and death."
>
> The lies altered them. Instead of blaring light, the beings hid in darkness. Wings fluttered, and arms and legs moved in the shadows.
>
> Pairs of eyes, luminescent and unblinking, appeared in a variety of hues. They looked like the eyes of felines with slits for pupils, but they didn't narrow and widen in the manner of felines in changing light. They writhed. The deep black recesses constantly changed shapes, curling and coiling in the shape of serpents.
>
> The eyes stared in four rows of six pairs, twenty-four in all, full of malice and hate. One pair in the first row was red, one green speckled with black, one cobalt blue, one brown, one purple, and one orange. The orange eyes changed to pink. In the second row the pairs were amber, sapphire blue, light gray, dark gray, white, and olive green. One pair in the third row was black, although a lighter shade than the ebony of its writhing pupils. Another pair was maroon, and four more eyes opened on that face for a total of six maroon irises. The rest of the eyes, four pairs in the third row and all the ones in the fourth row, were sky blue.
>
> The dark beings spoke more lies and finally a truth.
>
> "You have no hope."
>
> "We are invincible."

"You are doomed to destruction and death."
"We are the bondage lords of the Snarshyimt."

Rankling chains shackled their arms and legs, but they couldn't protest because they were gagged with rolls of parchment. A larger roll descended. The looks of malice and hate in the twenty-four pairs of eyes plus four changed to panic and terror. The big parchment had a knobby handle at each end. One knob grew longer, much longer, flattening and becoming shiny and sharp. The other knob molded into the parchment, transforming into a hilt for a great sword. The blade swung around, level to the necks of the bondage lords, and lopped off all their heads in one stroke. The eyes went dark.

Twenty-four broadswords, bejeweled and golden-hilted, danced in the night. White hands of light held the golden hilts. The arms with the hands were upraised from flashing bodies of brilliance.

Brutez squatted on his cloak over the warm, rough, and rocky floor. The brilliant apparitions with swords surrounded him, facing outward. Flashing light fluttered from their bodies like robes blowing in the wind. A gale whipped through his hair and beard, which had grown long. The tempest howled overhead where more light appeared, so blindingly bright Brutez couldn't look at it.

The howling became words, loud as thunder. "This one is mine! I have plans for him. You are not allowed to touch him. You are blinded."

A man was close, a cruel and pitiless man. He had a prize within his grasp, but he didn't see it. Another man, steadfast, loyal, and true, looked for the prize and found it.

Brutez saw glowing walls while sitting alone atop his cloak and coughing. The unbearded portions of his face and his earlobes stung from the onslaught of a straight-line wind.

Steam rose by the windward portcullis where inblowing snow met the heated floor. He hurried over to obtain relief for his parched and inflamed throat.

> *He heard his mother's voice. "You won't only be clanlord like your father but more."*
>
> *Five trees had grown in a line through the forest. Nothing remained of the first three except stumps. A strong sapling on the other end was chopped down. The fourth one grew tall, splitting into two trunks. The branches reached to the sunny sky and the limbs budded. The buds grew into red leaves shaped like Herkyim blooddrop pennants. They rustled in a warm breeze, breaking the sunlight into a fluttering array of speckles.*

Brutez's cough spattered blood on the floor, and his eyes and nose oozed with excretions. He had no sense how long he was confined at what he supposed to be Mapvin, the Black Citadel, but he guessed some weeks. The meals came twice a day or once every several days. The intervals were irregular so they were no good for tracking the passage of time. He couldn't have tracked time anyhow because he wasn't cognizant much. Often when he regained his senses, he found several meals waiting for him by the downwind portcullis.

> *A tower reached to the sky, but the men building it no longer understood one another. Nor did the people living on rings speak the same languages. The rings traveled through the night behind a gaseous ball.*
>
> *Bubbles formed on a watery surface. Each lucid membrane vibrated, speaking a different dialect or language. Some bubbles popped out of existence. The rest, except one, divided into new dialects and languages. The one speaking the Snarshyim language never changed, immune from the curse of the tower.*

Brutez coughed up more blood, spattering the floor. However long he spent in the windy cell with warm rock, he didn't think he would last much longer. Time was a relentless blur and all of it miserable. He wondered why he was abandoned and seemingly forgotten. *Why doesn't Matkulk do something with me?* He never had seen the vicious Jatneryim but heard enough about him to expect to be killed. *Why does he tarry?*

What's Grebnar doing? What's happening at Taubueth? How are my clansmen reacting to the death of my uncle and my disappearance with Grebnar? How's Aunt Yeemzal coping with her grievous loss? Is Chrenlon getting better? Is Heptor causing trouble? The questions bombarded him when he was alert, which wasn't often.

The moonstar was constant, brighter than any other point of light in the nighttime sky. It reflected sunlight at the same intensity all month as a consort to its larger companion, the moon, but the moon was gone and the moonstar appeared alone in space. It was a prism for a lightbeam that passed through, splitting some of the white stream into bands of red, blue, and green.

The red band reached the lands in the east and caught fire. The fire didn't consume but produced cities and roads spreading over the land and across the water. The Red Kingdom burned bright for a time.

A talisman glowed in the Red Kingdom, shining golden. It had plain structure, a pole joining the midpoint of another at a square angle. When the talisman faded so did the Red Kingdom.

The blue band of light landed in the west in various shades: azure, cerulean, cobalt, cyan, indigo, sapphire, sky, teal, turquoise, and dark blue. The ground absorbed the light, which remained cold and dormant until the coming of the Blue Kingdom. The talisman glowed again, gleaming like sterling, and grew. It was revered by the banners of the Blue Kingdom; a red blooddrop, a green and black standard, a cobalt blue triangle, a pair of brown triangles, a purple notched rectangle, an orange trapezoid, an amber forked tongue, sapphire blue tassels, light and dark gray triangles, a white egg, an olive green pennant, a black ribbon, a maroon patch with six flaps, and ten sky blue rectangles.

The Blue Kingdom's light fluctuated, shining and waning, but it lasted. It almost winked out under the powerful glare of the Green Kingdom from the south, where the talisman was dull bronze, but the blue light recovered more brilliant than ever. It reflected to the moonstar, which exploded in a blinding flash. The kingdoms reflected in the glittering pieces of the moonstar. They were reflections of a White Kingdom, an everlasting kingdom.

Brutez endured another coughing fit. When it abated, he heard a voice, *Grebnar's* voice. "Take him to the Green Citadel."

Another voice responded, "Boldness, he's near death. He won't survive."

"He'll live," said Grebnar's voice. "I've seen things about him."

"What things?"

"He has great deeds to perform, but a counterstrike is coming. We can't risk staying here."

"We have the forces to hold the citadel, Boldness. We don't need to leave."

"Enough men will stay to keep Matkulk worried, but I don't want the rest of us embroiled in a siege. Take him to the Green Citadel."

Brutez felt warm but not too warm. Cold air touched his face. It smelled fresh, lacking sulfur odor. He was wrapped in furs, wonderfully soft and warm. His body reclined, head higher than his feet. He shook, and he heard sticks scrape the ground.

Opening his eyes, he saw bared branches and limbs backed by blue sky and puffy clouds. Behind his head he heard the snorts and hoof-steps of the equine dragging his litter. The air was crisp enough to show his breath, and he saw plenty of snow to the sides, blinding under a winter sun. He coughed.

A man shouted, "Pay attention, fool. See the flap? Sir Grebnar will flay you alive if he freezes."

A furry pelt settled over his face. When the flap was off again, the air was balmy. Sweating within the furs, he saw the same scene above him, leafless trees and a fair sky. Water trickled from a thaw.

Vines covered a wall, so thick even without leaves, he couldn't have determined whether the wall was built from wood or stone, but he knew. This wasn't his first visit to the stronghold at Doenesh, the Green Citadel of the Jatneryimt and home of their leader, Sir Rendif, *or was his home*, since he could be dead. The walls were both wood and stone, timber atop a rocky foundation. When the vines sprouted leaves, the citadel truly would be green.

Doenesh was built on a flat parcel of ground, rare for this part of the Swanshyim Forest. A moat surrounded the citadel, and Brutez was dragged on the litter across a drawbridge to get inside. He was soaked in sweat, and grateful he soon would be indoors and able to get out of the furs, having completed his journey between citadels.

A girl stood over him, not a ravaging beauty, but comely. No, not a girl, she had the full pleasing form of a grown woman, but she looked *young*. Her chestnut brown hair dropped around her shoulders in curls. She had green eyes and a small upturned nose. Her rosy cheeks had dimples and a smattering of brown freckles.

He lay on a bed with a mattress below him and a feather pillow under his head. The hard pockmarked and bumpy rock, baking and cutting him, seemed like a bad dream. He still sweated under furs, although these weren't as thick. He tried to fling them away but was too weak to move. The girl, no the woman, touched his perspiring brow.

"You're burning hot." She had a pretty voice.

He swallowed a vile-tasting liquid she put into his mouth.

He saw the same parchment with knobby handles once transformed into a great sword. This time a Swenikyim pennant, a cobalt blue triangle with concave sides, fluttered from one of the handles. The parchment rolled open, and he saw it full of markings. The etchings lifted from the page and became waves passing through the air.

The waves spoke, "Consume the scroll and receive life."

He wondered. What was he being told to do? Eat it? How could he chew a parchment?

He looked at it and saw no parchment. It was a fresh-baked loaf of bread, wafting a sumptuous aroma to his nostrils. He ate, and the warmth spread from his stomach to the tips of his fingers and toes. He felt like he never would be hungry again but could eat more, in fact, to keep eating and never be filled. When he reached for the loaf to grab another piece, he discovered it remained whole. It was bread that never would run out.

He swam in a crimson ocean. The liquid was thicker than water, although it tasted salty like the sea. It was blood. He tried to remain afloat, but weights shackled around his ankles dragged him under. His lungs ached for air, and he no longer could hold his mouth shut. Blood poured into his nose and mouth, going down his throat and windpipe.

He choked to death, but he wasn't dead. The shackles were gone from his ankles, and he stood naked before a throne, covered head to foot in blood.

"You will live," said a voice. "I have work for you, great deeds to perform. Look, I have changed your heart."

He no longer was bloody but dressed in a white robe. He pulled aside the fabric from over his heart and saw his birthmarksign was removed, not flayed away like in the mountain clan, but replaced with unblemished skin.

The comely young woman sat at his bedside. She had a spoon but with tasty broth instead of awful medicine. As he sipped, he realized his mustache and long scruffy beard were shaved away.

"Your fever is gone," she said.

He swallowed and tried to speak, but only a croak came out. He wondered how long since he last used his voice. After a few more servings of wet broth, he managed some raspy words. "Who are you?"

She smiled, one of the loveliest sights he ever had seen. "I'm not allowed to tell you, Herk Brutez."

Best News

Herkt

ZAMTOTH **TAUBUETH**

Three boys played in a shallow river, wearing nothing but britches. They were the ones keeping cool on a sweltering day in high summer. His two other sons were with their mother on a grassy knoll under the shade of a leafy tree leaning over the riverbank. One of the younger boys was a weanling, the other not, the baby born during the winter and currently suckling. The rest of the family would have their picnic meal later after his brother's brood arrived.

Sitting on the grass higher up the knoll with his daughter, he admired the ruby tresses of his wife's hair. Although his locks were equally thick, she teased him because his were becoming gray.

He overheard her tell the little boy something but discerned only the last few words. "You won't only be clan-lord but more."

Zamtoth woke and sat upright in his cold, dawnlit chamber and wiped away the slobber, his daily nuisance of drooling into his beard. He was undecided whether the dream recalled a long-forgotten memory or came from his thoughts for his fourth-born son's potential—Brutez, the thoughtful son. Zamtoth, the son with his name, was the arrogant one. Makstim was unthinking, Hartezz was foolish, and Heptor was the rash.

He no longer thought much about his three slain sons, but still missed his wife, especially waking on a cold morning without her warmth beside him. Rising from bed, he stooped under the low-beamed ceiling in the uppermost chamber of Taubueth's donjon and scratched his birthmarksign under his bedclothes. The cursed lump itched more the older he became. He put on stagskin slippers and a cloak to warm his shivering body.

The room's tiny window presented a view of the sunrise over the forest where the trees were about to bud. This was the kind of fair day he wanted for sending Heptor on an assignment for the clan. He dreaded the recklessness of his youngest son but had no other choice because he no longer could travel. Shemjib would have been the best man if he was alive. With winter ending, the Herkt would realize Brutez was missing and clamor for a new clanlord. Zamtoth figured receiving heed from the clanlord's closest kin, even Heptor, would delay suspicion.

Zamtoth descended a ladder through a hole in the floor and took a short passage to a steep stone staircase curling inside the donjon's outer wall. On the second level, he pounded on a thick wooden door. The chamber belonged to Brutez, but Heptor lived in his brother's place while the clanlord was gone, having moved from a nook below a guardhouse. Nobody answered, not a surprise, so Zamtoth entered. He saw the backside of his youngest son sleeping with a leg wrapped over Nazzel and smacked the back of his curly brown-haired head.

"Heptor, get up!"

Nazzel squirmed to her back from under Heptor's leg. The bedsheet swelled over her enlarged belly with nearborn child.

Zamtoth smacked Heptor's head again.

"Get up!"

Heptor groaned. Nazzel sat upright, and the bedsheet fell away. The sight impressed Zamtoth, although he rather appreciated other facets of the female body.

Nazzel shoved her man's shoulder. "Wake up, Heptor."

She rolled him, and Zamtoth helped dump him over the bedside. Heptor landed with a thump on the planked floor.

"Curses, Nazzel, why did you do that?"

Nazzel covered herself with the bedsheet. "Your father's here."

Heptor stood, wearing nothing more than a tunic, but at least he wore *something*.

Zamtoth spoke before Heptor complained about being wakened so early. "I have something for you to do in the clanlord's name."

"Brutez is back?"

"Dolt, I'm the clanlord while he's gone."

"You want me to do something for *you*?"

"Yes, as if you were clanlord."

Heptor grinned, realizing his father meant for him to be acting clanlord. *Good for him to think of himself as important,* Zamtoth thought, so he would do as he was asked.

"Son, come to my chamber when you're dressed. Breakfast can wait until after we talk." Although he didn't care if Nazzel listened, making Heptor see him without her would give him more sense of importance.

Zamtoth climbed the two levels to his upper room and changed into his day clothes; boots, trousers, and a jerkin covered with a mantle made from red vulpine fur. The day had warmed enough not to need a cloak. Heptor arrived, eager as a retriever canine waiting for a stick to be tossed.

"Heptor, you must determine what happened to last year's tribute from the Swenikt. I expect it went to Vulrath's kin like the other years."

"I'll bring it here, Father."

"No, my son, they need it for their provision." *My youngest is rash*, Zamtoth regretted. "We have our own. You only need to let me know if they received it."

"Where do I ask?"

"The Blue River." Zamtoth doubted Heptor knew how to get there or what to do when he did. "Take some warriors, about a dozen." He figured that would establish Heptor's authority coming from the clanlord. "Include Larboelm. He lived there for years as Vulrath's bodyguard and will know who to see."

A breakfast of eggs, sausage, and flatsnout strips was served in the lower hall. Heptor immediately recruited Rankeb and Konrash to join his cadre of warriors.

Nazzel wasn't pleased about his upcoming absence. She rubbed her rotund belly. "Heptor, you'll miss the birth of our child."

"You have a few more weeks. Hold it in if you have to until I return."

Zamtoth laughed, hoping she became enraged enough to punch him. Then he lost his smile as he thought, *This is my emissary, my son of no tact?*

Alas, no punch came from her but more pleading. "You promised to be the first to hold our baby."

"The second," Heptor hedged. "You know Aunt Yeemzal will be the first when she guides the baby out. Whether I'm there or not, I promise we'll get married after you're thin again."

Still lacking tact, Zamtoth thought. Then he reconsidered. He never remembered Nazzel being *thin*. Perhaps his son was more tactful than he gave him credit by suggesting she once was.

Although pleased by Heptor's sense of responsibility for his progeny, Zamtoth preferred a more useful marriage for him. He didn't think much would be gained if this son took a wife from another clan or tribe, but a bride from Vulrath's kin at the Blue River could strengthen ties within the clan.

Zamtoth went to Yeemzal's chambers after breakfast. His grandson, Chrenlon, who had endured months of pain healing from his burn, lived there. The boy annoyed his aunt by jumping back and forth between two chairs at her table.

"Don't worry," Chrenlon told Yeemzal after she warned him to be careful. "This is easier than leaping between a boat and a dock."

Zamtoth knew Chrenlon enjoyed fishing, so he had promised to take him to the Taubueth River on the next nice day, and this was it. The river didn't have much for fish, but Zamtoth didn't think the boy needed to have his fun spoiled by knowing that.

Chrenlon followed Zamtoth outside. Several days of rain changed the yard from snow to mud slopping to their knees. Zamtoth saw his youngest son going about the stronghold, finding men to go with him to the Blue River and giving commands. *Heptor likes being in charge, being important*, the old man told himself.

Zamtoth seldom ventured outside Taubueth. The ladder was too difficult, unlike the one below his chamber, so he was lowered from the rampart by a rope beneath his armpits. Chrenlon barely held onto the ladder descending it. *How nice to be young*, Zamtoth mused before deciding he wouldn't want to live his life again. He had no desire to repeat the painful times, and the good things remained pleasant, as memories.

A Feldram named Tarberg, who was without one arm, used his one hand to descend the ladder behind Chrenlon, being invited by the boy to come along to the river. Zamtoth planned to have an escort anyhow, having recruited Jonerch and Gordib, so adding another man didn't matter. Tarberg was raven-haired like so many Feldramt. He had a forger's bulging bicep on his remaining arm. Zamtoth arranged for him to be armed with a massive maul hammer.

The snow outside the stronghold wasn't as melted where trees blocked direct sunlight, although trampled to slushy mud around the buildings. Zamtoth's group helped ready the mounts going to the Blue River. All was ready by mid-morning, and Heptor led the way to the Taubueth River. Zamtoth followed with Chrenlon and their escort.

The river was a raging torrent of melted snow. Zamtoth meant to speak parting words to Heptor, but before he had a chance, his son and the other mounted warriors passed out of sight downriver. Chrenlon found two hooked poles inside the shack to use for fishing. He gave Tarberg one, and they went to the river. Jonerch stalked into the woods with his bow to hunt something for lunch, and Gordib built a fire.

Zamtoth wandered from the fire and found a knoll like the one where he had sat with his family in his dream. He looked for the tree hanging over it, but if this was the place, it had collapsed into the river and had been carried away by a flood many springs ago.

Dream or memory, that time with his family was another life. His wife was gone forever, his daughter gone for decades, the three boys who had played in the river now slain, Brutez missing, and the baby, Heptor, was an impulsive warrior leading his men downriver. Zamtoth fingered his beard, once blond but now white as the snow around him. He sighed, *another life*.

Chrenlon caught no fish as Zamtoth knew he wouldn't, but Jonerch returned with a longear and a bushtail to cook over the fire. The meal was supplemented with bread, dried meat, cured cheese, and brew they brought with them.

Two dark-haired footmen appeared across river, carrying small packs over their cloaks. The taller one carried the only visible weapon, a bow on one shoulder. Jonerch readied his bow, Gordib clutched an axe, and Tarberg held his maul, but their caution wasn't needed. Zamtoth recognized the shorter man. He was a clansman named Vikth, one of the Herkt living southwestward on the ridge.

The newcomers continued downriver to reach a place to cross. Zamtoth sent Tarberg back to Taubueth with Chrenlon, not wanting any Feldramt around for the upcoming meeting.

Vikth and his taller companion arrived, joining Zamtoth, Jonerch, and Gordib around the fire.

"This is my half brother Zzuz." Vikth introduced the young man with him. "We have a message for you, Zamtoth."

Zamtoth judged Zzuz to be Heptor's age, some ten years younger than Vikth.

Vikth continued, "Two days ago some mounted Jatneryimt came to our place, frightening us out of our wits, but they only wanted to talk. Sir Grebnar the Bold sent them from Doenesh."

"You have a message from Sir Grebnar?"

"He spent a night with my half sister Vel while captive at Taubueth, telling her about his wife, dead sons, and daughter. She told him about us and where we lived. Our father berated her for that. He expected Sir Grebnar to attack us!"

"He sent couriers instead," said Zamtoth, understanding why Grebnar would send them to a borderland rather than all the way to Taubueth. Jatneryim riders wouldn't be welcome inside Herkyim territory. "What's his message?" *What about Brutez?*

Vikth threw off his cloak and unstrapped something hidden behind his back. He presented a bloodstained cudgel. "They gave us this."

Zamtoth recognized the weapon Brutez used against Klinteg.

Vikth passed the cudgel to Gordib around the fire. "Clanlord Brutez was captured by Matkulk's men and held all winter at the Black Citadel."

"The Black Citadel?" Gordib passed the cudgel to Zamtoth.

"That's what the Jatneryimt call their fortress at Mapvin. Matkulk never realized he had our clanlord. Grebnar rescued Brutez and sent him to Doenesh, where he's recovering from the hardship of his imprisonment."

Zamtoth shared jubilant glances with Jonerch and Gordib. Setting aside the cudgel, he stood and rounded the fire to give Vikth a heartfelt pat on the back. "You bring the best news, my man!"

Vikth smiled. "The Jatneryimt are waiting at our place. We'll return with any message you have for Sir Grebnar or Clanlord Brutez."

Zamtoth would think on that. For now, he wanted to celebrate. "Come with us to Taubueth for supper. I promise a feast!"

Reunions

Feldramt

MAJDEL **TAUBUETH**

Majdel worried about Chrenlon as she climbed the makeshift ladder up the wall of Taubueth. *Did her son die after all?* Although Sangern assured her she would find Chrenlon recovered, she knew how an infection could turn for the worse.

The trip from Agratuna was ending on another warm and mostly sunny spring day. Only patches of snow remained on the forest floor under budding trees. Majdel reached the rampart, where her husband waited after limping up the ladder.

They heard cheers inside the stronghold, coming from their people who spent the winter there, and Majdel saw Chrenlon. She ran down the steps ahead of her husband, who limped with a staff. Their son dashed into her waiting arms, but he yelped in pain when she embraced him.

She let go, dismayed. "Chrenlon, I thought you were better."

He looked at her with pain in his blue eyes, but with a

set jaw as he tried to hide it. "I'm fine, Mother. It only hurts sometimes."

Lord Chieftain Feldram caught up. "My boy, how are you?" He rubbed a hand through Chrenlon's tangled black hair.

What fool question is that? Majdel wanted to berate her husband. *Don't you see our son wincing in pain?*

"I'm good, Father, almost, like you." The boy pointed to his father's staff.

Feldram shook the four-cubit-high stick. "That's right, Son. Almost, but we're good enough."

More reunions took place in the courtyard as the ten warriors of the escort from Agratuna joined their fellow Feldramt who wintered at Taubueth. Majdel looked at any Herkt walking about, hoping to find her own reunion, although she didn't expect to recognize her surviving brothers, Brutez and Heptor, she hadn't seen since young ages.

Chrenlon helped her find someone. "Mother, here comes Grandfather."

Although Zamtoth approached with a spritely step, he looked *old*. Majdel remembered her father's mass of hair and beard, but it was so *white*. She supposed she looked more changed to him, having been a slim girl with long platinum blond instead of short silver hair the last time he saw her.

He recognized her no matter how much her appearance was changed. "Majdel, my dear daughter." He embraced her. "I despaired of ever seeing you again."

She was too overcome with emotion to say anything. Seeing her father alive, and knowing she wouldn't see her mother, made it more real to her that she was dead.

"I thank you for helping us, Wedlock Father," her husband told him. "Sangern wanted to come for more good times with his Uncle Heptor, but I needed him to stay home in my absence."

Zamtoth released Majdel. "No matter, Heptor isn't here."

Not here? Majdel was disappointed. Heptor would remain her baby brother in her mind until she saw the grown man.

"Father, where's Brutez? I want to see him."

His response brought more disappointment. "I regret he's away, too. He's clanlord and has duties."

Feldram made his own inquiry. "Where's my sister? Is Yeemzal here?"

"She's in her chambers. Chrenlon knows where."

Chrenlon tugged his father to follow. Majdel went along with envious thoughts about how her husband could see his sister, and she, not her brothers. She remembered the place in the donjon basement, but the hovel full of healing remedies didn't stand over the entrance in her day. Chrenlon hopped down the steps and through the curtain of skins at the bottom.

Majdel heard him call. "Aunt Yeemzal, guess who's here!"

The lord chieftain went down next, descending with his staff. Majdel followed and endured watching her husband's happy reunion with his sister.

Her eyes wandered to the impressive display of steel, jewels, and gold on the innermost wall. She hadn't thought about the clanlord's swords since she saw them before leaving Taubueth as a young bride. They belonged to her father then, now to Brutez. *What man did the little boy she last saw grow to be?* She had only Sangern's description of Brutez, remembering his words with a smile.

"He's strong but not as strong as me," her son had said. "He's intelligent but not as intelligent as me, and he's handsome but not as handsome as me."

Feldram finished embracing his sister, so Majdel exchanged greetings with Yeemzal, heartfelt as she thanked her for saving Chrenlon.

"Nephew, show your mother," said Yeemzal.

Chrenlon removed his tunic, and Majdel saw the area where the felled beam burned him, including where his birthmarksign and left nipple once were. The skin was gnarled, knotted, ridged, and whorled like driftwood on the Agratuna shore. Although looking like old leather, at least it was dry instead of bleeding and oozing pus.

Majdel realized Uncle Shemjib wasn't present and asked her aunt about him.

Yeemzal stiffened. "Brutez sent him to the Jatneryimt, and they killed him."

Majdel was perplexed. *Why would her brother send their uncle to the people who sacked Agratuna, burned Chrenlon, and crippled her husband? Is he trying to make peace, and why would he?*

She joined her husband giving Yeemzal their condolences, useless as they were. Yeemzal appeared neither grateful nor annoyed by their words, but asked, "How long are you staying?"

"We must leave soon, tomorrow would be best," Majdel answered.

She wished the Feldramt could stay until her brothers returned, but the Chrevramt were coming to Agratuna for Sangern's betrothal to Zabfrul that was arranged last autumn at Biepazz.

"I'm going with you," said Yeemzal. "Nothing's left for me here."

Her Pies are Delicious

Herkt, Jatneryimt

BRUTEZ   **GREEN CITADEL, DOENESH**

The great iron portcullis weighed more than any man could move without a series of chains, blocks and tackle, and counterweights that enabled Brutez, with exhausting effort, to open and close the Green Citadel's main gate. The traffic was steady all morning, going in and out through the portal on the near end of the lowered drawbridge; warriors arriving on foot and mounted, warriors leaving, a herd of flatsnouts for the butcher, grain and bread, a wagonload of coal for the foundry, loads of wood for hearth fires, carts of straw coming in, garbage and piles of dung going out, and whatever else the citadel needed to consume or discharge as if it was some giant living beast.

    Brutez opened and closed the portcullis for all, working alone pushing the turnstile and thinking, *Taubueth should have one of these.* Usually some guards turned it with little effort, and recently Brutez had needed help before he grew stronger. He supposed the Doenesh garrison considered him a prisoner being put to forced labor, for he remained under the constant watch of an escort, but every day he volunteered for whatever work could rebuild his emaciated muscles. He unloaded carts and wagons, shoveled coal and dung, and chopped wood.

The young woman brought him a basket lunch, and three guards relieved him at the turnstile. Brutez eventually convinced her to tell him her name, *Tersol*. They ascended the battlement and walked along the rampart around the courtyard, followed by the escort.

Vines sprouted leafy green on both sides of the wall. The trees of the Swanshyim Forest grew leaves, too, standing behind the town that shared the flat ground with the Green Citadel and its moat. The last snow disappeared a week ago.

A new Jatneryim banner flew from the citadel watchtowers and buildings in town, a combination of the separately colored Jatneryim banners. The black portion was an upright rectangle next to the pole with a triangular notch on the outer edge. The green was a half circle attached by its corners to the black.

Brutez and Tersol entered a porch next to the keep, and the guards posted themselves outside the entrance. She took out the lunch—a flask of brew, fresh bread with butter, boiled barn fowl eggs, salted flatsnout, and a special treat, spring berries.

Each day he pestered her with the same questions, and she gave the same unsatisfactory answers. *What is Sir Grebnar doing, and when will he return?* She didn't know . . . and didn't know. Brutez knew he was being kept at Doenesh until his former Jatneryim prisoner took time to see him. Now he was the prisoner, although no longer in the depths of the Black Citadel or even shackled by an ankle to a wall in his captor's quarters. *Did any news come from the Herkt?* She told him, *Not today.* He asked himself, *Did that mean news came from his clansmen on a previous day?*

She looked fabulous. Her hair was freshly washed and lush with chestnut brown curls, and hoops dangled from her ears.

She wore a form-fitting blue gown, the color of the sky, with white lacey trim and a plunging neckline showing a peek of her breasts. Brutez saw freckles on the lobes, and she was bigger than he had thought.

He wished he could take as much interest in her as she did in him. He enjoyed every moment with her, talking and laughing, basking in her green eyes and white smile, and the sight of her body pleased him, but she couldn't be his. He was clanlord and his marriage must bring some advantage to his clan.

The spring berries tasted sourly sweet. They turned Tersol's teeth and lips to violet, and Brutez supposed they did the same to his.

"I wish we had jam from these berries for the bread," she said.

Brutez thought of pie, *delicious* spring berry pie. One of his earliest memories was his mother making pies. "Pie," he said. "Nothing's better than pie."

Tersol flashed him a berried smile, setting aside the bowl of remaining spring berries. "Well then, Brutez. I'll make you a pie."

After he spent a grueling afternoon at the millstone, she brought a fresh-baked spring berry pie with their supper. Its sweet, fruity fragrance permeated the room. Brutez almost felt sorry for the ubiquitous guards who must smell without eating, but only *almost* sorry. He and Tersol ate half while the pie was still warm before their meal, and they consumed the rest after.

She didn't always join him for meals, and when she didn't, he ate alone. The Jatneryim guards refused to interact with him even when he offered to share his food. He had only the young woman for conversation, but she wouldn't tell him anything he wanted to know.

Waiting for Grebnar's return, he abrogated thought of escape, although anxious to return to his clan. He didn't want them picking a new clanlord in his absence. Although he had confidence of winning another tournament, he didn't want to waste the life of another warrior, and he wanted to keep his promise to Klinteg that never again would a Herk kill another Herk to lead the clan.

One morning a clap of thunder woke him. The sound rumbled through the Green Citadel's foundation. A torrential rain filled the view outside his window, and hail pelted the keep's roof one level above his. He dressed and stepped outside his door to tell the guards he was ready for breakfast.

They were gone.

He wondered, *Is Doenesh under attack?* He heard no mustering of troops or din of battle, but would he over the noise of thunder and hail? The corridor was dark without any torches burning, but light from outside showed rainwater seeping under the door to the porch. He went to the door and lifted the latch to swing it open.

The hail stopped, but the rain kept pouring. He fingered icy pebbles on the porch floor. Looking across the porch and over the battlements, he saw nobody but sentries huddled within the guardhouses. Outside the citadel, he saw only a shadowy silhouette of the town. The forest beyond was hidden behind a curtain of rain.

The place wasn't under attack, so where were his guards? *Was he being allowed to escape, and why?* He returned inside to look for Tersol. The keep was built from wood atop stone like the rest of the Green Citadel, so the walls changed from timber to rock going to the ground level.

He went to the main hall adjoining the keep. It was double the size of Taubueth's donjon hall, and twice as high. Torches lined the rock walls, and the gabled timber roof leaked. Two of the new green and black banners hung from rods protruding from the wall, one on each side of the main double doors at one end.

A bearded man, dressed in black except for green in his cape, sat behind a small table laden with food and drink. He looked up from breaking off a chunk of bread.

"Brutez, you're here for breakfast."

It was Grebnar. Brutez hadn't recognized him with a beard so thick it reminded him of his father's, except for being dark brown.

Brutez stroked his stubby whiskers. "I have questions."

Grebnar motioned to a chair opposite him. "Sit. Let's eat and talk."

Brutez took the seat, thinking what to ask, but a peal of thunder interrupted.

Grebnar spoke first. "I'm glad I returned before this thunderstorm." He looked at the leaky ceiling. "It's raining hard to be doing that."

Brutez had his question, an important one. "Am I free to leave?"

Grebnar set down his bread and laughed. "You always were."

Brutez frowned. *What about the guards?*

His host asked, "Didn't you try?"

Brutez couldn't say he did. No matter, he had a greater concern. "My clan needs to know I'm returning."

"I sent a message to Taubueth. Your father sent you this."

Grebnar pulled a cloth off a lumpy object between the bread and flatsnout strips on the table. Brutez saw the iron casting of the Herkyim blooddrop, taken from the top of its pole. The message was clear. *He still was clanlord.*

"What did he say?" Brutez wanted to know what spoken message his father sent with the unspoken one.

"Nothing." Grebnar tapped the casting. "This was it."

Although disappointed, *it* was enough. Brutez now knew that he hadn't been away from his clan for too long.

"I see you made a full recovery," Grebnar kept talking. "How do you like the young woman who took care of you?"

"She made me better." Brutez didn't know what else to say.

Grebnar gave a coy smile. "Do you like being with her?"

Brutez was suspicious. *Why was Grebnar trying to goad him into admitting she was desirable?* "I enjoy our conversation," he said, *although she resisted answering his questions.* "She made me a pie."

"Her pies are delicious." Grebnar grabbed a pitcher by the handle. "Do you like bovine milk?"

Brutez told him he did, although not his favorite. While the Jatneryim poured white foaming liquid into two mugs, Brutez asked, "Where have you been?"

"Chasing Matkulk into the mountains." Grebnar set down the pitcher and handed Brutez a mug. "If we're lucky the mountain clans will kill him and his remaining followers."

Brutez sipped from his mug but set it down when he spotted spring berry jam on the table. He cut himself a slice of bread as he listened.

"I met Mosik after the Boewint accepted my peace offer to stop attacking him. He leads the largest mountain clan, and he's a mountain himself, as huge as any Herk. His pike shaft is like the trunk of a white tree. He'll send me Matkulk's head on a pole if he gets it."

That would be a delightful sight, Brutez thought, although he wouldn't know the difference between Matkulk's head and any other man he never had seen.

Grebnar drank from his mug and resumed talking. "Our worst fears about my wedlock brother, Sir Rendif, were true. He was killed during the raid at Agratuna. The unanswered question is, *by which side?*"

Brutez paused from spreading jam on bread. "Did Matkulk plot his death?"

"Doesn't matter," said Grebnar. "It's easy to believe, so I used the suspicion to my advantage. My loyal men thought Matkulk arranged my disappearance. They took my wife and daughter from Doenesh into hiding before he got here. When I heard one of the men who took us at the Kipneesh River say they were missing, I knew I could seek my forces to find my family."

You abandoned me, Brutez thought. He wasn't angry, *yet*. He would listen to the rest of Grebnar's story.

"I found substantial loyal forces. A brute like Matkulk

has plenty of enemies. I soon recaptured this place, the Green Citadel. See, I recovered my cape." Grebnar stood and turned around to present the green and black garment. He pointed to a familiar-looking hilt protruding from a scabbard on his hip. "I regained my sword, too."

"I was taken to the Black Citadel at Mapvin." Brutez finished the slice of berry bread and started to prepare another.

Grebnar resumed sitting. "I knew you were there. I had my loyal servants among Matkulk's people, some of them boys like you were, Brutez, when you spied against me. One of the riders who took you to Mapvin belonged to me. Using the suspicion that Matkulk killed Rendif wasn't the only advantage I had against him. I knew everything he was doing. My forces were relentless in attacking him. I wanted to distract him from finding you. Even so, he went to Mapvin once. My followers protected you."

"I remember when you rescued me, Grebnar. You didn't think you could hold the Black Citadel."

"I could have, but I would have been trapped there. I launched a diversionary attack while you came here, so you see, Brutez, I saved you from other Jatneryimt like you saved me from other Herkt."

Brutez swallowed his last bite of berry bread. "Then we owe one another nothing." Grabbing his mug, he drank the rest of the milk in one swig.

"You owe the young woman who restored your health," said Grebnar. "How do you like her?"

Brutez wondered, *Why is he asking me about her again?* "What do you mean?"

"Do you *desire* her?"

Brutez felt his face flush. Why did he ask him *that*? The way Grebnar smiled made him feel more discomforted. He couldn't lie. Grebnar would know he was lying.

"I admit she's a comely woman. Any man would be delighted to have her, including me, but I can't."

"Why not?"

"I must marry to benefit my clan."

Grebnar's smile broadened to a huge grin, showing his teeth within a mass of beard and mustache. His next question stunned Brutez. "Why do you think marrying my daughter won't benefit your clan?"

His daughter? Confused, Brutez stammered, "Her name, her name is Tersol."

Grebnar laughed. "That's the name she used?"

Brutez held his head in his hands, bemoaning how he allowed himself to fall into Grebnar's snare. He caught him *desiring* his daughter. "She's Beksel?" He last saw her as a little girl.

"Look at me, Herk Brutez."

He had no choice but to look into the penetrating brown eyes of Beksel's father.

"She's my only remaining child. I saw how you treated the woman in your chamber at Taubueth, the woman named Vel. The guards here let me know how you treated Beksel with respect. Why do you think I had them watch you? Like I told you, they weren't there to keep you from escaping. I know no other man for my question."

Brutez wasn't thinking, only asking, "What question?"

"Will you wed my daughter?"

He should have known that was the question. As he recognized the new reality that Tersol was Beksel, that he could have her *and* benefit his clan, the answer became obvious. Even so, he hedged. "If she wants me."

Exasperated, Grebnar thumped his fists on the table. "You tell me, if she wants you! Do you have any doubt how much she desires you?"

Brutez had no doubt. "She desires me the same as I desire her."

"How about marrying her tomorrow?"

Tomorrow! Brutez asked, "Why so soon?"

"You must take my wife to Taubueth with Beksel."

"Why?"

"A powerful Warnekyim force is advancing up the Kipneesh River. I can't guarantee Doenesh won't be sacked."

The Warnekt! Why are they attacking the Jatneryimt? Do they perceive them weakened by their infighting? Brutez wondered what he missed during his imprisonment.

Grebnar answered before he asked, "The Warnekt are retaliating because Matkulk destroyed their towns around the lakes downriver last autumn during the time your uncle languished here in the dungeon. Shemjib was beheaded when Matkulk returned."

Brutez looked away, saddened by the reminder of his uncle. The green and black banners around the main double doors blurred in his vision.

Grebnar asked, "You see my new banners with both colors in them, the green and black? The Jatneryimt no longer fight under separate banners with allegiance to one citadel or the other. The Warnekt will be our first enemy to see the new banner when we fight under a single leader, *me*."

We Herkt have our single banner, Brutez thought. *The blooddrop!*

"I'm leaving the morning after next, so if I'm to see you marry Beksel, you must do so tomorrow. I hope the weather will be better."

Reminded of the inclement weather, Brutez didn't recall when the thunder stopped. Lighter rain pattered the roof.

He regretted his father wouldn't see his wedding unless he took Beksel and her mother to Taubueth and marry there, but then Grebnar couldn't attend. *No*, Brutez decided. His father saw a daughter's wedding when Majdel married Feldram, so Grebnar should see his daughter wedded, especially since she was his only remaining child.

Brutez had less regret over others missing his wedding. His childhood friend, Jonerch, wasn't family. Heptor wouldn't care, except for losing a chance to celebrate. Aunt Yeemzal, like a mother to him, wouldn't want to see him marry a Jatneryim.

Grebnar waved a hand before his face. "Brutez, you

look dazed."

"I'm considering who will attend the wedding." He wondered about his soon-to-be wedlock mother. "Where's Sejel?"

"She's been living in town so you wouldn't see her. She's eager to meet you."

Sejel   Green Citadel, Doenesh

The day was bittersweet for Sejel, the same as the mixed mood of the weather. Sometimes the sun broke through thick clouds between rain showers. She felt similarly ambivalent, happy at times for Beksel while thinking about sons she never would see take wives and have children.

Sejel gathered with Beksel and their immediate family members in the main hall next to the keep, a distressingly small group: her old uncle from her mother's side and his grandson Puutnam; her cousin, Tersol, on her father's side, who was married to a warrior in the Green Citadel's garrison; and her husband, Grebnar. Her only sibling, the Jatneryim leader Sir Rendif, had been killed by the Feldramt or Matkulk. Sir Rendif's wife died last year from an infection, and their son, Sejel's nephew, was long dead at the hands of the Boewint. Their two daughters, Sejel's nieces, were married to warriors still loyal to Grebnar and didn't live at Doenesh.

Beksel was dressed for marriage in a floor-length, long-sleeved gown of many layers of translucent material. Enough layers kept her breasts and hips hidden, but fewer layers elsewhere allowed inviting glimpses of her arms, shoulders, waist, and legs. The layers overlapped one another in petals like feathers on a bird. They were dyed in different shades of red, the color of her new clan, the Herkt.

The Herkyim red bothered Sejel. The Herkt killed Chakstim and Rendif, the son named after her brother, and today, her daughter *was marrying one*. Although Grebnar told her how Brutez saved his life and was much like him, and she was charmed when she met him, she didn't like seeing her daughter wearing the Herkyim red.

Sejel wore green, the color of her deceased brother's citadel. Grebnar claimed the black, too, so he wore both Jatneryim colors—a green jerkin, black trousers, and his green and black cape. His beard was trimmed. They were ready to give away their last remaining child in marriage. *Bittersweet.*

The weather seemed between rain showers, so Sejel escorted Beksel outside with the rest of the bride's family. The Green Citadel's courtyard and battlements were filled with people, including armed warriors, the citadel guard, servants, townspeople, cooks, craftsmen, stable hands, old men, women, and children. Green and black banners flew everywhere, from the watchtowers, the sides of the wall and buildings, and the raised speartips of the warriors.

The portcullis was open and the drawbridge down. Sejel, Grebnar, their daughter, the old uncle, the grandson, and the cousin walked through a gap in the crowd to the drawbridge. Beksel stood between her parents, holding hands with them. Brutez walked from the town through a crowd of townspeople gathered outside the moat. He came with two Herkt who had returned with Puutnam, the bearer of Grebnar's message to Taubueth that Brutez was at Doenesh. Although the bridegroom should have his family with him for a proper wedding, Sejel understood him coming with the only two clansmen available. The taller one carried an iron casting of the hideous Herkyim blooddrop atop a pole.

The trio stopped across the drawbridge. The bridegroom would leave his household, represented by his two companions, and the bride would forsake hers to establish a new household with her husband, so said the ancient words. Nobody knew the origin of the words, or why they were spoken at every wedding from the dawn of time. They simply were.

Brutez advanced to the drawbridge center. Sejel considered

him strong and handsome like her Grebnar. He was dressed in a light brown tunic, darker brown breeches, and boots. They differed from regular day clothes only by being new.

Brutez spoke the words of all bridegrooms, "It is not good for a man to be alone."

Grebnar said his part, "You will have a helper suitable for you."

Sejel and Grebnar released their daughter's hands. Beksel advanced across the drawbridge. A current of air over the moat ruffled the feathered layers of her gown. The effect was stunning, looking like flames of fire.

Brutez took his betrothed wife by both hands and looked into her face. "This is bone of my bones, and flesh of my flesh. For this reason, a man shall leave his father and his mother, and be joined to his wife, and we shall become one flesh."

Sejel was sad Beksel was leaving her household, although in a change to tradition, she would go with her daughter to the new household because the Warnekt threatened Doenesh. *More bittersweet.*

BEKSEL GREEN CITADEL, DOENESH

A long day of feasting and watching performers was past, and the time was come for the consummation. Beksel stood alone in the same chamber where she spent weeks caring for her husband, before he knew who she was. The room with a bed, a chair, and a single candle would be the bounds of their new household for one night. She waited for him in her wedding gown of flimsy red petals, looking perfectly still on the outside, but she was a churning broil of angst and excitement inside. Her mother gave her instructions and assurance. If Brutez was anything like her father, Sejel told her, she was about to experience feelings she had never imagined, but she worried, knowing she wasn't the first woman for Brutez.

Her father told her that before she hoped for him. She questioned herself. *Will Brutez be satisfied with me?* She didn't want to disappoint him.

The latch moved on the chamber's massive wood door, and Brutez entered. He swung the door closed and stood facing her a few cubits away.

"I regret this isn't my first time, but I took chances in my youth before I waited."

She wondered, *Why do men take their chances and then want maiden brides?* Yet, he waited after those early chances while knowing what he missed. She smiled, a smile of invitation, and hoped she didn't appear too nervous.

"Beksel, my love, let's savor this moment by watching one another disrobe."

She didn't know how she would react to him watching her, but she wanted to please him, so she nodded approval.

He asked, "Who goes first?"

She had seen him naked when she washed him after he arrived from the Black Citadel, near death, so she felt less apprehensive about seeing him again. "You."

He smiled and pulled his tunic over his head. That previous time, his arms and torso were pale and flaccid, the outcome from months of captivity, but now his muscles were sinewy and firm. His arms bulged, his shoulders and chest flexed, and his stomach was flat except for a contoured grid of tautened flesh. *He looked magnificent.* Even his birthmarksign was less unappealing, looking like another sinew of muscle over his heart. He removed his boots and finally his breeches. *Yes, magnificent!*

He basked under her appreciative gaze until she became flustered staring at him. She asked, "My turn?"

"Your body is yours to give me as you will."

My dearest husband, she thought. *I will to give you my body, all of it!* She peeled the first layer from her breasts, a crimson band of petals, then a lighter red layer and a burgundy one, and then more layers until she showed through. The whole time she watched him watch her. She switched to removing layers from below, dropping the petals into a growing pile by her feet. Eventually no part of her remained hidden, although the transparent gown left her with some sense of being dressed.

She saw her husband's loins before, but when she washed him they hadn't done *that*. A thrill quivered through her knowing she aroused him. He approached and helped remove more layers. The petals dropped faster until none remained.

His hand went behind her ear, and he fingered curls of her hair. The other hand swept across her opposite cheek and lifted her chin so she looked into his gray eyes.

"I want you to know, my love, the more you surrender to the pleasure I give you, the more pleasure for me."

She remembered her mother telling her something like that. Taking deeper breaths, she experienced within her body new and wonderful sensations. She joined her husband in a kiss, and they eased themselves to the bed without parting lips. He touched and caressed her in places to prepare her body for lovemaking.

They became one flesh.

BRUTEZ — GREEN CITADEL, DOENESH

Brutez sat for his first breakfast as a husband, between his bride and Sir Grebnar the Bold, *his wedlock father*. This was a reality he never could have envisioned while imprisoned so many months, or when Grebnar was captured, or while he spied against the Jatneryimt during the years they were mortal enemies of his clan.

Sejel sat on the other side of Beksel. Grebnar's wife was a comely woman for her age. Her hair was darker than her daughter's chestnut curls, shorter and straighter, but she had the same green eyes. She had rounder hips and fuller breasts with a concave curvature between. Brutez saw in her the future look of his wife.

His two clansmen, Vikth and Zzuz, sat across the table with his wife's second cousin Puutnam, who was Brutez's age and raven-haired like a Feldram.

Grebnar had an announcement. "Clanlord Brutez, I expect your marriage to my daughter to be the first of many between the Jatneryimt and Herkt. Puutnam is betrothed to one of your clanswomen."

Brutez asked Puutnam, "Did you meet her when you brought your message?"

"While I waited for Vikth and Zzuz to go to your father," said Puutnam.

"Puutnam is marrying my half sister," said Vikth.

Grebnar smiled. "You know her, Vel."

Brutez shrugged to downplay his surprise about Vel, the woman Heptor brought to his chamber the night before the tournament. "I expect Puutnam will go with us."

"He'll live with Vel at Taubueth as my envoy if you'll have him."

A resident envoy, Brutez mused.

Grebnar stood. "Brutez, my new wedlock son, I have a gift." He ordered two sentries to open the hall's main double doors. A man entered with an equine, appearing within the brilliance of a morning sunbeam.

"I showed you, I regained my cape and sword," said Grebnar. "Here's something from the Black Citadel I'm returning to you. This animal belonged to Chakstim."

Brutez saw the equine's ebony mane when it stepped out of the sunlight. He was aghast this was the mount Grebnar's son was riding when he was killed. "I'm sorry, Wedlock Father. Why didn't you ask me to switch mounts when we were riding away from Taubueth?"

"This mount is yours. Tell him, my wife."

"My dear Brutez," she said. "You're now our son."

His Name Is Thoiren

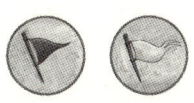

Swenikt, Hamuntht

HAMUNTH   **NEAR PINKULDA**

Where's Jorgis?

Chief Hamunth looked for his daughter's betrothed husband. The eastern room of the Swenikyim longhouse was filled with people standing in groups, sitting at tables, or in the case of children, running about. The woodbeam door at the far end stood open, letting in a refreshing touch of balmy spring air. Tree boughs, with new leaves, framed a glimpse of the Tauzzreen River flowing past outside.

He leaned toward Chief Thoiren beside him. "I don't see the bridegroom."

Thoiren's smile waned for a moment, but the chief reasserted his broad grin. "Chief Hamunth, you mention my most vexing problem. The bridegroom isn't here."

Hamunth suppressed a snort while thinking, *obviously*. He asked the obvious question. "Where is he?"

"On a quest."

Hamunth refused to ask the next obvious question. *What quest?* He waited for Thoiren to tell him.

The chiefs sat on a raised platform by the lattice wall that separated this room from the next in the longhouse. The back of Hamunth's chair had a pad of smooth-worn burnt brown leather for a headrest, bare wood armrests, and a cushion filled with wedgewing feathers. Thoiren's chair differed by having a higher back and a carving of the Swenikyim concave-sided triangle over his head. Hamunth's standard hung limp from a pole behind the chief's seat. In a stream of air, the amber pennant would spread into the shape of a forked tongue.

Hamunth's canine sprawled before the chief's feet on the edge of the platform, chin propped on its forelegs. The animal had sorrel fur, not unlike some vulpines, but was larger than such creatures. Although its head rested, the large brown eyes watched Thoiren, and Hamunth delighted how that bothered the chief.

Wary of the canine, Thoiren went behind his high-backed chair and opened a trap door in the platform floor. He extracted a roll of parchment as big around as a man's neck, holding it by handles on both ends.

"Jorgis found a stash of these scrolls in a cave between the two long lakes during his return from Chizdek last autumn. His quest is to translate them."

Hamunth held out a hand with an unspoken command. *Let me see.* Thoiren placed the roll on his palm. Hamunth unraveled it a cubit's length, enough to see its markings.

"These look like Chizdekyim symbols."

"Jorgis knows them," said Thoiren. "He didn't know what these say."

Now Hamunth allowed himself a snort. He rolled the scroll closed and stepped from the platform to bring it to the nearest table, leaving his canine behind. Thoiren followed with his wife, Befdaul, a short robust woman.

Hamunth's betrothed daughter, Larzil, sat at the table with the chief's two Chizdekyim bodyguards. Not much taller than Befdaul, she had scrawny arms and legs but a pudgy middle. She grew her blond hair so long it reached the backs of her knees when she walked. Her face almost was pretty until she smiled, showing crooked teeth. Her skin was fair like her Chizdekyim mother, whom Hamunth didn't marry and who disappeared after Larzil was weaned.

The bodyguards, Adam and Enoch, looked like father and son, although they weren't. They had broad noses and thick lips on hairy faces. Adam wore a sleeveless tunic, revealing his arms' solid muscles and the Chizdekyim branding marks on them. Enoch's sleeves went to his elbows, exposing Chizdekyim markings on his forearms. His arms were as huge as Adam's, although fleshy and not as muscled.

Hamunth set the scroll on the table and unrolled the same cubit-long section. He spoke in the Chizdekyim language, which he learned by living among the vagabonds as a youth. "Adam, what do you think of this?"

While the older Chizdekyim examined the scroll, two men came from a neighboring table. Kevyar, the only living child Thoiren acknowledged, left a woman at the other table who looked like she was about to give birth any day. Hamunth supposed the craggy-faced expecting mother with straight black hair to be Kevyar's wife, especially after some girls previously came to them, seeming to be their daughters.

The other man, looking a few years older than Kevyar, arrived with a tankard in one hand. He had introduced himself as Davlek when Hamunth arrived at the longhouse late last night. Once married to Thoiren's now-deceased daughter, he also seemed to have daughters because two girls had begged for his attention.

Everyone else present, including some dozen Hamunthyim and Swenikyim warriors, continued whatever they were doing—mostly drinking. Hamunth collected a tankard of brew from a passing server before Adam was ready to speak.

He used Snarshyim words. "This isn't the Chizdekyim language."

"Jorgis was right about these not being Chizdekyim words," said Befdaul.

"I think it's the Old Language."

"The Old Language?"

"My grandmother knew it," said Adam. "All the languages around here except your Snarshyim language are based on it: Chizdekyim, Yarsishyim, and Kendulyim."

Thoiren asked, "What about the Richeeyim language?"

"Richee?"

"The coastland south of the great eastern desert."

Adam shook his head. "I don't know of that place."

Thoiren's shoulders sagged.

Hamunth asked, "Did Jorgis go to Richee?"

"He left before winter with two scrolls." Thoiren smiled as always but looked strange until Hamunth recognized he was cringing. "We don't know when he'll return."

Larzil became distressed, asking in an unsteady voice, "Jorgis isn't here?"

Hamunth moved beside his daughter and let her bury her face into his side. *Shed big tears, my dear.* He planned to extract as much retribution from the Swenikt as he could. "I traveled far to see a wedding."

The blue strip of the Tauzzreen River outside the open door didn't appear so bright as before. The sky was clouded over. The Hamuntht had followed the river, going across the two long lakes between the high hills and the great eastern desert during their journey from Chizdek, which was located sixty-five horizons northward on the coast of the Chizdekyim Inlet.

Thoiren never stopped smiling. "I assure you, Chief Hamunth, you'll receive a husband for your daughter. I welcome her into my household until Jorgis returns, if she's willing to wait for him."

Hamunth knew Thoiren understood his challenge of finding a husband for a daughter from an unwed mother, and Jorgis was an ideal choice, being like the bride, a child of a chief and a Chizdekyim mother. Jorgis told Hamunth that secret so he would consent to the marriage. The young man's father wasn't some woodsman as Chief Thoiren claimed; it was Thoiren himself.

Chief Hamunth never married. None of his eight children had the same mother except for a pair of full brothers, and one of them, Buerosh, killed the other. Hamunth hardly could fault his oldest son, other than his foolhardy purpose of fighting over a woman, because he slew his older brother but for a better reason: to become chief.

He left Buerosh at Chizdek to let him think he was leading the tribe, and to see if the young man would dare organize a revolt while he was gone. Hamunth's most loyal men would make sure he didn't. The chief brought along his three other sons, who were young boys, to keep them safe from Buerosh. They were among the children running about, which included his two youngest daughters.

He stroked his oldest daughter's head that was buried in his side, asking in a soothing tone, "What do you say, Larzil? Do you want to stay here for Jorgis?"

She looked at him with teary eyes and nodded.

"I shouldn't have to pay the bridal price until Jorgis returns, Chief Thoiren, but I don't want to haul the livestock and foodstuffs back to Chizdek."

"Would gold and silver suffice?"

Hamunth didn't have much use for the shiny metals, but the Yarsishyimt who crossed the Chizdekyim Inlet to trade had enough liking for them to relinquish more useful items in return. "They'll suffice."

Thoiren clapped hands. "Then we both get something else we want, better relations between our tribes."

Hamunth didn't care much about that.

Thoiren continued, "I know you came here for a feast and a celebration. The sun's high in the sky, time to begin."

Hamunth raised his tankard. *Bring the food.*

Kevyar near Pinkulda

Davlek was passed out from too much drinking. His arms slumped on the table, so Kevyar amused himself by arranging fish heads from the meal to suck the fingers of his once-wedlock brother. An annoyed look from his wife added to his amusement. *If Jankwel wasn't annoyed by one thing*, he told himself, *it was another.* She frowned each time he tossed a morsel to Hamunth's canine, and no doubt she disapproved of the entertainment the visiting chief's consort performed for the mock wedding feast. The woman sang a bawdy song with provocative dance about a man's wife pretending to be his wench.

Chief Thoiren enjoyed the performance from his chair on the platform, leaning toward Hamunth next to him to trade lighthearted remarks Kevyar couldn't hear. The visiting chief had a thin face with a tuft of beard and balding gray hair. He wore a stagskin jerkin and taupe gray woolstock trousers on a twig body.

The consort removed her skirt, stripping to a short, lacey undergarment to play the part of the wench in her song. Kevyar stole glances of her long, shapely legs whenever he thought Jankwel wouldn't notice.

He wondered why his wife stayed. Their daughters and nieces had gone to another room with his mother, Befdaul, and the other children for a game and innocent stories. He supposed Jankwel remained on behalf of Larzil, the bride without a husband, who wasn't eating or speaking, but came to sit by them.

Some shouts from outside sounded like the revelry out there degenerating to a drunken brawl, but then a guard with a spear appeared in the doorway. He shouted in the shrill voice of a youth, "We're under attack!"

Thoiren bolted to his feet, and the canine by him yelped. Kevyar was halfway to the door before he heard his father ask who attacked them. The spearman didn't know.

Kevyar asked, "Which way?"

The young man tilted his speartip southward down the Tauzzreen River.

Kevyar thought, *Druogoint or Warnekt*. He saw the other warriors from the longhouse, including Chief Hamunth's men with the Swenikt, coming with weapons to follow him, at least the ones not too drunk.

"Stay here and protect the chiefs, women, and children."

The Swenikt moved to obey Kevyar. The Hamuntht looked to their chief.

Hamunth remained seated, having calmed his canine. "Men, we're staying here."

Kevyar felt foolish because he left his sword under the table in his haste to get to the door, and he wasn't going back for it, so he took the spear from the young guard before running south to meet the attackers.

The longhouse was part of a settlement of kitchens, foundries, stables, barns, pens, shops, and houses between the river and the forest along its western bank. The inhabitants scurried about, some calm and others shouting or shrieking in terror. Some climbed into boats to escape to the other side of the river, and more ran into the woods.

A few other warriors, armed with shortswords and throwing hammers, joined Kevyar along the path running among the riverfront buildings. The group of seven, Kevyar included, waded through a cluster of clucking barn fowl and passed by the stock pens holding Larzil's dowry. Although mid-afternoon, a roiling cloud deck blackened the sky and made the way as shadowed and dark as twilight. A chill wind blew over the river, churning the water as much as it stirred the clouds.

They crossed an ankle-deep creek marking the edge of the settlement and entered a sparse pattern of trees. A battle echoed among the tree trunks—clanging metal, the splintering of wooden shields, dull thuds against leather and flesh, combatants shouting, and the screams of the wounded and dying. Kevyar hurried forward with his men.

One hulking form appeared ahead, then another. They kept coming, dressed in skins and carrying axes, war hammers, cudgels, and maces. Kevyar saw hairy heads, since few wore helmets, and blooddrop pennants. *They were Herkt*, he realized. *They wouldn't attack except for tribute.* He suppressed the terrible thought.

His warriors released a flurry of throwing hammers. One's pointed end found its mark between the eyes of an oncoming Herk, a massive bulk of a man who flopped on the weapon embedded in his forehead. More came, outnumbering the Swenikt. Kevyar surmised the Herkt came down the Pultanik River in sufficient numbers to overwhelm the Swenikyim watchmen. The distance crossing to the Tauzzreen River was no more than a few horizons near Pinkulda.

The attackers stampeded through the Swenikt. Kevyar stabbed his spear into one's hip, and the looming hulk swung a cudgel. The iron mallet pummeled Kevyar in the stomach, making him lose hold of his spear. The speartip fell from the Herk's hip, and the enemy warrior moved past. Kevyar curled on the ground, thinking he would vomit, and gasped for breath. The blow struck only flesh, missing any bone, so he suffered no lasting damage.

He regained his breath and crawled to the riverbank under the confusion of more waves of Herkt coming from the south. Slipping into bone-chilling cold water to his neck, he moved upstream past the creek mouth on his left.

The Herkt rampaged through the buildings on the shore. Most occupants had fled. The stragglers were ignored unless they resisted or were women. Kevyar saw a stable hand with a pitchfork getting his brain bashed with a mace, and he heard the screams of violated women.

Moving along the western bank, submerged to his neck, he passed the stock pens, being emptied by the Herkt, and swam around the rafts on which the Hamuntht arrived from upriver last night. Boats lined the opposite bank, left by the people who escaped over there. They watched from the other side, looking ready to flee farther east if the Herkt attempted to cross.

Kevyar's limbs became numbed in the frigid water. Lightning arced across the sky. *Time to leave the river*, he told himself. He climbed ashore near the riverside entrance of the longhouse.

The Herkt hadn't reached the large building, opposed by the warriors Kevyar ordered to protect the place. He was aghast to see the door standing open and hurried dripping wet into the longhouse before the fighting reached there.

The two chiefs remained sitting. The Chizdekyim bodyguards, Adam and Enoch, and the other warriors from Chizdek ringed Hamunth and his canine. His consort cowered nearby without a skirt. A few Swenikyim warriors flanked Thoiren. Jankwel and Larzil hid behind an upended table, although not well hidden because Kevyar saw them. He wondered, *Why didn't they retreat to the inner rooms, and where's Davlek?* He didn't see the passed-out man anywhere.

The door was open against the inside wall. He began closing it, so the crossbeam could be lowered to secure it, but a mob of Herkt burst through. Kevyar was swept behind the swinging portal and pinned against the wall. A gigantic Herk stood against the mass of wood, leaving him helpless to do anything but watch.

The first wave of attackers engaged the warriors around the chiefs. Hamunth's canine joined the fight. The beast's growls and snarls mixed into the noise of shouts and combat filling the room. Two other Herkt, one taller with straight dark hair and a stout one with lighter hair, yanked the table from the front of Jankwel and Larzil. The terrified shrieks of the women added to the cacophony.

The tall dark-haired Herk tore into Larzil's clothes and violated her. The stout fair-haired one grabbed for Jankwel. Kevyar saw the stout one's ugly face, scabbed and warted, and strained against the wooden planks pressed against his body, desperate to rescue his wife.

A third Herk with curly brown hair lingered nearby. He was a young man, not much older than a youth but huge, and Kevyar heard his thunderous voice over the din. "Leave her, dolt! Don't you see she's ripe with child?"

The stout one released Jankwel and took his turn with Larzil. When finished, he drew a dagger and grabbed her hair. Kevyar feared he would kill her, but the Herk sliced off her long blond strands and wrapped them around his neck.

Hamunth's consort also was violated, but Kevyar realized the man on her was Hamunth. *At least the Herkt were kept off her.*

The defenders were overpowered by Herkt packing into the room. Kevyar saw two lying decapitated on the floor and others bleeding and dying. The rest, including Adam and Enoch, were restrained. Jankwel and Larzil held one another, sobbing. Larzil was a mess; hair cropped short, clothes torn, and bloodied between her legs.

Only the canine kept fighting. It leaped on the curly-haired man, fangs bared and snarling. The Herk barely had time to draw a dagger and stab it in the belly. The animal emitted an earsplitting yelp and collapsed to a whimpering pile of sorrel fur. The attacker held his bloodied dagger in a hand covered with his own blood because that arm was gashed open. More blood covered a shoulder from a bite in the neck.

Some invaders penetrated the inner rooms. Kevyar heard the high-pitched shrill of screaming girls, including his daughters and nieces, and feared for their safety, helpless to protect them. A Herk returned from the next room.

The curly-hair with the dagger asked, "Who are back there?"

"An old woman and children, mostly little girls, and a man too senseless to move," said the other Herk. "We're watching them."

Thoiren lurched from his chair with words of fury. "What's the meaning of this wanton attack? We pay tribute for this?"

The curly-hair approached him with his dripping blade and countered with his own questions, "You do? Where is it?"

"You should have it. We sent it last year as usual."

Kevyar felt doom knotting in his stomach that was aching from the cudgel blow. He ordered the tribute to be withheld, thinking the Herkt wouldn't miss it during their succession to a new clanlord. *A grievous mistake*, he fretted. He wanted to shout an explanation from his place pinned behind the door, but had none. No matter, he expected his father to placate the Herkt as he did with Chief Hamunth about Jorgis missing his wedding.

The young Herk shouted, "Aren't you the chief here, old man? Why are you lying? I see the herds in the pens, the tribute you kept from us."

"I'm chief, but who are you?" Thoiren seemed to force a smile, but Kevyar knew his father smiled from habit. "You're a boy."

The Herk pointed his dagger's bloody tip at Thoiren's face. "I'm the clanlord's man. He sent me to get the tribute."

Thoiren's smile widened. The chief leaned forward so his nose almost touched the dagger's tip. "He sent you, a foolhardy whelp? Why not ask for the tribute before attacking us, you feckless dolt?"

No, Father! Kevyar didn't understand why his sire would antagonize an enraged warrior holding a dagger in his face. He struggled again to free himself from behind the door, but the gigantic Herk leaned harder against it to keep him trapped.

The young curly-haired lead Herk swung his dagger low into Thoiren's stomach. Jankwel screamed and buried her face into Larzil's arms. Kevyar had the door pressed too hard into his chest to yell.

The Herk extracted the dagger and let Thoiren drop to the floor next to the wounded canine. He whirled, wielding the blade covered in the blood of two victims, and called, "Who will be the new chief? If this man has a son, where is he?"

Kevyar opened his mouth to speak.

"I'm the chief's son."

The words came from Chief Hamunth, who stood in a corner in front of his woman he violated to keep the Herkt from violating her.

Kevyar wondered, *What's he doing?*

"Take him," the lead Herk told the guards around Hamunth. "He's good for ransom." He noticed Adam and Enoch. "These men have Chizdekyim markings. They're going with us, too."

Hamunth and his bodyguards offered no resistance as they were escorted to the door. The chief glared at Kevyar as he left. His message seemed clear: *Protect my woman and children.* Kevyar nodded that he understood.

The lead Herk lingered at the platform, picking up the scroll left between the chairs of the two chiefs. He unrolled the first cubit for a look, rolled it closed, and handed it to the dark-haired Herk who had violated Larzil. "Keep this. It looks important."

He surveyed the platform a final time, spotted Hamunth's amber forked-tongue pennant, and snapped it off the end of the pole to take with him. *The fool*, Kevyar thought. *Doesn't he recognize the Hamunthyim standard?*

New Herkt entered with torches and pails of grease probably taken from the kitchens. The departing leader commanded, "Big flames."

One man dumped grease over the platform and chairs, and a torch set them on fire. Kevyar lamented, *the scrolls!* The rest of the parchments under the platform were doomed to burn. More pailfuls were splashed against the walls, setting them aflame. The Herkt vacated the fiery room, going outside and shutting the door.

Free at last, Kevyar rushed to Thoiren lying in a pool of blood on the floor. He ripped open the tattered front of his father's tunic. The wound was worse than a mere stab. The blade had wrenched the chief's belly, spilling entrails.

Kevyar looked into Thoiren's face. The dying man stared at the ceiling. The flames up there reflected in his pupils.

"Father, why?" Kevyar's voice was choked with anguish. *Why did you incite the young Herk to kill you?*

Thoiren's voice rasped. "I can't see! The light's too bright."

A look of recognition appeared in his face. "The scroll, it's so white!"

The canine beside him whimpered, and Thoiren extended a hand to stroke its head. His fingers passed over its snout, and the animal licked them.

Thoiren called again, gaining strength in his voice, "I see! I see a great red tree, and it's full of crowns. I see a son!"

Kevyar sobbed. "Father, I'm sorry." He should have paid the tribute.

His father didn't hear. The flame in his eyes glazed over. Chief Thoiren of the Swenikt died as he lived, with a smile.

"Kevyar!" Jankwel clutched her child-swelled belly, and Kevyar went to her.

Hamunth's consort helped Larzil stand, but they had nowhere to go. The room was engulfed in flames, and the door to the outside was set afire.

The burning platform blocked the way to the next room. Some warriors tried to quell the flames with cloaks. Kevyar recognized the best chance was hacking through the lattice wall, but the Herkt disarmed everyone. He remembered his sword and looked by the upended table. It was on the floor where he left it, unnoticed.

He swung the blade into the lattice, chipping the wood, blow by blow. He sweated in the intense heat, keeping his clothes drenched that were soaked in the river, and a hole appeared. A burly warrior rammed a shoulder into the broken lattice and crashed through.

Kevyar handed his sword to the next man to take with him through the opening. Then he guided his wife toward the next room. The noxious scent of charred wood and smoke afflicted his nasals and throat. He coughed, and his eyes watered. Jankwel suffered worse, coughing out of control. The consort and Larzil went ahead through the lattice. Kevyar could barely see the opening through the smoke. He encountered his mother on the other side.

Befdaul called in panic, "Where's Thoiren?" She tried to pass through to the burning room, but the people coming out blocked her path.

"Mother, he's dead." This was no time for Kevyar to be gentle. "Jankwel needs your help."

Befdaul's voice was shrill. "He's dead? I must see him."

"You must help Jankwel." Kevyar shoved his wife into his mother's arms.

Jankwel paused from coughing to clutch her stomach in another wave of pain.

"The child's coming!" Befdaul took Jankwel away from the fiery room.

The outflow of people escaping the room had ceased. Kevyar peered through the lattice. He saw nothing except churning smoke, not much different than the blackened clouds he saw outside. The ceiling cracked, and debris crashed down. Fire appeared within the smoke, falling in balls of flame. *How fitting*, Kevyar thought, knowing his father's corpse would have been burned on a funeral pyre anyway.

Fire licked through the lattice. Kevyar retreated to the third room, being the last person to vacate the second. He found Davlek sitting on a bed, recovering his wits.

"Kevyar, what's happening?"

"This place is burning down. We must go."

The last few others were leaving the third room to get to the last. Kevyar followed Davlek after them. His frightened daughters met him on the other side. The youngest embraced him around the knee, and he took her into his arms.

"Father, are the bad men gone?"

The room's back door stood open on the western end of the longhouse, so Kevyar concluded the Herkt who watched his mother and the children left that way. He asked his oldest daughter, "Did they hurt you?"

She almost was old enough to flow. Her hair was dark

brown like his and long and straight like her mother's. "They only scared us. Did they hurt Mother?"

He looked over her head at the great curtained bed of his parents where Befdaul tended to his wife. "No, but the baby's coming."

Jankwel wasn't hurt, he thought, but others were; Larzil for one, lying atop large pillows on the floor. Worst yet, *how would he tell his daughters about their grandfather?* He asked his mother about Jankwel.

"The child's coming," she said. "We need a safe place."

He agreed. The other end of their building was an inferno. Setting down his youngest daughter, he retrieved his sword from the warrior who had it and went outside.

The western end of the longhouse stabbed into the forest. Kevyar rounded the corner to the southern side and saw the pillaging Herkt setting more buildings afire. A drop of moisture touched his face.

He went to the northern side where no Herkt were. Steady rain started, renewing the wetness of his clothes. The fiery longhouse, collapsed at the eastern end, sizzled under a mounting downpour. The odor of soggy ashes mingled with the prevailing smell of burning wood. Kevyar thought the weather might put out the blaze. He returned to his mother and assured her they were safe. He sent Davlek to watch the fire's progress, or its demise, as he hoped.

Although the bed curtains provided some privacy for Jankwel to birth a child, Kevyar sent most everyone, including his daughters and nieces, to the next room. Only his mother, Larzil, and Chief Hamunth's consort remained. He changed from his drenched clothes to dry ones from his father's wardrobe that were a loose fit on his body, not caring that the women saw him.

Davlek reported the deluge extinguished the fire. Kevyar went outside to see a smoldering ruin. The rain was done, and the Herkt were gone, so he inspected the rest of the settlement. He saw empty pens and buildings saved by rain from burning. The people who fled across the river or into the woods were returning.

When the time neared for his next child to be born, he watched with fascination, having not seen the births of any of his daughters. He saw the dilated opening between Jankwel's legs and the top of the baby's wrinkled head, looking like a hairy raisin.

Jankwel pushed with all her strength and mighty loud shrieks, and a tiny head appeared. Kevyar saw closed eyes, a nose, and quivering lips, all covered in violet slime. Jankwel pushed again, and the rest of the infant came out. Befdaul handed the child to Kevyar, still attached by the cord to the mother. The baby was messy and bloody, and the father was joyful to see he had a son.

A son! Kevyar regretted his father didn't live the short time to see the grandson he wanted. The newborn looked perfect, ten fingers and ten toes, and unblemished except for his birthmarksign. Kevyar placed the crying baby boy into his wife's arms, and stroked sweaty black strands of her hair from her beaming face.

"Look, Jankwel. We have a son!"

She asked, "What will we name him?"

He paused, realizing they never discussed a boy's name because they expected another daughter. His response was the only proper answer.

"His name is Thoiren."

Rash

Herkt

Brutez   **Taubueth**

"You won't only be clanlord, but more."

More what? He asked his mother, but his mother wasn't speaking. The woman was younger, her hair not as red, green eyes instead of blue; she was his wife.

"All is going as planned."

The voice wasn't a woman's. *Who was he? His father? Grebnar?* He remembered the voice coming from a throne.

"Your deeds will be great."

Brutez woke to morning light entering through a shaft in his bedchamber and stared at the plank and beam ceiling, recalling the words from his dream. *Where did he hear them? The Black Citadel*, he remembered. He thought about the illusions he saw there; a scaly winged leviathan, the luminous multi-colored eyes of dark beings, dancing swords, talking bubbles, and colored lights and kingdoms. Three stumps, a sapling cut down, and a tall dual-trunked tree with blooddrop leaves, *what did that mean?* Another thought came to his mind, stronger than the others. He needed to find a scroll, and the Swenikt had one.

Beksel stirred beside him. He liked waking up with her warm body next to his. *He liked marriage.* He began many mornings by grabbing the woman. He still felt uneasy about using the same bed as Uncle Shemjib and Aunt Yeemzal, and by his father and mother before them, but his uncle and aunt were gone, and his father insisted the quarters belonged to the clanlord. His loins were ready, and this morning *she grabbed him.*

Brutez expected his father, Zamtoth, to welcome his bride with open arms when he brought her to Taubueth, and the old man didn't disappoint, embracing Beksel and thumping Brutez's back. Heptor was gone, so Nazzel moved out of Brutez's former chamber for Beksel's mother, Sejel, to stay there.

The parents, Zamtoth and Sejel, joined the recently married couple for breakfast in the main room. They were done eating when a familiar voice Brutez hadn't heard for a half year called for him down the stairs from the hovel.

"Come, Larboelm," he shouted.

Footsteps pounded heavy on the stairs and the huge bulk of the man burst through the doorway of skins. His sandy hair and beard were longer and wilder than last autumn, and a twisted nose remained from the beatings he endured from the Jatneryimt at Doenesh, although the rest of his face was healed.

"Clanlord, it's true! The men at the wall told me you returned." Larboelm laid his spiked mace on the furred floor and knelt over it. "My fealty remains yours."

Of that Brutez had no doubt, seeing no need for a demonstration of loyalty. He stood to vacate his chair. "Sit here, Larboelm. Have you eaten?" He swept a hand over the remnant of their breakfast—starch roots with bits of flatsnout, toasted bread, and spring berry jam.

"Yes, Clanlord," said Larboelm; nevertheless, he collected the uneaten portions when he sat.

Brutez was anxious to ask more questions, but before that, introductions were needed. He raised an open hand to indicate the older of the two women at the table. "Larboelm, this is Lady Sejel, Sir Grebnar's wife."

Larboelm's eyes opened wide.

Brutez reported his more startling surprise. "This is her daughter, Beksel, my lady wife."

Larboelm dropped a heap of starch roots from the utensil going to his mouth. It plopped on the edge of the table, half landing in his lap. "That means Sir Grebnar . . ."

"He's my wedlock father."

Larboelm's stunned look changed to a broad smile. "You made peace, Clanlord." He picked the mushy lump from his trousers, transferring it to an empty mug.

Brutez asked, "Where's Heptor?"

Larboelm hesitated.

"Speak freely," said Brutez. "I keep no secrets from my wife, and Lady Sejel listens for her husband."

"I left your brother in Swenikyim lands." Larboelm resumed eating.

"Left him? You returned without him?"

Brutez was concerned about Heptor being gone for more than three weeks on an assignment that shouldn't have taken more than one, and he *still* hadn't returned.

Larboelm swallowed. "Yes, Clanlord. I arrived last night, too late to see you, so I stayed at the stable until this morning."

Although wondering why Larboelm returned alone, Brutez wanted to hear his story from the beginning, having a foreboding about Heptor being gone so long, as well as not being where he was sent. "My father sent you with Heptor to the Blue River."

Beksel asked, "Where's the Blue River?"

Larboelm put down his next bite of starch roots. "I suppose you came down the Taubueth River on your trip from Doenesh, my lady."

"We did after leaving the ridge."

After Puutnam married Vel, Brutez recalled.

"Another day downriver and then south through the forest crosses to the Blue River." Larboelm looked at Brutez, who stood nearby since giving away the chair. "We did that, Clanlord."

Brutez asked, "What did you discover about the tribute?"

"They didn't receive it."

Brutez thought. *Where did Larboelm say he left Heptor, Swenikyim lands?* A conclusion came easy. "So Heptor decided to get it?"

"Not at first," said Larboelm. "Many Blue River warriors were gone on a raid, crossing to the Fall River."

The Fall River? Brutez was dismayed to hear about his clansmen attacking the Warnekt. Grebnar was dealing with retaliation from the Warnekt, and now the Herkt must worry about a counterattack.

Larboelm continued, having forgotten about eating. "Heptor wanted to go after them and join the raid, but one of his dimwitted friends, Rankeb or Konrash, I don't remember which one's the scab-face, gave him the idea to go after the tribute."

"Konrash," said Brutez. "He has the scab."

Larboelm looked at Zamtoth. "I urged your son to report to you as ordered, but he was lathered into a battle fever."

Zamtoth shook his head. "He's rash."

Larboelm spoke to Brutez, "I told Heptor we needed a larger force and should wait for the warriors to return from the Fall River, hoping he would become bored and forget about the tribute. I think he stayed the week for drinking and feasting more than anything else. I would have come here sooner with a report had I known how long before the warriors returned to the Blue River."

"You did what you thought best at the time," said Brutez.

"When the warriors returned, some joined our force, and we continued down the Blue River."

"You went all the way to the deep blue lake?"

"Not by the river. It goes out of the way to the southeastern corner of the lake. We cut across to the western shore."

"You went to the fishing town at the mouth of the Taubueth River?"

"Yes, Clanlord, that's where I lived as a boy. Rankeb and Konrash also come from there and know the local warriors. Enough joined our force so we numbered more than eighty."

Brutez asked what happened next, knowing he wouldn't like the answer.

"After some days of festivities, you know how Heptor enjoys those, we took boats along the northern shore to the eastern corner where the Pultanik River flows from the lake, and we attacked the Swenikyim town on the other side."

"What did the Swenikt say about the tribute?" Brutez asked, knowing the annual indemnity was gathered at that town.

"Nobody bothered to ask until after the place burned. I wanted no part in the attack and stayed back. The looting began before I entered the town."

"The men were out of control," said Zamtoth.

Heptor lost control, Brutez concluded.

"I thought so," Larboelm agreed. "I stopped some needless killing but couldn't do much by myself. The Blue River warriors started violating women."

Brutez was appalled, remembering what he heard about the raid at Agratuna. The actions of his Herkyim warriors, who declared fealty to him, sounded as bad or worse. He paced across the room to the hearth. "What about Heptor?"

"I found him on the edge of town. He said no tribute reached there, so we must go downriver toward Pinkulda."

Brutez bowed his head. The report kept getting worse. He told Larboelm to continue, expecting to hear how the raiders pillaged across Swenikyim territory.

"My pleas to stop were ignored, so I returned here."

"You came alone?"

"I took a Swenikyim skimmer across the lake to the town

where I lived as a boy. I acquired a mount there for the rest of the journey."

"You did the right thing, Larboelm," said Zamtoth.

Brutez agreed with his father, returning from across the room to pat Larboelm's shoulder. "You did the best thing. We needed to know our clansmen have started wars with the Warnekt and the Swenikt." *We have new enemies after making peace with the Jatneryimt for the first time in living memory*, he lamented.

Larboelm asked, "What will we do, Clanlord?"

Brutez watched for his father's reaction as he answered, "We must go toward Pinkulda with as many men as we can muster."

Zamtoth nodded approval but spoke an objection, one Brutez also held. "We don't have many warriors left. Taubueth will be woefully undermanned."

Unacceptable. Brutez couldn't leave Grebnar's wife and daughter at risk. Moreover, if he took the warriors he wanted—Larboelm, Jonerch, Gordib, and others—the most seasoned warrior at Taubueth would be Puutnam, a *Jatneryim*. He had a solution for both problems, sending Puutnam to have Vikth bring men from the ridge to Taubueth.

Larboelm went with Brutez upstairs through the hovel. Yeemzal's stock of remedies remained there for use by Beksel, who was well trained in the healing arts by her mother. Brutez was disappointed by his aunt's departure, almost as much as he was for missing his sister's visit, but not surprised. The Feldramt were closer kin for Yeemzal than any of the Herkt without Shemjib.

Brutez and Larboelm walked outside to a pleasant spring morning. "Prepare mounts and provisions for Puutnam and his escort," Brutez commanded. "I'll gather the force going with us. I want to leave after lunch."

Larboelm poked a thumb toward the sound across the courtyard of metal picks chinking Taubueth's stone wall. "What are they doing over there?"

"Making a proper entrance for this place."

Brutez was never more embarrassed than when his bride, wedlock mother, and the other Jatneryimt had to climb a rickety ladder to enter Taubueth. The workers were chipping through the wall for a more accessible entrance to the stronghold, after attempts to dig under were thwarted by bedrock or an older section of wall sunk into the ground.

Larboelm responded, "Why not build a ramp? We have plenty of trees around here to use for wood."

Curses, Brutez thought. *Why didn't I or any other Herk for the last centuries think of that?* A ramp could be torn down or set afire in case of attack, and cutting down trees out to the distance arrows could be fired was another good idea. He remembered the open space around the Green Citadel at Doenesh. Attackers couldn't sneak through the forest all the way to the wall there like at Taubueth.

"Mounts and provisions," he told Larboelm, too annoyed to acknowledge the man's suggestion for a ramp, although he determined to reassign the workers before he left Taubueth. "I want Puutnam gone before we are."

Thoughts of a Maiden

Feldramt

Sangern **Agratuna**

Sangern leaned over a slat railing on a fair, cloudless spring day, gazing into the sun over the sparkling water of the Snarshyim Inlet toward Agratuna on the nearby coast. He stood on planks hanging over the shore, enclosed by the handrail on three sides and backed by the outer wall of an island lodge. Recognizing some footsteps as his mother's, he didn't look at her when she leaned by him on the railing.

"The Chrevramt have arrived inside. Come, Son, and meet your betrothed wife."

He wasn't allowed to see them since they arrived by boats that came down the coast a day ago, although he visited some of the Feldramyim skilled craftsmen and herdsmen who had spent the winter in Biepazz and now returned home. He couldn't get any of them to speak about the Chrevramyim girl he was supposed to marry, so he only could rely on his mother's promise she was a beauty. *Of course she would say that,* he told himself. He rather would have his father's manly opinion, but the lord chieftain had no part in the selection and not seen Zabfrul until her arrival in Agratuna. Even then he refused to speak about her.

Sangern wondered, *Why doesn't my mother let anybody tell me about my future wife?* He stared over the water. "Yes, Mother, I'll go see this wife you picked for me."

Enough of a breeze wafted over the calm sea to ripple the water and keep the air from becoming too hot. Even at high tide, the rippling surface was some cubits down because the lodge was built high enough so it wouldn't be battered by a stormy sea.

His mother's hand rested on his shoulder. "I didn't pick her. She was offered."

"I understand. I have to take her so we could get some boatloads of food."

"Trust me; you're getting the good end of the deal. She's a lovely girl, sweet and vivacious."

He looked at her so she would see his sardonic smirk.

She patted his shoulder before removing her hand from it. "You're a good son."

A grown son, not a boy, he wanted to tell her, but didn't.

She had fussed for him to look his best. He was scrubbed clean and had his raven hair trimmed and combed. His patchy beard was gone. He wore everything leather and new—black boots, brown tight-fitting breeches, and a tan jerkin.

His lord chieftain father and brother Chrenlon met them inside the door. The lodge was constructed from the white bark trees that grew on the island. A spacious room ran through the center under a thatch ceiling that was fifteen cubits up at its highest point, and supported by two rows of thick poles. The three spaces between the rows of poles and walls were lined with banquet tables, waiting for food. Sangern was introduced to Lord and Lady Chrevram.

Their appearance worried him. Lord Chrevram was short and gaunt except for pudgy red cheeks. His ears flapped from the sides of his head, and most of his gray hairs were collected into a mustache. His wife was taller and full of girth, pale and pasty, and looked older. Her hair was lighter gray, and she had wrinkled skin. Sangern asked himself in dismay, *What does their daughter look like?*

"Zabfrul," said Lord Chrevram. "Come forward."

She was taller than her parents and Sangern's mother, Majdel. Sangern saw golden hair, the color of honeycomb, piled on her shoulders and waving down her back. She had glistening azure eyes, a dainty nose, and carnelian lips curved into a quaint smile. Her delicate cheekbones showed her smooth copper skin.

She wore a singular garment, leaving her shoulders and arms bare and cinched in the right places to present her slender form. The gossamer teal material revealed a hint of the rounding of her breasts. It pressed around her stem of a waist and clung to her hips, wisping to her ankles.

"My dear daughter," said Chrevram. "You've left the young man speechless."

Sangern realized his jaw dropped open and closed it. Zabfrul's father was right. He couldn't think of a word to say.

His mother rescued him with a suggestion. "Son, take Zabfrul by the sea and get acquainted."

He gave Zabfrul a look of invitation and her little smile broadened, making dimples by the corners of her mouth. She accepted his offer of taking hands and walked by his side to the rail overlooking the shimmering Snarshyim Inlet. Her flaxen hair fluffed in the breeze, catching the sunlight and smelling better than any flowers he ever savored. He shifted, guiding her with the hand he held so he looked into her face, and took hold of her other hand. She met his gaze. His soul swam in the azure expanse of her eyes. He had his words to say.

"My fairest of maidens, I'm delighted by your presence."

She looked away. When she spoke, her voice had a sweet and steady resonance. "True, I'm a maiden, but I must confess I don't have the thoughts of a maiden."

His heart paced. *What does she mean?* She wasn't as innocent as she appeared. "What thoughts?"

She looked straight at him with azure eyes, dainty nose, curling lips, dimpled cheeks, and golden hair. "Now that I see you, betrothed husband, I think about sharing our wedding bed, pleasing you and being pleased."

He took a deep breath to curb a surge of desire. "I'm surprised you think about such things," he said when he could speak again.

She smiled wide, showing rows of white teeth, and asked, "Why shouldn't I?" She leaned up with her lips and breathed more words into his ear, "We'll create life together."

He didn't know what to say, for he could barely think. His stomach was aflutter. The silence would have become uncomfortable except she wrapped her arm behind his back and didn't seem to expect him to say anything while they looked across the water. He set his hand over her opposite shoulder. She was tall for her age. The top of her golden-haired head reached his nose, and she was young enough to grow taller.

The words he knew he should say came to him. "My dear Zabfrul, may I seal our betrothal with a kiss?"

She looked at him. "I would find that pleasing."

His mouth met hers. Her lips seemed inexperienced at first but learned quickly.

"We should return inside," he said after they parted. He figured he more than followed his mother's suggestion to get acquainted.

They found their mothers with Aunt Yeemzal inside.

Lady Chrevram stepped away. "Zabfrul, come with me."

Zabfrul followed her mother but glanced back at Sangern as she went. "Sangern, my love, I'm anxious to rejoin you at the meal."

How could this be? Sangern questioned himself. They met a moment ago and were one mind.

His mother asked, "My son, what do you have to say about the Chrevram girl?"

"Mother, she's a vision!"

She gave Sangern a wry smile. "She's worth some boatloads of food, don't you think?" Then she scolded, "While she's here, have the courtesy not to go visiting your wenches."

He was aghast at the thought. "How can I? I belong to Zabfrul. I won't think about anybody else!" He didn't think he ever would visit a wench again.

The Chizdekyim Way

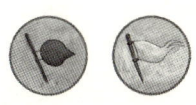

Herkt, Hamuntht

Brutez — **Swanshyim Forest**

Leafy slopes loomed higher on both banks as the Taubueth River descended a widening valley. The current flowed swift but smooth, unbroken by rocks like those that turned the water to raging rapids upriver. Here any leaf, twig or stick, fluffy white spore, drowned bug, or whatever else landed on the rapidly moving surface swept past without being churned under. Some log buildings appeared among the trees on the northern bank, and beyond that, a dark blue swath filled the distance to the edge of a lighter blue sky.

It was the deep blue lake.

Brutez assumed it was called that solely from its color, murky dark even under noontime sunshine, but Larboelm told him about the lake's depth, how an anchor on the end of a hundred cubits of rope couldn't reach the bottom.

The clanlord led a mounted column of twenty warriors. They followed a hard-packed path along the northern bank, the same side as the upcoming town, never needing to cross the river since leaving Taubueth two days ago. Brutez often rode with his friends, Jonerch and Gordib, but invariably he found Larboelm nearest him, holding the staff with the iron blooddrop. He ventured to learn more about the bodyguard he inherited from Vulrath and Klinteg.

"This is the town where you were a boy?" Brutez knew the answer, but the question opened a conversation.

"Yes, Clanlord." Larboelm spoke those words more than any others to Brutez.

"What's its name?"

Larboelm paused before answering, "I don't remember it having one."

Brutez considered a nameless town and a lake referenced by a description rather than a name, yet the Taubueth River had a name, the same as his stronghold. His father once told him Taubueth was a Chizdekyim name, but didn't know what it meant. "Do you have family there, Larboelm?"

"No, Clanlord."

A variation of his most common words, Brutez thought.

"I have no brothers or sisters. If I had other family, I never was told about them. I left for the Blue River with my mother when she went there for a new husband."

"What happened to your father?"

"He stuck a sword down his throat, a bloody mess."

Brutez remembered how his mother begged for death. "Was he sick?"

"Sick of life."

"Does your mother still live at the Blue River?"

Larboelm shook his head. "Her husband beat her to death. I killed him for that."

Brutez couldn't decide which disturbed him more, Larboelm's story or how he told it without emotion.

Larboelm tapped his macabre spiked mace by his leg on the side of his mount. "I mashed his head to pulp. Clanlord Vulrath saw me."

Brutez understood how Larboelm became Vulrath's

bodyguard, and also why he became his. *I'm the man's family*, he realized. The man should have more. "Do you have a woman?"

"I never thought about having one," said Larboelm.

"You never took chances?"

"My own, yes."

Brutez had resorted to *that* for many years, but he knew the ancient words. *It is not good for a man to be alone.* He had a worthy question for his man. "If I find you a wife, will you take her?"

"Clanlord, I'll do whatever you command."

The townspeople greeted their clanlord and fed the warriors fresh fish and roasted marshbill. They weren't so cordial the next morning when Brutez had Jonerch and Gordib cull portions from their herds of backhorns, woolstock, bovines, and flatsnouts, although he promised to replace them. Slowed by the livestock, Brutez and his warriors followed a path along the northern shore of the deep blue lake until nightfall.

> *Take, eat, and receive life.*
>
> *The scroll smelled like fresh-baked bread, but was nothing more than a roll of parchment. No, not parchment, it was blue cloth. It unraveled to a concaved triangle, and another. More unraveled, twelve Swenikyim pennants in all. Other triangles disintegrated to ashes. Then an amber pennant came, like a forked tongue, flapping in the forest, and two more like it appeared emerging from a glaring desert sunrise.*

Brutez opened his eyes to morning light. *Another dream about a scroll and being told to eat it*, he contemplated. He didn't know what it meant, but the Swenikt seemed to know *and so did the tribe with the forked-tongue pennant, the Hamuntht.*

The Herkt and their livestock reached the beginning of the Pultanik River at the northeastern corner of the lake by midmorning. The channel was wide, about two hundred cubits, carrying the same volume of water the Taubueth River, Blue

River, and various rivulets and streams poured into the lake. The near riverbank had nothing, not even a dock or pier. Any boats were moored on the Swenikyim side. Brutez wondered how Heptor's force crossed until he remembered those warriors took boats from the unnamed town at the mouth of the Taubueth River.

The Swenikyim town across the river was reduced to charred remains of collapsed timber. Some people resided in tents but most lived under animal hides propped on frameworks of branches. A thin middle-aged man in a rough-spun robe came from the devastated town by boat, rowed by two youth.

When they were near enough to one another for conversation without shouting, Brutez asked the thin man, "Are you the town leader?"

At a closer look, he concluded the thin man once was a fat man. The townsman had jowled cheeks, covered with a thin gray beard, and a wrinkled neck where he once had multiple chins. He kept his gray hair tangled on top to obscure a bald area up there.

"I lead nothing," said the man. "I fish, speaking for the town only when needed."

The oarsmen stopped the boat from coming closer than forty cubits. The craft drifted in a lazy current.

Brutez walked northward along the western bank to keep pace with it. "I'm Brutez, Clanlord of the Herkt. I didn't order the attack against your town."

"They were your warriors."

He's right, my warriors, Brutez thought. He was responsible and wouldn't make excuses, nor would words suffice, only retribution. "I'm going by Pinkulda to offer your chief amends. I'll restore my command over those warriors who attacked you. They won't bother you again."

The man in the boat bowed his head, a gesture of sadness and relief.

Brutez motioned to the bleating and squealing herd. "I'm

leaving these animals for you. They're a loan. When they produce offspring, deliver an equal number to the Herkyim town on the lakeshore west from here."

The man nodded agreement. "I'm Zuedon. My daughter, Jankwel, is married to our chief's son. Please let them know her mother and I are well."

"I'll do that." Brutez was glad to do something for him. *Perhaps a man who could return a favor*, he hoped, but Zuedon knew nothing about a scroll when asked.

The journey downriver northward along the western bank progressed faster without livestock. The river narrowed, and the current quickened. Brutez reached another river with his warriors before nightfall. The Red River came from the north, directly opposite the Pultanik River coming from the deep blue lake. The water churned as two currents slammed into one another before flowing eastward.

A large camp with blooddrop pennants stood across the mouth of the Red River. Brutez saw a herd of livestock several times larger than the one he delivered to Zuedon's town, which was why Heptor's warriors were slow to return. The camp included boats, so Brutez and his men had means to cross the Red River, although the churning confluence of water presented an unwelcome peril.

Heptor waited on the other side with a bandaged arm, a bandaged neck, and a broad smile. He called as Brutez approached, "Where have you been, Brother?"

Brutez stepped to solid ground. "A wedding."

Heptor lost his smile to a look of confusion, but he regained it and embraced his brother. Brutez accepted the gesture after not seeing him for five months, but regretted he wasn't able to return a month sooner, a month that couldn't be undone.

Heptor released Brutez, oblivious to the clanlord's lackluster response. "I see you found Larboelm. He's as good at disappearing as you, Brother."

Brutez took the iron-cast blooddrop from Larboelm to an open space within the camp, observing how Heptor's men had begun drinking and feasting for the evening. He pushed the pointed pole into the ground and stood by. "Brother, assemble all the men."

Heptor protested, "All? What about the ones on patrol or cooking supper?"

The mention of supper made Brutez think of his hunger, but he wouldn't be distracted from his purpose. "Every man."

Heptor's smile faded, and he left to obey. Brutez organized his warriors from Taubueth into two rows, armaments ready, and returned to his stance by the standard. The eighty or so warriors of Heptor's force gathered before him and his warriors.

Heptor stepped forward. "They're here, every man."

Brutez gazed over the ranks. He saw warriors standing at rapt attention, some shuffling feet, and others disinterested. "I'm your clanlord. Each man shall declare fealty, one by one."

Heptor came first and dropped his war hammer before Brutez's feet. "I declare fealty to you, Clanlord Brother."

Rankeb dropped an axe. "I declare fealty to you, Clanlord Brutez."

Konrash tossed down another axe. "I declare fealty to you, Clanlord Brutez." He wore strands of straw-colored hair around his neck, two cubits long, which Brutez thought came from a mount's mane or tail.

The warriors continued coming. Most first-comers Brutez recognized from the Taubueth garrison, whom Heptor selected the day their father sent him to the Blue River. Cudgels, more hammers and axes, maces, a few spears, and some swords and bows were added to the growing pile of arms. Each weapon was offered with the same words, "I declare fealty to you, Clanlord Brutez."

According to Larboelm, most of the next group came from the town by the deep blue lake at the mouth of the Taubueth River. Each new cudgel, hammer, axe, mace, spear, sword, or bow landed with a thud or clang atop the pile. The oath was spoken again and again, dozens of times, "I declare fealty to you, Clanlord Brutez."

The procession slowed. The remaining men hesitated. They were Blue River warriors, the kin of Vulrath and Klinteg.

"Come," Brutez commanded. "Declare your fealty."

One stepped forward, a large red-haired brute named Fenchrous, carrying a dual-bladed axe with a lead club on the other end of a thick shaft. He demanded, "Why must we declare fealty when we did at tournament?"

Brutez asked, "Why not repeat it?"

"What if I refuse?"

Brutez clutched the war hammer at his side. "Then by clan tradition, you make a challenge to become clanlord that must be resolved in tournament. We have sufficient numbers of the clan to hold tournament at this time and place." He heard his Taubueth warriors brandishing weapons behind him, while the warriors who declared fealty stood disarmed.

Fenchrous watched the Blue River warriors around him lower their weapons. His shoulders sagged, and he lowered his double-axed club. He thrust it to the stack where it landed with a clatter. "I declare fealty to you, Clanlord Brutez."

Each remaining warrior dropped an armament and repeated the words, "I declare fealty to you, Clanlord Brutez."

Brutez set his war hammer atop the discarded weapons, a pile reaching his waist. "I commit myself to the clan. Whatever I do is for the clan, no matter what's best for me." He took back his war hammer, and the warriors began retrieving their armaments.

Heptor stood by, waiting for his war hammer to be uncovered from the bottom of the stack. "You see the animals, Brother? I forced the Swenikt to pay their tribute."

"Father sent you *only to ask*," said Brutez. "Did you attack near Pinkulda?"

"The tribute was there." Heptor pulled an amber cloth from his tunic and handed it to Brutez. "We captured the new Swenikyim chief for ransom."

Brutez frowned at the banner in his hand. "What about

the old chief?"

"He didn't survive." *Another bad report.*

Brutez spoke to Fenchrous as the warrior took his axe club from the pile. "I'm told you raided the Fall River."

"We needed supplies." Fenchrous hefted his weapon's shaft over a shoulder. "The Swenikt didn't send their tribute."

"Did you burn any towns?"

"Doesim Falls and others." Fenchrous stepped away from the weapons pile so other warriors could reach it. "We did some killing and enjoyed the women."

Brutez regretted Fenchrous didn't challenge him to tournament so he could have killed him. "You can expect retribution. I haven't met Tribemaster Warnek, but my father tells me he's a spiteful man." *Although the Warnekt are busy retaliating against the Jatneryimt,* Brutez considered, but best for Fenchrous not to know that. "You must leave for the Blue River with your warriors at daybreak. I'll send other warriors with you." *Ones I can trust,* he thought.

"Yes, Clanlord," said Fenchrous.

Brutez relished hearing Larboelm's words from the Blue River brute. "Stay west of the river while returning to the deep blue lake, and don't bother the Swenikyim town there. Send messages to Taubueth and Larboelm's town if the Warnekt attack."

Curses, he wanted the town to have a name. *Could he call it Lake Shore?*

He waved for Fenchrous to go, pleased by reducing two concerns at once. Not only did he rid himself of the troublesome Blue River warriors, but sending them home blocked any Warnekt going toward Taubueth from the south. Sir Grebnar would protect Taubueth from the Warnekt at the Kipneesh River, if they came from the west.

Brutez's stomach growled, and he yearned to eat, but not yet. He turned to Heptor with a request. "I want to see the hostage."

HAMUNTH   SWANSHYIM FOREST

Blood pooled around Chief Thoiren's body. Not Thoiren, but Hamunth's brother. Some of the crimson absorbed into the ground. The pool bubbled, and drops floated into the air. A tiny mouth opened on each globule, and the brother's blood cried for justice.

Chief Hamunth woke in a sweat. His wrists were bound with rope, as were his ankles. He looked at his hands he had used to strangle his brother. *No blood was spilt*, he pondered, *so why did blood accuse him in his dream?* He rubbed his fists over his heart. His birthmarksign was inflamed again. Sometimes it irritated him so much he scratched it until he bled through his tunic.

Adam and Enoch were bound hand and foot, sleeping by him under a stag hide propped on a framework of branches. Adam's sleeveless tunic was torn. Hamunth saw the Chizdekyim's birthmarksign and envied the bodyguard for it not being inflamed.

The sun shined through a gap in the clouds, hanging in the treetops. Hamunth first thought he slept through the night, but the orientation of the rivers told him the sun was setting rather than rising, meaning he only took an afternoon nap. The surrounding camp had tents, cookfires, and livestock but no Herkt. This was an opportunity. Hamunth wakened both Chizdekyimt, and the three men sat with their backs together to untie one another's ropes.

His surrender as Thoiren's son was a spontaneous act. He mulled a reason why. Perhaps he didn't want the Herkt knowing his identity, but didn't his captors notice his forked-tongue pennant? At least Thoiren's actual son Kevyar was more likely to ransom Hamunth than his own son he left behind at Chizdek, who had little incentive to do so.

His true purpose, after some thought, was killing the men

who violated his daughter. He didn't get a good view of them while protecting his consort, but one brute identified himself by wearing Larzil's hair. Adam and Enoch confirmed that his constant companion was the other. He learned their names during the days traveling up the Pultanik River—Rankeb and Konrash.

Adam's fingers were loosening the knot on his wrists when three Herkt appeared from around a tent. Hamunth knew the one with curly brown hair was their leader named Heptor. The red-headed one by his side was the same height, not so stocky but bulging with more muscle. Both lead Herkt carried war hammers. The trailing Herk with lots of sandy hair and a smashed nose was larger and carried a spiked mace.

Heptor spoke as they neared. "The scrawny fellow with the two Chizdekyimt is Thoiren's son, the new chief."

The red-haired Herk asked, "How do you know that?" His hand without a war hammer was closed into a fist.

Heptor shrugged. "He told me."

The red-hair snorted. He stood over the three tied men and opened his fist, unfurling an amber forked-tongue pennant. "I'm pleased to meet you, *Chief Hamunth*."

This Herk is no fool like Heptor, Hamunth lamented. "That's me." He saw no advantage from a denial.

Heptor's bewilderment amused him. "Chief Hamunth?"

The more enlightened Herk ignored Heptor. "I'm Brutez, Clanlord of the Herkt. This is a mistake. Allow me to free you."

Hamunth smirked, thinking *sure*. Brutez released the amber pennant, which fluttered to Hamunth's feet. The clanlord dropped his war hammer and produced a dagger to cut the rope from the chief's wrists. Heptor stood by watching in stupefied silence next to the large sandy-haired Herk, who cradled the mace.

While the cords fell away from Hamunth's wrists, Brutez asked, "Who are these Chizdekyimt?"

"My bodyguards."

Hamunth untied his own ankles while the clanlord freed

the Chizdekyimt.

"You're free," said Brutez. "We'll take you with us toward Pinkulda, if that's where you want to go."

Heptor asked, "We're going toward Pinkulda?"

Brutez raised his empty hand, the one without a war hammer, to silence him.

Hamunth took his banner from the ground. "I'll go with you, but I want the two men who violated my daughter. She was to be married." *Perhaps no longer*, he fretted. "These animals in your camp are her bridal price."

"The animals will be returned," said Brutez.

Heptor protested, "They're the tribute, Brother."

They're brothers, Hamunth mused.

Brutez glared at his brother with narrowed eyes. "Don't speak," he commanded. "Or leave."

Heptor frowned, tightening his lips, and slumped into silence.

Brutez asked, "Chief, do you know which men violated your daughter?"

"I saw them. I want their heads, both Rankeb and Konrash."

"Brutez, *no!*" The outburst came from Heptor.

Brutez countered, "Heptor, silence!"

The big Herk with the mace stepped over to block Heptor from coming closer.

"Does your daughter live, Chief?"

"She does, Clanlord."

"Then death is too severe a retribution for Rankeb and Konrash."

"They took her from her betrothed husband." Hamunth knew the proper retribution. "They should be deprived from women."

"You speak about castration."

"I do. If I can't have their heads, I want their loins."

Brutez commanded the mace-wielding Herk, "Larboelm, gather some Taubueth warriors and bring Rankeb and Konrash here."

"Yes, Clanlord."

Heptor moved to leave with Larboelm, but Brutez commanded him to stay.

"Chief Hamunth," said Brutez. "What can you tell me about a scroll?"

Hamunth didn't know how to respond, not knowing what the Swenikt would want the Herkt to know about their scrolls.

Words from Heptor kept him from needing to decide. "I have it in my tent."

Brutez   Swanshyim Forest

Until Heptor mentioned the scroll, Brutez held nothing but fury for his brother. His wrath merely was suspended while he rolled open two cubits of the document on a rocky slab outside Heptor's tent, under the light of a torch held by Heptor. He saw the strange, undecipherable markings he knew represented words and wondered, *Why can't Snarshyim words be marked when a backward people like the Chizdekyimt can mark theirs?* He considered himself fortunate to have two of the vagabond people with him to interpret the meaning of the marks. They came with Hamunth when Heptor led the way to the tent. During the walk, the one named Adam revealed he knew the Snarshyim language.

Eat the scroll to receive life. Although hungry enough to think about chewing the parchment, Brutez deduced the true meaning. The words in the scroll would tell him how to save his life, or live longer. He invited Adam to look. "Tell me what the words say."

Hamunth gave the Chizdekyim permission to speak.

"I can't read them. They're written in the Old Language."

Brutez was disappointed. *Why would his dreams tell him to seek a scroll he couldn't understand?* "Does anybody know this old language?"

"The Swenikt sent a man named Jorgis beyond the desert with two scrolls to search," said Hamunth.

Brutez considered the trackless wasteland beyond the Tauzzreen River. He didn't know about lands on the other side but remembered his dream about two Hamunthyim banners emerging from a desert sunrise. Unrolling more parchment, he furled the free end into a second coil. The markings on the new section remained meaningless to him, but then a drawing appeared, starting with scribbled blue lines. Unraveling more, he saw a brown smudge and a large green splotch with more blue lines, and finally a reddened spot and blue lines.

Elation welled within him as he realized he looked at a map. He recognized the blue lines as coasts, rivers, and lakes. The red spot had to be the great eastern desert, and the green splotch, the Swanshyim Forest. He identified where Taubueth should be, located under blue lines that could be the Snarshyim Inlet. Sure enough, two irregular blue lines led to a blue rectangle, representing the Taubueth River and Blue River flowing into the deep blue lake. A longer crooked blue line coming from the brown smudge was the Kipneesh River flowing from the mountains.

With heightened interest, Brutez scanned the green splotch to see where the Swanshyim Forest ended in the west. He saw its limit at the bank of another long river, three times farther past the Kipneesh River than the Black Citadel at Mapvin, figuring a distance of more than one hundred horizons. Looking farther west, he saw land going southward off the bottom edge of the parchment, the northern coast continuing past the end of the mountains, and large bodies of water.

Some thick blue lines, coming from the west and ending with arrowheads east of the Kipneesh River, puzzled him. They didn't correspond to any coasts or rivers.

He tapped a finger on them. "What are these?"

"I don't know," said Hamunth. "They might signify travels."

Or an invasion, Brutez surmised. He recalled his vision of colored lights and kingdoms. The Blue Kingdom rose in the west, flying the banners of the Snarshyimt, including his clan's red blooddrop. He wondered, *Did the Snarshyimt come from the west?* The markings of the Old Language would say.

"We must wait for Jorgis to return." Brutez rolled the scroll closed and tucked it under one arm to keep.

The sun was down and daylight almost gone, time to return to the place Larboelm was commanded to bring Rankeb and Konrash. Heptor led the way with the torch.

Brutez started a conversation. "I think Taubueth means something in your language, Adam."

"It means rock water. You Snarshyimt pronounce it wrong. We say *Taubuet*."

Whatever the pronunciation *the name made sense*, Brutez thought, considering how many rocks were in that river. "What does Tauzzreen mean?" He figured its meaning must be something similar.

"Desert water."

Of course, that river ran along the great eastern desert. "What about Pinkulda?"

"Stonework."

Brutez nodded. A ruined fortress stood on the point of the ridge between the Tauzzreen River and Pultanik River. "Pultanik?"

"I don't know. It sounds like a Snarshyim word."

If Pultanik was a Snarshyim name, Brutez didn't know its meaning. *Did names always mean something?* He thought of one that didn't sound like a Snarshyim name. "Agratuna?"

"A Yarsishyim name, but not the way they say it or we Chizdekyimt. We don't combine sounds like you Snarshyimt do, and so we say *Agaratuna*."

For a man whose language didn't combine sounds, Brutez thought Adam spoke the word *Snarshyimt* well enough.

Larboelm waited at their destination with Rankeb and Konrash, who were disarmed and flanked by six armed warriors.

Brutez asked Hamunth, "These men violated your daughter?"

The chief yanked the straw-blond hair from Konrash's neck. It glimmered in the light of Heptor's torch. "This is her hair."

Brutez glared at Konrash. "Did you violate the woman who had that hair?"

The wart on Konrash's nose wriggled as he spoke. "Clanlord, I wasn't the first to use a woman."

You used the wrong woman, Brutez seethed. "You, too, Rankeb?"

Rankeb's downward gaze proclaimed his guilt.

Brutez faced Hamunth. "Chief, you'll get your castrations."

He ordered the guilty men bound and invited Hamunth and his bodyguards to join him for supper. They went to where Jonerch and Gordib roasted fish over a fire.

"Hamunth, what's the best way to castrate?"

"The Chizdekyimt often do it. Adam and Enoch are castrates."

Brutez was vaguely aware of the Chizdekyim custom. *No wonder they're a dying people*, he mused.

Hamunth continued, "The quickest way is the most painful, cutting. It's also the riskiest for infections, often fatal."

"Do you know a better way?"

"The Chizdekyim way. Although Adam and Enoch are unable to sire children, they're adept at producing more of their own kind. The way involves tying and withering, takes several days."

"With your consent, Chief Hamunth, I want your Chizdekyimt to stay here until the job is done. I'll give them mounts to go toward Pinkulda afterward."

Or Stonework, as the Chizdekyimt called the place.

"Agreed, Clanlord Brutez, and I want the shriveled loins." Hamunth raised the golden strands in his hand. "I'll cherish them as my daughter once adored her hair."

Prodigy of Banshim's Anvil

Warnekt, Druogoint

VINLON   **FENZDIWERP**

The meadow, the flattest parcel of ground anywhere in the vicinity, was an ideal spot for an exchange. It was several hundred cubits of open space with nary a tree. It was covered by tasseled grass and clovers less than knee high, allowing for no surprises, namely no ambush.

Vinlon never planned to be there, although he was tribemaster, but circumstances brought him. Two weeks ago, he was leading a force of two hundred heavily armed warriors up the Kipneesh River, which was gorged with spring melt from the distant mountains, and past all its lakes into the thick of the Swanshyim Forest. Although Jatneryim resistance stiffened, reports of enemy infighting explained their weaker-than-expected defense, and Vinlon hoped to reach Doenesh. He was determined the Jatneryimt would regret raising the ire of the Warnekt.

Even when a large force appeared to check Vinlon's advance, flying new Jatneryim green and black banners supposing a newfound unity among them, it was inferior in numbers to his. Nor was he intimidated by their shouts of "Boldness!" He didn't fear Sir Grebnar the Bold any more than he did Sir Rendif.

A message from the Fall River changed everything. The Herkt had raided there and must be dealt a counterblow. Vinlon considered going eastward to attack Taubueth, but knew nothing about the rugged way. He also expected the Jatneryimt would harass his left flank, so he took half his warriors back down the Kipneesh River to go over to the Pultanik River. The other half of his force withdrew to a defensible position north of the uppermost lake on the Kipneesh River in order to keep the Jatneryimt from repeating their attack against his territory.

He traveled ahead of his footmen in a mounted vanguard of ten riders. When the trees of the Swanshyim Forest thinned, they left the Kipneesh River and followed the border of the woods through a gap in the ridge leading eastward to the Pultanik River.

His memories after that were painful to recollect. He arrived at the final town before reaching the Fall River. Last autumn he feasted, celebrated with the people, and enjoyed watching a spirited competition between the local warriors, but this time he found an incinerated ruin. He listened to stories of violated women and killing. The Herkt took livestock and foodstores. The remaining residents, for many fled to Fenzdiwerp, were left with limited shelter and not much to eat other than fish from the river.

Fearing the worst for Doesim Falls and his favorite mistress there, Vinlon rode with his men to the devastated Fall River town. The mill and its clever waterwheel were a heap of charred wood and ashes. He found the two snot-nosed girls who supposedly were his daughters huddled inside a grotto with their grandfather on a nearby hill. The old miller was listless and covered in grime. Vinlon had to shake him to get news about the girls' mother. She was violated, and the Herkt took her along when they left. Her son who wasn't quite a yearling, and perhaps Vinlon's son, was left behind in the care of a wetnurse.

Even days later at the meadow, Vinlon gripped his sword's pommel so tight in rage, his hand cramped. It was his new sword, Banshim's masterpiece of artistry and utility. The hilt was as elegantly crafted as the forger promised. Its swirling handguard resembled the tangled brush on the shore by Habergenefinanch. Even better was the weapon's functionality. The dual-edged blade was sharper than any Vinlon ever wielded, and the lightness of weight and balance of the whole was a wonder. The magnificent sword deserved a name but would remain unnamed until Vinlon thought of one worthy.

Still enraged, Vinlon unclenched the pommel and flexed his hand to relieve the cramp. He wanted to pursue the Herkt to the Blue River but had to wait for the rest of his warriors, the footmen following him on the Pultanik River. When he returned to the junction of the Fall River flowing into the Pultanik, he encountered Radzig's cadre of warriors going upriver toward Fenzdiwerp with the armaments that Leenarth and Banshim crafted during the winter for ransoming Jaspich from the Druogoint.

Radzig convinced Vinlon to attend the exchange for his son while the tribemaster waited for his larger force, so here he stood on one end of the meadow with his friend and a line of warriors carrying the bows, swords, and spears for the ransom. A warm breeze ruffled the meadow foliage. Vinlon held a Warnekyim pennant and Radzig another on the tips of poles they butted on the downy ground. Although the breeze unfurled the long black ribbons, the crossway airflow flapped Radzig's banner before Vinlon's face.

Fenzdiwerp was close enough behind for its outlying buildings to remain visible. The local hill stood a similar distance eastward to the left, although no longer the steep slope it was by the river and waterfall. Bovines grazed within a fenced area to the right. Farmers with plowstock tilled the surrounding farmland.

Druogoinyim warriors lined the other end of the meadow several hundred cubits away. Vinlon knew their number matched the several dozen on his side because Radzig met his counterpart, a man named Nelber, to negotiate the details of the exchange. The Druogoint carried plenty of orange trapezoid banners, outnumbering the paltry two pennants on Vinlon's side. *Curses!* Vinlon wanted more banners, but his warriors were too loaded with the ransom weapons and their personal armaments to hold them.

An unarmed man stood among the Druogoint. They wrapped his arms to his sides and his knees together with rope.

"Looks like him," said Radzig.

Vinlon agreed. The captive was tall and brown-haired like Radzig's son Jaspich, which a closer look would confirm. The details of the exchange were meant to prevent duplicity.

When the tying was done, Radzig lowered his pennant, holding the pole out at waist level from the hip opposite his hatchet. Vinlon was grateful the black ribbon furled over the ground rather than flutter in his face. It was the signal for the Warnekyim warriors to unload the ransom payment. They stabbed each sword and speartip into the soft meadow turf. The bows were left leaning against the spears.

Radzig raised his pennant, and both lines of warriors advanced toward the other. The men took measured steps to maintain ranks, presenting themselves in unthreatening posture. Swords were left undrawn, mauling weapons strapped to sides or behind backs, and spears tucked beneath arms and behind shoulders. The Warnekt marched away from the row of bows, swords, and spears they relinquished to the meadow. The roped man, who was supposedly Jaspich, remained standing by himself behind the Druogoint.

Vinlon focused on a warrior in the middle of the approaching Druogoinyim line who was wearing a proliferation of orange. The gaudy color blazed from the quilted padding of his gambeson. It flashed from his bootlaces, the fishbone pattern stitching in his breeches, tassels on his upper sleeves, and his cape. Vinlon tensed with recognition, and the cramp returned to his sword hand, again clenching to a fist. *Curses*, he should have known Warlord Druogoin would appear at the exchange to gloat.

The warlord wasn't much changed from the last time Vinlon saw his wedlock father years ago. Druogoin had the same head of stubby hair, although the bristle had turned white. His beard was white-bristled, too. He was fit for his age, a patriarch in his late fifties with grown grandchildren.

The gap between the opposing lines closed until they stopped mere cubits between them, barely beyond reach from Radzig's standard if it was lowered again.

"A surprise, Warnek," said Druogoin. He had cold gray eyes and a permanent sneer. "I didn't think you would watch your people give me armaments."

Vinlon had no vexing words for a response, only perfunctory ones. "Let's do it."

"Nelber, now," Druogoin commanded the next man in his line.

Nelber was Druogoin's height, taller than Vinlon and shorter than Radzig, and defied the semblance of a singular age. He had a young man's shag of hair, not gray but faded sandy brown. Coming from the Druogoinyim line, he passed through the Warnekt, hands clasped together and head leaning forward.

Radzig dropped his pennant and dashed through the Druogoint toward the solitary rope-tied figure in the near distance. Vinlon was annoyed by a Warnekyim standard flung to the ground. He picked up Radzig's discarded pole, now holding one in each hand.

"Nelber will verify I'm getting your best weaponry, Warnek," said Druogoin. "He saw what you sent to Richee. Fine workmanship."

Vinlon watched Radzig over Druogoin's shoulder embracing the roped man, purging any doubt he was Jaspich.

While Radzig untied his son, Vinlon pondered Druogoin's mention of Richee and decided against asking his inimical wedlock father if anybody returned from the foreign land. He didn't want to give him reason to suspect he had more men with the Richeeyimt than Jaspich and Dekloes, who were captured. Moreover, no answer Druogoin gave could be trusted. Vinlon settled for a safe inquiry with possibility for news about his son who hated him.

"Chief Thoiren told me Hoj went to Richee." *With a Swenik named Jorgis.*

"I suppose Ranjin wasn't far enough away from you," said Druogoin.

Vinlon wanted to punch him in the face. He watched Radzig embrace his now-freed son, envious. His son, Hoj, remained so distant in place and affection; he may as well be dead.

Druogoin cocked his head, noting the joyful whoops of a father and son behind him. His icy eyes grew colder as he squinted, and his sneer intensified. "A family reunited is a delight, don't you think?"

Vinlon clutched his standard poles, cramping both hands.

"Concerning family," said Druogoin as the shouting from Radzig and Jaspich subsided. "I'm pleased to tell you, Warnek, you're becoming a grandfather."

Vinlon took a moment to realize what he meant, that Druogoin had switched to talking about his daughter. "Thigrel has a child coming from the servant?"

"I don't think of Pokyer as a servant, although he does whatever I tell him. He's part of my family."

And you're not, Vinlon knew he left unsaid. Thinking about Druogoin living with three generations of his offspring and himself with none galled him.

Radzig stood with Jaspich. Both men waved. Looking in the other direction, Vinlon saw Nelber pulling a bowstring and inspecting the spear that the bow had rested against. The Druogoin fingered the tip, flexed the shaft over his knee, and gazed along its entire length while holding the spear by the side of his face and pointing it to the sky. As he moved to the next sword, Vinlon realized he had scrutinized only a small portion of the delivery.

"Must we wait for him to look at them all?"

"He's meticulous," said Warlord Druogoin. "Let me send a man for a report."

Vinlon agreed, grateful his counterpart seemed as eager to conclude the exchange.

Druogoin's man went to converse with Nelber and returned to report. "He says they're the same quality as the ones going to the Richeeyimt."

Satisfied, Druogoin declared the terms of the ransom were met, and both leaders ordered their warriors ahead. The lines passed through one another, intermingling man by man. The Druogoint continued forward to retrieve their new weapons, and the Warnekt clustered to join Radzig and Jaspich.

Warlord Druogoin lingered before Vinlon, blocking the way to the tribemaster's warriors. He asked, "When did you start paying ransoms, Warnek?"

Vinlon had no answer.

"A travesty you didn't start years ago," said Druogoin.

Not my fault, Vinlon thought, but nothing he said would convince Druogoin to relinquish his hatred, and he passed this contempt to Gernthol, his daughter who was Vinlon's wife, and she passed it to her children.

Vinlon's silence agitated Druogoin. "You have nothing to say, Warnek? If Hoj wasn't my grandson, I would kill him to take away your son from you, but I've taken him already, haven't I? I have your daughter and wife, too."

Vinlon's arms shook, ruffling his black ribbons. *The man better shut up.*

Druogoin didn't. "Do you know why Gernthol allowed Thigrel to be a woman with Pokyer?"

Vinlon didn't know, and he didn't care. He only wanted Druogoin to *shut up*. He walked around him to leave. The warlord dressed in garish orange stepped sideway, and they bumped shoulders.

Druogoin sneered into Vinlon's face. The warlord's breath smelled like onions as he kept speaking. "She tried him first, and when he performed well, she couldn't deny Thigrel the experience."

Shut up!

"Don't be shocked, Warnek. Did you expect your wife to give up pleasures when she gave up you?"

Vinlon couldn't get away from Druogoin fast enough, and then a revelation struck him. *They were alone.* Their nearest warriors were no less than one hundred cubits away. This was an opportunity he might never get again.

He tossed his pennants at his antagonist. While Druogoin batted away the poles, Vinlon unsheathed his sword, the prodigy of Banshim's anvil: sharper, lighter, and balanced—*lethal.* The multitudinal-honed blade shimmered glaucous blue in the sunlight. It was virgin steel, never before used against flesh because Vinlon didn't engage in any swordplay against the Jatneryimt. His sword would know pleasure, consummated with his wedlock father's blood.

He swung up one-handed, intending to slash off an arm, but one pole still was falling to the ground. The sword sliced through the loose wood stake as though it was a marsh reed, but the blow deflected into Druogoin's side, and the warlord's orange-padded gambeson absorbed most of the impact. Druogoin drew a longsword while stumbling backward.

This first parry turned them around, so Vinlon saw the Druogoinyim warriors collecting their new armaments. They noticed the combat and ran closer. The time of opportunity was getting short. He swung low. The blade was so *light*, sailing through the air like a bird's wing. Druogoin met the blow with his thick heavy blade before Vinlon would have severed him at the knees. Vinlon whirled up and around. Druogoin's sword was too sluggish to follow. Vinlon came across with a backhanded slash, and his blade gashed through Druogoin's neck as easy as through a melon. The head lolled into the air, squirting blood from the sneering lips, and dropped to a cushioned landing on the meadow grass. It was a sight Vinlon would replay in his mind countless times with satisfaction.

The Druogoinyim warriors were almost upon him, but his warriors were closing, too. He regretted not having time to claim Druogoin's sword or head as prizes before he ran to join his ranks, holding his bloodied bluish blade before him. Reaching his men, he turned to face the enemy. Some Druogoint stopped at the head and body of their slain warlord. The rest trailed, hauling their booty.

Radzig came to Vinlon's side, wielding his hatchet. "I don't think they'll fight."

Vinlon agreed and ordered his warriors to halt. Sure enough, Nelber retreated eastward with an armload of bows, beckoning the other Druogoint to go with him to the hill marking the border of their territory. A brawny warrior hoisted the warlord's headless corpse over his shoulder. Blood drained from the severed neck. Another Druogoin took the warlord's sword, impaled the head on it, and went with the others following Nelber.

Vinlon planned to lead his warriors in the opposite direction to Fenzdiwerp, but first he needed to clean his weapon, kneeling to wipe the blade on the meadow grass. He had a name for the consummated sword, a worthy name—*Shut Up.*

JASPICH   FENZDIWERP

The inn was built against the hill that split Fenzdiwerp into lower and upper towns. Jaspich followed a plank walkway along the roofline toward the waterfall, a voluminous twenty-cubit descent of gleaming liquid. The torrent sounded like ocean surf, although steadier than the rhythmic crashing of waves, so on second thought, Jaspich likened it to the pounding of hooves. He had watched the Druogoint race mounts. Perhaps a hundred equines could thunder the same intensity as he was hearing.

The young man reached an open deck, bordered by squared logs instead of a railing on the edges. Jaspich joined his father, Radzig, with Tribemaster Warnek around a little round table set with a pitcher of brew.

The tribemaster, Vinlon, had a full head of silver-streaked hair and sunken cheeks. He continued the conversation in progress. "The footmen from the Kipneesh River will give us a total of a hundred and fifty warriors."

"Their number doesn't matter, Tribemaster," said Radzig. "We shouldn't attack the Herkt."

Vinlon slammed his tankard on the table, spilling some contents. "We're not attacking. We're *counter*attacking!"

Radzig finished a swig from his tankard. "We have enough other enemies. We're fighting the Jatneryimt, and today a war started with the Druogoint."

"I'm not worried about the Druogoint." Vinlon picked up his tankard. "They have nobody to lead them. Tell him, Jaspich."

Jaspich felt uneasy listening to his tribemaster and father debate strategy, thinking he didn't belong there. He didn't understand why Vinlon thought he had anything useful to say, so he asked, "Tell him what?"

"You spent a half year living with the Druogoint." Vinlon withdrew his tankard from his lips to talk instead of drinking from it. "Who do they have to lead them without the warlord? He had no other kin than my family, did he?"

"I never heard about any," said Jaspich, and he heard much. He was left for months under Nelber's charge, and the shaggy-haired man enjoyed talking.

Nelber imparted his knowledge on a plethora of interesting topics, although Jaspich wondered how he learned so much. The Druogoin talked about weapons, how to care for them and use them, and battle strategies. He scrutinized nature, studied the movements of fish in the Tauzzreen River and migrating birds, checked the growth of moss and fungus in the forest, observed the directions and sense of winds, and analyzed the colors at sunrise and sunset to predict weather and seasons.

More than any other topic, Nelber claimed to know about people. He told Jaspich he could recognize a lie from the twitching of facial muscles, although he failed to catch the four other Warnekt on the Richeeyim vessel that was driven ashore at Ranjin by the storm, but then Jaspich considered, *Maybe he did know.*

"Jaspich, you have more to say?" Vinlon's voice interrupted his thoughts, and he realized he did have useful information.

"The Druogoint have no obvious successor for the warlord." *Hoj might have been,* Jaspich thought, but Druogoin's only male relation was gone to Richee. "None of the lead warriors are fit to command. Grapnef is mentally unstable." *Too many Druogoint are.* "Pershnig is a drunkard." *Also in Gernthol's bed,* but Jaspich thought best Tribemaster Warnek didn't know that about his wife.

"What about Nelber?"

"He has no desire to command." *He only wants to know,* Jaspich thought. "He's more capable as an advisor."

Vinlon crossed his arms. "Listen to your son, Radzig. We don't have to worry about the Druogoint."

Radzig's shoulders slumped. "As you say."

Gazing from the deck, Jaspich overlooked a mill shrouded by glistening mist and spray from the waterfall. A waterwheel churned in the roiling pitch-blue stream. The Pultanik River flowed southwestward until its tree-lined banks pinched it from sight.

"Is Thigrel with child?"

Jaspich answered Vinlon's question, "The baby's coming this summer."

"The father is Pokyer, a servant?"

Jaspich nodded. "An affable fellow." He had eaten many

meals with Pokyer, the Swenik traveling with Jorgis when the Druogoint captured them.

"You confirm what Warlord Druogoin told me. Are they married?"

Jaspich didn't think so. The tribemaster asked about his wife, Gernthol, wondering about her physical appearance. A warm pulse came to Jaspich's face. He looked away, pretending to admire the waterfall, and hoped Vinlon and his father didn't notice him blush. Best for them not to know his tribemaster's wife showed him *all* of her appearance when she offered herself to him, the only time he didn't see her wearing pink. Although a good sight for an older woman, he must forget. He told Vinlon her hair remained red as flame, long and curled, and described her as *statuesque*.

He was relieved when Vinlon changed the conversation. "I know Hoj and a Swenik named Jorgis went to Richee. Did any Druogoint go?"

Jaspich was disappointed he never reached Richee, and he had Hoj to blame for exposing his identity. "The Richeeyimt refused them." *To protect the four Warnekt the Druogoint didn't know about.* "They took Hoj and Jorgis because they had the scrolls."

Vinlon knew nothing about any scrolls, so Jaspich told him about the two rolled parchments Jorgis and Pokyer found in a cave. Nelber became excited whenever he talked about them. Jaspich told Vinlon nobody returned yet from Richee. The tribemaster told Jaspich he was coming along to fight the Herkt, who were reported to have a new clanlord.

Radzig objected, "Yazdil is waiting at Habergenefinanch to see our son."

Vinlon scowled. "Let her wait. Jaspich will be tribemaster someday. He must learn to lead men into battle."

What did he say? Jaspich was stunned. *He was going to be tribemaster?*

Vinlon looked directly at him. "That's right, however much I delighted in killing Warlord Druogoin, I sacrificed any hope of Hoj returning to me. I have nobody to take my place but you."

Jaspich, Tribemaster of the Warnekt. The young man liked thinking it.

Amends

Herkt, Swenikt

Kevyar　　　　　　　　　　**near Pinkulda**

Thoiren's final words echoed through the forest. "I see! I see a great red tree, and it's full of crowns."

It was the largest of the giant trees near the headwater of the Red River at the red lake. The trunk was a limbless tower, ribbed by russet bark two hundred cubits high and as big around as a threshing floor or a pen for barn fowl. The scarlet-leafed canopy indeed was full of crowns, all sterling except one, lodged in the crooks of branches or wedged within knotholes, nineteen in all. The other crown, a golden diadem wider than the trunk, floated over the canopy.

At first the scarlet leaves resembled the blooddrop pennants of the Herkt, but a gust of wind stripped the branches bare. Swenikyim pennants grew to replace them, although the concaved triangles were scarlet instead of cobalt blue.

The branches of the great red tree stretched higher into an ivory sky. A city appeared on top within a circle of

> *the foliage, a lovely metropolis with wide streets running through a patchwork of alabaster buildings and verdant parks, dotted with crystal blue lakes. One structure seemed to be a palace, replete with towers, courtyards, and gardens echoing throughout with a baby's cry.*

Kevyar opened his eyes to darkness. He usually slept through Baby Thoiren's nocturnal feedings. Jankwel held the wailing infant beside him in bed, the same great curtained frame where the child was birthed. She began feeding, and blessed silence returned except for slurps from the suckling baby boy.

What does the dream mean? The question kept Kevyar awake. Was it the same his father saw or his own imagining based on the dying man's words? The crowns seemed clear concerning a king or kings, either Herkt or Swenikt, or perhaps the Swenikt replacing the Herkt. The Yarsishyimt in the north across the Chizdekyim Inlet had a king. Kevyar wondered, *What if the Snarshyimt, or at least some of the clans and tribes, had one?* Unity under a king would end raiding and pillaging. A monarch required homage and resources, but how was that worse than tribute?

What about the magnificent city? His father, Thoiren, didn't speak about any city. Perhaps he saw it and died before saying so. Whatever his last vision, it must have been gorgeous because he left life with a smile.

Kevyar saw a crevice of light in the curtain around the bed, the sign of a new day's dawn. Kissing his wife's brow, he stroked his son's downy scalp by her bosom and rose to get dressed. He found a jerkin, trousers, and boots in the dark.

Kevyar discovered Larzil was awake. Chief Hamunth's daughter spent nights on a straw-padded cot at the foot of the bed. She was inseparable from Jankwel after the Herkt violated her and took away her father. Kevyar often heard her weeping in the night. He invited the young woman to take his spot in the great bed, knowing his wife would give her comfort, and stepped outside into the woods with his sword and a cloak. Early mornings still were quite cool, almost cold, in the mid-spring.

The longhouse was burned to half its former size. Kevyar's mother, Befdaul, slept in the other intact room with her granddaughters. Chief Hamunth's consort and youngest children stayed there, too.

The next room was gutted, although the charred ends of the logs that were its side walls remained, the same logs still walling the two intact rooms. Fresh logs reinforced a new outer wall, once a lattice between the two middle rooms.

A burnt patch of ground remained after the charred debris and ashes of the easternmost room were cleared away. The twelve scrolls inside the platform under Chief Thoiren's seat were destroyed. Only crisped scraps survived. The other twelve scrolls were unharmed, stashed at the other end under the great bed on which Kevyar slept.

The worst memory was the blackened lump with gristly limbs that was his father's body. The remains were committed to a funeral pyre on one of Chief Hamunth's rafts set adrift down the Tauzzreen River. The charred corpses of Hamunth's canine and the warriors slain by the Herkt in the same room were included in the flames.

Kevyar remembered thinking, *Was Chief Thoiren of the Swenikt nothing more than fuel for a blazing raft floating downriver?* The Chizdekyimt claimed to converse with the deceased. Kevyar yearned to believe his father still existed, if only in spirit.

He found Davlek sitting over the Tauzzreen River on one of the Hamunthyim rafts moored to the bank. Stepping aboard the flat floating platform, he joined his once-wedlock brother to gaze over the water. The surface was smooth, like weathered rock the color of lead, on a day breaking without a whiff of breeze. The current was slow because the river was wide, more than two hundred cubits, and receded from its highest level that spring. A flock of quacking marshbills landed on the water.

This was the eastern edge of the Swanshyim Forest. The land across river was more pasture than trees, where the Swenikt kept their livestock to graze, and flat for the several horizons to the shore of one of the long lakes. Beyond the lake stretched the rocky barren waste of the great eastern desert.

Davlek spoke, "You're out of bed early, Kevyar."

Not as early as you, Kevyar thought. "The baby was crying," he said, although true but not the reason he stayed awake. He reconsidered not mentioning more. As chief, he needed loyal advisors, and here was a chance to try Davlek. "I had a dream. I saw the same as my father when he died—a great red tree full of crowns."

"The Chizdekyimt say dreams have meanings," said Davlek.

"They say other things I wish were true about speaking with the dead. I want to ask my father about what he saw and to get his forgiveness."

"I want my wife's forgiveness."

"The poisoned fungus wasn't your fault." Kevyar considered his sister, Davlek's deceased wife. *She was headstrong and wouldn't listen.*

Pounding hooves announced a rider on a lathered mount coming from the south through the town, a settlement saved from burning by the deluge of rain after the Herkyim raid. A Swenikyim concaved triangle flapped from his speartip. Kevyar intercepted the rider before he reached the longhouse. He had sent him for news, wanting to know where else the Herkt raided, whether his wedlock parents at the town by the deep blue lake were harmed, and if the Herkt sent any demand for Chief Hamunth's ransom.

The rider's beard was as lathered as his mount. "Chief Kevyar." Spittle sprayed from his lips.

The words still saddened Kevyar after a week. Although he liked hearing them, they meant his father was gone. He didn't like the rider's next words.

"The Herkt are returning."

"Where are they?"

"On the Pultanik River. They'll get here by the end of the day."

Some warning is better than none, Kevyar reasoned. He told Davlek to take their families and the Hamuntht to the nearby forest caves where the Swenikt stored foodstuffs in the cool depths. Then he summoned every available warrior, about thirty, intending to intercept the Herkt as far away as possible. He told the townspeople to evacuate across the river, taking every boat and raft with them.

The warriors were equipped with the usual Swenikyim armaments—shortswords, throwing hammers, and bucklers, also some helmets and hauberks, a few spears, and plenty of cobalt blue pennants. The men went to the pantry house to gather provisions for the day, which they slung in packs over their shoulders along with their drinking skins.

They marched from the town, dodging a herd of backhorns, and stepped across the shallow creek on the south side. The river split into two channels after a short distance, going around an island. The Swenikt followed the western bank until taking a well-worn path leading westward to the sharp bend that was the easternmost reach of the Pultanik River. That river turned there from flowing east to going southwestward one hundred horizons to the ocean.

The ruined fortress of Pinkulda overlooked them from a ridge on their left. It wasn't much more than heaps of boulders, except for a crumbling moss-ridden stone wall running between two mounds that once were towers. The forest nearly consumed the place, hemming it with trees and covering it with vines. Only a patch of bumpy gray rock below the fragmented wall remained free from growth.

The Chizdekyimt claimed their ancestors built Pinkulda. Kevyar believed them because Jorgis told him the name meant *stonework* in their language. Nothing in Swenikyim folklore remembered anything about the place's origin or destruction. Chief Thoiren told plenty of stories during his lifetime but none about Pinkulda. Kevyar hoped one of the scrolls told a story when it was translated.

They had passed the ruin when two riders appeared over a rise in the upcoming path, one small and balding, and the other huge with plenty of sandy hair and beard. The smaller one rode in the lead, holding an amber forked-tongue pennant. Kevyar recognized Chief Hamunth, who carried no visible weapons. The larger rider wielded a spiked mace.

Hamunth and his sandy-haired companion reined their mounts to stop a few cubits away. "Greetings, Kevyar. *Chief* Kevyar?"

Kevyar nodded and waited for Hamunth to say more, expecting to hear a tale about his escape. He wondered, *Does he know the Herkt are chasing him?*

Hamunth dismounted, leaving his banner with his equine. He wore the same stagskin jerkin and taupe gray woolstock trousers Kevyar saw him wearing before the Herkyim raid, now scuffed with a week's worth of grit. Kevyar saw three daggers on his person: stuffed into a boot, tied to his hip, and tucked into a chest pocket on the jerkin. He supposed Hamunth had others not visible. The menacing warrior with the mace stood behind, holding his weapon ready.

Hamunth asked, "How's my family? How's Larzil?"

"They're well." *Although hiding in a cave*, Kevyar thought. "Larzil's healed in body, but tormented. My wife comforts her. I think she wants to stay with us."

Hamunth presented a faint smile.

Kevyar asked, "Chief, how did you escape?"

"The Herkt set me free."

"Why would they do that?"

"They have a new clanlord. He knew who I am, not like his fool brother who believed I was you. This Clanlord Brutez doesn't want trouble with the Hamuntht."

The clanlord's brother killed my father, Kevyar contemplated. "So he released you, and all is forgiven?"

"Not quite. I'm receiving the justice I sought when I

pretended to be you."

"You wanted to avenge Larzil."

Hamunth extracted straw-blond strands from a pocket. "I got her hair. Adam and Enoch stayed behind to castrate the men who violated her, the Chizdekyim way."

"The Chizdekyim way?"

"Tying and withering." Hamunth returned Larzil's hair to his pocket.

Kevyar cringed. "This is your new bodyguard?" he asked about the mace man towering behind his fellow chief.

Hamunth looked at the spiked mace hovering over his head. "Clanlord Brutez ordered Larboelm to bury those spikes into my brain if I don't tell you his message."

"Then you better tell me."

"The animals from Larzil's bridal price are being returned. Brutez is coming to make amends." Hamunth swept back a hand, showing the way up the forest path. The hard-packed ground tunneled under a cover of leafy boughs before disappearing over the rise. "He isn't far behind."

Kevyar knew that. "Tell him I'll meet him. If the clanlord wants to make amends, I'll listen."

"I'm not going back." Hamunth crossed his arms.

"Then wait with me for him," said Kevyar. "Larboelm, too."

Considering Larboelm's stiff stance and stern face, Kevyar determined he wasn't leaving Hamunth's side. The rocky patch at Pinkulda would be a good spot to eat lunch from the provisions as they waited, providing an overview of the forest path. *The clanlord wants to make amends*, Kevyar thought. *I want justice.*

BRUTEZ 🚩   **PINKULDA** 🚩

Brutez walked beside his mount at the head of his column

of fifty warriors along the tree-covered path between the Pultanik River and Tauzzreen River. Heptor rode his mount. Brutez didn't speak much with his brooding brother, and he didn't care Heptor wasn't talkative because he remained angry with him for the trouble he caused. Only when Brutez told him about his marriage, did Heptor regain some of his cheery demeanor, asking him about Beksel's appearance and the size of her breasts.

Although the path undulated, the prevailing direction was up. Brutez supposed the land must rise to keep the Pultanik River from reaching the Tauzzreen. He led his men over a crest, where a gap in the leafy canopy revealed ruins on a ridge to the right, *Pinkulda, the stonework*.

A cadre of Swenikyim warriors blocked the path, displaying their cobalt blue triangle pennants. Brutez had ordered his warriors to conceal their blooddrops, his iron casting included, although Heptor still flew one from his bandaged arm, and Gordib had a blooddrop branded on his face.

"Chief Kevyar is waiting at Pinkulda." The lead Swenik pointed to the stony spot on the ridge. He was a grizzled warrior with a hole in one cheek, so he spoke with a gurgle of air sounding worse than a lisp.

Brutez saw darkened figures moving in a glare of noontime sun shining over the ridge. "How many warriors are up there?" He didn't expect the grizzled warrior to reveal the total number in the area, but he wanted to know how many men to take with him. "I'll go up with the same number."

"Twenty." The word sloshed from the man's mouth and the hole in his cheek.

Heptor joined Brutez in the lead group with Jonerch and Gordib, climbing a narrow trail behind a vanguard of Swenikt. They pushed through thickets and climbed over rocks. Emerging from the rough terrain, they stood on pitted and bumpy rocks that reminded Brutez of his cell in the Black Citadel at Mapvin, except it smelled of the ferns and moss growing from the cracks in its surface instead of sulfur.

The uneven gray rock was located at the base of the last crumbled wall of Pinkulda, providing a lofty view over the eastern fringe of the Swanshyim Forest. The blue ribbon of the Tauzzreen River flowed past around the ridge. The land shimmered below the eastern sky, possibly the watery surface of the long lake over there.

The twenty expected Swenikyim warriors waited in ranks. Chief Hamunth and Larboelm stood next to a lanky round-faced man with dark brown sideburns and thinning hair, whom Brutez supposed was Chief Kevyar. The clanlord waved Larboelm to come to his side while the last of his twenty warriors finished climbing to the open rocky space. When all the warriors were present, Brutez and the two chiefs approached one another in the gap between their men. Hamunth introduced Kevyar to Brutez.

"The Herkt and Jatneryimt have joined forces," Brutez told the two other leaders. He paused for the chiefs to consider the unsettling news.

Kevyar's furrowed expression portrayed the desired reaction.

Brutez continued, "Although we're battling the Warnekt, we seek peace between the Snarshyim clans and tribes. Chief Hamunth understands."

"The clanlord and I talked," Hamunth told Kevyar.

"I married the daughter of the Jatneryim leader, Sir Grebnar the Bold," said Brutez, informing the chiefs that his clan had a lasting relationship with the Jatneryimt. "Other Herkt are marrying Jatneryimt. The more we intermarry, the more we become one people, a Snarshyim people. We Herkt have amiable relations with the Feldramt because of marriages."

"I have more children to marry across tribes someday," said Hamunth.

"Chief Kevyar," said Brutez. "I'm aware you have daughters."

"I do, and a newborn son."

"I hope to be so blessed, perhaps a daughter for your son

to wed someday."

"I can envision that. We need amiable relations between us."

Brutez detected resentment in Kevyar's tone. "My clansmen attacked you without my knowledge. I recognize their actions are my responsibility, so I sent Chief Hamunth ahead to tell you I seek amends."

"Hamunth told me you're returning the livestock."

"True, and I brought other animals to your wedlock father's town. You can tell your wife her parents are well."

"My thanks," said Kevyar.

"I no longer expect tribute, but I hope to pledge helping one another."

Hamunth spoke, "Clanlord Brutez and I are pledged between us."

"I'll consider a pledge," said Kevyar.

He isn't committing yet, Brutez thought. *He wants something, perhaps the scroll.* "I'll return the scroll my brother took, but not yet. Hamunth told me about your man Jorgis, so I'm keeping it until he returns because I want to be invited to the translation."

"That's how it will have to be."

"Hamunth told me Jorgis took two scrolls with him. Do you have others?"

"All burned." Kevyar sneered in Heptor's direction. "You can blame your brother for that."

Brutez didn't believe it. If the banners in his dream were scrolls as he thought, he had the scroll represented by the Hamunthyim banner in the forest. Two more, the ones with Jorgis, would return from the great eastern desert. Although other banners in the dream burned to ashes, twelve Swenikyim pennants remained, so Brutez suspected Kevyar had that many unburned scrolls. No matter, the scrolls were useless until translated, and Brutez planned to gain Kevyar's trust so he would admit he had them.

"I can't replace the burned scrolls, Kevyar, but how else can I make amends?"

"Hamunth told me the men who violated his daughter are being castrated," said Kevyar. "I want justice, too."

Brutez knew he wanted retribution for Chief Thoiren's death, but needed Kevyar to agree that would be all. "I have too many warriors guilty of violating women and killing innocent people. I can't give you justice for everyone without decimating my forces and losing command of my clan."

"I require justice for *only* my father."

"I'll give you the man who killed him."

"Then you must give me your brother."

Larboelm was quick, grabbing Heptor and pinning back his arms.

Brutez asked himself if he would have offered Thoiren's killer knowing who he was, a question he didn't want to answer. Any man he gave Kevyar likely was someone's brother. How could he spare his by being clanlord? He remembered what he told the warriors when they declared fealty. *Whatever I do is for the clan, no matter what's best for me.* The best for the clan was *peace*, the end of the blood feud.

"You're going to kill him," he said.

"Or you will," said Kevyar.

Brutez wanted more time to think. He wanted to tell Kevyar his decision later but dared not show indecision. His decision must be rash.

Heptor cried out, "No, Brutez! Think about Nazzel and our baby." He was too distraught to offer resistance as Jonerch and Gordib disarmed him, taking his war hammer and dagger. "I beg you, Brother. Let me fight for my life."

Brutez glanced to Kevyar, although he knew how the chief would answer.

"My father was unarmed when he was slain."

Brutez wielded his war hammer. If he killed Heptor, he would be the most merciful and leave the body the least mutilated.

"Clanlord, allow me," said Larboelm.

"I don't want my brother's blood on your hands."

Larboelm released Heptor, who dropped to his knees. Brutez swung his war hammer in a wide arc with all his might into the side of his brother's face, hoping to knock him unconscious. Heptor spewed blood and teeth from his mouth. He reeled to his side on the stony ground and crawled to his hands and knees. *Curses*, he was tenacious. Brutez came down with a hammer blow on the crown of his head, dropping him deadweight to his stomach. Discarding the war hammer, Brutez overturned his brother and untied the bandage from the canine bite on his neck. He drew his dagger and slit Heptor's throat with the smallest incision that would finish him.

Stooping over the pitted gray rock reminded Brutez of the dungeon floor he knew for months at the Black Citadel, bringing back a memory: *Five trees, three stumps, a young tree chopped down, and a tall tree grown strong.* Five brothers, three slain before, and now the youngest cut down before his prime. Brutez was the last tree standing. All his brothers were gone—the last slain by his own hand.

He flung the dagger and his war hammer as far as he could into the foliage with a primal scream chafing his throat. He never would use those particular weapons again. Then he reviewed his warriors. The men were tense, fists clenched and grimacing, and their eyes were filled with fear, bordering on terror. *Good*, Brutez thought. He knew his clansmen no longer would violate women or kill the unarmed, for they would fear no man more than their clanlord.

Regarding Kevyar, he saw another awestruck man. The chief had his justice and would give his pledge. Hamunth's curious expression puzzled Brutez as if the chief understood his feelings about what he had done.

Brutez summoned Larboelm, Jonerch, and Gordib. "Take Heptor. He's going with us to Taubueth."

It's Your Color

Druogoint

NELBER   **RANJIN**

More warriors came in a longboat from up the Tauzzreen River, riding in the main channel's current. The previous group had come marching along the bank. Having returned from Fenzdiwerp with the ransom payment of weapons for releasing Jaspich to the Warnekt, Nelber no longer doubted the Druogoint were mustering for battle. He wrung his hands, knowing he must see the Pink Lady, a meeting he had delayed as long as possible.

The longboat entered a side channel. As it turned, Nelber saw a trapezoid banner silhouetted in the setting sun on a pole angling from the stern. The sky surrounding the dark shape was the same orange tint the banner would have appeared if in better light.

The Tauzzreen River splintered into branches like a watery tree before flowing into the bay by Ranjin. The Druogoinyim settlement wasn't as much a town as scattered huts on the delta's isles that were high enough to remain dry when the river flooded. Nelber's hut on his isle was a typical construction. A circular log fence was embedded in the sandy ground and walled by planks four cubits high. Long, flexible branches were anchored around the wall and lashed together at the top, forming a cagework frame for a thatch roof.

Nelber barely had a spot to sleep inside, although he recently made space for Jaspich to stay with him. The hut contained not only his herbs and other healing remedies, but also was packed full of commodities. Whenever a baker had more bread than he needed, a butcher more meat, a barn fowl farmer more eggs, a brewer more brew, a weaver more cloth, a tailor more clothes, a cooper more barrels, a forger more tools or weapons, or any other tradesman had a surplus, Nelber traded for the excess. He bought the commodities at a discount, and invariably somebody needed something, and would pay the regular price or higher.

He was grateful for Kulm, his strapping son, who helped him haul product from place to place, because his body, now beyond sixty years, didn't react well to heavy lifting. His offspring lacked some sensibility, for Kulm almost drowned as a youth, but was capable of performing tasks under Nelber's enduring direction. The younger man lived on a neighboring isle in a hut like Nelber's, which also was crammed full.

The servant Pokyer who was left in Ranjin by Jorgis the Swenik was Kulm's age. He hauled trade goods for Nelber, but his true worth was finding them as he wandered the isles of Ranjin, befriending the tradesmen. Everyone liked Pokyer.

Nelber liked him now for appearing at an opportune time with a boatload of barrels. The low ride of the boat told Nelber the barrels were full, meaning Pokyer came from a brewer and not a cooper.

Unloading the boat must wait. Nelber wanted Pokyer to paddle him to the Pink Lady's isle, where her father, Warlord Druogoin, lived before her estranged husband, Tribemaster Warnek, beheaded him. The head was sewn on the body before the corpse was interred within a hollow tree. Nelber shook his head, not comprehending the sense of restoring a head to a body and leaving a perfectly good sword with the corpse.

He had an empty boat available, a small craft for traversing the rivulets of the delta without hauling anything. Pokyer paddled him past Kulm's isle and up one of the broader channels in waning daylight to a pair of isles situated so close to one another they were connected by a bridge. Nelber wanted to go to the main isle, but the Pink Lady's daughter, Thigrel, saw them coming and waited on the other, so Pokyer stopped there.

She had stringy red hair, half as long, and a duller shade than her mother's fiery backlength tresses, and her face was bombarded with freckles. Her belly showed the bump of the child Pokyer put there, but only because her bodice was too tight, for she wouldn't have appeared any rounder than usual in looser clothing. Before the warlord's demise, Nelber wanted the child to be a girl, so a more-legitimate Druogoinyim heir could be born later, but now a male descendant was needed.

"Pokyer, you're home early," said Thigrel with her bucktooth smile, waving her arms and flexing her knees so she practically jumped on the shore. Her girlish delight was unrestrained.

Nelber intervened before Pokyer opened his mouth. "He's not staying. Pokyer, you have a boat of brew to unload."

Nelber walked to the bridge past some trees, thinking how his isle had no tree. His son had one on his, and he deserved to have shade on a hot day because he worked hard. Nelber spent the hottest days with his feet propped on a barrel of brew as he relieved the container of its contents.

The color of the trapezoid banner hanging from the bridge didn't seem right. The orange was faded more than Nelber thought it should be in the twilight. He shrugged and lowered his head in his resolve to get where he was going.

His destination on the larger isle was a hut constructed of embedded logs, planks, and thatch like his own, except for an elongated shape with rounded ends, instead of being a circle. Huts for a kitchen and servant quarters were scattered among the trees. The banners on the roofs had the same off-orange color.

The Pink Lady's paramour, Pershnig, met him at the door. He had the overhanging paunch of a man who drank too much brew. If he asked for some from Pokyer's latest delivery, Nelber resolved to charge him double, knowing he would pay.

The Pink Lady wore pink, what else? The neckline of this evening's gown plunged midway to her birthcordspot, and was lined with ruffles to mask her lack of curvature. Nothing masked the birthmarksign over her heart. Most people had a scabby lump the color of rusty iron, but hers was *pink*. More distracting than its unusual color, the full view of the birthmarksign showed Nelber how dangerously close the neckline came to not covering something else.

She maintained a rigid stance, appearing taller than her actual height, which was the same as Nelber's. Long red curls fanned down her back like flames of fire. Too bad she didn't wear green to match her piercing jade eyes, according to Nelber. He appreciated green on redheaded women, not that he desired this woman, nor did he want to. Her beaklike nose, not so smattered with freckles as her daughter's, should have warned any man she would peck out his heart.

She greeted him in a deceptively pleasant voice. "Nelber, why are you so long to see me? I've been calling for you."

"Lady Gernthol, I heard nothing from you. I've been busy." Only the latter statement was true.

"I've been deprived of your good counsel, such as you gave my warlord father."

Nelber sensed a trap. He would be wary, as if picking up a poisonous serpent.

"Nelber, you saw my wretched husband when he murdered my father. How did he look after all these years?"

Careful, Nelber, don't tell her what you saw when Vinlon slew the warlord. Tell her what she wants to hear. "The tribemaster seems to be losing his mind."

"I think the Warnekt are vulnerable."

Not because Vinlon is losing his mind, Nelber thought. *That's a Druogoinyim trait.* The Warnekt were vulnerable because they were fighting the Jatneryimt *and* the Herkt. "I see the warriors arriving, Lady Gernthol. Where are you planning to attack?"

Pershnig stepped in front of Nelber, much closer than he should, and close enough for Nelber to know he ate spicy sausage for supper. Nelber also noticed a rarity: for once Pershnig didn't reek of brew.

The abstaining drunk spoke with a blast of sausage breath, "That should be obvious, the site of the treachery, Fenzdiwerp."

No, what was obvious, the man was a dolt. Nelber stepped back to get away from smelling his supper. Fenzdiwerp was the worst place to attack. Nelber himself saw the town aplenty with Warnekyim warriors. Moreover, considering its Druogoinyim and Swenikyim inhabitants, what was more foolhardy than harming their own people, and upsetting their cordial relations with the Swenikt?

He asked, hoping to hear dissent, "Lady Gernthol, do you like this plan?"

"Why shouldn't I like my own plan?"

Curses, he must convince her to change the plan, and he knew logical arguments would be useless. He needed to channel her wrath in a different direction.

"Why attack Fenzdiwerp? Vinlon doesn't care about that place. If you want to wound him, sack his ancestral town, Habergenefinanch." Nelber turned to Pershnig, who would be more responsive to reason. "It's easier to reach and practically undefended. It's a tinderbox, easy to burn."

"How do you know that?"

The question came from the Pink Lady, surprising Nelber. *She responded to reason?* He answered, "Jaspich told me."

Not in plain words, but when Jaspich mentioned things like a foundry sharing a timber wall with a stable in Habergenefinanch, Nelber deduced the vulnerability of the town. Keeping a forger's fire next to a building full of straw was folly he didn't expect from the Warnekt.

"Habergenefinanch," said the Pink Lady. "We can destroy it!"

Nelber saw flame in her eyes, terrible to behold, to match the wildfire of her hair. "When do the warriors march?" He didn't want to attack anywhere, but if the Druogoint must assault someplace, better Habergenefinanch than Fenzdiwerp.

"You tell me, Nelber. What do you see ahead in the weather?"

Nelber thought about the orange sunset, a sign for foul weather, but the northwest wind all day was warm, so the temperature wasn't changing. "Gentle rain," he guessed.

The Pink Lady twitched her peaked nose. "That doesn't sound good for a fire."

"The rain will be done by the time our forces reach Habergenefinanch." Nelber had to convince her to attack there. "We've had fair weather for a week. The place should be dried out. A brisk wind could fan an inferno in a few days."

The Pink Lady threw back her head so her hair cascaded past her buttocks. She laughed with an unsettling shriek. "The place is going to burn!"

Nelber rubbed his fists. This wasn't the first time he lamented being born among the Druogoint. He would continue accepting the life he was given and persevere to the next day.

The Pink Lady commanded, "Pershnig, find Grapnef and ask him if enough warriors have arrived for us to leave tomorrow morning."

Pershnig's departure left Nelber alone with the maniacal woman, not his favorite situation. She once was a serene young lady, but too many years of sharing her father's resentment had twisted her mind.

"Nelber, I have something to show you, and I want your opinion."

Nelber rubbed his fists harder. *This can't be good.* She led him to her bedchamber, *not where he wanted to go.*

He remained thankful she never took an interest in him, although he took offense at not being offered. *Why didn't she consider him?* He was comelier than Pershnig, and what did she possibly find appealing about Pokyer?

Kulm's mother was long gone. Nelber had other women through the years, none lasting long enough to consider marrying, and he was done with that. A good thing about aging was thinking about that less.

The Pink Lady showed him a Druogoinyim trapezoid banner. His mouth gaped. *It was pink!*

"Nelber, I see you like it. You're awestruck."

"My lady, my lady," he stammered. He almost said, *my pink lady*, but caught himself. "It's your color." He had nothing else to say.

"This will show the warriors I'm leading them into battle."

Nelber clasped his hands behind his back to keep them from shaking. *A woman leading warriors to battle? Insanity!* "The warriors must follow a man."

"Pershnig will be at my side."

"When's the last time he went to battle?"

Nelber didn't think it was in her lifetime. *Why did she bed him?* His girth had to smother her, and he was old enough to be her father. Suddenly Nelber realized Pershnig looked like her father, at least above the neck, which was most disturbing.

"Grapnef goes to battle," said the Pink Lady. "He'll be with us."

Nelber restrained a scoff. Grapnef was no capable leader, a man who chopped off his own thumb to prove he didn't need it. Then Nelber reconsidered, thinking Grapnef would be a good man for committing mass arson. "The warriors will follow." *If they don't balk at a pink banner*, Nelber mused. *The Pink Lady should ride naked. Then they would follow.*

Realizing an opportunity, he took the pink trapezoid to the main room, feigning to use it as an illustration so he could leave the bedchamber. "The best way to hold the loyalty of the warriors is to command in Hoj's name. He's the rightful heir and will be warlord when he returns." He turned to confirm the Pink Lady followed him to the main room.

"Nelber, you speak words of reason."

Somebody must, he thought. For her to say so was the most sensible thing she uttered during their meeting, and this moment was his best chance to present his proposal. "We must consider the possibility Hoj doesn't return." He leaned the pink banner against a wall to get it out of his hand. "Thigrel must marry Pokyer if she births a son. Then you can command in the boy's name."

"Nelber, you're brilliant!"

He knew. He was brilliant. The boy would have Druogoinyim, Warnekyim, *and* Swenikyim blood. The potential was great.

Leaving the Pink Lady, he was in a better mood than he anticipated possible, until he stepped outside. The banner flapping on her hut's roof reminded him how the color of the banners seemed wrong when he arrived. They were strange because they were *pink*. Would the Pink Lady force the warriors to carry pink banners? Nelber shook his head, and crossed to the smaller isle, hands behind him.

Where was Pokyer? His small boat was gone. Nelber went inside the isle's main hut to ask Thigrel where Pokyer went, and she said, "You told him to unload a boat."

Curses! He didn't mean for Pokyer to leave without waiting for him. He was stranded on the two isles until he returned. Hungry for supper, he wasn't going to wait to join his son, but he didn't want to return to the Pink Lady's isle so he convinced Thigrel to bring him something from the kitchen over there.

He sat with his brew and meal on the shore to wait for Pokyer, glad this was the warmest evening that spring. Still waiting after supper, he turned his attention to the forever-fascinating dome that was the nighttime sky.

The moon was a few days past full phase with a surface that was freckled like Thigrel's face. The pattern shifted in a four-month cycle. This month a cluster of the freckles resembling a swarm of insects had moved from one side of the disc to the other. Next month, a dark blotch splattered like spilled brew would appear on the other side.

Nelber numbered the days in a year by counting ten moon cycles, each thirty-four days long, and four more days. The stars rotated during the year, except the four brightest ones strayed from the fixed pattern. The brightest one, the moonstar, pierced the night within the brilliance of the moon. It was an unwavering beacon, calling to Nelber more than any object in the heavens. He sensed intelligence up there and wanted to communicate with it.

Pokyer arrived too long after in the larger boat he had used to haul brew. Nelber smacked his head, calling him a dolt, and demanded to know where he had been. *At the inn drinking brew.* Nelber wondered how Pokyer didn't fall overboard and drown for he couldn't handle much brew.

Pokyer left him at his son's isle to check whether Kulm ate supper. Nelber found him sleeping inside his hut, so he took Kulm's raft to his own isle and went to sleep.

He was wakened in the dark by shouts from across the main channel. Stepping for the door, he knocked over a rack of barn fowl eggs. *Curses!* That was a mess to be cleaned later.

A red band rimmed the eastern sky. Torches blazed across the water on the western bank of the Tauzzreen River. The warriors were leaving for Habergenefinanch, *but why so early?* A slender figure moved in the torchlight with a sweeping plume of hair and a swirling skirt. The pinkness of Gernthol's clothing was indistinguishable in the darkness, and Nelber liked how the same was true for the banners. Maybe the warriors wouldn't notice the color of the trapezoids until they marched under daylight.

Pokyer left the small boat at the isle, so Nelber paddled it to Kulm's isle to wake his son and return with him. Dawnlight revealed the mess of eggs in his hut. The two men cooked whatever could be salvaged for breakfast.

The Pink Lady and the warriors across the channel left for Habergenefinanch. Some men and youth came to Nelber's isle by boat and raft to get provisions for the supply carts that would follow the warriors. They took all the bread and salted meat, so Nelber sent others to Kulm's isle for more. They also claimed the entire shipment of brew that Pokyer had stacked next to Nelber's hut. Nelber carved markings on a stick to record the quantities of goods for payment later. Pershnig ordered the supplies on the Pink Lady's behalf, so Nelber marked down double payment for the brew.

The rising sun disappeared behind clouds. The last supply raft left Nelber's isle, and Pokyer arrived in time to miss all the work. He came with important news. A sail was spotted on the bay. The Richeeyimt were back.

Nelber was grateful the visitors came after the Pink Lady's departure, allowing him to deal with them without her interference. He commissioned Pokyer to row him in his larger boat down the main channel to the bay. A misty rain started before they reached the seawater, proving Nelber's guess about the weather to be true.

They emerged from the mouth of the Tauzzreen River, and the Richeeyim vessel came into view offshore to the right. It looked the same as the one blown into the bay by the storm last autumn, at least how that other vessel would have looked not cracked down the middle. The sail was down, and the oars were pulled in. The visitors finished lowering an anchor.

The water was calm because the wind blew from shore. The trees on the coast didn't grow so dense like the Swanshyim Forest ten horizons northward. Nelber scanned the landscape to be sure no departing warriors remained close enough to see the vessel. Pokyer rowed him to its side.

The same captain as last autumn welcomed Nelber. "Nelbee!" The Richeeyim couldn't pronounce the last part of his name.

Nelber didn't remember the captain's name, nor did he want to. His aging mind had limited space for new information, and he didn't want to waste it on things he didn't care about. Neither man spoke the language of the other. Nelber climbed aboard the vessel, leaving Pokyer in the boat.

Like last autumn, none of the crew spoke the Snarshyim language. Some scrubbed the deck, making use of the light rain landing on it. Stripped to their waists, the foreigners showed birthmarksigns with the same scabby lump pattern as the Snarshyimt.

Nelber recognized two sailors leaning against the mast and approached them. They had dark hair and beards, appearing to be the same age as Kulm and Pokyer. "Did you fellows have a good trip?"

They shrugged, as if they didn't understand him.

"I'm not fooled. I know you're Warnekt."

They still pretended not to know his Snarshyim words.

"Do you think you fooled me last time? You wore different clothes, didn't understand this vessel, and never spoke, like mutes."

One man stiffened so he no longer leaned on the mast.

Nelber continued, "I don't want to capture you. I want to know about our man Hoj and the Swenik who traveled with you."

The man relaxed, shouldering the mast again. "They spent the winter with us in Richee but couldn't get a translation for the scrolls."

The scrolls! They gave Nelber some of the thrill he used to get when he thought about women. He lamented, *No translation, curses!* "Where are they now?"

"They left Richee a week before us. They went farther east, across a strait to a place named Kendul, thinking somebody might translate the scrolls over there."

Nelber identified four Warnekt on the vessel last autumn masquerading as Richeeyimt, and now he knew the two others stayed in Richee.

The Richeeyim captain stood nearby, listening to each word and understanding none. Nelber placed a hand on his shoulder and asked the two Warnekt, "Have you learned this fellow's language?"

They knew enough to translate an agreement between Nelber and the captain to meet later and discuss trade. The Druogoint excelled at clothesmaking, and looking at the crew's tattered clothing, Nelber figured his tribe had much to offer in terms of garments.

He had something else for the Warnekt to translate. "Tell him to sail directly to Pultanik. Don't stop at Habergenefinanch."

The Richeeyim perked at hearing a word he understood, although he didn't pronounce it the same. *"Aber genefi nanot?"*

Nelber gave a false reason. "The place is stricken with a pestilence, a burning fever."

A Strong Man

Herkt, Jatneryimt, Warnekt

VINLON **TAUBUETH RIVER**

Vinlon found an outcropping at the top of a small cliff on which he could view the Taubueth River on an overcast morning. The rapids churned white and sprayed. The tribemaster marveled how the same liquid sometime later would flow by the fortress the Warnekt were constructing by the ocean. He knew from an ill-fated campaign years ago how the Taubueth River flowed into a deep blue lake at the headwater of the Pultanik River, which flowed eastward before doubling back to Fenzdiwerp and the coast.

His current campaign fared better, although he didn't find his Doesim Falls mistress. The Warnekt overwhelmed the Herkt at the Blue River. The blooddrop warriors scattered in three directions retreating upriver westward, downriver eastward, and northward between valleys to the Taubueth River. Vinlon pursued the northbound group, leaving half his force to pillage the Blue River settlements and protect the way of his return to the Fall River in Warnekyim lands.

Jaspich stood with him. The young man was so much like Radzig in stature that Vinlon sometimes forgot the taller figure by him was the son rather than the father, although Radzig was at Habergenefinanch and what little hair he had wasn't brown.

Vinlon heard the same resonating voice as Radzig's when Jaspich spoke. "Are any Herkt down there, Tribemaster?"

"Let's go see."

The warriors were ready to march after spending the night on higher ground. Vinlon didn't like descending to the valley but had no choice if he wanted to reach Taubueth, which he really did. The Jatneryimt escaped the brunt of his retribution when his force didn't reach Doenesh, so he wanted to sack Taubueth.

Jaspich led the force of eighty warriors on foot around trees, through thickets, and over rocks downhill to the river. Vinlon considered the young man's potential to be tribemaster. The men were responsive to his leadership somewhat because he resembled his father, but more than that, he proved himself steady in battle at the Blue River. The young warrior's swordsmanship impressed Vinlon, whose own son was lost to him, so he fancied treating Jaspich as one.

Taubueth was located upriver, although Vinlon didn't remember which side. No matter, the rapids offered no crossing, so the Warnekt followed the southern bank westward. At Jaspich's suggestion, Vinlon sent a patrol downriver. The son was so much like the father. Radzig would have recommended the same precaution.

The way along the river challenged them. The course twisted and turned, and one obstacle after another lined the water's edge—streams, jumbles of fallen branches and trees, clumps of rock, and mushy spots.

During a stop for lunch, the patrol reported a large Herkyim force was coming on the other bank from downriver, the opposite direction from Taubueth where Vinlon expected opposition. The tribemaster decided to wait for them so he could assess their strength from across the river. He stationed his archers in the foliage and mustered his other warriors into lines, displaying every Warnekyim black-ribbon pennant they had.

The cold river churned like boiling water. A jagged stone pinnacle jutted from the maelstrom, narrowing to a point at the height of a man. A swift current tumbled over a rocky ledge spanning the banks. Vinlon scoffed at the tiny waterfall, compared to the great falls at Fenzdiwerp, or more modest drop-offs on the Fall River.

The Herkt appeared eastward on the other bank with red blooddrop pennants and mauling weapons, although some carried swords or spears. They took positions facing the Warnekt thirty cubits across the rushing water. Vinlon figured they had the same numbers as his side, assuming some remained hidden, and was pleased his force carried more long black pennants than theirs did blooddrops. *They'll have more blooddrops after the fight*, he mused.

Two Herkt, wearing chain links and brawny as any from their clan, came on foot from a group of riders. The bigger one, with a wild tangle of sandy hair, seemed familiar to Vinlon. He held a spiked mace in one hand, and a shaft topped by an iron casting in the other. Vinlon remembered the casting, recognizing its iron blooddrop, and his full memory returned. The Herkyim clanlord had the same standard during the ill-fated campaign years ago, and Vinlon wanted the sandy-haired man dead.

The shorter Herk with russet-red hair held no weapon. He gave commands to the warriors around him and stood facing the Warnekt, flanked by his man with the spiked mace and blooddrop standard. Vinlon figured he was looking at the new clanlord, the one who attacked his lands.

The clanlord called to him, but the noisy river swallowed his words. Vinlon raised the steely blue blade of *Shut Up* and swiped down. The Warnekyim archers hiding in the foliage let fly a flurry of arrows. Some Herkt dove for cover, and others huddled behind shields. The large mace-wielding Herk used the iron blooddrop to deflect an arrow from drilling the clanlord.

Rustling foliage on the far bank gave warning that a return barrage was coming from Herkyim archers in the woods. Vinlon dodged a shaft going past his head and scurried for cover with his warriors. The longer-range Warnekyim bows offered no advantage in the confines of the forest.

The Herkt hurried westward upriver. Vinlon deduced they were going to a familiar place to ford the river, and he couldn't allow them the advantage of reaching it first. He ordered his warriors westward on their southern bank, but the Herkt disappeared from sight. Vinlon supposed they had a well-beaten path on their side, while the Warnekt had to circumvent more tangled trees and shrubs at the water's edge.

Vinlon decided his best option was to wait from higher ground, so he ordered his warriors to a defensive position upslope. They passed time in silence, listening downhill for the enemy's approach among the trees. The forest provided its own cadence of sounds—treetops wisping in a warm afternoon breeze under a clouded sky, chirping birds, and twigs snapping from the scamper of bushtails. Vinlon dozed against a tree.

Jaspich nudged him awake, and Vinlon heard branches cracking downhill. Whatever was coming was bigger than bushtails. Looking around his tree, Vinlon saw thick-bodied men among the trunks closer to the river. Then a wave of more men with swords appeared from the left side, shouting, "Boldness! Boldness!"

Vinlon last heard that at the Kipneesh River and spotted the combined green and black Jatneryim banners he first saw there. Sir Grebnar the Bold had come to the Taubueth River.

The stocky warriors emerged from the trunks with Herkyim blooddrops, shouting "Brutez! Brutez!"

Vinlon's fear was confirmed. When the Jatneryimt attacked at the Kipneesh River, and the Herkt at the Fall River fifty horizons apart at different times of the year, he could rationalize they acted independently, but he no longer could deny they joined forces. He wondered, *What would the skeptic Radzig say?*

"Tribemaster, I can't believe it, the Jatneryimt *and* the Herkt!" Jaspich speaking beside him may as well have been Radzig. The son's voice was the same as the father's and his words were what Radzig would say.

Vinlon knew he was overmatched against a foe reinforced with Jatneryimt. "We must withdraw to the Blue River."

Grebnar   Taubueth River

Grebnar found Brutez atop the slope. "The Warnekt have retreated, Wedlock Son." *Matkulk still lives, but the cursed Warnekt are no less troublesome*, Grebnar fretted. He had wondered why they withdrew down the Kipneesh River when they had Doenesh within reach. Now he knew. *They were fighting the Herkt.*

"My thanks for your timely arrival, Wedlock Father," said Brutez.

Not timely but inevitable, Grebnar thought. When he became convinced the Warnekt only meant to defend the Kipneesh River, he took a cadre of warriors to bring his wife home, but waited at Taubueth for Brutez to return. Staying with Sejel in the room where he was a captive was a surreal experience, although delightful with her in the bed. A report came from the Blue River of the Warnekt attacking, so Vikth mustered a force from the garrison to march down the Taubueth River. Grebnar went along with his Jatneryim warriors, including Puutnam, and so their arrival wasn't timely but inevitable. They encountered Brutez and his force at the ford and crossed together.

They also fought together. "Brutez, it's good for my forces to be seen helping yours." If Jatneryimt and Herkt ever fought together in the past, nobody remembered.

Larboelm flanked Brutez with the clanlord's iron blooddrop standard. Gordib, branded with a blooddrop on his cheek, stood by with Vikth.

Brutez asked, "How many Blue River warriors fled to Taubueth, Vikth?"

"Several dozen. All are with us."

Brutez paused in thought. Grebnar knew he was counting numbers, the same as he did as a battle commander.

"A similar number came to Lake Shore."

Grebnar wondered, *Where's Lake Shore?*

Vikth asked, "Lake Shore?"

"The town by the deep blue lake," said Brutez. "The place needed a cursed name, so I gave it one."

"Lake Shore, a good name," said Larboelm.

Brutez continued, "I reinforced the Blue River warriors with ones from Lake Shore and sent them to counterattack the Blue River from the east. I encountered more Blue River stragglers while coming up the Taubueth River and added them to my force."

Grebnar remembered how he had spent the winter collecting his forces and sending them against Matkulk.

Brutez sent away Gordib with commands. "Add the Blue River warriors from Taubueth to our force from Pinkulda. Retake the Blue River and wait for me."

Grebnar asked, "Where are *you* going, Brutez?"

"I'm returning to Taubueth with Vikth's garrison and my brother's body."

"Heptor is slain?"

Brutez told Grebnar about Heptor during their return downslope to the river, including a story about meeting Chief Hamunth and the castrations of two warriors, who were recuperating at Lake Shore, their hometown.

Grebnar told his wedlock son about a new nephew birthed by Heptor's mistress. "Our wives helped deliver the child."

The corpse didn't smell as terrible as it should after so many days. A shiny, slick substance had been smeared on Heptor's smashed and purpled face.

Brutez explained, "We met the Chizdekyimt, Adam and Enoch, after they unloined Rankeb and Konrash. They found this forest slime to help preserve the body."

Some of the long mid-spring day remained, but not enough to reach Taubueth before dark, so Grebnar and Brutez ordered their men to camp on both sides of the ford and encouraged them to mingle at the cookfires. Grebnar and Puutnam shared a fire with Brutez and Larboelm on the northern bank. After a meal of fish brought from the deep blue lake, Brutez retrieved a stagskin bundle from his mount.

"I have something to show you, Wedlock Father." Brutez extracted a roll of parchment from the stagskin. "A Swenik named Jorgis took this scroll from a cave between the two long lakes on the Tauzzreen River. Heptor grabbed it when he attacked near Pinkulda."

Grebnar had some curiosity. "Open it."

Brutez spread the stagskin on level ground where no sparks from the fire could reach, and unrolled a portion of the scroll over it. Although cloudy, and the day was waning, enough light illuminated the yellowed page for Grebnar to see its markings.

"Jorgis traveled east looking for a translation. Chief Kevyar will send for me when he returns."

Grebnar snorted, thinking, *If he returns*. Without a translation, the scroll was nothing more than a useless artifact.

As if to prove him wrong, Brutez unrolled more of it. "Look at this map."

"I see," said Grebnar, gaining interest. He recognized how the blue lines represented coasts and rivers, although he didn't know which ones.

"The green area is the Swanshyim Forest." Brutez pointed to the green edge nearest the beginning of the scroll next to a blue line. "This shows how the western side ends at a river."

"I've been there, far past the Black Citadel."

"I hope you can tell me more about the west, Wedlock

Father. You told me last autumn about tribes speaking dialects of another language, and clans among them speaking the Snarshyim language."

"The Kaligt and the Nitzent live here." Grebnar touched the map in a spot west of the Swanshyim Forest. He moved his finger to the land going off the bottom of the parchment. "Nobody speaks the Snarshyim language in the lands farther south. The Kaligt told that to my wife's cousin, Puutnam's father, when he visited them."

"My grandmother was a Kalig," said Puutnam, standing behind Grebnar.

Brutez asked Grebnar, "The map has green for forest, red for desert, and brown for mountains, but what's this land like in the west with no color?"

"I've seen the land beyond the Swanshyim Forest. It's rolling hills with scattered trees, much like the Warnekyim lands by the coast."

"What about farther west?" Brutez tapped the beginning of the map, an open space with rivers between some coasts.

"All grass."

"Like the Yarsishyim lands across the inlets?"

"I suppose. I've not been to either place. The Moeleenzyimt live in the western grasslands."

"Who are the Moeleenzyimt?"

"A people who speak the Snarshyim language."

"How do you know that, Wedlock Father?"

"My wedlock father told me. He traveled there when he was a young man."

Brutez tapped the thick arrow-headed blue lines in the center of the map that didn't correspond to any coasts or rivers. "If the people speak the Snarshyim language in the west, do you suppose the rest of us came from there?"

Grebnar tapped the markings preceding the map. "These words will be the answer—when we can read them."

Brutez   Taubueth

A stump-ridden swath by the wall next to the outlying buildings at Taubueth was merely the start of clearing the trees around the stronghold, exposing a good amount of sky. Brutez wasn't accustomed to basking in so much sunlight as he approached the wall.

He hoped for more progress, but the lack of it was to be expected considering Taubueth's manpower shortage during his absence. At least he no longer needed to climb a flimsy ladder to get inside, for a crude ramp had been constructed from the felled trees. It wasn't large enough to accommodate equines, so he entered the stronghold on foot.

Larboelm, Jonerch, Vikth, and Zzuz carried Heptor's bier up the ramp to the top of Taubueth's wall. The corpse was shrouded and emitted its worst stench, overpowering the Chizdekyim balm. Brutez supposed anyone enduring the reek wondered why he brought back a rotting body, but he knew no better way to tell his father and Nazzel.

He descended the stairs inside the wall, followed by the bier. Grebnar and Puutnam came into Taubueth with the rest of the returning Herkt. The other Jatneryimt remained outside to camp.

Nazzel came to Brutez, holding a baby. "Where's Heptor?" The excited expression on her face changed to a nose-turning snarl as she whiffed the answer to her question.

Dreading the coming commiseration, Brutez motioned to the bier being lowered to the ground. Nazzel started with a throaty groan, which rose to a howl and a shriek. She shoved the infant into Brutez's arms and dropped to her hands and knees by the rancid corpse. Her soft mane of brown hair brushed over it as she bowed her head and wailed. None of her anguished words were intelligible except for Heptor's name.

Brutez groped to better grip the baby, never holding one before. The newborn's head flopped, so he put a hand under it to keep the neck from snapping. He studied his brother's posthumously born son, a boy who never would know his father. *Undoubtedly Heptor's offspring*, he considered the baby's squarish head and undersized ears. The child was barely jolted from a nap, keeping his eyes closed as he yawned. Brutez checked inside the swaddling clothes. *A boy*, he assured himself. He knew the baby's name would be Heptor, according to the Herkyim tradition for first-born sons.

Sejel and Beksel were with Grebnar, regarding Brutez with looks of amused astonishment. Beksel approached, meaning to relieve him of the baby, but he waved her away. Nazzel continued weeping, and Sejel stooped to console her.

Brutez went to Larboelm and transferred Baby Heptor to the big man's hesitant arms. "Take him."

"Yes, Clanlord."

Larboelm never tired saying those two words. Brutez showed him how he must support the baby's wobbly head. Gaining a good hold, Larboelm smiled.

"You're now responsible for him and his mother."

"Yes, Clanlord."

If Larboelm and Nazzel developed any affection for one another, Brutez reasoned, he found the wife he promised his bodyguard. "Nazzel can live in my old chamber with the baby after my wedlock parents go home."

"Yes, Clanlord."

Brutez asked Beksel to accompany Larboelm for as long as he held the baby.

Where was his father? The old man usually was quick to greet arrivals to Taubueth. Brutez sent Zzuz to find him and coaxed Sejel to take Nazzel away from Heptor's body. Zzuz returned, saying Zamtoth waited inside the donjon. Brutez gathered the bier-bearers, and took Larboelm's spot to carry the corpse to the donjon's main hall.

The grim-looking Zamtoth sat at the end of the great table, which was cleared of everything, even candles. Brutez guided the other bearers to set the bier before his father and told them to leave. Alone with his father and slain brother, he shifted from foot to foot, tensely waiting for the old man's response.

Zamtoth reached for Heptor's head and peeled away the shroud, exposing the smeared, bloody, bruised, and decomposing mess. "You did *this*?"

"Yes, Father." *How did he know?*

"You had a reason."

Brutez heard his father's words not coming as a question, *but did his father know the reason?* "Heptor killed Chief Thoiren, an unarmed old man, by his own hand. I restored peace with the Swenikt."

Zamtoth closed the shroud over Heptor's smashed face. "I'm not sure this had to be done."

The tense feeling within Brutez changed to queasy disappointment. He hoped his father would understand, as they agreed on many matters, especially this time when he wasn't sure he did right. Saying no more, Zamtoth rose from the table and went upstairs.

Brutez stared at the shrouded corpse, unable to form a cogent thought over his crushing sense of remorse. He summoned the bearers to dump the body in the forest. The corpse served its purpose, and the main hall must be readied for the evening meal.

Zamtoth didn't come from his chamber atop the donjon, and the meal was subdued. Brutez walked alone in thought along the rampart afterward under twilight.

Vikth came with a stout and curvaceous woman. "Clanlord, this is Darjil. She's from the Fall River. A Blue River warrior captured her when they raided there."

"Fenchrous," she spoke the warrior's name. Her auburn hair was thick and wild.

"He violated you," said Brutez.

"I didn't resist, so he didn't hurt me. He thought that meant I liked him, so he took me with him to the Blue River before leaving for another battle."

"With Heptor, my brother."

"Yes, Heptor. He liked to celebrate, and he kept looking at me. After Fenchrous went with him, I thought about returning to Doesim Falls."

"Do you have family there, Darjil?"

"My baby boy and two little girls are with my father."

"How did you think you would return home?"

"I heard the Warnekt were coming, but Fenchrous returned first and sent me up the Blue River with a group of women, children, and old men."

"Darjil came with Blue River warriors and their people retreating to Taubueth," said Vikth.

Brutez deduced the rest. Vikth saw an appealing forlorn woman and fancied her. "What do you want to do, Vikth?"

"I want to help Darjil rejoin her family."

"I'm leaving tomorrow morning for the Blue River," said Brutez. "If we chase the Warnekt to the Fall River, you may take her with us."

She assaulted him with an embrace. *Curses*, she was strong!

"Clanlord, I don't know how to thank you," said Vikth.

Brutez considered it a small concession to win the undying loyalty of a man. "I'll have Jonerch replace you as garrison commander." He freed himself from Darjil's hold and put her into Vikth's arms. "Keep watch over her on the march, especially if we encounter Fenchrous."

"No need to worry. A Blue River warrior told me the Warnekt killed him."

Good riddance, Brutez thought. He retired to his quarters in the donjon basement to spend time with his wife. She sat at the table in the main room with a candle, looking over the scroll from near Pinkulda. Larboelm was entrusted with the parchment and gave it to her.

"Brutez, this is a map. Where did you get this?"

He was distracted by her green eyes, quaint freckled nose, and inviting lips, but knew if he indulged himself with a kiss, their upcoming conversation wouldn't happen. He stood behind her chair, viewing the map over her shoulder, and told her all he knew about the scroll, including what her father, Grebnar, told him about the western end of the blue, green, red, and brown drawing.

"This is a wonder, Brutez. I want to know what these words say."

Brutez reached over her shoulder. Chestnut locks of hair caressed his face, and he sneaked a peek down her breasts. *Later*, he promised himself. *For now, the scroll.* He unrolled the parchment past the map to a place he didn't show Grebnar or any other Jatneryim. Beksel no longer was a Jatneryim. *She was a Herk.* He was saddened because he wanted to show the same spot and the rest of the scroll to his father, who presently wasn't speaking to him.

Beksel gasped. She looked at the wall lined with the relic broadswords and back to the scroll where a drawing matched the mounted arrangement, twenty-four great swords speckled with jewels on the handles. "Brutez, this will tell us about your swords."

This time he didn't ignore the invitation of her lips, and the conversation ended.

BEKSEL **TAUBUETH**

Beksel woke, knowing it was the middle of the night because the shaft providing light to the bedchamber from outside was dark. The only light flickered from the other room through the part-open door.

She was alone in the bed. She didn't want to be alone, not for a moment on this single night when Brutez was there, before leaving to fight the Warnekt. Too many lonely nights were ahead, and this time her mother wouldn't be there. Beksel's parents, Grebnar and Sejel, were leaving for Doenesh in the morning with the rest of the Jatneryimt except the resident envoy Puutnam.

The flickering light summoned Beksel to the other room. Brutez sat in a chair, turned away from a candle on the table. He stared at the broadswords on the wall, but wasn't looking at them. His gaze was elsewhere.

She knelt on the fur-covered floor to look into his eyes, but his blank fixation persisted. "My dear Brutez, you're troubled."

"The Warnekt won't make peace. I faced Tribemaster Warnek across the river and tried to talk. He raised his sword, and the arrows came."

She knew that wasn't the greatest of his troubles. He needed to tell her. Placing a hand on his knee to steady herself, she took hold of his arm with her other hand to get his attention. His sorrow brought his gray eyes to the brink of producing tears.

"I'm your lady wife. You don't have to be strong with me like before your men."

"The cost is so high, Beksel." The first tears streamed down his face. "I traded a clansman's life for your father's. I sent my uncle to his death to make peace with your people, and to make amends with the Swenikt, I slaughtered my own brother." He wagged his head, and more tears flowed as he languished. "What else can I do? The Warnekt won't make peace."

She caressed his teary cheek in a bare spot above his beard. "Dear husband, you see a future. You see what nobody before has seen, the Snarshyim clans and tribes as one people, but first you must weep for your dear brother, Heptor. I mourned for my brothers, and I'm here for you."

He leaned forward in the chair, sobbing. She accepted his head into her bosom and stroked his luscious reddish hair as he wept, body shaking. *This is a strong man,* she told herself, and she loved him.

General Conflagration

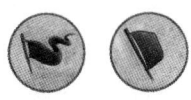

Warnekt, Druogoint

Radzig   Habergenefinanch

Radzig wouldn't acknowledge the color he saw, but how could he see it wrong? Broad daylight allowed no shadow, and wispy clouds were no hindrance to the sunshine. The Druogoinyim banners flapped in full view in the breezy air, and they *looked pink*.

    He watched the enemy warriors from atop the Habergenefinanch palisade, lingering out of range from the town's defending archers by the nearest line of scattered trees on the backside away from the bay. Some were mounted, including a slender rider with a long mane of red hair and dressed in pink. Gernthol! Radzig thought Vinlon should have anticipated this, but didn't. The tribemaster's wayward wife had led the Druogoint to Habergenefinanch when the town was most vulnerable. Many of the local warriors were gone fighting Jatneryimt or Herkt. Radzig had barely enough archers to cover the whole town, and certainly not enough men to launch an attack outside the wall.

Several forays were repulsed by the precise marksmanship of the defending archers. The Druogoint fired flaming arrows at the town, but they couldn't get close enough against the longer-range bows designed by Leenarth. The few fiery darts reaching the palisade were doused without much harm.

This time the enemy archers approached from the northside behind the cover of other warriors with shields, better withstanding the longer-range shots of the defenders as they marched into firing range, and their flaming shots started clearing the palisade. One flew over Radzig, stabbing the nearest building's plank wall with a twang. The flame flared, but an occupant of the structure used a rug to beat it down.

Bigger fires on the opposite side of town were greater reason for alarm, too large to be easily quelled, and threatening a general conflagration that would burn all of Habergenefinanch. Radzig's foremost concern became his wife and daughters. Their house stood next to the southern wall in the vicinity of the developing inferno.

The anxious husband and father leaped with his hatchet from the palisade down a series of platforms and ran into town. *What started the fires on the southern side?* No flaming missile could have reached there from the northside assault, and the other side was too narrow by the bay for an effective attack. He concluded the southside fires were set from inside the town. The Druogoint must have infiltrated Habergenefinanch before their warriors arrived, posing as farmers or merchants bringing goods for sale. The northside attack was a diversion.

Radzig pressed against a crowd of people and animals fleeing *the* fire, for the smaller blazes were fast merging to a heat-blasting holocaust. The flames licked toward him on his approach, fanned by the warm breeze coming off the bay. He found a gap to enter the inferno through the middle of an abandoned commons. Flaming buildings surrounded him as the blaze spread through the top levels, sprouting yelloworange dancing tongues from upper windows, and belching sooty billows from entire roofs that had become chimneys. Habergenefinanch was doomed, a waiting pyre of wood and straw to be devoured.

He scurried from the commons along a street that led to the large commons by the tribal longhouse, which was crowned by fire. The tribemaster's residence on the knoll was a bonfire. The Warnekyim pennant flying over its roof was the only part not aflame, black as the smoke roiling around it, but then it toppled into the burning structure.

The street leading to his house was a fiery tunnel, but some buildings facing the commons weren't as much ablaze as the others. He passed through a tanner's shop, hung with skins catching fire. Terrified flatsnouts squealed in the back across an alley. He chopped through their pen with his hatchet, releasing the panicked animals.

Stumbling through smoke, he girded the hatchet and pulled his frock over his face, trying to keep the noxious fumes from his eyes and nose. Breathing was like sucking ashes, irritating to nose and throat. He choked and coughed, and his eyes streamed tears. The flames moved closer, relentlessly hotter than any foundry. Sweat poured from his body, trickling into his ears and stinging his eyes. The air buffeted like the blast from a potter's furnace.

He groped for a way out of whatever building he had entered. Kicking through a burning wall, sizzling hot boards burned him as he passed through. He collapsed, sputtering and coughing, in a pocket of breathable air on the other side. The packed and rutted ground told him he had reached a street.

Rubbing his eyes to open them, he couldn't see more than a few cubits. Thick smoke hovered over the ground in a dark gray fog, churning like a thundercloud. Fire raged all around. Flames flashed within the smoke, the lightning within the storm. He didn't know where to go and wondered whether his family would discover what happened to him. *Would anybody recognize his charred body?*

A horrific mewing of a feline burning alive pierced the

air. Radzig longed for the poor beast to die. The sound was worse than Birdbane's worst. *Birdbane!* Vinlon's feline was showing him the way to his house, where the creature lived while the tribemaster went to war. Radzig stumbled toward the mewing, escaping the fogbank of smoke, and followed Birdbane's sable form along his home street on the southern side of town.

A look at the flames leaning northward across roofs told him the bay breeze slowed the fire's advance into his neighborhood, but the extra time was running out. He entered his house, trying to call his wife's name, but his throat was too raw and tongue too swelled for him to utter more than a croak and grunt.

His younger daughter of twelve years, blond-haired as his wife, appeared in the main room, calling, "Mother's trapped!"

He allowed her to show the way. Yazdil was stuck inside a storeroom. His older daughter of fifteen years, brown-haired like his son, tried to open its door.

"Mother went in there to get rope." Her pimpled face was wet with tears of fear and frustration. "The door closed, and we can't open it."

He tried the latch, discovering the bolt on the crude wooden handle was broken and held the door closed.

His wife's voice from inside was panicked. "Get me out!"

Since Radzig couldn't talk, his daughter told her mother he was there. If Yazdil was assured by his arrival, the urgency of her shouting didn't show it, and she had good reason to be concerned. The house was catching fire, and the place thickened with smoke.

He used the hatchet to knock away the useless handle and chopped the doorframe. The effort incited a debilitating coughing spasm. He leaned on his knees, choking up a sooty discharge of mucus and the grime that he had breathed. Both daughters watched helplessly. He stopped coughing and pried open the storeroom door with the hatchet.

Yazdil came out with a coil of rope, looking at the flames

all around. "Hurry, we must get over the wall."

He followed her with their daughters up the house stairs. A window on the uppermost level overlooked the town's southern wall, and he kicked open the shutters. The view of the bay sparkling under the midday sun was marvelous because nothing out there burned. Refugees fled across the piers over the bog along the shore to boats.

Radzig took the rope from Yazdil and motioned for her to loop an end below her armpits. She objected, wanting to send down their younger daughter, but he urged her to go first. He tied the rope snugly and lowered her out the window fifteen cubits to the base of the wall. She untied herself, and he pulled up the rope. The younger daughter went next. She needed help from her mother to get untied, which was why Radzig insisted his wife go ahead of the girls. The shutters burned around the window as he knotted the rope under his older daughter's armpits. Smoke blocked the bay scene, and the floorboards felt hot under his feet. The sill caught fire while he lowered the girl.

The rope slacked from his daughter reaching the ground, and he searched for a place to secure his end so he could descend. Squinting through the tears of smoke-wracked eyes, he spotted a post in the middle of the room. He leaned against it through another fit of coughs. Tying the rope around it, he saw that the length over the sill was burning through and wouldn't hold his weight. He had no more time. The floor was too hot for standing. He stumbled to the window, coughing through a cloud of smoke, and leaped through the rectangle of fire framing the aperture.

His foot hooked the fiery sill, flipping him into a headlong fall. The last sounds he heard were his wife shouting his name, the screams of his daughters, and the crack of his broken neck.

Jaspich   Habergenefinanch

At first sight, Jaspich was astounded Habergenefinanch still smoldered two weeks after the fire, especially after several days of drenching rain, but then he realized he saw campfires. Dislocated residents lived all around a town-sized scar on the land, the heap of blackened wood and ashes that once was the ancestral home of the Warnekt. The remnant of the tribemaster's residence piled higher than the rest of the ruin because it once stood on a knoll in the center of town.

Jaspich sensed Vinlon's fury. The tribemaster sat straight as a spear on his mount, clutching the hilt of his custom-forged sword, *Shut Up*. Jaspich's tension came more from anxiety than anger. He worried about his family—his father, mother, and sisters who were inside Habergenefinanch when it burned. The news of the destruction didn't come to the Blue River from Radzig, which didn't bode well for the fate of Jaspich's father.

Most of the force that raided Herkyim lands was with them, more than one hundred warriors. Many came from Habergenefinanch, and Vinlon dismissed them to search for their families. Jaspich began his own search, accompanied by the tribemaster. They dismounted and led their equines outside the jumble of charred wood that remained of the town's western wall.

Some families camped nearer the scorched area than the others. Their shelter built from scraps of salvaged timber had only a roof to keep them dry during rain. The late spring nights were warm enough for them not to worry about cold.

The lead man introduced himself as a carpenter. "Most people escaped the fire," he said. "Some made it to the boats and ferried to safety, but even those of us who fled to the open countryside weren't much pursued by the Druogoint. Their leader, a fat man, offered any tradesman a new life for returning with them to Ranjin."

A fat man, Jaspich mulled. He had to be Pershnig, and he wasn't the leader.

"You declined," said Vinlon. "What about the others?"

"Some were enamored by the pink woman."

"Did she have red hair?"

Of course she was Gernthol, Jaspich figured. He knew Pershnig wasn't the leader.

"Long flaming tresses," said the carpenter. "She told us we were spared because none of us were the Warnek she wants to kill."

Jaspich traded a knowing glance with Vinlon, whom Gernthol wanted dead.

Vinlon asked the people how they were surviving. The group had no more food, having consumed a flatsnout they found wandering after the attack. Vinlon gave them a portion from his provisions, promising more to come from Fenzdiwerp. The tribemaster had sent warriors there to secure supplies for stricken Habergenefinanch. His last gift was the most appreciated. The carpenter accepted Vinlon's personal black-ribbon pennant with wistful eyes.

Jaspich and Vinlon were greeted by a mewing black feline as they continued their trek along the sooted edge of the former town. Vinlon stooped to give Birdbane's sable fur a purr-inducing stroke. The creature ran ahead in the direction from where it came. Hope surged within Jaspich as he realized Birdbane led the way to his family.

They rounded the southwestern corner of the blackened ruin, putting the bay into better view. The water appeared more gray than blue under the day's clouds lingering from the recent storm. More campers packed the narrow strip of firm ground between the wreckage of Habergenefinanch and the coastal bog. Following the prancing black furry form with upright tail, Jaspich smiled. He should have guessed his family would stay close to their former home next to the southern wall.

Vinlon found a path for their mounts through the cluster

of refugees. Jaspich saw his mother and sisters outside the gutted remains of their house. He gave Vinlon his mount's reins and ran forward to embrace them.

Their mournful sobs weren't from joy, and he knew. His gut churned. "Father didn't survive."

His mother looked at him with sodden face. "He gave his life saving us, here at this spot." She pointed down.

Jaspich scanned the patch of beaten ground around their feet next to the disfigured pile of the southern wall. Two weeks had passed, but he asked nevertheless, "The body is gone, Mother?"

"It was sunk into the bog with the others."

Vinlon offered condolences. Then Dekloes arrived, and Vinlon asked, "You came from Pultanik?"

"Yes, Tribemaster. The Jatneryimt didn't attack at the Kipneesh River, so I went to check the project at Pultanik, as you ordered. The outer wall almost is completed."

"Then you heard about the attack and came here?"

"I was halfway here when I met a messenger."

Vinlon frowned. "Why were you coming here?"

"Two of our men returned from Richee, saying their voyage skipped stopping here at Habergenefinanch."

"They saw it destroyed while sailing past?"

Jaspich shared Vinlon's confusion. Who told Dekloes about the attack, the messenger or the men returning from Richee?

"They stopped at Ranjin," said Dekloes. "A Druogoin there, a fellow with a mop of light brown hair . . ."

"Nelber," Jaspich interrupted.

"I agree the description fits Nelber. He warned about a pestilence here."

"He knew the attack was coming," said Vinlon. "He warned away the Richeeyimt without betraying his tribe's plan."

"Of course I hurried here for news," said Dekloes. "I arrived a week ago, Jaspich, and kept watch over your mother and sisters."

Jaspich was thankful. He owed Dekloes much, not only

for watching his family, but also for his role in arranging his ransom from the Druogoint.

"The Druogoint left without slaughtering anybody other than the victims of the fire," said Vinlon.

"They were gone when I arrived," said Dekloes.

"They left the day after the attack without bothering us," said Jaspich's mother, Yazdil.

Vinlon walked off to look over the carnage of the town, and Jaspich followed, leaving his mother and sisters with Dekloes.

"We have a hundred warriors," said Vinlon. "We're going to Ranjin."

"Tribemaster, we shouldn't."

Vinlon was angry. "Why not, Jaspich? Look what they did to your family's house. They killed your father."

"Nobody will stop the Herkt from reaching Fenzdiwerp if we go to Ranjin."

"You're like your father, not wanting to counterattack."

Angered, Jaspich no longer withheld words. "If you had listened to my father, Habergenefinanch wouldn't be this incinerated ruin."

Vinlon thrust forth his chest in a challenge. "You speak bold words to your tribemaster."

The menace in his voice chilled Jaspich, but he refused to relent. "You're tribemaster, but you told me I'm the next one. I know you intend to treat me as a son. If you want to be my new father, you must listen to me."

Vinlon said nothing, staring Jaspich in the eye. He looked down Jaspich's tensed body to the young man's feet and back to his face. "I chose well." He allowed a smile. "You're not intimidated against speaking your thoughts, even after I threaten you. You're worthy to advise me, so speak, and I'll consider."

"I share your desire for revenge, Tribemaster. How can't I? He was my father!" Jaspich considered that Lady Gernthol burned Habergenefinanch merely to avenge her father. *How would the cycle of revenge end?* "This was my town as much as for any Warnek, but we should do what's best for the tribe. Let's send a force back to the Pultanik River to defend Fenzdiwerp. Let's take as many of these good people we can to Pultanik. We're going to need the fortress we're building there."

"I know we should do as you say, but I want vengeance."

Jaspich knew Vinlon needed an argument to convince his heart as well as his mind and was glad he had one. "You heard the carpenter back there, saying your lady wife wants to kill you. If we go to Ranjin, you'll have to kill her. Do you want that?"

Vinlon didn't need to speak his answer. It was written on his face for Jaspich to read. He still loved the woman.

Sudden Family

Herkt

BRUTEZ   **DOESIM FALLS**

Brutez thought he might as well be looking at the backside of the Doesim Falls, as if his tent was a cave in the cliff behind the falling water. The runoff from the downpour pelting the tent's gabled roof was a streaming curtain in the open entrance.

The actual waterfall was a more substantial cascade than any of the cataracts on the Taubueth River. Brutez had been eager to see it after listening to a description from Darjil, the furiously red-haired woman with Vikth. It was a fluid staircase of three steps, wide as the river, some thirty cubits.

The Herkt entered the valley of the Fall River wondering where the Warnekyim forces went and were wary of an ambush. Only after Zzuz and the other scouts reported none of Tribemaster Warnek's warriors were present in the area did Brutez then venture to the base of the Doesim Falls, and to the town with the same name.

Alone in the tent while Larboelm left on a gallant quest

for firewood in the downpour, the clanlord wondered why the Warnekt would abandon a town in their own lands after resisting at the Blue River for ten days. Even their withdrawal from Herkyim lands seemed rather abrupt, not forced from any decisive victory by the Herkt, so after a few more days to oversee the return of refugees and to collect his forces, Brutez crossed between the river valleys to investigate.

Vikth arrived, stripped to his breeches, which the clanlord thought was sensible in this pouring warm rain. The newcomer carried the same cudgel Brutez had used against Klinteg at the tournament. Vikth wiped rainwater from his face. "Darjil and I found her family, Clanlord."

Brutez wondered what next, knowing Vikth fancied Darjil and wouldn't want to leave her.

"I want to marry her." Vikth answered the unspoken question. He swiped his bared chest, flaying water from his birthmarksign.

"She has what, two little girls and a baby boy?" Brutez wanted Vikth to consider all. "You'll have a sudden family."

"I was married, Clanlord. None of our children survived, and the last birth took my wife's life, so gaining healthy children appeals to me."

Brutez understood. "You must take her to the ridge. You can't stay here in a Warnekyim town, abandoned by them or not."

"Her father accepts that."

"I want to speak with him, Vikth. Bring him to me at once." Brutez reasoned Darjil's father would be more forthcoming with information than the other townspeople, whom he determined not to threaten or abuse.

The rainfall was lighter when Vikth returned with Darjil's father, a man named Tetharng, so the newcomer arrived in reasonably dry clothing. He had tangled hair similar to his daughter.

"Your daughter will become a Herk," Brutez told him.

"My father was a Herk," he said. "The warriors have come

from the Blue River other times to violate women."

"My warriors won't. We'll help rebuild your town."

"Is that so? What if I don't want to stay here?"

"My future wedlock father wants to go where Darjil goes," said Vikth. He was better clothed, having added a threadbare tunic to his attire.

"I'm as much a Herk as a Warnek," said Tetharng.

Brutez was pleased, seeing a chance to gain knowledge for his clan. Darjil's description of her father's mill, and how the water turned its wheel, fascinated him. He planned for his warriors to learn how it worked when they helped rebuild it but better the miller came to his lands with the knowledge.

"Do you know why Tribemaster Warnek retreated?" Brutez expected Tetharng to provide information, being as much a Herk as a Warnek.

"We got news the Druogoint burned Habergenefinanch to the ground."

The Druogoint, Brutez mused. Vinlon didn't have friendly relations with any of his neighbors. "The tribemaster went to Habergenefinanch," he concluded. "I suppose we have time for a wedding." He smiled, but Vikth seemed uneasy.

"Vikth, your clanlord must know." Tetharng looked at Brutez. "My daughter was Tribemaster Warnek's mistress. She claims he's the father of her children."

A startling revelation, Brutez pondered, although not knowing to what advantage.

Tetharng continued, "I'm not convinced. The baby's lineage is difficult to judge, but the girls look nothing like the tribemaster. Darjil has been with other men."

Brutez asked Vikth, "How do you know you'll be her only man?"

"I'm the one who wants to marry her."

Brutez hoped the best for him. Darjil and her father would become Herkt. *Herkt who spent time with Warnek Vinlon.* "Tell me, Tetharng. When the tribemaster wasn't alone with your daughter, you ate with him, didn't you?"

"Many times. He's well known for dining with his people."

"What did he talk about when you filled him with brew?"

"Pultanik."

"Pultanik? The river or the ocean?"

"Where the river meets the ocean. Vinlon's building a great structure there."

"What sort of structure?"

"One made of rock. The tribemaster boasts it will be impregnable."

"I must lead my forces to see this wonder." *And destroy it while I can*, Brutez left unsaid. He commanded, "Vikth, go home with your new family to get married there, and take Zzuz with you. When you pass by Taubueth, send Puutnam to Grebnar with a message about the mighty structure at the mouth of the Pultanik River. We must sack it before it's finished."

What I Have For You Better Stab your Heart

Warnekt

JASPICH　　　　　　　　　　**PULTANIK**

The more Jaspich thought about Tribemaster Warnek's instructions, the more they vexed him.

"Go to Banshim's place for supper," Vinlon told him. "You must ask him for something, but you can't ask until you find what you're getting."

A sweltering foundry wasn't where Jaspich wanted to go on what was the hottest day yet that summer, and plenty of sunfilled daylight remained even at suppertime. He wore a loose-fitting sleeveless tunic and breeches that didn't reach his knees. He walked barefoot along the main street through the shacks of the camp at Pultanik, going against the traffic.

More people heeded their leader's call to take what they valued to the fortress, for they soon would be under attack. The Herkt were coming down the Pultanik River from the Fall

River. The Jatneryimt already had pushed to the mouth of the Kipneesh River and were poised to move against Pod's Peak, eight horizons westward where the stone for the fortress was quarried.

While Jaspich brought his family and other refugees from Habergenefinanch to Pultanik, Vinlon led his warriors on the Pultanik River to delay the advance of the Herkt until the fortification's outer wall could be completed. Then he came to Pultanik to oversee the preparations for a siege, leaving Dekloes in command of the Pultanik River warriors.

Vinlon's white male feline, Spear, accompanied Jaspich. The young man couldn't figure why the beast would go with him, other than to get away from Birdbane, the ever-demanding black feline from Habergenefinanch.

They pressed to the side of the street by the steps to the streamer to avoid a flock of woolstock being herded toward the fortress. A family pushing a cart of furniture, and a potter with his wheel, also went by. A short distance farther, after the street cleared, Jaspich took a side alley with Spear to Banshim's foundry and residence.

Approaching the door, he pondered again the vexing question of what to ask. Vinlon gave him one clue. Banshim's apprentices weren't allowed to touch whatever the master forger had for him.

Banshim opened the door before Jaspich finished knocking. Jaspich didn't recall the remnant of the forger's hair ever appearing so gray, but then he didn't remember the fellow not being covered in soot. Had he used bathwater?

"Good, you brought the furry ferocity," said Banshim, looking at Spear, tail erect, passing by his feet through the door. "I have more vermin around here for him to kill."

While the feline disappeared to hunt for supper, Banshim offered Jaspich a seat at his table. None of his apprentices were present. His lame daughter was the only other one seated, a girl whose name Jaspich didn't remember.

Banshim's older daughter appeared with the first serving, a

crustacean soup. Jaspich remembered her name, Zzinel. When she was younger, and his sisters were small girls, they played together. The gangly girl from those days, now womanly, had turned more intriguing to Jaspich.

"Tell me," said Banshim while scooping soup into his mouth. The creamy broth dribbled on his chin as he talked. "Is it true the tribemaster used the sword I made for him to kill Warlord Druogoin?"

"I saw it," said Jaspich. "The warlord had no chance against such a fine weapon." Vinlon let him brandish *Shut Up* on occasion, a magnificent instrument of death.

"I put all my skill into forging that blade, accepting no help from my apprentices."

Banshim's apprentices weren't allowed to touch it. Jaspich became elated with a realization. He was getting a sword like *Shut Up*! All he had to do was find it. He ate his soup in as much haste as he could, but Banshim finished his first.

"Master Banshim, while we wait for the next serving, let me look at your forge."

Banshim put a hand by his mouth, supposedly to wipe away his slobber, but Jaspich saw a smirk. "I don't know why, Jaspich. My coals aren't even fired."

Jaspich realized the place wasn't so ghastly hot as he dreaded. "You know why I'm here. I must look." He was in no mood to parry words.

Banshim waved to the foundry. "Look all you want," he said in a more disinterested than challenging tone. His disinterest was feigned because he went with Jaspich. "You see, my anvil is sent to the fortress."

Jaspich saw the empty space, but the rest of the workplace was filled with raw metal, tools, and unfinished projects. He saw ordinary swords and speartips along with more mundane items, such as hoof rings and nails.

Banshim continued, "Tell me, Jaspich. Do you think everyone will fit inside the stronghold when the Herkt and Jatneryimt arrive?"

"The place is immense. It even has a channel from the river so we won't lack fresh water."

Disappointed by his failed search, Jaspich returned with Banshim to the supper table and the forger's younger daughter. Zzinel came with a pitcher and poured her father a tankard of brew. She lingered longer pouring brew for Jaspich. His heart paced and his breathing increased by the nearness of her womanly body. Her form was pleasing, augmented by a tan leather bodice.

"Tell me, Jaspich." Banshim's upper lip frothed with brew. "What were you looking for in my forge?"

Jaspich couldn't say. He wasn't supposed to ask until he found it. "Something special."

"Special indeed," said Banshim. "There's only one."

Zzinel brought woolstock chops, starch roots within their crispy brown skins, buttered greens sprinkled with pepper, and a tureen of gravy. She caught Jaspich staring, but a small smile curling at the edges of her mouth told him she enjoyed his attention. He was enthralled for a moment, falling into the muddy pool of her dark brown eyes.

His appetite took over, and he ate hearty. Finishing a third or fourth tankard of brew, Banshim excused himself to the streamer. Jaspich had an opportunity.

"Little girl," he said to the younger daughter, wishing he remembered her name. "Do you know where your father keeps the sword he made for me?"

The girl fingered a buttered green she didn't want to eat. She looked at him, brown-eyed like her sister. "Why do you think he made you a sword?"

Jaspich pondered. *If not a sword, what else does a forger make? Hoof rings and nails, what's special about those?*

Zzinel came to clear the meal. Her father returned, appearing much relieved.

"I came for something from you." Jaspich hoped for a clue from Banshim. "Would it be able to stab me through the heart?" An answer would settle whether he looked for a sword or at least a speartip.

The forger smiled. "What I have for you better stab your heart."

Jaspich became more perplexed than ever. He noticed Zzinel smiling like her father. He would have thought she mocked him except for the inviting lure of her lips. The young woman left the dining room with the last used dishes and returned with frosted raisin cakes. She had served an entire meal without speaking, and Jaspich thought finally they should talk.

"You prepared this meal?"

"I like preparing food. My father's the best-fed man in our tribe."

Banshim laughed, patting his rotund stomach. "She speaks the truth."

"Someday your husband will be well fed, Zzinel." Jaspich wondered why none of Banshim's apprentices gained her favor.

"I hope so. My father tells me a man has many appetites, and not all for food."

"I warned her about manly appetites," said Banshim.

Of course he had to, Jaspich thought, considering the virile young men the apprentices were. *The apprentices weren't allowed to touch!* Vinlon's clue hammered into his mind. He met Zzinel's gaze, sinking into the mud of her eyes, and considered himself stabbed in the heart.

"Master Banshim, I know what to ask. What I ask for is special. There's only one, this one your daughter."

The Tribemaster Likes His Banners

Herkt, Jatneryimt, Warnekt

BRUTEZ   **PULTANIK**

Brutez sighed from relieving his gorged bladder into the streamer. The long ceramic trough ran along the rooflines of shacks in the town the Warnekt called a camp. This streamer flowed to the ocean, buttressed over the streets on pairs of crossed poles. The other one went to the river. Although accustomed to innovations from the clever Warnekt, Brutez didn't see the value of this one in improving sanitation. Livestock and wandering canines and felines still defecated in the streets. The urination trough was better used by women who dumped used water from their cooking, cleaning, and laundry.

The platform offered a decent view of Tribemaster Warnek's rock structure on the land point between the ocean and river. It had an inner building and outer wall, the same as Taubueth, but it was immense. Warnekyim black-ribbon pennants smothered the edifice. None of the structure's stone protrusions seemed without one. No matter how many Herkyim blooddrops Brutez added to the rooftops of the shacks in the town he controlled, Vinlon hoisted more pennants.

Grebnar's forces didn't participate in the gamesmanship of banners. The Jatneryimt camping across the river on the northern bank displayed the same modest amount of green and black as when they arrived a few days ago.

The Herkt crossed the river many horizons upstream in boats from a town on the northern bank. They brought the craft downriver and used them as ferries, since the Warnekt left no boats in the vicinity before retreating into their fortress.

Brutez descended to the street and hurried to the forger's place where he resided, expecting Grebnar's imminent arrival with Larboelm. The Jatneryim leader was newly arrived at the mouth of the Pultanik River, after lingering by the quarry at Pod's Peak for several days.

Brutez saw a white feline scurry across the alley leading to his destination. He passed through the dormant foundry on his way to the residence. The anvil and any tools of value were gone. Only raw material, refuse, and unfinished projects remained.

Puutnam came with Larboelm and Grebnar.

After sending Larboelm on another assignment, Brutez asked his wife's second cousin, "How's married life?"

"I miss Vel," said Puutnam.

"You newly married don't think about much else," said Grebnar.

"Not true, Wedlock Father," said Brutez. "I think about the troublesome Warnekt and their cursed structure. You see the place is formidable."

"It's more impressive than the Black Citadel."

"The wall looks finished. We're too late to attack it."

"My Jatneryim warriors want to try."

"That would be folly. The Warnekyim bows have longer range than ours. We must learn a new method of warfare to attack such a fortification."

"My men will comply if I decide against attacking, but sometimes it's better for them to learn a hard lesson. My son, Chakstim, was the reckless one. He wanted to ride standing on his mount, the same one you have with the black mane. It took a broken arm to convince him it was a bad idea."

"We might not need to attack if I can meet with the tribemaster." Brutez hoped so because his warriors had been fighting since the snow melted, but Vinlon didn't want to talk, considering all the envoys who didn't return.

Grebnar asked, "How do you plan to arrange this meeting?"

"I have one of his tribesmen to use as a messenger."

The last one, Brutez told himself. He knew the tribemaster was thinking him a fool to keep sending Warnekt as messengers, in effect freeing them when they didn't return, but he had a message he expected would get a response.

"You're prudent to send a Warnek," said Grebnar.

Brutez agreed best not to send his own men. He didn't want another head returned. Larboelm made a timely arrival with the last messenger.

"Here's the man," Brutez told Grebnar.

The new arrival barely was a man, but a maturing youth, growing what must be his first beard.

"Tell your tribemaster how well you were treated," Brutez told him. "Then give him my one-word message. It's a name: Darjil."

Vinlon   Pultanik

Vinlon contemplated how the Pultanik Ocean rarely was this calm, caressed by a soft breeze coming offshore. Jaspich took advantage of the unusual circumstance when proposing how to meet the Herkyim clanlord without risk of treachery, at least any risk that could be anticipated. The supposedly risk-free arrangement Jaspich's father, Radzig, had negotiated for ransoming the young man at Fenzdiwerp hadn't prevented Warlord Druogoin's head from flying through the air, a fond memory for Vinlon.

The tribemaster coasted in the prow of a small boat, rowed by the Herk who was sent to his side to verify he came without a missile weapon, namely the longer-range Leenarthyim bow. Gordib was branded by his clan's blood-drop on one cheek. Vinlon was glad the two Warnekyim pennants flying from the boat's stern outnumbered the one banner on his enemy's face.

Jaspich rowed the oncoming other boat, since he insisted on being the one in his plan to verify Clanlord Brutez came without bow or spear. The clanlord was the same red-haired man Vinlon saw that day across the rushing Taubueth River.

"Tribemaster Warnek," Brutez called when his boat came close enough for him to be heard. "Your structure has my attention."

Vinlon allowed himself a look at the magnificent construction on the point of the nearby coast, framed by a blaze of late afternoon sun. All the pennants wafting in long dark streams against a pale blue sky were spectacular.

Brutez continued, "I'm glad my last message got your attention, too."

Vinlon clenched his fists. He wouldn't be swayed by any threats against Darjil, his favorite mistress, but his curiosity had him here listening. Gordib and Jaspich rowed the two boats closer for easier conversation, but no less than twenty cubits apart.

"Clanlord, what did you do to Darjil?"

"Nothing, Tribemaster. My clansmen attacked Doesim Falls while I was a prisoner of the Jatneryimt. The man who took her is dead, killed by your warriors at the Blue River."

Vinlon liked hearing that but wanted to know more. "Where is she?"

"She married one of my warriors after he brought her to Doesim Falls to get her family, including her father, Tetharng.

They live near Taubueth."

"How do you expect me to believe that?" Vinlon didn't know which angered him more, being duped into meeting Brutez by a lie, or the possibility he told the truth about Darjil marrying a Herk.

"Doesn't matter if you don't," said Brutez.

Of course not, Vinlon fumed, now that he was here, he must listen. *Curses*, he couldn't leave. The man rowing his boat was a cursed Herk.

Brutez continued, "You can verify what I say next. My forces helped rebuild Doesim Falls and the other towns my clansmen ravaged."

Vinlon's jaw dropped. The lie was so brazen he couldn't respond with words.

Brutez kept talking. "Your townspeople along the Pultanik River told me how you visit them each autumn on a harvest tour. Ask them on this year's tour, and you'll discover I speak the truth."

Vinlon didn't know what to think. As unbelievable were the words he was hearing, he could see for himself if he wasn't besieged. "How can I take a harvest tour while you surround me?"

"I propose we withdraw," said Brutez. "I told you my clan attacked your tribe while I was a prisoner. The Jatneryimt sacked your Kipneesh River towns when Sir Grebnar was my prisoner. Neither of us wanted to fight the Warnekt."

His talk about one or the other being the other's prisoner confused Vinlon. If Brutez was lying, why tell it so complicated except to better obstruct the truth? "Then why were we attacked?"

"Sir Grebnar and I weren't in control, but now we are."

"Why weren't you in control?"

"Our previous leaders, Sir Rendif and Clanlord Vulrath, were killed. The changes in leadership took time."

Vinlon understood, remembering the reports of infighting among the Jatneryimt. "What do you want for your withdrawal?"

"If you stay out of our lands, we'll stay out of yours."

"Then go away, and I won't bother you."

"We can if you make a token surrender. Our warriors must think they won."

A token surrender! Vinlon's anger returned. He was being tricked.

"Not an actual surrender," said Brutez. "Lower your banners. Then we'll withdraw to our lands, taking nothing from yours except what we need for provisions."

Vinlon fumed. He only could know the truth by lowering his pennants. *Curses!*

BRUTEZ   **PULTANIK**

Brutez drank brew with four others in the waning light of a late summer evening. They sat by the riverbank where they could watch the Warnekyim edifice from out of range of the defending archers.

Gordib asked, "Do you think he'll lower his banners?"

The meeting with Vinlon ended when Gordib swam to Brutez from the tribemaster's boat while young Jaspich swam the other way. Brutez would have sent Larboelm to the meeting if his bodyguard was a better swimmer.

"I don't know," said Grebnar. "The tribemaster likes his banners."

"I like his fortress," said Brutez. "I want one."

Puutnam asked, "Did you ask him how his tribe learned to build such a colossal structure?"

"Why would I? Why would he tell me?"

Larboelm called, "Look! One's coming down."

Brutez watched the first black ribbon descend within a backdrop of sunset colors, and then another and another, until only one remained, left flying from the highest point on the keep.

"Good enough." Brutez turned to Grebnar. "We'll withdraw in the morning, but I'm leaving a blooddrop to fly over this town."

Knowledge

Recorded Year 863

Mark of Cain

Hamuntht, Hojyimt

HAMUNTH   **CHIZDEK**

"My life is wrested from me."
"You were my keeper."
"Murder, you're guilty!"
The burgundy drops floated from the ground. The blood mouths accused him. They spoke with his brother's voice.
"Justice is required."
"The blood must be repaid!"

Chief Hamunth awoke and sat upright, sweating in his bed, scraping the stinging sore that was his birthmarksign. Blood covered his fingers.

Curses! For months he knew relief from the recurring dream that started tormenting him two years ago during his trip to the Swenikt. Now his hope to never have it again was dashed.

The dream returned at the worst time. This was the day he declared the fate of Buerosh, his son held in the dungeon. The young man's plot to become chief by arranging a stray arrow to kill him on his hunting trip was foiled by an informer within his son's cadre of friends.

He decided against descending to the depths to see Buerosh a last time, fearing his resolve would weaken. His oldest child must die, even if new dreams of blood, a son's blood, made accusations from the ground as in his other dream. Not only would Buerosh threaten Hamunth's life for as long as they both lived, the young man was a danger to his siblings born from different mothers, having slain his brother from the same mother.

Hamunth stepped outside to a terrace overlooking the Chizdek River where it flowed into the Chizdekyim Inlet. A town sprawled across the valley in a random arrangement of buildings roofed with carnelian tiles. The streets varied in width and pattern, fanning from a central plaza like a webspinster's snare.

The castle backing Hamunth's terrace was a wilting structure of loose stones, built by the Chizdekyimt centuries ago when they ruled from Chizdek. It rambled on the valley slope, a collection of walls and towers as mixed as the buildings in the town.

The sunrise tracked farther north with each day as they approached high summer, so when a sail caught Hamunth's attention northeastward on the inlet, the chief shielded his eyes with one hand for a better look. He saw a Kendulyim vessel, a craft with a cabin on deck astern, and oars plying the water from below. Returning inside, he sent Adam to the harbor.

Enoch joined him for breakfast, drinking and eating everything first to check for poison. Adam returned at midmorning, breathless and excited. He spoke in the Chizdekyim language. Jorgis, and a Druogoin named Hoj, came on the Kendulyim vessel, and they brought scrolls. This was an occasion to meet in the castle's great hall. Hamunth commanded that Jorgis and Hoj appear before him there.

The chief sat in a great stone chair, a sculpture of hooded serpents built into the wall. Hamunthyim banners hung from the stony mouths, giving the serpents amber forked tongues. Hamunth's part of the seat was carved from a tree stump set in the rock. The chief had cushions for his personal comfort. A golden-furred canine slept at his feet, and Enoch stood by.

The ceiling was high, at least twenty cubits, and supported by pillars lining both sides for forty cubits. The original stone roof collapsed generations ago and was replaced by timber. Ribbed daylight illuminated the hall, slanting through crevices in the stony walls on both sides. The vertical gaps were spaced five cubits apart, extending almost to the ceiling. They were boarded over in the winter.

Jorgis and Hoj entered, carrying armloads of scrolls. Adam brought as many as he could hold. Hamunth asked himself, *Didn't Jorgis leave with only two scrolls?*

The travelers stood before him in sandy brown pleated robes that were uncinched at the waist and reached midway between knees and ankles. The sleeves wrapped their arms tight to the elbows, and the cloth curled into collars at their necks.

Jorgis, who was supposed to marry Larzil, was thinner than he was during his previous visit to Chizdek. He seemed a decade older, although less than three years passed, gaining gray hairs in his beard and wrinkles on his face. His bald spot bared more scalp. He had a flatsnout skin flask slung over one shoulder.

The other man, Hoj, was younger and slightly shorter than his companion. He had faint freckles on his nose and cheeks, scraggly whiskers, and a full head of tan hair. His sapphire blue eyes blazed with an intensity belying his relaxed demeanor.

"Jorgis, you asked to marry my daughter your last time here." Hamunth enjoyed watching Jorgis squirm. The canine raised its head with a growl, startling Jorgis, but Hoj didn't flinch. Hamunth calmed the animal with a pat on its shoulder.

Jorgis composed himself to speak. "Chief Hamunth, I hope

to make amends with news of our quest and amazing discoveries. I'll understand if Larzil is given to another."

Taken, not given, Hamunth thought. He figured Jorgis must be desperate for news of the woman he was betrothed to marry. After waiting for two years, as did Larzil, the chief planned to keep the wayward bridegroom in suspense.

"When you missed your wedding, Chief Thoiren told me you went on a quest to translate some scrolls. Tell me about your journey."

Jorgis and Hoj stacked their scrolls on the stony floor in front of them. Adam came from behind to add his portion to the pile.

Jorgis began his tale. "I left the chief's longhouse near Pinkulda with my servant, Pokyer, and we were captured by the Druogoint. Hoj is Warlord Druogoin's grandson. He took an interest in my quest and supplanted Pokyer as my traveling companion."

"The scrolls enthralled me," said Hoj. "I was compelled to go."

Hamunth recalled, "Adam says they're written in an old language."

"The Iriack language," said Jorgis.

Hamunth tried to pronounce the difficult name. "Eereeak?" The Chizdekyim language had similar names with too many connecting sounds. This one even began with a connecting sound.

"You say it well, Chief," said Jorgis.

"Adam says his Chizdekyim language is based on this older language."

"Many languages are, including any spoken in the east."

"You must have traveled past Richee." Hamunth figured a journey taking three years went *somewhere* far.

"We went farther east than Kendul, crossing a sea to a vast land before we found anyone knowing the Iriack language."

"Did you learn the language?"

"Not to speak but to read."

"More than that," said Hoj. "Jorgis devised a way to write the translation in our language, the Snarshyim language."

Hamunth didn't want to misunderstand. "You're able to put Snarshyim words into scrolls like the Chizdekyimt do with their words?"

"I based the Snarshyim symbols on ones from the Iriack language," said Jorgis. "The symbols for all the languages having them—Chizdekyim, Kendulyim, Yarsishyim, and others—are based on Iriack ones."

Hamunth pointed over his sleeping canine to the pile of scrolls in front of the three men before him. "You left with two scrolls. What are these others?"

"We acquired some in Kendul, written in their language, and more written in the Iriack language." Hoj opened a hand over the pile and beheld Hamunth in his piercing sapphirine gaze. "Some of these are the translations into the Snarshyim language."

Hamunth stood, wakening the canine. "You must read from one to me!"

Hoj had the set jaw of a man with a purpose. He selected a scroll, a specific one because he took it after finding a blue tassel on its handle. "This one's translated from one of the two we took with us." He rolled it open. "It's the most important."

Hamunth returned to his seat. "Why do you say that?"

"Listen to the first sentence." Hoj read, "In the beginning God created the heavens and the earth."

"*Earth?*"

"The Iriack word is unclear," said Jorgis. "It can mean ground, land, or the entire surface of the world in which we live. I think of it as everything below, whereas *heavens* refers to everything above."

"I think of the earth as the seen, and the heavens as the unseen," said Hoj.

Hamunth asked, "Unseen, you mean like the wind?"

"I mean a spiritual dimension, which can't be seen the same as our physical dimension. The words in the scroll say

God created both."

Hamunth considered the words. *In the beginning God created the heavens and the earth.* "Which god?"

Hoj's eyes flared. "The one God."

The canine went to Hoj, who set down his scroll to pat the animal's head.

Hamunth was annoyed. His canine wasn't supposed to be friendly. "Adam tells me the Chizdekyimt pay homage to many gods."

"They're deceived," said Hoj. "For God to be God, he must be the only one."

Such as my tribe must have one chief, Hamunth thought. "One God makes sense."

"A one and true living triumvirate God."

Hamunth didn't know the meaning of *triumvirate*. "Triumphant?" He couldn't remember the word.

"Triumvirate. It's an Iriack word meaning a group of three."

"Now you say God is one and three. I'm confused."

"We can never fully understand God. We must accept what the words say." Hoj picked up the scroll he had set down. "This recounts how God created land and seas, plants, the sun and moon, stars, and animals. Then it quotes God saying, 'Let us make man in our image.' Note the plural referring to God. The words also say *he* created male and female, in particular one man and one woman, named Adam and Eve."

Hamunth exchanged looks with his Chizdekyim bodyguard standing behind Jorgis and Hoj. "Adam, you have the name of the first man."

"Our Chizdekyim names must come from the time of the scrolls," said Adam. "My mother's name was Eve. I wonder if anyone's named Enoch in there."

Enoch stirred beside Hamunth. The bodyguard had withdrawn into a stupor while listening to the Snarshyim language, which he didn't understand.

Hoj rolled the scroll more open and pointed to a spot on the parchment. "Here it says Enoch was Cain's son."

Hamunth asked, "Who was Cain?"

"He was the son of Adam and Eve who killed his brother."

Hamunth's birthmarksign flared. *Curses*, it burned. The birthmarksign tormented him, and he wanted to tear it from his chest. He clawed at it through his tunic. "What happened to him, Hoj?"

"God heard his brother's blood crying from the ground and cursed him."

"The same as I dream. My brother's blood speaks against me."

"God planted a moral code into your heart. You hear it in your dream, and you have a physical ailment to go with your inner conflict."

"My birthmarksign." Hamunth scraped it.

"The scroll says Cain told God his punishment was too great to bear. He feared he would be killed, so God marked him with a sign so nobody would slay him."

Hamunth bled through his tunic. "A birthmarksign?"

"The Mark of Cain. We all have one, being descended from Cain."

"What am I to do? My dream says I must repay in blood."

"Your tainted blood is worthless." Hoj stepped around the canine, and returned the blue-tasseled scroll to the pile of the others. "One of these is a scroll of traditions. It has words about the pure blood, the only blood worthy for repayment, poured by God."

"How do I get this blood?"

"The references are vague about the pure blood, but the traditions say sacrificing animals represents pouring it. That custom was replaced by a more convenient ritual."

Hamunth hoped the ritual was convenient enough to perform at once. His chest felt afire. "I want the ritual now."

Jorgis unslung the flask from his shoulder and gave it to Hoj.

"This contains fermented vinefruit." Hoj offered the flask. "Drink, Chief Hamunth. This is the pure blood, poured by

God for repayment."

Hamunth hoisted the spout to his lips. The biting liquid cooled his tongue and throat. When it reached inside his chest, the burning on his outer flesh cooled, too. After returning the flask to Hoj, he peeled away his tunic to examine his birthmarksign, which remained a bleeding mess, but it was soothed.

"You have my gratitude, Hoj."

"You owe your gratitude to God. You've been cleansed; God's free gift, and now you can consume the scroll and receive life."

Hamunth frowned. "Consume? You can't mean for me to eat it."

"I mean for you to allow what it says to transform your thinking."

"I must learn the Snarshyim symbols first."

"Jorgis and I are traveling onward, but we'll teach anyone who comes with us."

"I'll send Adam with you. He knows the Chizdekyim symbols, so learning the Snarshyim ones should be easy for him." Hamunth had refused his bodyguard's offers to teach him the Chizdekyim symbols, but he wanted to learn the Snarshyim ones from him. "I'll send my son, Fidrek, too." That would keep the boy away from the influence of anybody sympathetic to Buerosh, and he would learn something.

"I'm anxious to return to my father near Pinkulda," said Jorgis. "Will Adam and Fidrek be ready to go with us by tomorrow?"

Hamunth had unwelcome news for him from two years past. "The Herkt attacked Chief Thoiren's longhouse when I was there to hand over Larzil for marriage. They killed your father before my eyes. Kevyar is chief."

Eyes widened, Jorgis asked, "What happened to Larzil?"

"She survived."

"Where is she?"

"She lives in Chief Kevyar's household, waiting for a

husband if you'll have one another." Hamunth would say no more. Jorgis had a decision to make about Larzil, and best the choice not be presented to him until he was with her.

The chief had a decision to reconsider, which he did in his bedchamber after lunch. He fingered the straw-blond strands of Larzil's hair that Konrash cut from her head after he violated her. The decision soon was remade.

After some arrangements, he descended to the castle foundation. His son had an unusually comfortable accommodation for a dungeon, well lit with torches and furnished with a padded mattress bed and a table stocked with food and drink.

Buerosh's thick, bony brow gave him a fearsome presence. His black hair grew in a long tail from the center of his head, shaved on the sides by his ears. The young man snarled his question. "Father, are you here to kill me yourself?"

"I'll have no more blood accusing me from the ground. I'm sending you with the Kendulyimt to the slave market, but I'm keeping part of your body." Hamunth smirked as Buerosh turned white in the face. *Let him think he's getting the Chizdekyim way.* The chief only wanted his son's long tail of hair to keep as a memory with Larzil's straw-blond strands.

Consummated in Blood

Herkt, Feldramt

BRUTEZ   **AGRATUNA**

Brutez refrained from tears as Majdel embraced him. His heart leaped with joy to see his only remaining sibling after so many years. He forced a steady voice when he spoke. "Sister, I can't say how delighted I am to see you."

He wasn't sure the silver-haired woman with Aunt Yeemzal and his nephews, Sangern and Chrenlon, was her until she was introduced with her husband, Lord Chieftain Feldram, a raven-haired man leaning against a staff.

She asked, "How's Father?"

"Feeble," was all Brutez would say.

Zamtoth lost whatever remained of his spritely step after Heptor died. Although the old man became reconciled to a cordial relationship with his last living son, Brutez no longer discussed matters of the clan with him.

Tarberg, the lord chieftain's one-armed resident envoy at Taubueth, had led Brutez and fifteen others across the barren salt flat of Kradig on a flawless track to Agratuna, a town rebuilt since the Jatneryimt destroyed it. The visitors settled at an inn in town before coming by boat to meet their hosts on one of the coastal islands.

Brutez introduced the comely young woman with him. "Lord Chieftain and Lady Feldram, this is my lady wife, Beksel, daughter of Sir Grebnar the Bold, Lord of the Jatneryimt."

Beksel held a little boy's hand. Majdel stroked his dull red hair.

"Our son, your nephew," said Brutez.

"Your name is Brutez," Majdel said to the boy, who nodded.

Clanlord Brutez placed his hands on the shoulders of a slightly older blond-haired boy. "Here's another nephew."

The boy announced his name, "Heptor!"

Brutez went to young Heptor's mother and stepfather. The stepfather held a sleeping infant. "This is Nazzel and her husband, Larboelm, with their baby daughter."

The clanlord introduced one more family. "This is Puutnam, my wife's kinsman and Sir Grebnar's resident envoy at Taubueth, with his wife, Vel, and their daughter."

Brutez declined to introduce the warriors of his escort. The Feldramt would remember Rankeb and Konrash, who came to Agratuna with Uncle Shemjib, and perhaps they knew Jonerch and Gordib from their visit to Taubueth. They wouldn't know the warriors from the ridge, Vel's brother, Zzuz, and half brother, Vikth, whose wife and stepchildren were left at home.

Lord Chieftain Feldram invited all to the island lodge for supper. "I'm glad we get time together before the Chrevramt arrive."

The Chrevramt, the bride's family for Sangern's impending wedding, Brutez mused, glad for a chance to meet them.

He dreaded seeing Aunt Yeemzal. *Did she still blame him for her husband's demise?* They met before supper, standing at the rail overlooking the Snarshyim Inlet.

"I sent Shemjib to his death." Brutez didn't know what else to say.

Yeemzal's thick, long gray hair blew in the wind as she gazed over the water. "You married our enemy's daughter."

He gulped. "I'm sorry."

She locked blue eyes on him and scolded, "Why are you sorry? You made peace. No battles have been fought in our part of the land for two years. You could travel here in safety, bringing babies."

"I'm sorry you're angry."

"I'm not angry at you. I'm angry Shemjib was our last casualty fighting the Jatneryimt. I'm angry each time I crawl into a lonely bed, and I miss him."

Brutez dared to ask, "This winter Beksel is expecting another child. If we have a son, do we have your blessing to name him Shemjib?"

"My dear nephew, nothing would please me more."

WIKSTON   AGRATUNA

Wikston listened to Tribelord Boewin argue with his father.

"I keep telling you, Cousin, the Yarsishyimt will reach Neshim by the end of summer. You must help me fight them."

The argument hadn't changed since Boewin arrived at Biepazz, Wikston supposed, and continued while Boewin's family joined Wikston's to travel to Agratuna for his sister Zabfrul's wedding. Wikston was glad to have missed the arguing, being sent ahead by boat to tell the bridegroom's father, Lord Chieftain Feldram, the Chrevramt were delayed while waiting for the Boewint to come from Neshim.

His father Lord Chrevram responded, "They were peaceful until you attacked them. I warned you I wouldn't become involved."

Now Wikston had Boewin's finger pointing at him. "I know the problem," said his father's cousin. "This son of yours likes the Yarsishyimt too much."

Too true, Wikston thought. The Yarsishyimt were friendly and ate well. He enjoyed his two years with them northward in the Langech peninsula learning stonecraft and seeing a pretty green-eyed blond girl.

"He's here now to fulfill his obligation," said his father.

The obligation, Wikston lamented, one that couldn't be postponed any longer. He was required to choose a second cousin to marry. Although his sister knew Boewin's four daughters, he didn't because he was living with the Yarsishyimt when the Boewint visited Biepazz three years ago. Zabfrul claimed they were pretty. Wikston considered the task could be pleasant selecting which pretty maiden would share his wedding bed.

Boewin beckoned, "Come, boy."

Boy, indeed, Wikston bristled within. He was nineteen, a man. Even so, he dutifully followed Tribelord Boewin, leaving his father behind at the harbor inn where the Chrevramt stayed at Agratuna.

They passed an inn with a blooddrop pennant hanging from its signpost, where the Herkt stayed, and came to one flying the sapphire blue tassels of the Boewint. Boewin paused by the door. The tribelord had an imposing stature, but Wikston refused to be intimidated. He never saw a man growing hair in as many places as Boewin, even where he shouldn't, such as the backs of his hands.

"The oldest two are twins." Boewin talked about his daughters. "I warn you. If you pick one of them, the other might be jealous, and you'll have to marry both."

Of course he jested, at least so Wikston hoped. If marrying a second cousin didn't seem proper, marrying twice certainly wasn't.

Boewin continued, "The youngest doesn't flow yet, so you must be willing to wait if you want her."

His wife, Lady Boewin, waited inside the common room's door. She was an excited, stout woman, babbling about how long she waited for this wonderful day.

"Go away, woman," Boewin told her. "Our future wedlock son doesn't need you flustering him. Go back and send in his choices, one by one."

He invited Wikston to join him at a table and ordered brew for them both.

The twins arrived together. Boewin growled, since he wanted them to come one by one. Wikston never would have thought the pair was twins. One was short and the other tall. Their hair was different shades of brown. Although he didn't consider them ugly, he thought they appeared ordinary.

The third daughter was more comely in the face, brown-eyed and black-haired, but Wikston suspected the body hidden under her loose-fitting gown wasn't as slender as most girls her age and would grow larger with age, like her mother's. He liked her cheerful disposition more than her skittish twin sisters', but not the obnoxious squeal she had for laughter.

His last hope remained with the youngest daughter. He almost resolved to choose her unseen, reasoning circumstances could change while he waited for her to come of age so he wouldn't have to marry any of Boewin's daughters. When the girl showed herself, she was too decidedly ugly for him to take the risk.

After the last daughter departed Boewin faced him across the table over their tankards of brew. "Which one?"

Wikston didn't want to answer—and he had a legitimate objection. "I don't know them." Their father hadn't bothered to tell him their names.

Boewin folded his hands around his tankard and leaned forward with a menacing stare from his hairy face. His voice became more foreboding, speaking in a mutter, "We're men talking here. You know as well as I do, we consider a woman's appearance, and then we know. Your loins should know which one they want."

The problem for Wikston was his loins didn't want any of them.

Boewin continued, "I grant you a short while to decide.

You'll have a chance to spend time with my daughters at the wedding. Your sister knows them. Ask her which one she prefers to have for a wedlock sister."

Wikston already decided. He didn't want Tribelord Boewin to be his wedlock father.

Brutez   Agratuna

"It is not good for a man to be alone."

Brutez watched Sangern stand between his parents, saying the ancient words. The bridegroom wore a tan jerkin, brown breeches, and black boots. A blast of thunder overwhelmed Lord Chieftain Feldram's response about his son getting a helper. Rain pelted the island lodge's thatch roof.

Lord and Lady Chrevram released their daughter's hands for her to cross the room and join hands with Sangern, who would be her husband when he finished reciting the ancient words. Even the drab brown of her wedding garment, the color of her new tribe, the Feldramt, looked appealing on her lithe form. A waving cascade of honey-blond hair poured to the middle of her back.

"This is bone of my bones, and flesh of my flesh. For this reason a man shall leave his father and mother, and be joined to his wife, and we shall become one flesh."

The feast began. Brutez sat with the other Herkt, between the Boewint and Chrevramt, on the side of the room nearest the Snarshyim Inlet. Tribelord Boewin and Lord Chieftain Feldram started an animated conversation across the room. Sensing trouble, Brutez commanded his warriors to refrain from drinking much brew and approached the two other leaders.

"I told you some were killed," Boewin was saying. "The rest are fighting for me. Some took Boewinyim wives."

"I refuse to believe so few of my warriors wanted to

return to their own tribe," said Feldram. He acknowledged Brutez arriving. "Clanlord Wedlock Brother, we're discussing the warriors Majdel brought with her to Biepazz when she arranged this wedding. My tribe was short on means to feed everybody after the Jatneryim raid, so the warriors were sent with my cousin here to fight the mountain clans."

"That fight ended two years ago." Brutez knew Grebnar negotiated peace between Mosik and Boewin.

"My cousin's been using my warriors to fight the Yarsishyimt in the Langech peninsula. I don't want them fighting the Yarsishyimt."

"They choose to fight," said Boewin. "See for yourself, Clanlord Brutez, with your mighty Herkyim warriors. You speak about the Snarshyim clans and tribes becoming one people, so help me purge from our lands these Yarsishyimt who speak another language."

Brutez wasn't sure he wanted to be embroiled in that fight and certainly didn't want to discuss the matter at a wedding. "Let's talk about this another time."

He convinced Boewin to return to the table by his kin where the tribelord increased his intake of brew, but only after urging Feldram to leave so the argument would end. Anticipating more trouble, Brutez returned to his seat and reminded his Herkyim warriors to keep refraining from brew.

The trouble came when Boewin stumbled under the influence of brew across to the Chrevramt, shouting for all to hear, "This wedding's done!" He stopped behind the chair of a young, curly blond-haired man whom Brutez remembered was the bride's brother, Wikston.

"Here's the bridegroom for the next one." Boewin placed his hands on Wikston's shoulders. "We only need a bride. Tell us, my boy. Who is she? Which one of my daughters do you choose?"

Wikston flinched from his touch.

"Why don't you choose? Are none of my daughters pretty enough?"

Brutez gripped the cudgel at his side and watched his men, all seven, reaching for weapons. *Good.*

Lord Chrevram, a short, gaunt man, confronted his cousin. "Tribelord Boewin, stop harassing my son."

Boewin backed away, giving Brutez hope that the situation would diffuse, but the tribelord's tirade resumed. "Why don't you call me *cousin*? I'm the kin you won't help against invaders." He stumbled toward the newlywed couple, motioning to the bride, Zabfrul. "Your son thinks my daughters are ugly, and you have this stunning beauty for a daughter."

Brutez saw metal in his hand and leaped from his seat, followed by his warriors.

"What if I make her ugly, too?" Boewin's arm swung, and blood squirted from Zabfrul's face as the dagger in his hand sliced across her cheek and mouth.

Women and girls screamed. Small children cried. Chairs tumbled to the plank flooring, and tables of food and drink overturned in a crash of broken pottery as warriors from all sides came to their feet, drawing weapons.

The Herkt had the lead against the others.

"Protect our families," Brutez commanded Larboelm.

The massive bodyguard shielded Beksel and Nazzel with their children behind his body and spiked mace. Puutnam huddled with Vel and their daughter.

Brutez led his other warriors to interpose between the Feldramyim and Chrevramyim warriors about to engage in a bloodbath against Tribelord Boewin and his warriors. Although outnumbered, the Herkt were sober and most everyone else was not. They also were mighty, as Boewin called them. Order was restored without more bloodshed. Brutez held Boewin, arms pinned behind his back, more for his protection than to restrain him, because Sangern was coming with a meat cleaver.

"Come no closer, Nephew," he warned the bridegroom. "I'll club you senseless."

"Clanlord Uncle, he maimed my wife!" Sangern yelled, but

stopped there.

Wikston also came, holding daggers in both hands. Brutez's menacing glare warned him away.

Zabfrul wailed on the floor, hands over her face, blood everywhere, a wedding consummated in blood and tears. Aunt Yeemzal was with her, and Brutez called over Beksel to assist while their little boy, Brutez, stayed with Larboelm.

The opposing warriors were disarmed and herded into tribal groups away from one another. All women and children were cleared from the room, including Yeemzal and Beksel with Zabfrul.

Brutez floored Boewin with a punch in the jaw. *The cursed fool*, he thought. The man was desperate to find husbands for his daughters, and Brutez had three warriors here who needed wives, five if Rankeb and Konrash still had loins. Something could have been arranged. The clanlord had watched Zzuz showing interest in Boewin's black-haired daughter.

He had instead the vexing task of maintaining peace. The Boewint must leave, and the Feldramt and Chrevramt wouldn't want them passing free through their lands. Brutez stood over Boewin prone on the floor. "My warriors will go with me to escort the Boewint home. I need someone to show me the way."

Lord Chrevram waved forward a sandy-haired and bearded man. "Steebnaf will guide you."

Lord Chieftain Feldram spoke, "While you're gone with your men, Wedlock Brother, your women and children will be our honored guests. We owe you much for preventing tribal war."

Kill Grebnar

Jatneryimt

Sejel   **Black Citadel, Mapvin**

"We must kill Grebnar."

The words Sejel heard from below froze her in place on the stairs. Fear gripped her throat, and she resisted an urge to flee.

Another voice, a young man's voice, asked, "When?"

"When we have the most favorable odds for our survival," said the first voice, a gruff one. "The Boldness is a fearsome warrior."

The voices came from around a corner, down the stairs carved into the rock of the Black Citadel. They echoed off craggy walls, allowing Sejel to hear every word. A growling stomach had her awake early, sooner than her chambermaid expected, so she was descending to the kitchen in her bedclothes for something to eat.

"He'll inspect the citadel after he returns, perhaps alone."

"That will be the best chance to ambush him."

Those were two more voices, one lilting and one raspy. *How many were there?*

"We need a remote spot, somewhere on the backside," said

the gruff voice.

"Not by the hot spring," said the lilting one.

The hot spring was Sejel's favorite part of the Black Citadel, where she could soak in sweaty warm water to her neck. She didn't like much else about the place.

"Agreed, too many people there," said the raspy voice. "How about attacking from the dark well?"

"A good place for an ambush," said the gruff one. "The dungeon's empty, so no guards are down there."

Sejel heard enough. She took a first step upward, slow and careful, heart pounding and barely daring to breathe.

The youthful voice asked, "What if the Boldness has too many men with him?"

Sejel climbed more lava rock steps, one by one.

"He won't," said the lilting voice.

A scullion came from the top of the stairs with a banging of the pots she carried.

The gruff voice shouted, "Who's there?"

Footsteps sounded from around the corner below. Sejel sprinted for the top to the outside and mingled into a fortuitous group of wash maids going past. She fretted. *Did any of the conspirators see her?*

Grebnar hadn't wanted her to come to the Black Citadel, but she knew he rarely would travel the distance to Doenesh while fighting Matkulk. He made regular stops here at Mapvin, and was due for another appearance any day.

The danger of the Black Citadel, why her husband wanted her to stay at Doenesh, suddenly was distressingly apparent. At the Green Citadel, she knew whom to trust. She could have gone to her cousin Tersol's husband in the garrison. Nobody at the Black Citadel was familiar to her except the chambermaid. Most of the garrison certainly was loyal to Grebnar, but Sejel dared not go to any of them, not knowing which few plotted against her husband. She left the wash maids to return to her chamber.

Cursed Matkulk! Sejel knew he instigated the plot. He should have been killed two years ago when Grebnar and Mosik from the largest mountain clan almost had him, but the Warnekt invaded and he found refuge with a rival mountain clan, the one that was his mother's. He was familiar with that clan after growing to manhood there, according to what Grebnar told her about Matkulk's life. When Matkulk's father, the Lord of the Black Citadel, discovered he had a son, he invaded that clan and killed Matkulk's mother before the young man's eyes and brought him to Mapvin to live as a Jatneryim.

Sejel pondered, *How come I know more about Matkulk's early life than my husband's?* Grebnar claimed to have no knowledge of his parents and family. He was an orphan who became a mighty warrior, won the hand of his leader's sister, and became Lord of the Jatneryimt.

She encountered the chambermaid outside her door, returning with an empty chamber pot. The hunched-over old woman had her head wrapped within a green and black scarf Grebnar gave her. She was deaf and couldn't speak. Sejel changed into her day clothes while the other woman worked on the bed.

After the maid departed, Sejel realized how foolish she was to be alone. If any of those men saw who she was, her life was in mortal danger. The grip of fear returned, and she lowered the beam behind the door to make herself secure within the chamber.

She sat on her bed to settle the panic from her mind. How could she warn her husband about the plot against him? She decided she should leave a message in case she couldn't tell him herself, and the message must be one *only* Grebnar would understand.

Although no fire burned in the hearth on the near-summer day, old coals remained, and the walls of the chamber were gray stone, rather than black lava rock. Taking a sooty piece from the cold hearth, she used it to draw rings and chains on the wall in the same place relative to the bed as the shackles in the chamber where Grebnar was imprisoned at Taubueth.

That would get his attention, but provide no clear message. She moved a table to the same spot where the one was at Taubueth and rubbed the coal on one edge, leaving an obscure mark that would get her husband's attention when the drawing on the wall compelled him to investigate. Tipping the table on its side, she sketched an oblong oval and a looping line on the bottom to represent the ridge and the Black Citadel's half wall of lava rock. She put a final clue, a crossmark, where the conspirators planned their ambush at the dark well, and turned the table upright.

Remaining locked within her chamber until her husband's return wasn't feasible, but she determined to spend any time outside her quarters with as many other people as possible. Her door had a viewport, and she waited for some women and children to pass by outside before venturing out.

She spent all day with groups, usually women, but also anywhere enough men congregated for her to be certain all of them couldn't be conspirators, which was the case at mealtimes. She listened to the voices of the men when they talked, not knowing what she would do if she recognized any of the group she overheard.

The sun was setting, leaving the Black Citadel in the ridge's shadow, when she retired to her chamber. She brought along wash maids for cover, including some she mingled with that morning, under the premise of giving them clothes to be laundered. The deaf chambermaid came to prepare her bed, and Sejel gave her discreet motions not to clean the coal markings from the wall, and to leave the table where she placed it.

She secured the door after the other women left and reclined on her bed in the dark, trying to calm herself enough to fall asleep. If only her husband would return. She longed for tomorrow to be the day he did.

Faint taps attracted her attention, which she figured to be a small rodent before realizing someone knocked on her door. Resisting a wave of fear, she peered through the viewport and relaxed. A hunched figure with the look of the old chambermaid, wearing a green and black scarf, stood under the light of a torch ensconced in the wall outside. Sejel opened the door.

The figure loomed larger, and a hand clamped over her mouth before she could scream. The assailant held her helpless within his grasp, leaving her no opportunity to scratch or kick him. She saw his face for a moment in the torchlight, gnarled like the bark of an old tree with a wart on one cheek like a knothole.

Having entered the chamber, he kicked the door closed and dragged her to the bed. He flung her there, keeping his hand over her face, and straddled her.

"Don't worry about me violating you." He was the one with the gruff voice. "I'm doing that after I kill you."

She squirmed and thrashed. A pillow pressed over her face. Her mouth gaped wide, sucking for breath, but she took in nothing but linen and feathers. Her lungs burned as if fire flamed within them. She faded, falling asleep, and her struggle ended.

Consummated in Tears

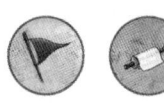

Swenikt, Hojyimt

Jorgis   **near Pinkulda**

"Here's a map of our travels." Jorgis unrolled a scroll on a table before Chief Kevyar sitting across from him.

"This looks like the one you showed me before you left." Kevyar placed a finger on the spot near Pinkulda. His once-wedlock brother, Davlek, leaned over one shoulder, and his mother, Befdaul, stood over the other, holding her weanling grandson, Thoiren.

"A copy," said Jorgis. "I didn't want to draw the path we took on the original." He indicated a red line that squiggled in a large loop all over the map. "I updated it from the original to show the lands the way they are today, writing the names in the Snarshyim language."

Kevyar opened his mouth in wonder. "How's that possible, Jorgis?"

"I devised Snarshyim symbols like the Chizdekyim language and others have. Each sound in our language has a symbol, twenty-two framing sounds and fifteen connecting ones."

Befdaul asked, "What do you mean by framing and connecting sounds?" Young Thoiren squirmed in her arms, and she let him go.

"Consider our names. Jorgis, Befdaul, Kevyar, and Davlek all have two parts, and each part has a connecting sound between two framing sounds."

"My name is the same except it has only one part," said Hoj. He stood by Jorgis with Adam and Chief Hamunth's son, Fidrek.

"Look here where it says Pinkulda." Jorgis pointed to the spot on the map. "The name has three parts, but the last part has no framing sound at the end so it's written with eight symbols."

"It's a Chizdekyim name," said Adam. "Our names often start or end with connecting sounds, like mine starts with one."

Kevyar asked, "Does every Snarshyim word have symbols?"

"Each word is some combination of the thirty-seven framing and connecting sounds," said Jorgis.

"How many of these scrolls in your pile are translated into our language?"

"All."

"Chief, your son," said Hoj.

Jorgis looked to where his companion pointed and was horrified to see the little boy unrolling a scroll from the pile.

Kevyar commanded, "Mother, take him to Jankwel. Then bring Larzil here."

The mention of Larzil renewed the intense anticipation within Jorgis that became more unbearable as the years of waiting to rejoin his betrothed wife became months, weeks, days, and now *moments*. His emotions included anxiety. What did Chief Hamunth mean by saying Larzil waited for him—*if they would have one another?*

Befdaul grabbed Thoiren and snatched the parchment from his hands. The boy responded with a tantrum, and his grandmother took him away.

Jorgis was glad to be rid of the young child. "We hoped to get the scrolls translated in Richee," he said. "The Richeeyimt speak a dialect of the Kendulyim language, but they told us the scrolls are written in an older language they don't know, the Iriack language."

Kevyar tried to say the name. "Eereek?"

"Iriack. We don't have multiple connecting sounds in the Snarshyim language, so they're difficult to say. Hoj and I learned how to say them during our winter in Richee. That's when we learned the Kendulyim language well enough to use as we traveled."

Kevyar pointed at the red line on the map passing through Richee, and followed it eastward across a strait between the Pultanik Ocean and a giant inland bay. His finger reached the tip of a peninsula coming from the north, bounded by the bay westward and a companion sea to the ocean eastward.

"You went here," he said.

"That's Kendul. Although the Kendulyimt and Richeeyimt speak nearly the same language, they're enemies. We had to take a neutral vessel to get there." Jorgis pointed along the red line where it followed the peninsula northward from Kevyar's finger. "We traveled the full length of Kendul and found nobody who knew the Iriack language."

A mountain range along the entire peninsula continued northward beyond the reach of the westside bay. The great eastern desert ended at the same mountains Chief Thoiren noticed when Jorgis showed him the original map. The sea still bordered Kendul eastward on the opposite side of the mountains from the desert. The map showed a separate large landmass farther east across the sea.

Jorgis moved his finger to the end of the mountains, from where a river flowed westward to the end of the Chizdekyim Inlet. Then he traced the red line as it turned eastward to the end of another peninsula.

This peninsula was a long phallic nose on a coast with

the likeness of a face. Two protrusions of land farther south resembled a pair of lips, and the coast farther north was shaped like an eye socket and a forehead. The nose nearly reached the other landmass across the sea where the red line crossed a narrow strait.

"We went farther east." Jorgis placed his hand over the eastern landmass. "These lands were the core of the Iriack Empire."

Kevyar asked, "This empire no longer exists?"

"It collapsed centuries ago about the time the scrolls that Pokyer found were hidden in the cave. The Iriack language hasn't been widely used for centuries."

"That's why we weren't finding anybody who knew it," said Hoj. "Then we heard about the Iriack Masters living in a city named Filok."

"Flok," said Kevyar.

His pronunciation was off, but Jorgis withheld comment. He pointed to the easternmost extension of the red line on the map, a good distance overland within the interior of the eastern land mass. "Filok was the northern capital of the Iriack Empire." He tapped the spot. "Today it's the capital of a kingdom named Sokeel. We stayed there almost a year with the Iriack Masters."

Kevyar opened his mouth, and Jorgis supposed he was about to ask who were the Iriack Masters, but Hoj preempted him with the answer. "The Masters are keepers of the knowledge of the Iriack Empire, including the language. They taught us how to translate the scrolls."

"What do they say?"

The question came from Befdaul as she returned from taking away young Thoiren. Jorgis wondered, *Where's Larzil?*

"The scroll with the original map recounts the westward expansion of the Iriack Empire," said Hoj. "The empire reached our lands six centuries ago, but our Snarshyim ancestors weren't living here."

"Mine were," said Adam.

"The Chizdekyimt were the original inhabitants of this land," said Jorgis.

Kevyar asked, "What about the scroll you took with you that had the pictures?"

Hoj placed a hand on the scroll with a blue tassel. "These are the words of the one and only God."

"Why is this God the one and only?"

"Only he self-exists."

"He created all else simply by speaking," said Jorgis.

"He has all power and knowledge, and is present everywhere at once," said Hoj.

"My Chizdekyim gods are worthless compared to the self-existing God," said Adam. "He's everlasting, unbound by time."

Kevyar asked, "If this God is so great, why doesn't anybody know about him?"

Hoj answered, "The first man and woman rebelled against God's sovereign authority, and their descendants chose to forget him."

"The scroll tells us about five generations from our ancestor Cain to a man named Lamech and his family," said Jorgis.

Kevyar asked, "That's it, nothing beyond that?"

"It has another lineage from Cain's brother, Seth, to a man named Noah and his three sons."

"Do any of these other scrolls tell us about the time between our earliest ancestors mentioned in God's words and the Iriack Empire?"

"No, but they contain plenty of other useful knowledge." Jorgis picked through the pile. "The Iriack Empire developed laws and methods of calculations. The imperial scholars studied the skies and recorded their observations." He found the scroll he wanted. "This one translated from the Kendulyim language describes how to make something like parchment from trees, called paper."

"We have plenty of trees for making paper," said Kevyar. "I have twelve more scrolls to translate that the Herkt didn't destroy."

"Clanlord Brutez has another one," said Adam.

"Somebody must go to Taubueth and tell him to bring it here." Kevyar nudged his once-wedlock brother, who hadn't spoken a word. "A good mission for you, Davlek."

Davlek made a guttural sound, a mix between a grunt and a groan.

"I hate thinking about the lost knowledge in the twelve burned scrolls," said Jorgis.

Kevyar motioned to the pile. "You brought plenty more. How did you carry them from Flok?"

"The Iriack Masters sent servants with us." Jorgis traced the red line of the return journey with his finger on the map. "We returned to Kendul and followed this river from the mountains to the Chizdekyim Inlet. The servants left us there, returning to Filok, and we boarded a Kendulyim vessel for Chizdek."

"A dangerous journey," said Befdaul. "You traveled a great distance."

Jorgis understood her reasoning, since travel through Snarshyim lands never was safe, at least before Clanlord Brutez brought peace between the clans and tribes. "Lady Befdaul, we passed through stable kingdoms now hospitable to travelers."

Farther east, beyond Sokeel, wasn't so stable, where petty lords fought one another to expand their lands.

"We were under God's protection," said Hoj. "He has a purpose to become known by the people of our land. We were destined to return."

Kevyar leaned with one hand on the table. "Jorgis, do you believe what he says about this great God?"

"Absolutely."

Kevyar regarded Jorgis with a steely gaze. "He didn't protect Larzil. You believe in him after what happened to her?"

Jorgis was stricken with dread. "What happened?"

"Didn't Chief Hamunth tell you?"

"He only told me she's waiting for me."

Kevyar asked Befdaul, "Mother, where's Larzil?"

"She refused to come."

"Have Jankwel convince her to see us," said Kevyar. "Everybody else go, too. I must speak with Jorgis alone. Davlek, get the twelve scrolls from under my bed for Hoj."

When everyone was gone, leaving Jorgis with Kevyar, the chief extracted a pouch from a fold in his tunic and tossed it over the map.

"Chief Hamunth left these for me to give you. I thought he told you."

Jorgis dug into the pouch, feeling fleshy soft pieces within, and extracted shriveled loins.

"From the two Herkt who violated Larzil."

Disgusted, Jorgis stuffed the loins back into the pouch and tucked the package into a fold of his robe.

Kevyar continued, "Larzil has a son. We don't know which Herk, Rankeb or Konrash, is the father. Neither will sire another child. You and Larzil must decide what you're going to do."

Jorgis remembered Chief Hamunth's words, their meaning coming known to him at last. *She lives in Chief Kevyar's household, waiting for a husband, if you'll have one another.* Jorgis knew his decision; his anxiety came from not knowing Larzil's. "I'm staying here," he said. "Whether or not I marry Larzil, my journey is done. Hoj will leave for Ranjin in a few days without me."

Hoj planned to go alone, an easy trip drifting down the Tauzzreen River in a one-man boat.

Jorgis continued, "Adam and Fidrek are staying until I finish teaching them the Snarshyim symbols. Then they'll return to Chizdek to teach Chief Hamunth."

"I want you to teach me," said Kevyar.

Jorgis was glad, thinking the more Snarshyimt who learned their new written language, the better. Then they could send messages to one another on paper, as did the eastern peoples. Knowledge would be retained in writing, including knowledge of the one and true God.

Kevyar continued, "Hoj spoke about his destiny. I wonder about mine. I had a dream, I think the same as the vision my father saw when he died."

"The one God sometimes shows us things in dreams or visions," said Jorgis. "What did you see?"

Kevyar told him about a giant red tree full of nineteen sterling crowns and a golden one, a tree with a magnificent city and leaves changing from Herkyim blooddrops to scarlet versions of the Swenikyim triangle pennants. Jorgis knew what it meant. He didn't know how but simply did. God must have put the meaning into his mind.

"The dream is clear about a Swenikyim line of kings."

"I thought so," said Kevyar.

"Herkyim kings rule first. The nineteen sterling crowns mean there will be that many Swenikyim kings. The golden crown is God's kingdom in the spiritual dimension. Our physical kingdoms are a mere representation of his authority."

"What about the city?"

"I think it represents a physical city and a spiritual one." Then Jorgis reconsidered. "The second city is more real than the first. It will last forever."

"If it's the last thing my father saw, it made him smile. I want to ask him."

"You can't."

"The Chizdekyimt think I can."

"Hoj and I discussed this with Adam, and he agrees his people are being deceived when they think they're communicating with the deceased."

"Who's deceiving them?"

"Dark spiritual forces," said Jorgis.

Kevyar looked distressed. "Then I never can get my father's forgiveness."

"Not true. The one living God is the source of all forgiveness. He forgives with the pure blood. The pure blood is a mystery, but we have a ritual to receive it."

Jorgis offered Kevyar the flask of fermented vinefruit. "Drink, Chief Kevyar. This is the pure blood, poured by God for forgiveness."

Larzil arrived with Kevyar's wife, Jankwel, surprising Jorgis with her drastic change in appearance. She had no more hair on her head than Hoj did. The long straw-blond strands were gone, and her body had become as scrawny as her arms and legs.

"I'll wait outside," said Kevyar, leaving the room.

Jorgis wanted to embrace Larzil after waiting three years, but she wouldn't look at him, staring at the floor. "Larzil, I want you to be my wife. I'll take your son as my own child."

She buried her face into her hands. Jorgis didn't think she was crying, but she almost was.

Jankwel wrapped an arm around Larzil's shoulder. "Go with Kevyar. He's outside the door. Jorgis only wanted to see you. You waited so long to see one another. You'll see him later, and soon, won't you?"

Larzil nodded, and Jankwel guided her out the door.

Kevyar's wife returned with words for Jorgis. "When she birthed the child, she wouldn't hold her son. I was the baby's wetnurse. Larzil later learned to love the boy more than anyone in the world, and so her love for you will come anew."

"What's the boy's name?"

"He doesn't have a name. You can name him when you become his father."

Jorgis walked alone outside to think. His quarters were a two-room log house Kevyar gave the four travelers from Chizdek. It was part of a new timber-walled town built on an island in the Tauzzreen River a short distance downstream from the older town where half of the tribal longhouse remained. Kevyar had a new three-room longhouse built in the center of the island's town. A Swenikyim cobalt blue triangle flew over the central room.

Jorgis walked out the town's western gate to the river's edge, gazing over the tranquil water under a late afternoon sun. He asked the one and true God some questions. *Why was an innocent young woman forced to become a mother? Why was Chief Thoiren killed? Why did a God with all power, knowledge, and presence allow anything bad to happen in the world?*

The words of the living God came to mind, bringing more questions. Jorgis knew they came from God. *Why did the first Adam eat the forbidden fruit? Why did his wife believe the deceiver?* God's questions answered his own. Nothing done by evil men was God's choice. God gave each man, woman, and child the freedom to choose.

Jorgis flung the pouch of loins into the river.

Returning to the quarters, he found his three companions looking through Kevyar's twelve scrolls, although Hoj was the only one able to read the Iriack language.

"Some of these have the same knowledge as our other ones." Hoj held up a scroll. "This one describes celestial observations. Nelber will be excited to study it."

They already had a scroll from the Iriack Masters about the nighttime sky, translated into the Snarshyim language. Each translation had two copies so Jorgis and Hoj both had one after they separated.

Hoj held up another scroll. "Here's another copy of the traditions."

Disappointed, Jorgis asked, "Did you find anything new?"

Hoj pointed with the scroll in his hand at the stack of the others. "One of these describes how to improve the harvest by changing the crops planted in the same soil through different years."

Valuable knowledge, Jorgis told himself, but uninteresting.

His stomach was gaining interest for supper, so he welcomed a knock on the door, hoping for a meal call. He saw Kevyar and Jankwel, knowing they weren't there to announce food. Larzil followed, looking at the floor.

"Larzil has something to say," said Kevyar.

Hoj motioned for Adam and Fidrek to leave with him.

Kevyar raised a hand. "Stay."

Larzil raised her head, and Jorgis looked into her blue-gray eyes for the first time in three years. They were moist to the brink of tears. He longed to see her smile.

"Jorgis, I want to be your wife, but I don't want a wedding."

He wondered, *What does she mean about not wanting a wedding?* Even so, he couldn't stop smiling.

She continued, "You must say the words, of course, but I don't want any feast or celebration. I want to become your wife before anybody leaves this room."

"It is not good for a man to be alone." Jorgis recited the ancient words.

Whenever a bridegroom said them, nobody knew from where they came. Saying them himself, Jorgis knew he quoted the words of the one and true living God, spoken before he created a wife for the first man.

Kevyar asked Larzil, "Who will say your father's words? You consider Jankwel to be your mother, and I'm her husband, so I can say them."

"You're from my betrothed husband's household," she said. "I wear your color."

Jorgis admonished himself. He didn't notice she changed to a cobalt blue gown for her second visit to him that day.

"Somebody from my father's household must say the words," said Larzil. "I want Adam to say them."

Adam had tears in his eyes. No doubt he felt honored, especially since he never would have his own daughter to offer for marriage. The Chizdekyim's voice quavered. "You will have a helper suitable for you."

Jorgis quoted the first bridegroom, adding some words forgotten over time. "This is bone of my bones, and flesh of my flesh. She shall be called Woman, because she was taken out of Man. For this reason a man shall leave his father and his mother, and be joined to his wife; and we shall become one flesh."

At that moment, he became a husband and a father. The question about when he would meet his son was answered after Kevyar called outside to his mother. Befdaul entered with a weanling light-haired boy.

"Jorgis, your son needs a name," said Kevyar.

Jorgis had one. "The first man and woman had a son who was innocent and loved by God. This boy, my son, is innocent and loved by God, and so his name is Abel."

Kevyar motioned for his mother to leave with Abel. "You'll see more of your son tomorrow. Spend the rest of this day with your wife." He invited Hoj, Adam, and Fidrek to go with him to alternate quarters.

Jorgis reminded Hoj to take Kevyar's scrolls to resume studying.

Jankwel lingered after the others left. "Supper will be sent," she said before leaving.

The first moments alone with Larzil were awkward. Her reticence discouraged Jorgis from asking her about life with the Swenikt, and he resorted to giving her a monologue about his travels with Hoj and their discoveries. During supper he offered to teach her the Snarshyim symbols he devised. She surrendered a first small smile, and his heart soared.

She became skittish and distraught as the time neared for retiring to bed. He coaxed her to sit next to him fully clothed on the edge of their straw mattress.

"Larzil, you decide when to give yourself to me."

His loins were ready, but she wasn't. Her body shook, and she wept holding her face in both hands. He wrapped an arm around her and pulled her to him, with her head under his chin, on his wedding night that was consummated in tears.

The Biggest

Herkt

BRUTEZ　　　　　　　　　　　**BIEPAZZ**

Brutez craned his neck to examine the stony ceiling of the hall at Biepazz. His wonder mixed with angst. *How does the weighty rock stay up there?* He sat between Jonerch and Puutnam on the male side of the long supper table according to the Chrevramyim seating arrangement by age.

Lord Chrevram hadn't returned from the bay, where he was fishing with his son, Wikston, when the Herkt arrived at Biepazz that afternoon, so Brutez went in the older direction from his seat to consult the guide he had followed since Agratuna. "I admire your lord's hall, Steebnaf. Where did the knowledge come from to build this place?"

"The Yarsishyimt built it."

"It doesn't look that old." Brutez thought about Taubueth, another place built by previous inhabitants of the land.

"They built it for Lord Chrevram's grandfather."

Brutez wondered if he could get Yarsishyimt to build the mighty structure he wanted since seeing Tribemaster

Warnek's fortress at Pultanik. He waited for Lord Chrevram to arrive. The short, gaunt man came with his son midway through the meal, leaving Wikston at the younger end of the table.

Brutez intercepted him going to the older end. "Lord Chrevram, when did you return from Agratuna?"

"A few days ago, Clanlord. How was your journey with my quarrelsome cousin who I no longer consider to be my cousin?"

Brutez considered the days traveling with Tribelord Boewin. "I restrained myself from killing him."

Chrevram accepted a full tankard from a server. "You have more restraint than most men."

Brutez waited while he gulped his entire serving of brew.

Chrevram then resumed talking. "You kept one of his daughters."

Brutez heard the squealing laughter coming from Boewin's black-haired daughter downtable. "My man, Zzuz, took her. Boewin should have been happy to find a husband for a daughter, but he was upset Jonerch and Gordib didn't want the twins."

"He refuses to be happy," said Chrevram. "I've never seen him smile. Did you go to Neshim for this momentous occasion, the wedding of a Boewinyim daughter?"

"We left the Boewint at the border of their lands."

"How was my man, Steebnaf, as a guide?"

"He showed us the best way."

To skip past Biepazz while traveling with the Boewint, Steebnaf deviated from the usual route along the western coast of the Snarshyim Inlet by leading them inland through the Swanshyim Forest. When they reached a river, called the Biepazz River because of where it flowed, they resumed the path toward Neshim. After parting from the Boewint, Steebnaf led the Herkt downstream to Biepazz.

"Steebnaf knows the land," said Chrevram. "He likes going places."

Good. Brutez intended to ask about Steebnaf going to Taubueth as a resident envoy, but first he wanted to discuss building a stone fortress. "Steebnaf told me the Yarsishyimt built this place. Could I get them to build something for me?"

"Ask my son, who lived with them. He knows their stonemasters."

Brutez went to Wikston. "I want the Yarsishyimt to build me a stone fortress at Taubueth."

"They'll teach you," said Wikston. "Send some men with me, and I'll translate."

"You're returning to the Yarsishyimt?"

"Why not? I no longer must marry a Boewin."

Brutez considered which men to send. *Ones without families,* he decided.

Wikston asked, "What size fortress do you want?"

"The biggest."

Consummated in Love

Feldramt

SANGERN **AGRATUNA**

From the moment Sangern beheld the Snarshyim Inlet, he knew this was the day. The water was smooth as a Yarsishyim mirror, and somewhat as reflective. The young man saw the same scattered clouds shimmering in the sea as in the sky. The day already was hot under a summer sun, even better for what he planned.

He left the water's edge and passed through the lodge to the commons among the cluster of the island's buildings, all built from white bark trees. Finding Aunt Yeemzal, he enlisted her to make preparations. He went to his quarters for a change of clothes, putting on the same tan leather jerkin and tight-fitting breeches he wore on the days he became betrothed to Zabfrul and married her. The items practically were new, only the third time he used them. He remained barefoot instead of wearing the black leather boots.

Yeemzal told him all was ready, and he crossed the commons to meet his maiden wife for the day. She waited, sitting in a sleeveless gown of her favorite color, teal. The veil covering her lower face was the same shade. Her honey-golden hair appeared fresh-washed, adding curl to the long wavy tresses. Sangern was pleased. Yeemzal had given Zabfrul notice he was coming, and she looked fabulous.

"Dearest wife, how are you feeling?"

Too many of her days were spent with his two aunts, the healers, Yeemzal and Beksel, but the weeks of the worst pain seemed to be past, at least her physical pain.

"I'm weary of being inside these quarters," she said.

Sangern smiled, almost a smirk, knowing how she would respond to his next question. "Will you join me for a picnic on the water?"

He didn't see her smile behind the veil, but he saw it in her eyes, pools of azure beckoning him.

"I would find that pleasing."

He led her to the shore, and where the ground became rocky he lifted her into his arms, although her soft-soled slippers were more footwear than he had, which was none. His pulse quickened from contacting her body, warm against his and scented by some pheromatic ointment from Aunt Yeemzal. He considered Zabfrul's bare, slender arms wrapped over his shoulders, and fancied seeing more of her.

They reached a small pier and a rowboat.

"Sangern, this is delightful."

He had to agree with his wife. Yeemzal exceeded his expectations for making preparations. The boat was furnished with enough pillows and blankets to fill its entire bottom. Sangern set Zabfrul's slippered feet on the pier and assisted her boarding the craft. He found a jug of brew onboard with a basketful of bread, cheese, sausage, butter, nuts, and berries. Not a boatload of food, he judged, but loaded enough.

Zabfrul reclined on pillows and blankets in the prow. He rowed the boat on the tranquil Snarshyim Inlet. The sun reached high, and he sweated. Pausing from the oars, he unlashed his jerkin and removed it. Rowing again, he feigned not to notice Zabfrul's eyes fixed on him, admiring his physique, although he supposed he didn't fool her. She knew he enjoyed her admiration. He contemplated that's how the pleasure worked, feeding on the other's pleasure.

She rubbed her feet against one another to remove her slippers. The teal folds of her gown lifted above her knees, teasing Sangern with her shapely legs, and she dangled her feet into the water. She leaned on one arm and arched her back, presenting a rounder sight of her breasts. Her golden hair draped away from her body, curling on the bedding below her. She was, as Sangern once told his mother, a vision.

No other boats on the inlet were close to their inshore position by the island. Sangern rowed around an outcropping of white bark trees hanging over the water into the middle of a secluded cove and tossed the boat's anchor overboard to hold them there.

He stood, legs parted to maintain balance. "Zabfrul, my dear lady wife, are you thinking like a maiden today?"

"Dearest husband, I must confess to having no maidenly thoughts since I saw you arrive in your wedding clothes."

He gazed over his birthmarksign, down his bare torso to his breeches. "I have only half left."

"What are you saying? I must beg to see the rest of you? What about our lunch? Aren't you hungry?"

He hungered but not for food, and he was ready to end his fast of two years. "Zabfrul, you're unkind to taunt me."

She swung her legs into the boat and turned forward to the prow with her back to him, sitting on pillows and holding her knees. "My love, I think you're unfair to be the only one bared in this heat."

His heart pounded and his breathing deepened. Her head swayed, and tendrils of golden hair brushed her back. He lifted the honey-blond locks forward over a shoulder, then untied and unclasped the fasteners of her gown, starting at the neck and going down. She wore no bodice underneath. Sunshine glared from the smooth copper skin between her shoulders, for the rowboat's stern was placed closest to the hot orb in the sky. The sun's rays came from their highest point of the day over the white bark trees that cordoned the cove in a ring of shade.

The two halves of the gown clung to Zabfrul's shoulders as the garment parted. Sangern continued down, delighting in his unhindered view of her narrowing torso. He reached the last knot and clasp where her hips widened, then traced the crease of her bared back on two fingers of one hand, going up. She shivered under the tingle of his touch. He stroked the back of her neck before tapping there to let her know the next step was hers.

She flipped the waving length of hair to her back and extracted her shoulders from the hold of the gown. The garment dropped away, and Sangern's anticipation escalated. She spun on her buttocks in the pillows, presenting herself unclothed to the waist. The gown covered her hips, and her legs folded at her knees.

She spoke from behind the veil, "This is fair, isn't it?"

Fair indeed, he agreed, but half measures wouldn't suffice. He tugged the hem of the gown down by her ankles.

"You want more than fair," she said, laughing, a delightful sound. She wriggled the teal wrapping from her hips and upraised thighs over her knees.

Sangern did the rest, pulling the cloth from her ankles. He beheld copper skin, gleaming in daylight, slender legs and form, her curves, the points on her body that were ready, and the place she had for him. He recalled his words from the day he met her. *Mother, she's a vision!*

He wanted more, or to better put it, less. He wanted to see nothing on her—and the veil was *something*. "Zabfrul, you don't need the veil."

The sparkle in her eyes saddened, and her voice wavered. "Sangern, my face is marred."

He looked to the sunny sky, scattered with puffy clouds. "Look up with me, Zabfrul. What do you see?"

"I see the sun and clouds."

"Do you remember that first day? It was as fair as the maiden who captured my heart, not a cloud in the sky."

"I remember, a glorious day."

"Is this day with some clouds any less fair? My dearest lady wife, as the sun shines this day with some clouds, your beauty outshines your marred face."

He saw tears glisten in her eyes, tears of happiness, not sadness. She reached behind to release the veil. The gossamer teal cloth fell from her face.

The wound was reddened and healing. It gashed across one cheek, sliced her lower lip by the corner of her mouth, and nipped the middle of her upper lip. He delighted that her cute dainty nose was untouched. His heart leaped. None of her body was hidden from him.

"Zabfrul, you're a vision."

"This isn't fair. How come I don't get to see all of you?"

He had to be fair. He reached by his bulging loins to undo the breeches and pulled them off. She reclined on the pillows and blankets, head by the rowboat's prow, and opened a path between her legs for him to approach. He nestled over her, propped on his arms to withhold a portion of his weight from her, and his face came to hers.

The wound wasn't healed enough for him to kiss her mouth, so he planted a path of kisses from her brow to her unmarred cheek. He nibbled her ear. While there he whispered, "We'll create life together."

He moved his attention downward. He touched, caressed, licked, fingered, and prodded. Watching her respond to the pleasure he gave her thrilled him. He wouldn't join with her until she begged.

"Sangern, now," she gasped. Then she howled, "Now!"

They were one flesh. He found the places within and without to heighten her pleasure. He was most pleased when she was pleased. That's how the pleasure worked. The rowboat rocked, not side-to-side but prow to stern.

"Sangern, my love," she cried out, and after that, she no

longer could say anything.

She did something that enraptured him, and he wondered how a maiden knew to do *that*. Lady Chrevram did her mother's duty and taught her daughter well, or maybe Aunt Yeemzal told her to do *that*. He cried out in his mind. *Zabfrul, I'm yours!*

He cried out, "Zabfrul!"

His marriage was consummated in love.

Hojyim Colors

Druogoint, Hojyimt

HOJ   **RANJIN**

Hoj saw the Tauzzreen River breaking into channels as he reached the isles of Ranjin. How convenient that he arrived in a boat, he mused, because he would need it to move about the Druogoinyim settlement.

During the trip, he had hauled the craft from the river at night. It wasn't much longer than he needed to sleep inside. His scrolls were sealed within ceramic jars that would float if the boat overturned.

He paddled toward his mother's isle under an overcast sky. The isle once was his grandfather's, but he knew Warlord Druogoin was dead because Chief Kevyar told him. Kevyar also mentioned pink trapezoid banners, which Hoj saw flying from the buildings. He docked at the neighboring isle where he had lived with his mother and sister before his long journey. Seeing nobody nearby, he reluctantly left the jars full of scrolls untended in the boat and approached the three circular huts on the small plot of land.

The center thatch-roofed structure used to be his mother's,

and he supposed his sister lived there now. He entered the side hut that had been his quarters. Although not surprised to find his belongings were moved, he didn't expect to see a small boy sleeping in a child's pen. He guessed the blond-haired child to be two years old.

The boy's eyes blinked open before Hoj could retreat outside. Hoj didn't want him to be alarmed, so he smiled and waved. "Little boy. What's your name?"

The boy stood, smiled, and waved.

Hoj asked again, "What's your name?"

"Toush."

Hoj realized the boy was in his family. Toush was the name of his deceased uncle. He wondered, *How does my sister have a son?* He heard footsteps and his sister's voice in the connecting passage from the center hut.

"Toush, are you awake?"

"I'm here with the man."

"What man?"

Thigrel arrived in a worried flurry of wispy red hair. She saw Hoj and lunged to him for an embrace. Hoj didn't remember she could squeeze so hard. He felt a lump in her belly and knew Toush was getting a brother or sister.

She released him and lifted Toush from his pen. "Look, Toush." She held him in one arm. "This is Uncle Hoj."

The boy waved. "Hoj."

"My husband's not here," said Thigrel. "He's helping Nelber."

Hoj supposed her husband was Nelber's son, thinking Kulm was somewhat old for his sister. "Your husband?"

"Pokyer."

Pokyer! Hoj didn't expect the passive fellow to have the gumption. A more stunning thought struck him. *Pokyer is my wedlock brother.* "Pokyer," he said, as if saying the name aloud made the reality more real.

"Hoj, have you seen Mother?"

"I'm going to her now, but I'll return for supper."

He crossed to his mother's isle over the bridge, which was lined with pink banners. When he rapped on the doorpost to her long hut, which he previously knew as his grandfather's place, Grapnef appeared wearing only breeches. He had the ugliest birthmarksign Hoj ever saw, twice as lumpy, and looking like a clump of maggots.

"*You*," he said with a snarl. His tone would have made more sense for greeting a regular nuisance, rather than somebody gone for three years. He rubbed an eye with the stub on his hand missing the thumb. "Your mother's getting dressed."

Mother hasn't changed, Hoj thought, going to bed in the middle of the day. Evidently Grapnef regained her favor and Pershnig no longer had it, although Hoj couldn't exclude the possibility they both had it—and maybe together.

She came out dressed in pink, of course, showing parts of her body Hoj didn't want to see. Nor did she display any shame for appearing so before her son, but at least her flaming red tresses covered some spots.

She spoke in a level voice, "Hoj, I surrendered all hope of seeing you again."

Not the emotional greeting he expected. The mother he knew would have put him into a more crushing embrace than Thigrel's, although given the current state of her undress, he was glad she didn't.

"Jorgis and I traveled a vast distance," he said.

His mother showed no interest, watching Grapnef return to the bedchamber. Hoj was dismayed. Didn't she wonder where he went? Didn't she want to know if the scrolls were translated, and what words were in them? What would she think about writing words in the Snarshyim language?

Hoj knew who would listen. "Mother, I'm going to Nelber."

"You should see your sister."

"I did, and I met my nephew."

"My grandson." Hoj's mother tossed her long red tendrils. "I don't look like a grandmother, do I?"

Hoj turned away to leave. "I'm eating supper with Thigrel

if you want to join us."

He encountered a brighter day, the result of the clouds breaking apart, and he sweated while paddling his boat to Nelber's isle. Nelber sat on the shore, holding a brew and propping his feet on the barrel containing his refills. Pokyer was nowhere to be seen.

Nelber lurched to stand when he saw Hoj. "Did you translate the two scrolls?"

"Every word." Hoj pointed to the jars in his boat. "I brought others."

Nelber chortled and rubbed his hands together in glee. He helped to haul the boat ashore and to unload the jars. Hoj asked for a mallet and broke the ceramic pots. Nelber collected the scrolls, handling them with care like the treasures they were, and stacked them in a neat pile by his barrel of brew. He gathered a second mug and another stool from his premises, and offered Hoj a seat with an invitation to the brew.

"Tell me all." Nelber sat with a refill.

Hoj took the scroll with the blue tassel. "These are the words of the all-powerful, all-knowing, and ever-present God."

"My son should hear this."

While Nelber went to Kulm's isle, Hoj checked to ensure he had all the scrolls and sorted them into an arrangement he could remember.

Kulm arrived, taller than his father and barrel-chested. His dark brown hair was tamer than his sire's, and he had no beard. He had a perpetually calm disposition and bright, cheery, blue-gray eyes.

Nelber resumed his seat with a brew. "Let's hear the words of the all-powerful God."

Kulm declined tapping from the barrel and sat cross-legged on the turf.

Hoj read the scroll from beginning to end, the first words even said, "In the beginning," and the last ones were the names of Noah's sons. Nelber and Kulm listened in rapt attention, remaining silent after Hoj finished.

Hoj said nothing, allowing the men to think about what they heard.

Nelber raised his hands. "I've looked up many nights and wondered about the all-knowing and ever-present God. I didn't know to call him that, but I knew he was there. I want to declare fealty to this God. Do you have a ceremony?"

Hoj remembered something in the traditions. "One of these other scrolls mentions one. I'll study it and let you know."

Nelber nudged his son. "He's going to study."

Kulm was wide-eyed.

"I'm impressed," said Nelber. "The scroll is written in another language, but you read it in the Snarshyim language."

Hoj smiled. "This copy is written in the Snarshyim language."

Nelber dropped his brew and nearly tipped from his stool. Kulm's serene expression didn't change, as if a written Snarshyim language was no more surprising than watching the river flow.

Nelber went behind Hoj to look. "The scribbles look the same as before."

"Jorgis based these symbols on the originals when he devised them for our language," said Hoj.

"You must teach them to me, so I can read God's words."

"I'll teach anybody who wants to learn."

"Read God's words again."

Hoj did, starting with "In the beginning," while Nelber watched over his shoulder. Nelber asked him to repeat some words about cursing a serpent.

"I declare war between you and the woman, and between your seed and her seed; he shall crush your head, and you shall bruise him on the heel."

Nelber asked, "What does that mean?"

"It's a prediction," said Hoj. "We won't know the full meaning until it happens."

"The woman's seed must be one of her descendants, one of us."

"He beats the serpent that enticed the first man and woman to disobey God, stomping its head."

"A mortal wound," said Nelber.

Hoj read the rest of God's words, ending with "Shem, Ham, and Japheth."

"This is remarkable to have these words recorded in our language," said Nelber. "What's in the other scrolls?"

"These two will fascinate you." Hoj pointed to a pair on the ground. "They describe what we see in the sky."

Nelber picked up one. "You're right. I *am* fascinated."

"That one's translated from one Jorgis and I acquired during our journey. It has a means for naming the days of the year."

"How so?"

"Each moon cycle is split into two seventeen-day periods, which are named. The four extra days—deep winter, high summer, and the two days when daylight equals night—are interspersed by five half cycles of the moon between each."

Nelber set down the scroll. He frowned and twittered his fingers, doing calculations. "I see. That makes sense."

"That scroll also describes the timings of the wandering stars," said Hoj.

"What about the moonstar?"

"One curious passage says it appeared a thousand years ago."

"A thousand years." Nelber seemed awed by the number.

"The Swenikt have twelve more scrolls." Hoj took the other scroll that described the sky. "I convinced Chief Kevyar to let me take this one. I haven't translated it yet. Maybe it will tell us more about the moonstar."

A growling stomach told him to return to his sister's for supper, but Nelber compelled him to stay by producing fresh crustaceans from his vast supply of food. *Cursed Nelber*, he thought. *He knows crustaceans are my favorite food.*

While Kulm built a fire to boil water, Nelber asked, "Hoj, how did the Pink Lady react to your return?"

Although amused by the term for his mother, Hoj

maintained a stoic expression.

"I'm sorry." Nelber wrung his hands. "I should call her Lady Gernthol."

"She was strangely *unpleased* to see me."

"Understandable. She's grown fond of leading the tribe in the name of Toush, your nephew."

Hoj rubbed his scraggly chin, realizing the sense of Nelber's assessment. His return meant he was warlord, not needing anyone to lead in his name.

While the crustaceans boiled, he took out his copy of the map showing the red line of his journey, and told Nelber and Kulm about his travels. He talked about the Iriack Empire throughout the meal, and afterward, read from the scroll about the empire's westward expansion. As daylight waned, he collected the two scrolls with God's words and the traditions to take with him.

"Keep the rest safe, Nelber."

Nelber's mouth gaped as if he was entrusted with a pile of gold.

Having missed supper with Thigrel, Hoj stopped to see the most skilled clothier of the Druogoint, rather than return to his sister. Hoj's sandy brown pleated robe from Kendul was tattered and riddled with holes, and it stank. The clothier gave him a new tunic and breeches, but Hoj wanted another robe and had a particular desire for its colors. The man promised to have it ready by midday tomorrow.

Returning to his sister's isle, Hoj found Thigrel readying Toush for bed. "I was with Nelber," he told her to explain missing supper. "He likes talking."

"Pokyer says that, too."

Where is Pokyer? Hoj didn't care, so he didn't ask. He had a different question. "Did Mother come for supper?"

Thigrel shook her head. "When the servants brought supper, they told me Mother was eating with Grapnef and two other men."

Three men! Hoj decided not to see his mother that evening.

Toush asked for a bedding story, so Hoj volunteered to give him one. He unrolled the scroll with God's words and began reading, "In the beginning, God created the heavens and the earth."

NELBER   **RANJIN**

Curses, where's Hoj? Nelber asked himself while eating lunch with Kulm outside his hut. He considered the pile of scrolls secured within his abode, desperate to know more about what was in them, and was frustrated he couldn't read them.

He was rolling the day's barrel of brew, ready to spend another hot afternoon relaxing by the water's edge, when he spotted Hoj approaching in his one-man boat. The Pink Lady's son wore a new robe, much like his old one, except its colors. The uncinched waist, hemline between the knees and ankles, and sleeves wrapped tight above the elbows, were the same, but the new garment was black, not a good color for a hot day, and the pleats were cursed pink.

Nelber propped the barrel upright next to his stool. "You put on *your mother's* color?" He hoped with Hoj as leader, the Druogoinyim banners would revert to orange.

Hoj paddled the last few cubits to the shore. "My father's color, too."

The Warnekyim black, Nelber realized. *Since when did Hoj consider the father he hated?* "You're finally here, Hoj. Half the day is gone."

Hoj hauled his boat from the water. "Nelber, you asked me about a ceremony for declaring fealty to God. I read the traditions this morning until I found it."

Nelber rubbed his hands together. "What must be done?" He expected an elaborate process.

"A ritual drowning, called the Water Ritual."

"What does it mean?"

"Adam and Eve brought death upon themselves, and all of us as their descendants, when they disobeyed God."

Nelber waved for his son to come over from cleaning up after lunch.

Hoj continued, "He's a God of infinite love, so he longs to restore us to life."

Kulm arrived to listen, watching with wistful wide eyes.

"We must die to be restored. The pure blood is the death making that possible. The Water Ritual is a ritual death, a burial in the water, so we can begin to be restored during this life, a down payment for the new life we get after we die."

Nelber considered his aging body, the soreness in the morning, his waning hearing, his intermittent stream, his loins no longer as active as he liked, and a myriad of other ailments. He could use some restoration but supposed Hoj meant a different kind.

Whatever it meant, Nelber wanted to declare fealty to the all-powerful God. "Let's do it."

Hoj stepped into the channel. "Come."

Nelber followed, standing in waist-deep water. Hoj held him under, saying words he couldn't understand from below the surface. He heard some after Hoj let him up.

"You're cleansed and ready to live a new life."

Nelber looked at his son.

"I want the ritual," said Kulm.

Hoj held out an inviting hand. While he dunked Kulm, Nelber heard him speak the words of the Water Ritual. "Kulm, I drown you with pure blood in the name of the triumvirate God. Rise, you're cleansed and ready to live a new life."

Kulm stood dripping from the top of his head as did Nelber. "Do I get a robe?"

No, Kulm, Nelber wrung his wet hands. Hoj's robe had nothing to do with the all-knowing God. The man merely wore the colors of his parents.

Hoj asked, "Do you want one?"

Kulm's wide smile told Nelber his son would be honored

to wear what he thought to be the garment of the ever-present God. Nelber wouldn't deny his son the honor.

"I'll wear one, too. We'll wear your Hojyim colors."

HOJ   RANJIN

"I like your new robe, but an all-pink one would be better."

Never, Mother, Hoj thought. He was glad she wore more pink than the last time he saw her. Her gown covered everything, including her neck.

"I'm wearing pink and black, your color and Father's. I no longer consider myself merely a Druogoin or a Warnek."

They stood on the bridge between their two isles where they met when both were crossing to look for the other. The sun was setting into a band of clouds over a channel between two neighboring isles.

"You're not a Warnek."

"I'm going to see Father."

He expected anger from her and saw cold fury in her jade eyes, but her voice remained calm. "Why would you see the cursed man who murdered your grandfather?"

"During my travels I encountered the infinitely loving God. He reconciles with me, so I must reconcile with Father."

"You're no longer my son." She wasn't angry but on verge of tears. "I've lost you."

"I *am* your son, which means I lead this tribe." Hoj saw coldness return to his mother's eyes.

"You can't be our leader. You told me a moment ago you're not a Druogoin."

"Mother, listen to what I'm saying. I'm leaving to see Father, and I don't know when I'll return. You'll lead the tribe in *my* name instead of Toush's."

His forearm rested on the bridge's railing, and she clutched it with bony fingers. "The banners," she said. A line of pink trapezoids draped over the railing.

"You decide their color in my name."

She embraced him. "I see your plan, Hoj. Your father is so desperate to see you, he'll be careless. You'll get a chance to avenge your grandfather."

Her hatred saddened Hoj, and he lamented that for too many years he did the same. He would go to his father, Vinlon, Tribemaster of the Warnekt, and listen to him.

Written in the Snarshyim Language

Herkt, Jatneryimt

BRUTEZ   **TAUBUETH**

Brutez returned to Taubueth with same number of traveling companions as when he left. Jonerch, Gordib, Rankeb, and Konrash were gone north with Wikston to the Yarsishyimt in the Langech peninsula. Steebnaf, his wife and adolescent daughter, and Zzuz's wife with her annoying laughter, replaced them in the group. Steebnaf was coming to be Lord Chrevram's resident envoy at Taubueth.

    The stronghold stood across a thousand cubits of open space under a hot summer sun. The felled forest was put to good use for constructing a ring of solid timber buildings around the outer wall, and a ramp up the wall that was suitable for mounts. The ramshackle old buildings once nestled among the former trees were gone. Even with new buildings, Brutez considered Taubueth to be an unworthy seat of his power as clanlord, and inadequate for housing resident envoys. He wanted a larger stone fortress.

A Jatneryim green and black banner flew over Puutnam's residence, and Brutez supposed a messenger from Grebnar waited there. Another house had a Swenikyim cobalt blue triangle. Brutez wanted to see the guest from the Swenikt, who might bring news of translated scrolls, and told Vikth to bring him to his quarters before supper. He would wait until the meal to see Grebnar's messenger.

Arriving home in the donjon basement quarters with Beksel and their travelworn young son, Brutez took the crabby boy to the bedchamber for a nap and found his father asleep. Seeing the white-haired old man cheered little Brutez, who curled next to his grandfather on the bed. Grown Brutez had envy because he wanted a nap.

The Jatneryim at Puutnam's house was no messenger but Grebnar himself, who came to the clanlord's quarters with Puutnam. His grim expression, thin-lipped and misty-eyed, filled Brutez with dread. Beksel embraced her father, and he clung to her. Brutez figured the news must be bad for Grebnar to deliver it himself. The father broke away from his daughter and asked her to sit.

"Dear daughter, your mother's dead."

She dropped to the furred floor in a sobbing heap. Brutez and Grebnar went to her, almost colliding. They coaxed her to stand, each holding an arm. Brutez allowed Grebnar to take her. He held her next, wiping tears from her face.

"You can be proud of your mother, Beksel," said Grebnar. "She warned me about a plot against my life, and Matkulk's men killed her at the Black Citadel. I knew where to expect the ambush, and none of my attackers survived."

He snapped his fingers. Puutnam handed him a flat, floppy item, which he passed to Brutez. It was wrinkled skin with a wart, and Brutez thought he should recognize it.

"I flayed that from the leader's face as he screamed for mercy," said Grebnar. "I gave him as little as possible."

Brutez remembered. He was holding part of the tree bark face of the man who captured him and brought him to the Black Citadel. Not wanting it, he returned it to Grebnar.

Grebnar waved the skin in one hand. "I won't rest until I've done the same to Matkulk, cursed be his name."

Vikth arrived with a lanky balding man.

"Clanlord, this is Davlek from the Swenikt. He was married to Chief Thoiren's daughter before she died."

"Chief Kevyar wants you to know Jorgis returned," said Davlek.

Vikth flinched, seeing Grebnar, and saw Beksel's red swollen face streaked with tears. "Should we return later?"

Brutez wanted them to stay, but his wife needed comfort. She made his decision, speaking in a choked voice, "I want to hear about the scrolls."

Brutez smiled. He couldn't have a better wife. "I want all the envoys to hear." He commanded Vikth to find Tarberg and Steebnaf for a meeting in the hall upstairs.

Davlek stepped forward with a sheet of parchment. "This message comes from Jorgis."

Brutez took the sheet, covered with scribbles like the scroll already in his possession. "What does it say?"

"I don't read much yet, but Jorgis told me what he wrote. It says, 'Greetings Brutez, Clanlord of the Herkt, I can translate the scroll in your possession. This message is written in the Snarshyim language.'"

"It looks the same as the Old Language."

"Jorgis altered the symbols so our language can use them."

Brutez showed the sheet to Beksel. Grebnar's mouth gaped.

"Show me, Davlek." Brutez flattened the parchment on the table. "Which symbols say my name?"

"They're grouped by words." Davlek pointed at the sheet. "The words start here."

Brutez understood. Davlek's finger covered *Greetings*, so the next group of symbols was his name. He saw five symbols. The first was a circle with a hook, the next pointed up in three spots, the third went across and down, the fourth pointed up in two spots, and the last was a hook below a line.

σ ω ⌐ ᴧ ⊂

Mesmerized by seeing his name in writing, he took his dagger and carved a copy of the symbols into the table. He set the blade on the surface alongside the carving.

"This discussion should continue with Tarberg and Steebnaf upstairs."

Brutez asked Puutnam to show Davlek the way, and they left. Beksel went to the next room to check their son, leaving Brutez alone with Grebnar.

"That fellow Davlek was here when I arrived," said Grebnar. "He refused to meet with me."

"How long ago did you get here, Wedlock Father?"

"A week. Your father told me you were a month late returning from Agratuna, so I waited."

"I went to Biepazz," said Brutez, and he told Grebnar why.

"Boewin is fortunate you're so restrained." Grebnar raised the skin in his hand. "I would have flayed his face."

Then the tribes would be at war, reasoned Brutez.

Grebnar continued, "I'll have no restraint when I catch Matkulk."

Brutez asked, "Are you close to getting him?"

For two years, Matkulk's demise seemed close, but didn't happen.

"He's elusive," said Grebnar. "You know that."

Brutez remembered. Last year, he led the Herkt, together with Grebnar and the Jatneryimt, into the mountains. They joined forces with Mosik, the leader of the largest mountain clan, to subdue the clan Matkulk was born into, but Matkulk escaped.

Grebnar continued, "The peoples in the west who don't speak the Snarshyim language are attacking Jatneryim lands. I think Matkulk is living among them."

Curses! Matkulk's demise wasn't getting any closer, Brutez fretted. "How can I help?" He joined forces well with Grebnar last year, sometimes leading his wedlock father's warriors, but was reluctant to go on another campaign because he wanted to take his scroll to Jorgis for translation.

"Let me borrow some warriors," said Grebnar. "You should go to the Swenikt with the scroll."

That's exactly what Brutez wanted to do. "How will you use my men?"

"I'll put them on the Kipneesh River to watch the Warnekt, so I can send more of my warriors to the west."

Done, Brutez concluded a deal with his wedlock father. He would pass through Lake Shore on the way east and send a contingent to Vikth on the ridge. Vikth could lead them from there with ridge warriors to the nearby Kipneesh River.

Beksel returned with their son and Zamtoth, the grandfather the boy knew, to see the other grandfather. Grebnar last saw little Brutez during the year of his birth, although his wife saw their grandson twice a year. Sejel traveled to Taubueth each spring, and Beksel took young Brutez to Doenesh in autumn.

The boy was confused by being introduced to a second grandfather, and he pointed at Zamtoth, saying, "Grandfather."

Beksel motioned toward Grebnar. "This man is your other grandfather, Brutez."

The boy pointed again at Zamtoth. "He's Grandfather. Where's Grandmother?"

Beksel sat in a chair with her son on her lap, tears flowing again. "My dear son, you won't see your grandmother again."

Name Change

Warnekt, Hojyimt

NELBER   **NANCH**

Nelber found his son, Kulm, where he had spent much of the voyage, at the rail overlooking the Richeeyim vessel's prow. Fascinated by the sea, Kulm found wonder in every new sight, having never traveled before.

The bay at Habergenefinanch opened before them as they moved past the last barrier island. Their pink and black robes buffeted in the wind blowing through the passage, but the air and waves calmed after the vessel passed through.

Kulm pointed at a gap in the shoreline foliage. "Habergenefinanch, Father?"

Nelber nodded, seeing indistinct structures, some dull gray, and the rest gleaming white in sunlight. The Richeeyimt reported for more than a year the Warnekt were rebuilding Habergenefinanch, but they never mentioned that the old, highly flammable wooden town was being replaced by one constructed from stone.

Hoj knew their dialect of the Kendulyim language. He told the gap-toothed captain about the one and true living God and translated a copy of God's words to give him in his language.

Nelber rather wanted Hoj to translate more of the scroll from Chief Kevyar. It didn't mention the moonstar but described calculations with angles that determined the distance to the moon was ninety thousand horizons. Ninety thousand horizons!

The scroll claimed the world was a ball eight thousand horizons around, circling the sun. Nelber made some sense of the diagrams explaining the spatial relationships causing the moon to phase, but he determined to study them after he returned to land, experimenting with balls around a lighted torch.

The Richeeyimt rowed their vessel to a spot to drop anchor, and Nelber went ashore with Kulm and Hoj by boat. The three men in pink and black robes carried armloads and sacks full of scrolls. The new stone wall of Habergenefinanch was almost completed, and they approached the main gate.

Hoj asked a sentry, "Is Tribemaster Warnek here?"

"Who are you?"

"We're the Hojyimt," said Nelber. "The tribemaster will want to see us."

VINLON   NANCH

"The Hojyimt?" Vinlon repeated what the sentry told him, and wondered, *Who are these men calling themselves by my son's name?* He sat within his residence, a temporary wood structure until the stoneworkers finished his place that wouldn't burn, and anticipated lunch. "What do they look like?"

"They're wearing pink and black robes."

A curiosity, Vinlon thought, but it told him nothing. "What about their physical appearance?"

"One is somewhat old."

Somewhat old? Vinlon fumed. *What does that mean? Is he old or not?*

The sentry continued, "The tallest one is younger, but not young. The youngest seems to be the leader."

"This young leader." Vinlon was curt, wanting details. "What color is his hair? What about his eyes?"

"His hair is some lighter color. I don't remember his eyes."

Vinlon chided himself. Why did he hope the young man was his son who hated him? Hoj wouldn't come to him. The men were calling themselves Hojyimt to taunt him. He was about to order the sentry to send them away when he noticed him holding a cylindrical object. "What's that, a scroll?"

"The young one told me to give you this." The sentry handed Vinlon the roll.

The tribemaster didn't bother opening it, knowing he would see only meaningless scribbles. "Do you know how the men arrived here?"

"They came with the Richeeyimt."

They came from Richee! Vinlon guessed one of them could be Jorgis, the Swenik his son joined on a journey to translate some scrolls three years ago. Jorgis would have good sense not to return with Hoj to Ranjin to the duplicitous Druogoint, and have to pass through Warnekyim lands to get home.

Vinlon saw opportunity to improve his relations with the Swenikt to the detriment of his wife, who led the Druogoint. "Bring the Hojyimt to me."

Hoj   Nanch

The sentry led the way to a wood structure, one of many scattered within Habergenefinanch. Although the outer wall was almost completed, not much stonework was built yet inside the town.

Hoj asked Nelber, "Will my father recognize you?"

"He should. I was there when he killed your grandfather,

but don't worry. He won't notice me when he sees you."

Hoj was filled with excitement and angst. His father hadn't seen him since he was a boy. *How would he react?* He paused outside the door where the sentry left him with his companions. Then he knocked. The door opened, and the father he hadn't seen for thirteen years stood there.

Vinlon saw past Hoj. "Nelber, what the curses are you doing here?" The surprise passed in a moment, and then he brandished a sword in one hand and a dagger in the other.

Hoj supposed his father thought they were Druogoinyim assassins, wearing pink and black. "Father, Nelber's with me."

Vinlon paused. "Hoj, is that you?" The tribemaster studied Hoj's features, and he lowered his two blades. "It *is* you." He stepped aside from the doorway. "Hoj!"

Hoj entered with his load of scrolls. He didn't need to signal Nelber and Kulm to remain outside with theirs. Nelber had the sense to stay where he was, and his son followed his cue.

The room had no floor, only hard-packed ground, and was sparsely furnished with a table and a single chair. A comely blond woman occupied the chair in one corner, feeding an infant. Hoj supposed he was about to meet a stepmother, younger than himself, with a half sibling. He unburdened his scrolls on the half of the table without a pitcher and two tankards of brew. His father sheathed his sword and dagger, saying nothing, and watched. Hoj felt unease standing by the table. He came to say things, *but what first?*

Nelber and Kulm stacked their scrolls outside the door. Hoj wondered. *Where's the scroll I sent?* "Father, I gave you a scroll."

"You're not getting it back," said Vinlon.

A tall young man entered from another door. Hoj recognized Jaspich, who was shipwrecked at Ranjin three years ago. He couldn't blame Jaspich for sneering at him because he betrayed him to Warlord Druogoin, who held him captive for ransom.

The newcomer carried a tray with three bowls of steaming

creamy broth, and Hoj salivated to the aroma of crustacean soup. Jaspich shoved his tray on the table, pushing scrolls to the floor. Hoj picked up the documents to keep in his arms.

Jaspich asked Vinlon, "Why is he here?"

"A good question. Did your mother send you, Hoj?"

"She thinks I'm here to kill you."

"Are you?"

"I no longer hate you, Father."

Vinlon went to the table to drink from one of the tankards. Jaspich approached the young mother in the chair. Hoj suspected he was the child's father, not Vinlon.

Vinlon set down the tankard. "Why do you no longer hate me, Hoj?"

"The question I ask myself is why I *did*. I listened to what Mother told me happened to Uncle Toush."

"I suppose she told you the Herkt killed him when I refused to pay ransom."

Jaspich feigned a cough to get Vinlon's attention. "Should Zzinel and I go?"

"Stay, and listen, and eat the soup before it gets cold." Vinlon waved for Nelber and Kulm to come inside. "You listen, too."

Hoj watched Jaspich eat soup, wanting some. "Mother told me as you say, Father, about your refusal to ransom Uncle Toush." *And more*, he recalled, but no use mentioning the rest of what his mother believed, that Vinlon allowed the Herkt to kill Toush so Hoj would be Warlord Druogoin's heir.

"I didn't refuse to pay ransom," said Vinlon. "The Herkt wanted a stack of weapons, but I needed time to collect them. What was I to do? I wasn't going to disarm my warriors, so I asked their clanlord for time, and he gave me *no* time. Vulrath never wanted a ransom. He ordered his bodyguard, a brute with a spiked mace, to decapitate your uncle while I watched from across the Taubueth River."

Hoj watched his father's anguished face, beaded with sweat. "Father, I wronged you. I hated you before knowing the entire truth, and I didn't give you a chance to tell me. Will you forgive me?"

"My son, I long to forgive you." Vinlon held open his arms.

Hoj went to him, and they embraced.

His father asked, "Have you forgiven me for killing your grandfather?"

Hoj broke from the embrace and offered a weak smile. "Did he deserve it?"

"I think so."

"Mother never will forgive you."

"Will Thigrel?"

Although Hoj didn't think his sister cared what happened to Grandfather, blissfully living her life with Pokyer and their son, he didn't envision a change in her thinking about what Mother told her over the years about Father. "I'll tell her what you told me, but don't expect her to come here. She has a family." He told his father about a grandson named Toush and another grandchild coming.

"I'm glad Thigrel's happy," said Vinlon.

Jaspich and the blond woman, Zzinel, had switched places so he now held the infant, and she ate soup, convincing Hoj they were husband and wife. When Zzinel finished her bowl, Vinlon asked her to get three more for the Hojyimt, and a replacement hot one for him, and she took away the tray. Hoj placed the scrolls he was holding on the open space of table, cheered by his upcoming bowl of crustacean soup. Vinlon took three tankards from a shelf for Hoj, Nelber, and Kulm to drink brew.

"Tell me, Hoj." Jaspich still regarded him with a sneer. "I haven't heard why you stopped hating your father and came here willing to listen to him." He sat in the only chair, holding the baby, while the others stood around the table.

"I serve the all-forgiving God," Hoj told him. He turned to Vinlon. "Father, the scroll I gave you contains his words."

Vinlon shrugged. "Not much use to me written in another language."

"Your scroll is written in the Snarshyim language."

"Don't taunt me. I wish it, but our language has no writing."

Hoj set his tankard on the table among the scrolls there. "All these scrolls are written in the Snarshyim language. They're translated from the originals, using symbols my partner Jorgis devised."

Vinlon asked him to read a scroll, picking one at random. Hoj recognized the selected scroll, a translation from a Kendulyim one that was translated from the Yarsishyim language before he acquired it.

"This one's interesting. It's the account of a Yarsishyim who traveled to the far west, farther west than Jatneryim lands."

He read, "A curious resurgence of the Snarshyim language occurs in the far western lands. No tribes there speak other languages such as some living in the westernmost reaches of the Swanshyim Forest and beyond. Every tribe in the far west speaks the Snarshyim language, but they don't call themselves Snarshyimt, although their words are the same as the peoples farther east speaking the same language. They call themselves the Moeleenzyimt."

Zzinel arrived with the four fresh bowls of soup.

After they ate, and Zzinel took away the empty bowls, Vinlon looked inside the scroll Hoj had read. "How do these symbols work, Hoj?"

"Each one corresponds to a sound in our language, thirty-seven in all."

"They look like meaningless scribbles."

"They're not complicated." Hoj knelt on the dirt floor. "Think of two squares side by side." He sketched them on the ground with a finger, sharing a side between them.

"Each symbol uses different combinations of the sides of these squares. The symbol for the first sound in your name, Vinlon, uses all the sides of the first square, including the side it shares with the other square. It also uses the top and right sides of the second square, but not the bottom side."

Hoj sketched another copy of the two squares, leaving out the bottom side of the second square. Then he sketched a circle with a hook. "When we write this symbol, we curve the corners to look like this."

"I want to learn all the symbols," said Vinlon. "I must know how to read and write the Snarshyim language."

"I'll teach you, Father, and anybody else in Habergenefinanch who wants to learn."

Jaspich kept scowling. At least the child in his arms was happier, making cute baby sounds. "This place is no longer called that. Habergenefinanch no longer exists."

"This new town we're building has a new name, *Nanch*," said Vinlon. "The old name was too long."

Hoj liked the name change. "I'll stay in Nanch long enough to teach the symbols."

Jaspich's mouth curled in the beginning of a smile. "You're not staying?"

"You see me wearing the colors of the Druogoint and the Warnekt. I choose neither tribe."

"You'll choose when you take a wife."

"I won't have a family. I'm devoting myself to tell people what the scrolls have to teach us, including knowledge of the forgiving and merciful God."

Hoj thought someday to visit the Moeleenzyimt.

Vinlon asked, "You'll have no offspring?"

"I'm not your heir, Father."

Jaspich smiled.

Downfall of the Empire

Herkt, Swenikt

Jorgis   near Pinkulda

Jorgis thanked the one living God that he could spread the knowledge of the scrolls without traveling to the Snarshyim clans and tribes. They came to him.

The beginning class convened around several of the round tables in the central room of Kevyar's longhouse. The eleven students were four Herkt; Clanlord Brutez, his bodyguard Larboelm, and their wives; a Jatneryim named Puutnam and his wife; a one-armed Feldram named Tarberg; a Chrevram named Steebnaf, with his wife and daughter; and Davlek. They had parchments and coal sticks to practice writing.

Doors to the sun-brightened outdoors stood open on both sides of the room, allowing a refreshing breeze to waft through on a hot late-summer day. Jorgis wiped a stream of sweat from his brow.

Brutez had questions. "Why did you change the symbols for our language from the ones for the Old Language? The two languages have the same sounds, don't they?"

"The languages based on the Iriack language don't combine

framing sounds like ours does," said Jorgis. "I devised the Snarshyim framing symbols so they could be combined."

"Is that why my name has five symbols, although it has six sounds?"

"That's right. The combined symbols follow the pattern of three squares. The first square comes from the first square of the first combined symbol, and the rest of the squares come from the second combined symbol."

"This is too complicated," said Larboelm. "I'm glad my name doesn't combine sounds."

"It does at the end," said Brutez.

Larboelm slammed his coal stick on the table. "Curses!"

The symbols for the two framing sounds at the end of Larboelm's name couldn't be combined. Only the most common cases could combine symbols, and the end of Larboelm's name wasn't one of them.

The frustrated student could be glad the lesson was over because the members of the advanced class were arriving for theirs. They were Kevyar, Jankwel, Befdaul, Larzil, Adam, Fidrek, and the older daughters of Kevyar and Davlek. The newcomers found spots around the unoccupied tables in the room.

The members of the beginning class remained seated so both classes could discuss topics of mutual interest. The first class would depart after lunch.

Jorgis started the session the same as every day by reading from God's words or the traditions. This day he read about the serpent's curse.

"The serpent is our enemy, opposing any good God means for us," he said after the reading.

"I'm reminded what I dreamed in the dungeon at Mapvin," said Brutez. "A monster flies over our land, angry and hateful, wanting to destroy us."

"He won't succeed," said Jorgis. "The woman's seed will defeat him."

Beksel asked, "Who is the woman's seed?"

"We won't know until he comes, but the traditions tell us he'll shed the pure blood to bring victory."

"I want to know more of what the scroll Clanlord Brutez returned to me says," said Kevyar. "What new passages have you translated, Jorgis?"

Jorgis raised the copy of his latest translation. "The clanlord was correct when he supposed the map's thick blue lines marked a migration by our ancestors." He gave the parchment to Adam, the student knowing most about the written Snarshyim language, and asked him to read.

"I've traveled the western frontier and experienced the wrath of the Snarshyimt. They're a maelstrom, coming from the lands of the setting sun to devour all in their path. Their ruthlessness can't be exaggerated. Even our Iriack soldiers tremble before their crude weapons of wood. They refuse any treaty, for their desire to maim and kill renders payment in gold, silver, or goods worthless to them. The sight of an artificial structure infuriates them, and they aren't appeased until any such thing is razed to the ground.

"These aren't ordinary barbarians because they hold no superstition, nor gods, nor religious rites. Herein is the secret of their terror. They're unrestrained by conscience, feeling, or primitive belief. They fear not the wiles of nature, heavenly signs, or the apparent superiority of our empire. What soldier, however brave, or what army, however equipped and trained, can withstand the onslaught of these hellish warriors?

"I suspect within the dormant heart of the Snarshyim lies ingenuity akin to the life inside a seed. His energy is boundless. If only he could overcome his thirst for blood and passion to destroy, his feats and the height of his civilization would exceed imagination."

Adam lowered the parchment. "Now I understand why the Snarshyimt overran my ancestors."

"Our Snarshyim forefathers were no better than Matkulk," said Puutnam.

"Not all your Jatneryim forebears were Snarshyimt," Jorgis

told him.

"We speak the Snarshyim language."

Jorgis explained, "The scroll says the first wave of Snarshyimt passed through the middle lands four or five centuries ago, coming here to the east. That's why so many people living between the lands of the Jatneryimt and the Moeleenzyimt don't speak the Snarshyim language. The original inhabitants of the Jatneryim lands were a peaceful people called the Swansh."

"The forest must be named after them," said Larboelm.

Obviously, Jorgis thought, but he praised his frustrated student, "Good insight, Larboelm. The lands of the Swansh were the farthest west the Iriack Empire expanded, so the territory was called the Swanshyim Forest."

Puutnam asked, "How does this relate to the Jatneryimt?"

"The Snarshyim forebears of the Jatneryimt were the second wave. They occupied the lands of the Swansh, killing all the men and boys."

"That's why the Swansh no longer exist."

"The Jatneryimt took the Swanshyim women and raised the girls to be wives, so you warriors of the Green and Black Citadels are descended from the Swansh and the Snarshyimt."

"I suppose the first wave didn't intermarry with the original inhabitants," said Brutez.

"That's why the Snarshyimt and Chizdekyimt remained separate peoples," said Jorgis. "Other peoples under the Iriack Empire, the Richeeyimt and Yarsishyimt, were expelled from these lands. The Snarshyim migration initiated the downfall of the empire."

"Adam read something about our ancestors not tolerating structures," said Kevyar. "Is that what happened to Pinkulda?"

"I'm still translating that part. It mentions the Herkt and some swords."

Servers appeared with brew, so class was over and lunch starting. A distressed young woman entered, going to Larzil, so Jorgis went to his wife to listen.

"Your son is hurt!"

She was an attendant watching the young children during the classes. Jorgis and Larzil followed her outside. They passed around the kitchen and entered an enclosed space, paved with stone and filled with little children, babies, and their caregivers.

An older woman held a wailing weanling, the boy Abel, whose knees were bloodied. Larzil tried to take him, but he thrashed too much, so Jorgis held the boy tightly until he calmed.

Beksel came. "I'm a healer."

"She'll help you feel better, Abel," said Jorgis.

The boy sniffled. "Yes, Father."

Joy filled Jorgis. He exchanged smiles with Larzil. For the first time, Abel called him *Father*.

Brutez   near Pinkulda

Brutez carried young Brutez as he went with Beksel for her to check Abel's knees before supper, an opportunity for him to ask Jorgis about the latest translating.

The man who invented the written Snarshyim language lived in a two-room log house near the town wall by the Tauzzreen River. Scrolls littered the main room, including the one Brutez kept for two years. It rested on a desk with a fresh parchment and writing implements, unraveled to the drawing of the relic broadswords.

Jorgis was home with his wife and the child he took as his son. Beksel went with Larzil and Abel to the back room.

Brutez placed his son on the floor. "Don't touch anything." He pointed to the desk. "What have you translated about the Herkt and the swords, Jorgis?"

"The scroll doesn't mention your clan by name, but it says the Snarshyim barbarians who assaulted Pinkulda carried pennants shaped like drops of blood."

"My Herkyim ancestors." Brutez remembered the shattered ruin where he killed Heptor. The ancient Herkt didn't leave much standing. The destruction testified to their fury, angered by an artificial structure as Adam had read. Brutez wondered why his ancestors spared Taubueth the same fate.

"Pinkulda was the Iriack Empire's most formidable stronghold in these lands," said Jorgis. "When the Herkt sacked it, imperial power was broken."

Brutez checked his son, who sat against a wall inspecting his fingers with an intense fascination. He went to the desk and placed a hand by the drawing in the scroll that tantalized him for two years while not knowing the meaning of the words. "What does this say about the swords, Jorgis?"

"Davlek told me you have them at Taubueth, Clanlord."

"We Herkt have had them as long as we can remember."

"Your ancestors took them from Pinkulda. They're the Imperial Swords of Power, one for each magistrate in the spiritual realm. They're a representation of God's authority in our physical world."

Brutez had wondered how long before Jorgis would mention his one and true living God. Not long, never was. He considered Adam's reading how the ancient Snarshyimt—fearing no superstition, gods, or religious rites—made them so terrible, not only terrifying but no better than Matkulk. *No better than Matkulk*, he pondered. *Perhaps fearing a one and true living God would be good.*

Jorgis continued, "The scroll tells a legend of the swords coming from the sky, which some Iriack scholars interpreted to mean they came from God. I believe they came from God, but only in the sense of the artistic mastery he gave the men who forged them."

Swords in the sky reminded Brutez of his dream during the long winter at the Black Citadel, or a vision, he wasn't sure which. He remembered twenty-four broadswords, the same number, dancing in the night and held by spirit beings, perhaps the magistrates Jorgis spoke about, and hearing a thunderous voice, the voice of God?

"This one is mine! I have plans for him."

"You speak about things coming from God, Jorgis," said Brutez. "Do you think a dream or vision can come from him?"

"I do. Have you had one?"

"Several. I saw a Red Kingdom, prospering in the east with cities and roads, and it faded. I think about it every time you talk about the Iriack Empire." Brutez had no difficulty pronouncing *Iriack*.

"I see the similarity."

"Then I saw a dormant Blue Kingdom coming from the ground with Snarshyim banners, some I recognized, and others I didn't."

"That's happening now. Our people are rising from ignorance."

"The Snarshyimt are destined to be a great nation." Brutez remembered what the end of Adam's reading claimed about the Snarshyim warriors who brought down the Iriack Empire, and their potential for a civilization exceeding imagination.

He considered his role in making the Snarshyimt great. "I saw something else, five trees representing my brothers and myself. Four trees were chopped down, the same as my brothers are slain. My tree grew tall, sprouting Herkyim blooddrops for leaves."

"Chief Kevyar had a similar dream," said Jorgis. "He saw a tree with Swenikyim pennants replacing the blooddrops for leaves. I told him it meant Swenikyim kings, but first Herkyim kings."

Brutez felt a little hand tugging his breeches, and he took his son into his arms. "I'm the forebear for a Herkyim line of kings."

"Or its founder."

One detail from the blooddrop-leaf tree puzzled Brutez. "I saw my tree split into two trunks."

Jorgis shrugged. "Two Herkyim lines of kings."

Abel came from the other room with fresh bandages on his knees, followed by Larzil and Beksel. Brutez left the house with his family. Little Brutez ran ahead.

"Jorgis and Larzil have been married for weeks without having relations," said Beksel. "I told Larzil how wonderful the pleasures are."

"Hasn't Kevyar's wife, Jankwel, told her? She's like a mother to her."

"I don't think Jankwel has experienced the pleasures to her full potential."

Brutez looked over his wife, relishing her chestnut hair, green eyes, and inviting bosom.

"I know what you're thinking," she said.

"I'm thinking about your potential."

Beksel motioned toward their son, happily jumping over a stick in his path. "My love, let's leave him with Larboelm and Nazzel after supper."

Jorgis   near Pinkulda

Two visitors surprised Jorgis after supper. Nelber and Kulm wore robes of the same design as his, except pink and black. Jorgis asked Larzil for food and drink, and she left with Abel to get some.

"Hoj stayed in Nanch," said Nelber. "He's teaching his father and other Warnekt the written Snarshyim language."

Nanch? Jorgis wondered. *Is that short for Habergenefinanch?* "Why did you leave, Nelber?"

"We Druogoint aren't welcome in Nanch, so we came here for news from you."

"I'll write something for you to give to Hoj the next time you see him. Why are your robes pink and black?"

Nelber told Jorgis that he and his son started wearing the robes after the Water Ritual. Jorgis was overjoyed to hear they embraced the one and true living God.

"We're called the Hojyimt," said Kulm.

Jorgis supposed he was a Hojyim, too, and maybe Adam. *Did that mean they must wear pink and black?*

"I'm seeing all kinds of banners in this Swenikyim town," said Nelber. "The Hamuntht, the Herkt, the Jatneryimt, the Feldramt, and the Chrevramt, they're all here?"

"They're staying until they learn the written Snarshyim language," said Jorgis.

Nelber thumped Kulm's chest. "Hoj has been teaching us."

He's also teaching Warnekt, Jorgis thought, *so the knowledge is spreading to practically every clan and tribe in the region, thanks to the all-knowing God.*

Larzil returned with bread, meat, and brew. Abel wasn't with her. She disappeared into the back room.

Jorgis told Nelber and Kulm that Adam and Fidrek were returning to Chizdek. Nelber wanted to go with them to see the cave between the two long lakes where the scrolls were discovered.

"We looked for the cave when we came here from Chizdek," said Jorgis. "It seems to have collapsed."

When the guests were gone, Jorgis heard Larzil call from the back room. "Come, Jorgis. I thought they never would leave."

He found her on the bed, wearing nothing.

Greatness

Recorded Year 868

Done by High Summer

Herkt

BRUTEZ **TAUBUETH**

Brutez watched the portcullis and smiled. The double-lattice iron gate rumbled downward, thrusting two staggered rows of pointed metal teeth into a matching iron grid embedded in the ground. Hazy mid-afternoon daylight slanted through the grating from the south within the shadow of the gatehouse, adding warmth to some cool early spring weather. The portcullis bars left a distorted copy of themselves across the patch of light. Brutez walked into the gridded shadow and watched the dark lines bend over his body. He grabbed two bars and shook the closed gate. *Solid*, he observed with satisfaction. The iron was resolute.

Stepping back, he waved to the gatekeeper to raise the lattice, and the thing rumbled upward. Three small figures stood nearby, watching.

"Look at that, boys. Isn't it marvelous?"

The oldest, almost seven years, asked, "Uncle, may I hang from it?"

Before Brutez could tell him not, young Heptor ran to the rising portcullis and wrapped his arms around its lowermost crossbars. Brutez watched him go up and up until his little legs dangled overhead. He was amused as his nephew cried for help.

"Let me down! Let me down!"

He turned to his two sons, Brutez and Shemjib, aged six and four. "Do you see what happens when you do something without thinking?"

They replied together, "Yes, Father."

Brutez walked below Heptor and patted one of his feet to let him know he was there. "Let go, and I'll catch you." He let his nephew almost hit the ground before grabbing him.

Young Brutez pointed out the gateway. "Father, somebody's coming."

Brutez saw two riders in the sun's glare, dark forms with capes, crossing the open space surrounding Taubueth. Pink stripes appeared on the capes as they came out from the glare, and their robes under the capes were pink and black. They were Hojyimt, but which ones? One was a large man, possibly Adam, but he had no beard. The pair came to the gate where Brutez waited with his nephew and sons.

Brutez didn't know the smaller rider but recognized the big one. He was Kulm, one of the Druogoint who came five years ago to the town on the island in the Tauzzreen River, which the Swenikt called the new Pinkulda. They called it that, meaning *Stonework* in the Chizdekyim language, after they started replacing the original timber structures with stone.

Kulm's companion spoke from atop his mount, "I'm here to see your clanlord."

"I'm Clanlord Brutez."

"This is an impressive structure, Clanlord."

Brutez liked hearing that. He thought Taubueth should be called the new Pinkulda, *Stonework*.

The smaller Hojyim continued, "It's like the one my father built at Pultanik."

If his father was Warnek Vinlon, Brutez realized he was speaking to Hoj, of whom all the other Hojyimt were namesakes, *and what did he say?* Taubueth was comparable to Pultanik. Brutez relished hearing that. "Let me show you a better view," he invited, pointing to the rampart.

Hoj dismounted. "I would like that. Where may Kulm take our mounts?"

Brutez told his nephew and sons to show Kulm the way to the stable. Leading Hoj up a steep and narrow stairs, he turned back to speak, "Your tribemaster father used Richeeyim expertise to build his fortress. The Yarsishyimt helped build mine."

"I see," said Hoj in a tone that seemed to ask, *Why did they do that?*

Brutez wondered at times, for the Herkt didn't have much to offer. When Zzuz suggested making payment with relic broadswords—the Imperial Swords of Power—Brutez refrained from stabbing him with one. The Yarsishyimt had an affinity for precious metal, so Brutez collected most of his clan's gold and silver, and he traded for more from Chief Kevyar and Chief Hamunth. He closed the deal by promising to help the Yarsishyimt defend their lands in the Langech peninsula.

The Herkt once marched with the Chrevramt to defend the Yarsishyimt against the Boewint, who were allied with Mosik's mountain clan and Sir Grebnar's Jatneryimt. Brutez remembered the intense anger in his wedlock father's eyes when they met under truce that last time they saw one another three years ago. Grebnar couldn't attack the Yarsishyimt without fighting the Herkt and Chrevramt, so he resumed hunting Matkulk.

The rampart provided a view of its entire circuit, shaped not like a square or circle but something between those forms. The bulwark was finished, but only in the sense of surrounding the fortress.

"The wall isn't done," Brutez told Hoj. "It needs watchtowers and more parapets, and I want permanent barracks and storerooms inside the perimeter. Most Yarsishyimt are gone. Enough Herkt have learned stonecraft to finish almost everything."

A most difficult task remained, building a stone roof for the great hall. It stood next to the previous Taubueth stronghold on one side of the open space inside the fortress, dwarfing the old donjon. The long rectangle was twice the area and twice as high as the Chrevramyim hall at Biepazz. A timber roof served as a framework for the upcoming stone one, taller than the trees clustered within the confines of old Taubueth.

Brutez took Hoj along the rampart toward the old structure. The stable was near the old wall where Kulm and the boys were seen arriving with the mounts. It was a temporary lumber structure, like most buildings within the fortress, until a permanent stone one was built.

Stone structures housed the resident envoys. Brutez made constructing adequate quarters for them a priority. Six different banners identified the places near the great hall: the Chrevramyim purple notched rectangle, the Feldramyim dual brown triangles, the Hamunthyim amber forked tongue, the Swenikyim cobalt blue concaved triangle, the Druogoinyim pink trapezoid, and the Jatneryim green and black.

Rounding the wall's southwestern curve, Brutez saw wagons pulled by bovines on a path emerging from the forest. Most contained one large rock, while others carried smaller ones, but no wagon carried more than a few rocks.

"The rock comes from a bluff a few horizons away," Brutez told Hoj.

They came to where the rampart passed closest to the stable. Brutez led Hoj down another steep, narrow stairs to the ground level, and they left the steps behind.

"Tell me about your journey." Somewhere in Hoj's account Brutez hoped to learn the reason his visitors were passing through Taubueth.

"Kulm and I visited the Moeleenzyimt."

"The Moeleenzyimt," said Brutez, referring to the people

in the far west. "Sir Grebnar told me about them. Is it true they speak the same Snarshyim language we do?"

"It's not even a dialect, which is astounding because languages change."

Brutez recalled his revelation of the language bubbles when he was held at the Black Citadel. The Snarshyim bubble never changed. "A work of the true God perhaps."

Hoj gave him a startled look. "His work indeed."

Brutez supposed he wasn't used to somebody mentioning God before he did. "You say not even a dialect? They pronounce the words the same?"

"They do, although they have different ways of saying some things."

"What do you mean?"

"A good example is *maybe*. They say *bemay*."

They finished crossing to the stable, a place resounding with boyish laughter. Kulm held Heptor upside down by the ankles, shaking him, and the two other boys jumped in circles around them.

"Father, we want to play more with Kulm," said young Brutez. "He's fun!"

Kulm wore a broad smile.

Agreeing not to interrupt the fun, Brutez and Hoj entered the stable to retrieve some traveling bags Hoj wanted and brought them to the clanlord's quarters. Brutez still lived in the donjon basement with his family. A fire smoldered in the hearth. Beksel sat suckling their almost-weaned daughter, Sejel. The little girl was named after Beksel's deceased mother.

Hoj told Brutez about his journey. "It was longer than my trip with Jorgis, in time and in distance."

Brutez asked, "How have you traveled all the way here since winter?"

"Kulm and I spent winter with Mosik's mountain clan like we did going to Moeleenz. I taught them the written Snarshyim language, and told them about the creator God while we were with them."

Brutez figured how they traveled past the hostile area where Matkulk roamed. "You took a northern route."

"We followed the mountain foothills all the way from Mosik's clan to Moeleenz and back."

"Then you followed the Kipneesh River to get here?"

"That's right. We would have continued following it to the sea and Pultanik, except Kulm is anxious to return to his father at Ranjin."

That's why they were passing through Taubueth, Brutez learned. The three rivers of Taubueth, Pultanik, and Tauzzreen would take them to their destination.

"Tell me more about Moeleenz, Hoj."

"You can read what I wrote for you." Hoj extracted a stack of parchment from one of his traveling bags.

Brutez saw the rectangular pages were attached to one another along one of the short sides. "What's that?"

"It's a binding, more efficient than a scroll." Hoj gave it to Brutez. "The Moeleenzyimt call it a book."

Brutez flipped through the pages. "They knew how to write?"

"They had a crude system. I taught them to use the symbols Jorgis devised, which work better."

"That's good." Brutez closed the book. "If the Moeleenzyimt use the same spoken language, they should have the same written one."

Beksel Taubueth

Beksel ignored the nudge. It came from empty space. Then came another, and she wakened. She saw nothing in the dark, but heard Brutez.

"Beksel, please come."

"Come where? It's the middle of the night."

"It's almost sunrise, and I want your help before the

children waken."

He moved away, no longer blocking the candlelight flickering on the other side of the bedchamber door. Beksel saw him wearing the same clothes as last night and wondered, *Didn't he come to bed?* She went to the other room, keeping quiet so their three children stayed asleep in the bedchamber.

Brutez leaned over the table by the candle. He placed his hand on the open pages of Hoj's book. "I've been reading Hoj's account of his journey to the Moeleenzyimt."

He has been up all night, Beksel realized. How did he appear more awake than she felt?

Brutez continued, "The Moeleenzyimt live in tribes like we do here in the east, ten of them."

Beksel's sleepy mind became more alert with a recollection. "Didn't you see that in your revelations?"

"That winter in the dungeon, yes. I saw ten pairs of sky blue eyes among the bondage lords, and ten rectangle banners of the same color."

She was amazed how well he remembered the dreams and visions he experienced during those incoherent months. According to Jorgis, his revelations and recall of them came from the one and true living God. The Hojyimt talked about the one God any chance they had.

Brutez stabbed a finger into the book a series of times. "It says here they meet in one place every several years. They feast for days, engage in contests of physical prowess, and arrange marriages between their sons and daughters. It promotes unity among their tribes, Beksel, we should do that!"

He closed the book.

"We should," she said.

"What better place to meet than this magnificent new fortress of Taubueth?"

"No better place." Beksel knew her husband was proud of his stone edifice.

He handed her sheets of paper and a writing stick. "We need to write messages inviting the clans and tribes to come here."

"Now?"

"Why not now? The sun's rising. It's a new day. I'll tell you what to write."

"Why not write the messages yourself?"

"Your writing's better."

She agreed. His ragged scribbling sometimes looked as much like nonsense as before she learned the symbols from Jorgis.

She wrote the words he told her. The message to Lord Chieftain Feldram was the easiest. He needed no convincing to meet between kin. The message to Lord Chrevram was meant for his wife, baiting her with a chance to see her daughter, Zabfrul, and granddaughter living with the Feldramt. The messages to Chief Kevyar and Chief Hamunth emphasized opportunities to arrange marriages for their progeny. Writing to Lady Gernthol of the Druogoint, Brutez was lost for words. He never met the woman.

"She'll come," said Beksel, and she reminded him about Hoj. "You have her son here to convince her."

Brutez told her to invite her father, Sir Grebnar, in her own words. She was finishing the message when her young sons came from the bedchamber. Brutez told their oldest son, the one who shared his name, to get Larboelm. Beksel was suckling her little daughter when Larboelm arrived. Brutez commanded him to have the resident envoys come there to his chamber before going to breakfast.

"I want to see Hoj and Jonerch, too."

"Yes, Clanlord."

The envoys came. Steebnaf represented the Chrevramt, and the one-armed man, Tarberg, represented the Feldramt. Chief Hamunth's envoy was his young son, Fidrek. Chief Kevyar's man was Davlek, who came to Taubueth five years ago with his maiden daughters. The Druogoinyim envoy was a corpulent man named Pershnig who complained about living in exile. Beksel's second cousin Puutnam came for the

Jatneryimt.

"I have messages for you to take to your lords and chiefs," Brutez told them, indicating the folded papers on the table. "I'm inviting your kinsmen to a grand gathering of the Snarshyimt, never before seen in this part of the land. This meeting of the clans and tribes will take place here at Taubueth on high summer."

When Hoj arrived, Brutez asked him to go to his mother, Gernthol, with Pershnig when he delivered his message, and encourage her to accept the invitation.

"I'll do more than that," said Hoj. "Give me an invitation for my father, and I'll take it to Nanch."

Beksel was amused by her husband's smile, knowing how he would like to show his new fortress to Tribemaster Warnek.

Jonerch was the last to answer his summons. Brutez commanded his foreman of construction, "The Snarshyimt are coming to Taubueth, and I'll need the great hall. It must be done by high summer."

All Our Forces

Jatneryimt

GREBNAR   **BLACK CITADEL, MAPVIN**

Grebnar spread his arms along the edge of the pool, and slouched up to his neck into the Black Citadel's hot spring. A splash of the water wet his lips with a taste of salt.

For a long while, he couldn't go to the spring no matter how much he wanted to relax sore muscles, because his wife's naked body was found there, where her killer had dumped it, as if she drowned. Then one night, when Grebnar was drunk and had a wench, he was able to break his memory of Sejel and return to the pool. Thereafter, he indulged in the hot spring whenever coming to Mapvin.

While sweating in the water, he recalled meeting with Puutnam that week when his daughter's second cousin came with a written message. He perused the random markings on the paper from Beksel, unable to read it. *Curses!* Even Mosik could read since some Hojyimt visited him.

Grebnar thrust the page before Puutnam's nose. "What does it say?"

The message was an invitation to come to Taubueth on

high summer. Grebnar still hunted Matkulk after seven years, seeking him among the peoples not speaking the Snarshyim language who lived in the western Swanshyim Forest and beyond. Brutez built a fortress, instead of fighting battles. Grebnar hadn't seen his wedlock son since he fielded a force to protect the Yarsishyimt from his attack.

A shout echoed through the hot spring's dark, torchlit cavern. Grebnar reached for his sword resting on his green and black cape next to his clothes on the lava rock slab outside the pool. He reconsidered when he realized the foolishness of wielding a weapon in the nude. His bodyguards, Shrigen and Waenkth, would protect him.

Mosik appeared, shouting, and Grebnar refused to fret. If the enormous warrior wanted to kill him, nothing he or his bodyguards could do would stop him. Mosik's beard was as tangled as his hair, both long enough to reach his elbows. He wore ursine-skin clothes and carried a thick-shafted pike, topped by a human head.

"I promised you years ago, Grebnar, to give you this on a pole."

The head was decomposing, but Grebnar recognized the mustache downturned around its mouth. *Matkulk!* Grebnar rejoiced the nemesis likely complicit in the demise of his wedlock brother, Sir Rendif, was dead. Now his wife, Sejel's, death was avenged.

Mosik left the cavern, parading the head on his pike. His triumphant howl reverberated from the walls, and Grebnar hurried to join him. Coming from the water, he skipped drying himself and put on his trousers. He left off the tunic and donned the jerkin without fastening it in front, keeping his muscle-sculptured chest exposed. He put on his boots, draped the green and black cape over his shoulders, took his sword, and ran after Mosik, flanked by Shrigen and Waenkth.

They passed through a labyrinth of corridors hewn from black rock. The passages twisted and intersected, going up short staircases of a dozen or so steps here, and going down others there, but more stairs went up than down. The roughhewn walls changed to stone block in the outer passages, and daylight shafted through gaps in the ceiling. The citadel's occupants—wash maids, cooks, scullions, and such—streamed through the corridors going to the main courtyard.

Grebnar reached the plaza with his bodyguards. Matkulk's head danced on the pike within the gathering mob, and Mosik's booming voice shouted the news. Cheers resounded from the walls, battlements, and balconies. Grebnar gave his sword to Shrigen and entered the crowd. He reached Mosik among a group of his jubilant clansmen and took the headed pike. Matkulk's severed head dripped rotting flesh on his arms. He climbed a wide set of steps with a balustrade leading to the rampart, and Mosik followed. They went past a line of smiling citadel garrison, standing at attention with spears. Two Jatneryim captains, Fidezz and Varnzper, the husbands of Sir Rendif's daughters, waited atop the rampart overlooking the courtyard.

The people down there jostled and waved arms, becoming louder in their clamor. Mosik's warriors waved their banners, maroon patches with two flaps. The green and black banners of the Jatneryimt flew from the battlements and hung from balconies and windows. Jatneryim warriors in the courtyard, and those manning the battlements and towers, carried more standards. Some had the citadel's old black-only banners.

More citadel residents joined the throng as word passed throughout the black lava fortress. Women waved bedsheets and screamed. Boys took off tunics and flapped them as they jumped in excitement. One scullion hoisted a giant soup pan.

Grebnar raised Matkulk's head against a darkened sky. His muscles tensed on his bared chest. The cheering blasted his ears. A chant came from Fidezz and Varnzper, and Mosik joined them.

"Boldness! Boldness!"

The line of the garrison along the balustrade took up the chant.

"Boldness! Boldness!"

They pounded the ends of their spears on the steps.

"Boldness!" Thump! "Boldness!" Thump!

The chant spread to the courtyard.

"Boldness! Boldness!"

The crowd waved green and black banners, black-only banners, and maroon patches with flaps, as well as bedsheets, tunics, and a soup pan.

"Boldness! Boldness!"

The chant resounded through the citadel, and Grebnar knew he had a problem.

A fire blazed in a nearby brass cauldron on the rampart over the main gate. Tribelord Boewin stood by it with his warriors. One warrior held the sapphire blue tassel banner of the Boewint. Grebnar went to the cauldron.

He had negotiated peace between Boewin and Mosik the year he rescued Brutez from the Black Citadel because he needed Mosik's help to hunt Matkulk in the mountains. A year later, Brutez joined forces with Grebnar and Mosik to subdue the mountain clan Matkulk was born into. Matkulk escaped and instigated the western tribes that didn't speak the Snarshyim language to invade Jatneryim lands. Boewin joined forces with Grebnar, Brutez, and Mosik to repulse them.

Boewin remained a loyal ally, joining the hunt for Matkulk in the west after Grebnar and Brutez parted forces, so Grebnar gave the pike with the head to the tribelord. Boewin raised the trophy before his men, and they shouted. Whatever they yelled was overwhelmed by the cheering everywhere else. Boewin stuffed the head into the fire, and the remains of Matkulk's face burned, removing a scourge from the world.

Puutnam   Black Citadel, Mapvin

The courtyard celebration echoed through the corridor as Puutnam followed Shrigen to Sir Grebnar's chamber, hoping for a more favorable response to the message from Taubueth, now that Matkulk was slain. Grebnar stood by the chamber's back wall with his other bodyguard, Waenkth. Tribelord Boewin sat behind a table in the only chair. Fidezz and Varnzper flanked both sides of a fresh-stoked fire in the hearth.

Mosik, the huge mountain clansman, towered beside the door. "The swamp tribe brought Matkulk to me," he said.

Puutnam knew about the tribe living southward in the Wiskrakil swampland. They didn't speak the Snarshyim language and had speared his father to death.

Grebnar asked, "Matkulk was in Wiskrakil?"

The wall behind him had a curious drawing, somewhat faded in coal on the gray stone, but still discernible. It looked like chains.

"I encountered them in the Swanshyim Forest," said Mosik. "I don't know if they captured Matkulk from another tribe or betrayed him after he joined them. They wanted to make sure he was dead, so they let me take only his head."

"We should rejoin the celebration," said Tribelord Boewin.

"I've had enough adulation." Grebnar walked across the chamber and rested a hand on Puutnam's shoulder. "My daughter's second cousin lives at Taubueth with the Herkt. He brought a message about festivities my wedlock son, Clanlord Brutez, plans for high summer to bring together the Snarshyim clans and tribes."

Tribelord Boewin asked, "Which clans and tribes?"

Puutnam recited them. "The Chrevramt, the Feldramt, the Hamuntht, the Swenikt, the Druogoint, and maybe the Warnekt."

"What about the Boewint? Did Brutez send a message to Neshim?"

Puutnam shook his head, indicating not.

"I thought not." Boewin leaned back from the table and crossed his arms. "I'm not invited."

"I invite you," said Grebnar. "Mosik, too. We're going with all our forces."

Varnzper asked, "All, Boldness?"

"All. We must leave now to reach Taubueth by high summer."

To Taubueth

Warnekt

JASPICH　　　　　　　　　　**NANCH**

Jaspich looked at his wife reclining against one elbow on the bed. They were done, but he was glad she seemed to be in no hurry to reclothe. He refrained from dressing so she wouldn't get a notion to either. Their square stone room was brightly lit through sunslots near the ceiling and a window.

Zzinel twirled a lock of her brown-streaked blond hair in her fingers. "Your mother thinks we're leaving for Pultanik this week. Has Tribemaster Vinlon told you anything about that?"

"He hasn't," said Jaspich. "Even so, I think Mother's right."

The signs were evident. Jaspich saw wagons loaded with stores. Since Nanch was built over the ashes of Habergenefinanch, Vinlon resumed his annual habit of relocating to Pultanik during summer, until time for the harvest tour.

"I hope so," said Zzinel. "I want to know Father's getting well fed."

Jaspich wandered to the window and its view to the bay. They were inside a stone block keep, built on the knoll in the middle of Nanch. The keep centered the generally circular wall of a castle Vinlon commanded to be built within Nanch. The castle stable, foundry, kitchen, bakery, servant's quarters, and storehouse were long stone structures connecting the hub of the keep radially to the wall like spokes of a wheel. The outer town surrounded the castle with its own exterior wall, the first line of defense for Nanch.

"Your sister's lame, not helpless," said Jaspich. "She's able to feed your father."

He wished Banshim came with them to Nanch, but he wouldn't leave his foundry. Zzinel would have preferred staying in Pultanik, but Jaspich and his family went where Vinlon did.

Somebody knocked, and they quickly dressed. Jaspich opened the door to admit his mother.

Zzinel asked, "Where are the children, Wedlock Mother?"

"Don't worry, they're with your wedlock sisters," said Yazdil. "Jaspich, the tribemaster wants to see you in his chamber."

Jaspich noticed his wife's hopeful look and knew her desire, that Vinlon would announce their imminent departure for Pultanik.

Vinlon's chamber was located on the ground level next to the formal meeting hall, which protruded from the keep between the kitchen and the bakery. Two poles with Warnekyim black-ribbon pennants flanked the door. The tribemaster didn't sleep there, so the windowless candlelit room was furnished with cushioned chairs and low tables without a bed. Jaspich was dismayed to see Hoj, whose four-year absence had given him hope of never seeing the tribemaster's son again.

Vinlon sat with Hoj before a table with bread, cheese, and brew. "Have a seat, Jaspich."

Jaspich crossed his arms and remained standing. Although Hoj foreswore having a family and renounced himself as Vinlon's heir, Jaspich considered his presence a threat to his future as tribemaster. "Greetings, Hoj," he said, not meaning it. "You're back from visiting the Moeleenzyimt?" A stupid question, he considered. Obviously Hoj returned.

"I came from Ranjin," said Hoj.

"And Taubueth." Vinlon held a paper. "Tell Jaspich what's in this message, Hoj."

"Clanlord Brutez is inviting his Snarshyim neighbors to a gathering of the clans and tribes."

Jaspich asked, "Why?"

"Feasts, warrior games, marriage arrangements, and so forth. It's a Moeleenzyim tradition the clanlord wants to bring here to the east."

Jaspich was dismayed. "You're not considering going to this gathering, are you, Tribemaster?"

"It's a chance for me to scout the clanlord's lands without hostilities. I must see if the new fortress at Taubueth is as impressive as Hoj claims."

Jaspich suspected another reason. "Why did you go to Ranjin, Hoj?"

"I saw Kulm home to his father, and I went with Pershnig to deliver Brutez's message to my mother."

"Is your mother going to Taubueth?"

"She went before I left to come here."

Jaspich realized Hoj's devious plan of making certain Gernthol went to Taubueth so Vinlon would be compelled to go.

Hoj continued, "My sister and nephews are going, too."

Curses! Jaspich wanted to pummel Hoj for his guile. Vinlon wouldn't spurn the chance to see his daughter who he hadn't seen since she was a young girl, and grandsons he never met.

"I'm going with you, Hoj." Jaspich knew Hoj would go, and he couldn't allow the other clans and tribes seeing him at Vinlon's side as if he was heir, rather than himself.

"Of course you're going, you and your sisters," said Vinlon.

Jaspich wondered, *Why them?* He hoped his family would go to Pultanik, perhaps with Dekloes or Leenarth.

"Why do you want my sisters to go, Tribemaster?"

"You heard what the message mentioned about arranging

marriages. Your sisters need husbands, don't they?"

"Don't you want them to marry within our tribe?"

"The other clans and tribes are intermarrying. They're getting more familiar with one another, *too* familiar."

Jaspich recognized Vinlon's concern about the Warnekt becoming isolated.

The tribemaster continued, "Your sisters know the written Snarshyim language. If they live with another clan or tribe, or even better, they find husbands from two different clans and tribes, they can send information."

Jaspich couldn't refute Vinlon's logic, realizing how much more he could learn about being tribemaster. Vinlon considered the betterment of the tribe by habit, except in matters involving his wife who left him.

"My mother must approve any marriage arrangements," said Jaspich.

"Of course." Vinlon raised both hands in a gesture of surrender.

Jaspich was amused how the tribemaster feared his mother, who still resented him for her husband's death. "When are the clans and tribes gathering at Taubueth?"

"High summer," said Hoj.

"Must be soon." Jaspich was dismayed. The recent days were about as long as they ever became.

"A week."

A week, curses! Jaspich fumed. If Hoj hadn't lingered in Ranjin so long, making sure his mother left for Taubueth, they would have more time, *sufficient* time. He returned to his chamber in a foul mood.

Zzinel was cheerful. "When are we leaving for Pultanik?"

Jaspich ended her cheer. "We're not. We're going to Taubueth."

Battle Pennants

Herkt

Yeemzal　　　　　　　　　**Taubueth**

"Consider it a young man's dream," Yeemzal told Chrenlon. "You're going to spend the day eating, drinking brew, and looking for the prettiest maiden you can find."

Although tall herself for a woman, she had to look upward to see into the blue pools of her nephew's eyes. The strapping youth was grown taller than his brother, Sangern. He wore a loose tunic of Feldramyim brown with gaps below the arms for wearing in hot high-summer weather. The gnarled scar from his horrible burn eight years ago showed from one side.

"Why must I hurry to find a wife? I'm only eighteen."

Chrenlon's mother, Majdel, flattened a rumple in the tunic. "No hurry, but maidens are here from all over the land."

They were inside a tent, one of many within the new Taubueth fortress. It was like the others, square with a center pole supporting a pointed roof. The Druogoint brought them, all made from red and white fine-spun cloth that was translucent to daylight.

Yeemzal had a suggestion. "Go to the Swenikt, Chrenlon.

Chief Kevyar has daughters and nieces. They're lovely girls." *And bashful*, but they were maidens who would revel in some attention from a handsome fellow like Chrenlon.

The young man stroked his gorgeous raven hair. "Lovely girls, all right, I'll go."

Yeemzal followed him outside the tent. A Feldramyim banner flapped from the pointed roof. Chrenlon left in the direction of tents that were flying Swenikyim cobalt blue triangles.

Each clan and tribe prepared a banquet, welcoming any visitors. The Feldramt offered selections from the sea, fish and crustaceans. Their cooks set the seafood on a long wood slab propped atop barrels.

A lean woman, almost as tall as Yeemzal, sampled the fish. She wore a pink gown with barely enough of a bodice to cover her tiny breasts. Her graying bright red hair was as long as Yeemzal's, but not as thick.

"I like the taste of this fish better than ours," she told the shorter man with her, who was missing a thumb.

"Maybe the Feldramt will share their recipe," he spoke in a guttural voice. He noticed Yeemzal was listening. "Won't you?"

"Send over your cook," said Yeemzal. "Tell him to say Lord Chieftain Feldram's sister invited him."

The pink woman asked, "The Lord Chieftain is your brother?"

"I'm Yeemzal, and our host, Clanlord Brutez, is my nephew."

The woman held out a pale, bony hand. "My name is Gernthol. I lead the Druogoint, and this is my man, Grapnef. Do you like the tents?"

Yeemzal shook the hand, thinking the red and white cloth structures were nice.

Gernthol didn't wait for her answer. "Your clanlord nephew requested them after my envoy told him about our Druogoinyim tents. My tribe is most skilled with cloth. Brutez wanted them in his red color, although pink would have been better."

Yeemzal now understood the Druogoinyim pink trapezoid banners.

Gernthol kept talking. "You're a comely older woman. Your face is smooth, and I've never seen more luscious gray hair. How do you keep it that thick?" She fingered her wisping tresses. "Mine's getting so thin I fear I must cut it short."

"I have creams and tonics," said Yeemzal. "I'll make sure you get some."

Gernthol smacked Grapnef's chest. "You see, I told you we should come here."

Yeemzal's nephew, Sangern, came with a group of three other youthful adults and a small blond girl. "Aunt Yeemzal, have you seen Chrenlon?"

"I sent him to meet the Swenikyim maidens."

Gernthol looked Sangern over—tall, dark-haired, and handsome—and Yeemzal couldn't begrudge the woman admiring her gorgeous nephew.

"We came from the Hamuntht," said Sangern. Zabfrul stood beside him, holding their daughter's hand. "The chief has a comely maiden daughter Chrenlon should meet."

Gernthol's attention now was on Zabfrul. "You're quite a beauty, but what happened to your face?"

Zabfrul fingered the jagged scar across her cheek and lips. "This?" She laughed, looking at Sangern. "Things got rough on our wedding day."

Yeemzal smiled, wondering where Gernthol's imagination went with that. The other woman with them, whom Yeemzal remembered was Tribelord Boewin's daughter who married a Herk named Zzuz, loosed a grating shriek of laughter.

"These are Sangern, my nephew, and his wife Zabfrul with their daughter," said Yeemzal. "He's Lord Chieftain Feldram's son, and she's Lord Chrevram's daughter."

Zabfrul introduced the other young man. "This is my brother, Wikston."

The woman with the annoying laughter spoke, "I'm their

second cousin."

Gernthol offered her hand. "I'm the leader of the Druogoint." She glanced away toward Grapnef, who had walked away, and lowered her hand. "I'm sorry. I must go."

After she left, Sangern asked, "That woman leads the Druogoint?"

Yeemzal answered with a question, "Why do you think their banners are pink?"

Zzuz's wife responded with another round of cackling laughter, making Yeemzal glad the couple had no children.

"Wikston and I are going to swordfight," said Sangern. "Are you coming to the competition, Aunt Yeemzal?"

"I'll bring ointments to treat your wounds," said Yeemzal.

She wanted to ask Lord Chrevram about his stomach ailment she was treating, but hadn't found him in his tribe's camp, so she asked his son and daughter where he was.

"We left him with Chief Hamunth, talking about the Yarsishyimt," said Wikston.

Yeemzal supposed Chrevram knew the Yarsishyimt well, having one for a wedlock daughter. Wikston's petite blond wife wasn't looking so thin these days as a first child grew within her, and a second, Yeemzal suspected. She knew about birthing twins.

Going to the tents with Hamunthyim amber forked-tongue pennants, Yeemzal saw Taubueth's great hall through a gap between camps. Although some supporting woodwork remained, the arched roof was stone.

The new Herkyim blooddrops, now flying over the stone roof, were backed by rectangular fields of white. Clanlord Brutez called them the peace banners of the Herkt. Henceforth, the all-red blooddrops would be seen only in battle.

The cooking smells in the Hamunthyim camp told Yeemzal they served barn fowl. She found Chief Hamunth, a bald man without brawn, inside a large tent occupied by more than a dozen people. This included children and four men in the pink and black robes of the Hojyimt—but not Lord Chrevram.

The chief was speaking to a skinny young woman with short straw-blond hair. "You have nothing to fear, Larzil. Clanlord Brutez told me the men who violated you are gone cutting stone from a bluff several horizons away, so go with Jorgis and enjoy the festivities. Take Abel, too." Hamunth glared at a boy of about seven years who was jumping into a pile of pillows.

The youngest Hojyim—Jorgis, Yeemzal supposed—grabbed Abel by the torso. "Join us, my wife," he beckoned to Larzil. "Kulm will come, too."

A large Hojyim—Kulm, Yeemzal supposed—smiled, and Larzil joined them.

Abel was delighted. "Mother, we'll have fun!"

Hamunth spoke to a spindly young man with dark brown hair. "Go with them, Fidrek, and look for a wife."

"I know the woman I want to marry," said Fidrek.

Hamunth snorted. "Nonsense, how many years have you lived here without getting any interest from Steebnaf's daughter? You complain about it in every message you send me."

"Not every message."

Hamunth motioned to a comely dark-haired girl in the back of the tent. "Take along your sister so some husband can find her."

Yeemzal assumed the maiden was the one Sangern mentioned for Chrenlon to meet. "Go to the Swenikt," she said.

"They have all daughters," said Fidrek. "Two live here with their father, Davlek."

"My nephew is with the Swenikt, and he's as handsome as his older brother who visited you a short while ago."

Hamunth gave Yeemzal a thorough look as if first noticing her presence. "Lord Chieftain Feldram's son, the one married to the marred beauty?"

"Sangern," said Yeemzal.

"Yes, him." Hamunth turned to his dark-haired daughter.

"You want to meet his brother, so go with your brother."

The tent became more spacious upon the departure of Hamunth's son, two of his daughters, a wedlock son, the grandson Abel, and Kulm. Three men, an adolescent boy, and two younger girls remained with Hamunth and Yeemzal. One of the three men was an older Hojyim. The two others had Chizdekyim markings on their arms.

Hamunth had more to say to Yeemzal. "Sangern told me about you, his aunt."

"I'm Yeemzal." She wondered what Sangern told him.

"He talked about how you cared for his wife after Tribelord Boewin stabbed her face at their wedding."

The older Hojyim spoke, "You're the Feldramyim healer I want to meet for comparing remedies. I'm the healer for my tribe."

Yeemzal asked, "Which tribe?"

"The Druogoint," said the man in pink and black. "My name's Nelber. I'm getting too old to travel, but I wasn't missing this grand gathering of the Snarshyimt."

Yeemzal knew about Nelber. Tarberg met him years ago at the town now called Pinkulda. "Let's discuss our healing arts, Nelber, and include Beksel."

"The clanlord's wife," said Nelber. "Kulm and I met her when we visited the Swenikt five years ago."

Yeemzal asked Chief Hamunth about where Lord Chrevram went, so she could treat his stomach ailment. Chrevram was looking for Yarsishyimt, some who remained to help finish the huge stone roof, according to Hamunth, and the chief offered Yeemzal to help find him.

She didn't need his help but sensed his interest, and her body had feelings, things she hadn't felt since her husband was alive. "Come along," she said, adding a smile.

Hamunth commanded the Chizdekyim who was wearing pink and black robes, whom he called Adam, to stay with his three youngest children in the tent. Nelber stayed to take a nap on a cot with pillows from the pile Abel had jumped into earlier.

The younger Chizdekyim followed Hamunth and Yeemzal from the tent.

"Don't mind Enoch," said Hamunth. "He doesn't know the Snarshyim language."

He led Yeemzal up nearby stairs to the rampart. She doubted any Yarsishyimt would be found atop the wall, but she asked herself, *We're not looking for Lord Chrevram, are we?*

Hamunth's words made clear they weren't. "Yeemzal, you're a ravaging older woman, most exciting to me."

They paused inside an empty blockhouse, newly constructed on the rampart. Enoch took a vigil outside the door.

"Chief Hamunth, you're fortunate I have a weakness for bald men. How would you like the rest of your hair removed?"

"I wouldn't miss any of it. You name the time and place."

"The time is when we're married, and the place is our wedding bed."

"Surely you jest. You restrict the pleasures to marriage? How long has passed since your husband was slain?"

"Too long, but I care for myself. You could be the right man to change that."

"If I marry you."

"New experiences are the flavor of life. Consider this. I know positions, and my age doesn't keep me from doing them."

Hamunth gulped. "You're willing to live at Chizdek?"

She scoffed. "Curses, no!"

"You can't expect me to come to Agratuna. I'm a chief."

"Why do you think being married means we live in the same place?"

Hamunth frowned, and Yeemzal continued, "You visit me once each year, and I go to you. That's twice per annum."

"Only twice," he said.

"Twice in terms of trips, not opportunities, and when your capability wanes with age, I have herbs to help you."

"I sired eight offspring without marriage. I suppose your flow is done so I could be married without siring more children."

"You may suppose that thing but not another. As my husband, you'll have no other women. I know what your Chizdekyimt did to Rankeb and Konrash. If I discover you to be untrue, my method won't be the Chizdekyim way."

"I'm not sure I can resist."

"Here's a test. Go to the fiery woman in pink who leads the Druogoint, and when you withstand her overture, you'll know you can resist."

Hamunth raised his arms to signify triumph. "A test to win the hand of my Yeemzal, I'll do it!"

"I'll be watching my nephew and his wedlock brother in today's swordplay. You might encounter the Druogoinyim woman if you go."

"If not there, certainly when the Druogoint race equines, a spectacle that Hojyim Nelber told me not to miss."

A horn, shrill and sustained, blasted from down the rampart. Yeemzal followed Hamunth from the blockhouse, expecting to see whatever heretofore unannounced event the horn signaled. Enoch pointed outside the fortress across the open space surrounding it. A line of banners came from the edge of the forest a thousand cubits away. Another rank of warriors followed the banner bearers, and another, and more. They kept coming, rank after rank, marching in step with shields, spears, and swords.

"Jatneryimt," said Hamunth. The banners were recognizable coming out from the forest's shadow into afternoon sunshine, black along the poles and green on the outer edges.

Yeemzal spotted sapphire blue tassels with another contingent emerging from the trees. "Boewint, too."

The lead ranks parted, moving laterally to surround Taubueth from other directions, and more continued pouring from the forest to fill the gaps behind them. Yeemzal wondered, *Why the battle array? Why the show of force?*

"Whose banner is that?"

Yeemzal followed the line along Hamunth's arm, and saw

riders flying maroon patches with pairs of flaps. "I've never seen that one."

Hundreds of armed warriors lined the ground outside Taubueth.

Hamunth spoke to Enoch in the Chizdekyim language, and then reverted to the Snarshyim language. "Yeemzal, allow Enoch to escort you to your family. I must go to Clanlord Brutez."

Vikth   Taubueth

Vikth was attracted to the Swenikt because they roasted a flatsnout, but regretted coming when Chief Kevyar introduced him to a young woman with stringy red hair, and also to a pair of boys under age eight. "This is Thigrel, the daughter of Tribemaster Warnek and Lady Gernthol, and her sons."

Vikth considered how to introduce his family. Thigrel didn't need to know his wife used to be her father's mistress, and his stepchildren could be her half siblings. "My wife, Darjil, our children, and my wedlock father," he introduced them, including the old miller, Tetharng.

They stood by the pit fire, which sizzled from dripping pork, within a circle of the red and white tents flying cobalt blue concaved triangles. Kevyar stopped his son, Thoiren, another boy under eight, from getting too close to the blaze. His wife, Jankwel, gave him a ball to distract him, and sat with him at the entrance of one of the tents with an old woman whom Kevyar had introduced to Vikth as his mother.

Kevyar placed a hand on the head of Vikth's stepson, who recently reached his eighth birthday. "All these boys the same age should play together."

Vikth didn't want *that*. He wanted to get away from Tribemaster Warnek's progeny born within wedlock. The timely arrival of three youthful adults, yet another boy, and two

Hojyimt gave him a chance to signal his wife and her father they should leave.

Young Thoiren held up his ball, calling to the boy in the new group, "Abel, let's play catch!"

Abel's mother, a woman with short straw-blond hair, let her son go with him. Thigrel's two sons went, too, but Darjil held back her son.

Thigrel spoke to the smaller Hojyim. "Greetings, Jorgis. I haven't seen you since you left on the long journey with my brother."

Jorgis asked, "Where's my old servant, Pokyer, your husband?"

"He stayed behind in Ranjin."

"He's taking care of my father's trade goods," said the larger Hojyim.

The young man Vikth knew was Fidrek spoke next. "I brought my sister here to meet a handsome Feldram. Where is he?"

Kevyar laughed. "That young man, Chrenlon, came and took all my daughters and nieces with him. He gets more attention from maidens than I ever did."

Vikth left with his family, passing among tents flying Chrevramyim purple notched-rectangle banners. A long horn blast pierced the festive day. The family of six hurried through a crowd looking at the rampart. They reached the stone house where they stayed with Puutnam's family, Vel and two children. Vikth saw that his half brother, Zzuz, was there, but not his half sister, Vel, so he asked, "Zzuz, where's Vel?"

"She's with Puutnam."

"Puutnam is back from delivering the message to Sir Grebnar?"

"He returned this morning and left with his family."

"Something's wrong."

Zzuz left to search for his wife. Vikth went to the main gate, arriving as it clattered closed. He saw Jatneryim warriors through the grating, mustered on the open space outside

Taubueth. They chanted something Vikth couldn't understand at first over the bursts of the horn, but then he did.

"Boldness! Boldness! Boldness!"

The horn stopped blowing. A single arrow flew over the gate, stabbing into the ground a few dozen cubits behind Vikth. He unraveled a folded paper from its shaft and read on the outside, *Clanlord Brutez*.

A sentry called from the rampart, "What is it?"

"A message for the clanlord," Vikth called back. "I'll take it to him."

He hurried to the ancient part of the fortress and ascended a stairs between the new great hall and the old wall. At the top, Jonerch showed him where to find Brutez. The clanlord stood with Larboelm, surveying the scene around Taubueth from a porch outside the great hall. Vikth followed their gaze to see what they were watching.

Curses! An overwhelming force of Jatneryimt and the cursed Boewint filled the field, glinting sunlight from the points of their spears and swords. Other warriors carried the maroon-flapped banners of Mosik's mountain clan.

Vikth climbed a stairs to the porch and delivered the message. Brutez frowned while reading it. He commanded Vikth and Larboelm to summon the other leaders.

Vikth passed Chief Hamunth on the lower stairs, going up as he went down. The other leaders were easy to find, since all were coming to Brutez. The clanlord met them atop Taubueth's ancient wall at the bottom of the stairs to the porch.

He read the message, "Sir Grebnar the Bold, Lord of the Jatneryimt and the warriors of the Green and Black Citadels, demands immediate surrender. All Snarshyim clans and tribes within Taubueth are to submit to his authority, or attack is certain."

Brutez crumpled the paper. "What say you, lords and chiefs? I'll accede to your decision."

"I don't care what the others decide," said Hamunth. "I refuse to submit."

Lord Chieftain Feldram spoke next. "I submit to your protection, Clanlord Wedlock Brother."

"The Druogoint don't submit," said Gernthol, a woman Vikth met that morning. Her graying red hair and pink gown waved in a sudden breeze.

"I don't know this Grebnar," said Chief Kevyar. "Clanlord Brutez, you have my trust."

The leaders who had spoken turned to the one who remained.

Lord Chrevram shrugged. "What am I to say? I'll not be the lone dissenter. We don't surrender."

Brutez surveyed the group. "Are you certain? This fortress is more filled with our families than warriors, and its defenses are incomplete."

The lords and chiefs proclaimed their certainty with defiant words. "No surrender. Cursed be us if we submit. Grebnar be cursed."

Brutez swept an arm over the ancient stronghold. "This place is the most secure. Bring your women, children, and aged here." He commanded Jonerch, "Battle pennants."

Vikth watched the banners change over the great hall's stone roof. The white rectangles with blooddrops on them came down. Up went naked blooddrops, the battle pennants of the Herkt.

Lord of the Snarshyimt

Herkt, Jatneryimt

BRUTEZ **TAUBUETH**

A rider approached the main gate on a cantering mount, having left the Jatneryim force. He was a caped figure, silhouetted against the scarlet rays of a setting sun. Brutez supposed he was Grebnar while watching him from the battlement outside the gatehouse. Paces away, Jonerch notched an arrow into his bow and pulled the string.

"Put down your weapon, Jonerch." Brutez knew striking down Grebnar would precipitate an immediate attack. He shouted for all his men in the vicinity to hear, "Let him come. Open the gate."

The portcullis rattled upward, and Brutez went down by the gate with Larboelm. As the incoming rider came near, within the gathering dusk, Brutez saw lighter and darker stripes in his cape, undoubtedly green and black in better light, and a straight mustache on his unbearded face.

The rider was Grebnar. "Wedlock Son, your refusal to submit portends a fateful confrontation."

"A confrontation of your making, Wedlock Father," said Brutez. The nose of Grebnar's mount came within his reach. He grabbed the bridle, and the Jatneryim leader dismounted with a swirl of cape.

"A necessary one. I'm here to tell you what must transpire."

Smoldering anger flared within Brutez, not because Grebnar threatened him but because he thought he could be intimidated. "You may tell me, but your daughter must hear." Beksel would have to soften her father's hardened attitude.

"Agreed. She must know what will transpire."

"Come. Your mount can stay here." Brutez handed the bridle to Larboelm. "Secure Sir Grebnar's mount, and then join us in my quarters."

"Yes, Clanlord."

Brutez led Grebnar through the nearly abandoned campsite within Taubueth, tents interspersed with fading cookfires and uneaten feasts. "This was a peaceful gathering, a vision for the Snarshyim clans and tribes I thought you shared, Wedlock Father."

"I do, but my warriors don't."

They approached the original Taubueth stronghold and the new great hall.

Grebnar studied the darkened mass of arching stone against the twilight sky. "I see why you protected the Yarsishyimt, Brutez. They built you an impressive structure."

"Better than that, they taught *us* how to build it."

Chief Hamunth came. He regarded Grebnar with a sneer, and stepped to the opposite side of Brutez from him. "Clanlord, tell me where to put my men on your wall."

Brutez had something else in mind, knowing a meeting would be needed after Grebnar left. "Gather the other leaders in the old citadel, Chief." He pointed to the ancient donjon standing behind the old wall, and Hamunth departed.

"Brutez, you command the loyalty of the other leaders," said Grebnar.

"They respect me."

Brutez took Grebnar up the stairs between the old and new portions of the inner stronghold. They saw the interior courtyard from the rampart, filled with women, children, and the aged, a scene Brutez intended for Grebnar to see.

"I'll fight for these people with my life, Wedlock Father."

"You will indeed."

Grebnar followed Brutez into the old stronghold. He was an imposing figure walking stiffbacked in the cape, although not visibly armed. The Jatneryim stared ahead without giving heed to the hushed crowd in the courtyard.

Brutez saw the old fisherman, Zuedon. He was Chief Kevyar's wedlock father from the destroyed town by the deep blue lake. Brutez promised him no harm back then, wishing he could say so now. A strange sensation, he pondered, feeling responsible for people from tribes outside his own clan.

A new stone outbuilding replaced the healer's hovel once used by Yeemzal and inherited by Beksel. Brutez took Grebnar inside and downstairs through a new wooden door. The candlelit main chamber appeared the same, floored by furs and adorned with the twenty-four Imperial Swords of Power on the far wall.

Brutez saw his aged father, Zamtoth, dozing on a stack of furs on the low bed-sized table in one corner. The boys, Brutez and Shemjib, played with cousin Heptor by their sleeping grandfather. Beksel sat at the table with her newly weaned daughter, Sejel, who was asleep. Nazzel also sat there with a daughter, young Heptor's half sister.

Beksel lurched from her seat, holding Sejel. "What are you doing, Father?"

Sejel remained asleep, but Beksel's outburst wakened Zamtoth. The old man sat on the edge of the low table, and young Brutez wasted no time joining him.

"What's best for the Snarshyimt." Grebnar went to his daughter. "Let me see my granddaughter for the first time."

Beksel held out the sleeping child, cradled across her arms. Grebnar stooped to kiss the brow of the grandchild named after his deceased wife.

"Sejel, my love." Moisture softened the intensity of his eyes.

A tear ran along Beksel's cheek until a wisp of her chestnut hair absorbed it.

"My daughter, I must see you alone with your husband."

Nazzel took Sejel, and Beksel went with Brutez and Grebnar to the adjoining bedchamber. Brutez accepted Beksel's hand taking his. He stood with his wife by the foot of the bed, facing Grebnar.

"The Snarshyim clans and tribes have two great lords," said Grebnar.

"You and me," said Brutez. "You think one's enough?"

"That's the confrontation, but it need not involve our warriors."

Brutez had inkling for what he meant, but didn't want to consider it.

Grebnar forced him to consider. "You Herkt have a tradition for deciding who commands, a way to keep your clan from tearing itself apart."

"Tournament," said Brutez.

"A fight to the death," said Grebnar.

Beksel broke away from holding hands with Brutez. "Father, you're deranged! You or my husband will die?"

Grebnar fixed his penetrating gaze on her. "Daughter, call for your firstborn son."

She returned an emerald-eyed glare, glistening like the jewels on the sword hilts in the other room. Brushing past him with a sweep of chestnut hair, she poked her head into that next room. "Wedlock Father," she called. "Bring Brutez."

Zamtoth shuffled into the room with small Brutez under the cover of one arm.

"Grandson, come," said Grebnar.

The boy cringed and clutched his paternal grandfather. Beksel peeled him away. "Be brave, Brutez. This man won't hurt you."

The boy went from one grandfather, an old man who barely

could walk, to the other, a powerful warrior. Grebnar stood behind his firstborn grandson, resting his hands on the boy's shoulders. He wore a black gambeson beneath the green and black cape, patched with green over pleated padding. His forearms were equipped with vambraces, metal coverings etched with patterns of the Jatneryim Green Citadel banner.

"You're right, Daughter, one will die. The other will become the solitary Lord of the Snarshyimt. Either way, this boy is heir."

Beksel pleaded, "Why must you fight to the death?"

"My warriors are loyal only to me, although they once fought battles with Brutez leading them. Any loyalty for Brutez was lost when he defended the Yarsishyimt, and I don't know how else for him to regain it, except my warriors will declare fealty to him if he kills me."

Young Brutez looked up. "Mother, what's he talking about?"

Zamtoth called the boy to him by the door and put a hand on his shoulder. "Tournament, Grandson. This one will be the last."

Zamtoth withdrew to the other room with his grandson. Larboelm arrived, taking the spot by the door.

Beksel appealed to Brutez. "You told me the tournament against Klinteg was supposed to be the last."

"I promised never again would a Herk kill another Herk to lead the clan. Your father's not a Herk."

"The stakes involve more than leading the Herkt," said Grebnar. "We'll decide who leads all the clans and tribes. My warriors have agreed to follow the victor. Brutez, you must convince your allies to declare fealty to me if I kill you."

Brutez commanded Larboelm to take Grebnar to his mount.

Grebnar paused in the doorway. "Brutez, you choose the weapons."

"Cudgels."

Beksel faced Brutez when they were alone. She wiped away a tear, but her voice was steady. "Brutez, you must kill my father."

HAMUNTH TAUBUETH

Chief Hamunth went to the tents that were flying pink trapezoids, finding the Druogoinyim woman and a one-thumbed man mustering their warriors under a cluster of torches. "Come with me, my lady, to the old citadel."

"I'm a leader. I don't cower with women and children."

"Clanlord Brutez wants to see us after he meets with Sir Grebnar the Bold."

"The Boldness is here inside Taubueth?"

"I saw him myself."

"I want to see him, the greatest warrior in the land."

The woman left her men to go with Hamunth to get the other leaders. While they walked, she asked, "Why doesn't Brutez kill Grebnar while the man's under his power?"

"He's his wedlock father."

"He wouldn't be the first man to kill his wedlock father."

Hamunth considered how he never had a wedlock father. He was alone with the pink-gowned woman for the first time. That other time in her presence, when Brutez called for battle pennants, the lords and chiefs disbanded to their tribes. They walked below a torchpole. He noticed and wondered, *How did such a small breast show itself from her bodice?* He didn't care she caught him looking.

"We should meet sometime," she said. "It would improve tribal relations."

Hamunth imagined an unclothed lithe body and long red hair, *graying* red hair. She was another well-preserved older woman. Then he remembered Yeemzal, thinking of her positions, and restrained his thoughts of the other woman. *He would pass his test.*

They found Feldram, Chrevram, and Chief Kevyar before going to the meeting place. The donjon hall was illuminated by torches ensconced on the walls. Clanlord Brutez came up a stairs and invited everyone to sit around the long table. He stood at the end opposite the main entrance.

"We Herkt have a tradition called tournament. When someone makes a challenge to lead the clan, the matter's resolved by dueling to the death."

Hamunth thought his method was better, murdering a rival, except for the tormenting dreams that came later.

Brutez continued, "Sir Grebnar won't attack if I meet him in single combat. His warriors will declare fealty to me if I prevail. Will you declare fealty to him if he slays me?"

The Druogoinyim woman stood. "I will."

Considering her admiration for Grebnar, Hamunth wondered if she wanted him to win. Perhaps she wanted to improve relations with him. *Wasn't Grebnar's wife slain?*

Lord Chrevram remained sitting. "I see no alternative."

Feldram stood. "As you wish, Wedlock Brother. I have every confidence in your victory. You're two decades younger than Sir Grebnar."

"I dreamed of a tree," said Kevyar. "Jorgis told me about your dream, Clanlord. You're destined to prevail."

Hamunth wanted to say, *no!* He never would declare fealty to Grebnar.

Brutez asked, "Chief Hamunth, do you pledge fealty to Sir Grebnar if he wins?"

Hamunth never would but could pretend. He didn't speak, but offered a nod, and remained in his seat.

BRUTEZ   TAUBUETH

Brutez stood by the closed portcullis, dressed for combat in traditional tournament attire. A coif hooded his head, and more chainmail covered his neck and shoulders. His tunic's sleeves were tucked at the elbows into vambraces attached to his gloves. A leather jerkin covered the tunic over his torso. He wore tanned trousers and black leather boots.

He was glad the ritual of the tournament challengers

standing naked before one another wasn't needed. Grebnar wouldn't use poison, and Brutez rebuffed Chief Hamunth's proposal to lace a dagger with serpent venom, which Beksel or Yeemzal could have supplied.

Vikth brought a cudgel.

The weapon felt familiar to Brutez. "I used this against Klinteg." He remembered Vikth kept the weapon from that other tournament.

Grabbing the iron mallet in one hand and gripping its shaft in the other, he ordered the portcullis to be opened. The metal lattice rattled upward. Brutez stood spreading his feet shoulder width apart at the front of two columns of warriors, one led by Vikth and the other by Chief Kevyar. Each of the twelve warriors carried one of the Imperial Swords of Power.

The portcullis snapped into place overhead, and Brutez walked forth from his new stone fortress. He looked back to his family watching from the gatehouse. Beksel stood with their two sons, Brutez and Shemjib. Sejel was left with the caregivers of the smallest children. Zamtoth sat in a raised chair, flanked by Nazzel and young Heptor.

A crowd of men, women, and children from the clans and tribes within Taubueth packed the rampart. Brutez gazed up to a blue dome, bereft of clouds, and felt the scorching heat of the high-summer sun on his face—perhaps for the last time.

The Jatneryim, Boewinyim, and mountain-clan warriors massed in a half circle around the main gate. Sir Grebnar the Bold appeared from their ranks, followed by twelve warriors carrying Imperial Swords of Power that Brutez sent to them that morning. The tournament winner would take all twenty-four ancient broadswords.

The ranks commenced a chant.

"Boldness! Boldness! Boldness!"

They butted spear shafts on the ground.

"Boldness!" Thump! "Boldness!" Thump! "Boldness!" Thump!

Brutez and Grebnar approached one another, followed by

their entourage of swordsmen. Grebnar was bare compared to Brutez—no chainmail, no vambraces, no gloves, no tunic, and no jerkin—only trousers and boots, and a cudgel. His bulging musculature was impressive for a man with a half century of years: flexed biceps, contoured pectorals gnarled with his birthmarksign, and a taut grid for abdominals. He held up his hand without the cudgel, and the deafening chant from his warriors ceased.

Brutez dropped his cudgel and took off his gloves and vambraces. He removed the coif from his head and the chain links from his neck and shoulders, dropping them next to the gloves and vambraces on the ground. Unlashing the jerkin, he took it off and finished stripping to the waist by pulling the tunic over his head.

Something about Grebnar's intense brown-eyed gaze seemed different until Brutez realized he shaved off his linear mustache. Brutez picked up his cudgel and stared his opponent in the face.

The twenty-four swordsmen formed themselves into a square around them, six to a side. One by one they stuck their blades into the ground, keeping hold of the hilts with both hands at their waists. The six on one side were Vikth, Zzuz, Jonerch, Gordib, Sangern, and Chrenlon. The jewels in the hilts sparkled in the sunlight. The six behind Brutez were Kevyar, Chief Hamunth, Lord Chieftain Feldram, Lord Chrevram, Wikston, and Grapnef. Brutez recognized Puutnam among the Jatneryim contingent of swordsmen, and also Sir Rendif's wedlock sons, Fidezz and Varnzper, whom he fought alongside in battle.

Brutez and Grebnar stepped away from one another so Larboelm could implant the pole with the iron blooddrop into the ground between them. Larboelm gathered everything Brutez discarded, and took it away from the square. A youth stood outside the square with the helmet and shield Brutez no longer planned to use.

Brutez grabbed the standard pole below the iron blooddrop,

fixing his eyes on Grebnar, and gripped his cudgel tighter in his other hand, shouting, "Hail the Snarshyim warrior, Sir Grebnar the Bold! If I fall, do you pledge fealty to him as your lord?"

The twenty-four swordsmen responded, "Hail the Snarshyim warrior, Sir Grebnar the Bold! If you fall, we pledge fealty to him as our lord!"

The men, women, and children on the wall of Taubueth, and the ranks of warriors outside the fortress, over a thousand voices, yelled, "Hail the Snarshyim warrior, Sir Grebnar the Bold! If you fall, we pledge fealty to him as our lord!"

The warriors massed in a half circle resumed their chant.

"Boldness! Boldness! Boldness!"

Grebnar grabbed the standard next to where Brutez held it. When the chant from his side diminished, he shouted, "Hail the Snarshyim warrior, Herk Brutez! If I fall, do you pledge fealty to him as your lord?"

"Hail the Snarshyim warrior, Herk Brutez! If you fall, we pledge fealty to him as our lord!" the swordsmen shouted.

"Hail the Snarshyim warrior, Herk Brutez! If you fall, we pledge fealty to him as our lord!" the assembly repeated, everyone except the Boewinyim warriors with the sapphire blue tassel banners.

Brutez and Grebnar readied cudgels. They dodged around the blooddrop standard for some time before Brutez decided to step away from it.

Grebnar charged, cudgel held against his body, and knocked Brutez to the ground.

"Boldness! Boldness! Boldness!"

The combatants were sprawled on the ground, so Brutez could hear Grebnar talking into his ear. "The adulation of my warriors is misplaced."

Regaining their feet, they leaned toward one another swinging cudgels. They traded blows, sounding loud cracks off the wooden handles of their weapons. *Curses!* Grebnar was strong! *And quick.* Brutez soon knew he couldn't win. His opponent's blows came faster and became more furious.

"Boldness! Boldness! Boldness!"

Brutez tired. Grebnar was on him during a lapse of concentration, wrapping an arm around his throat. Brutez dropped his cudgel, gasping for air.

"Boldness! Boldness! Boldness!"

Grebnar's voice hissed into his ear. "You once told me, Brutez, you don't care if you live or die. Is that still true?"

Brutez thought about his wife and sons watching from the gatehouse, and his sweet little girl Sejel. He didn't want to die.

"I thought not," said Grebnar. "Good for you, I still don't care."

His chokehold loosened, and Brutez welcomed an influx of air. Brutez elbowed Grebnar in the groin and escaped his wedlock father's grasp. The chant around them changed as another cheer mingled into the shouts of *Boldness!*

"*Brutez!*"

Brutez recovered his cudgel and resumed exchanging blows with Grebnar. His opponent matched him blow for blow, but Grebnar no longer was faster or more furious. The cheering dissolved into wordless shouting as the parries continued. They paused under the hot sun to rest. Sweat poured from their faces and slicked their bared torsos.

"A convincing fight, Brutez," said Grebnar. Brutez heard him because the crowd's cheering had subsided. "Finish it."

Grebnar lunged, and Brutez blocked his thrust. Crack! The blows quickened. Crack! Crack! Then Grebnar was slow to react, and Brutez landed a blow against his ribs. Crack! That wasn't the meeting of handles, but an iron mallet breaking bone. Grebnar lost hold of his cudgel and reeled back, clutching his side. The spectators gasped.

Brutez advanced. "Wedlock Father, what are you doing?"

"What's best for the Snarshyimt," said Grebnar, wincing in pain.

Brutez lowered his cudgel. "I won't do it."

"Remember your cousins. I never told you I slew them

after they yielded, the sniveling cowards."

Rage surged through Brutez, and he swung his cudgel hard into Grebnar's hip. The pelvic bone was crunched and Grebnar fell to his back. Brutez stood over him, needing to make a final blow.

He looked to the gatehouse. Beksel remained standing between their sons. She gave a signal, pounding a fist into the palm of her other hand. Brutez raised his cudgel in both hands over his head and looked into his wedlock father's brown eyes.

"Dagger," said Grebnar.

Brutez set the cudgel on the ground next to the prone man. He took the blade from his hip and knelt beside him. Placing the knife's edge along the Jatneryim's throat, he looked into the piercing brown eyes for a last time. Grebnar's larynx moved, showing Brutez a desire to speak, so he delayed slicing him.

"Hail Brutez, Lord of the Snarshyimt."

Grebnar closed his eyes, speaking his last, "Twenty-nine."

Twenty-nine, Brutez remembered, the number of Herkt Grebnar had killed. Brutez wouldn't be the thirtieth. He slit Grebnar's throat and placed the dagger on the ground beside his cudgel. He never would use that particular pair of weapons again.

When the last slurping sound of breathing ceased coming from the final cut, Brutez stood and stepped beside the iron blooddrop on the pole. The twenty-four swordsmen still surrounded him in a square, silent as everybody in the crowd.

His men with broadswords came first. Vikth, Zzuz, Jonerch, and Gordib stuck their blades into new spots of ground, this time before his feet. Each gave their oath.

"We declare fealty to you, Brutez, Lord of the Snarshyimt."

Chief Kevyar stabbed his sword into the same area. "The Swenikt declare fealty to you, Brutez, Lord of the Snarshyimt."

Another chief was next. "The Hamuntht declare fealty to you, Brutez, Lord of the Snarshyimt."

Lord Chieftain Feldram came with his sons Sangern and

Chrenlon. Feldram declared, "The Feldramt declare fealty to you, Brutez, Lord of the Snarshyimt."

Lord Chrevram came with his son Wikston. "The Chrevramt declare fealty to you, Brutez, Lord of the Snarshyimt."

Grapnef added a twelfth sword sticking into the ground before Brutez. "The Druogoint declare fealty to you, Brutez, Lord of the Snarshyimt."

The twelve Jatneryimt formed a line, raising their broadswords overhead.

"Brutez, you're Lord of the Jatneryimt, the warriors of the Green and Black Citadels," said Puutnam. "We declare fealty to you, Lord of the Snarshyimt." He stabbed his sword into the ground with the other ones and recited the names of the eleven other Jatneryimt while they did the same. "Fidezz. Varnzper. Shrigen. Waenkth."

Brutez didn't listen to the remaining names, looking to the gatehouse. He saw his father, Nazzel, and Heptor, but his wife and their sons no longer were there. They came from the fortress with Larboelm, passing under the upraised portcullis. Beksel held each son by a hand. She reached Brutez as the last Jatneryim warrior stuck his Imperial Sword of Power into the ground. Brutez accepted the hands of their sons from her, and she collapsed over her father's body to weep.

Standing near, Larboelm shouted, "Hail the Snarshyim warriors! All hail the Snarshyimt!"

More than a thousand voices from Taubueth and the warriors outside the wall repeated the shout to a clear blue sky on a high-summer day. "Hail the Snarshyim warriors! All hail the Snarshyimt!"

Larboelm shouted, "Hail Brutez, Lord of the Snarshyimt!"

The more than thousand shouted, "Hail Brutez, Lord of the Snarshyimt!"

A Snarshgim Kingdom

Herkt, Warnekt

Vinlon   **Taubueth**

"We're almost there, Father." Hoj rode beside Vinlon. His pink and black robes draped over the sides of his mount. "Taubueth is located a horizon from the river."

They headed a column of other riders and carts containing baggage, women, and children traveling along a forest path that wound through the comforting shade of trees on a hot high-summer day without a breath of wind.

A roar like the battle cry of charging warriors echoed through the tree trunks. Vinlon raised a hand to halt the column and turned around. Jaspich was next behind on his mount, and then the carts that transported his wife, son and daughter, mother, and sisters. More warriors came after, including Dekloes and Leenarth. Many of the men brought families, too. Every man, woman, and child, except Hoj, carried the black-ribbon pennant of the tribe. Jaspich's little girl had wrapped hers around her face. Vinlon would have no shortage of banners.

Commanding the warriors to the front, the tribemaster ordered some to remain as guards, and led the rest forward with Hoj and Jaspich. They came to a broad clearing. The way was flat, devoid of pits and rocks. Another roar erupted from a shouting host. Vinlon unsheathed *Shut Up*. His warriors brandished weapons, too.

The shouting men massed outside a wall across the clearing, but they weren't attacking. They only stood watching and waving arms. Vinlon realized the uproar wasn't a battle cry but celebratory cheers. He wondered, *Did somebody sack Taubueth?*

A dust trail moved between the crowd and the wall from one side to the other at the rate of galloping mounts. Vinlon saw riders moving amid the dust, higher than the heads and waving hands of the cheering men, and then he realized equines were racing.

He missed the Druogoinyim spectacle of equines racing, not witnessing one since his last trip to Ranjin decades ago. He abandoned attempts to hold such events among the Warnekt. His tribe preferred archery contests as a means for wagering.

The cheering abated as the racing equines disappeared in a cloud of dust around the far edge of Taubueth, going in a circuit around the fortress. Vinlon sent Dekloes to get the warriors and family left behind on the wooded trail and waited. A resurgence of cheers announced the racers coming around. The shouting reached a crescendo, and the riders stopped by a gate in the wall. The race was over.

The rest of the Warnekt arrived. Vinlon sheathed *Shut Up* and raised his black ribbon, a signal for the others to do the same. He led the way across the open space. Approaching the back ranks of race spectators, the tribemaster was dismayed to see green and black banners among them, but no other standards. His group was advancing into a horde of Jatneryimt.

Too late, they saw, but Vinlon relaxed when their ranks parted, allowing his entourage to pass through among them. He doubted any of them saw Druogoint racing equines before, but they knew the concept of wagering. Men all around transferred whatever they used for currency—food rations, valued weapons or pieces of armor, and precious trinkets.

The fortress loomed ahead. Vinlon thought Hoj exaggerated its size, but he hadn't. The tribemaster saw the great hall's stone roof high inside the fortress and wondered, *How did the Herkt learn about Richeeyim arches?*

Looking for Druogoinyim banners, he spotted pink trapezoids atop the wall. If his estranged wife was watching, he expected her to be easy to spot in a pink gown. He saw pink clothing, but it was only the pleats of Nelber and Kulm's robes.

A woman with wild auburn hair and three children, two girls and a boy, caught his attention. He recognized Darjil, his former mistress from Doesim Falls, and the offspring she claimed were his. Then he saw her father, Tetharng the miller, and a younger man he supposed was her Herkyim husband.

He no longer cared about Darjil and kept looking for the red-haired woman wearing pink. His heart leaped. A red-haired woman he saw didn't wear pink, but the duller shade of her strands was unchanged since he last saw her as a young girl. *Thigrel!*

Hoj nudged him. "Father, here comes the clanlord."

The russet-haired man approached from the open gate with two young boys and a comely chestnut-haired woman holding a weanling girl. A big sandy-haired warrior followed, whom Vinlon remembered he wanted dead. The tribemaster dismounted and stood before his mount. Hoj and Jaspich did likewise.

Clanlord Brutez extended a hand. "Tribemaster Warnek, I'm pleased you're here."

Vinlon shifted the pole with his pennant between his hands and took Brutez's forearm, grasping him at the elbow, while Brutez gripped his. This was the first of their three encounters when the two men actually touched one another. The first time, they came no closer than the Taubueth River between them. The second time, they spoke from boats on the

Pultanik Ocean.

"My son, Hoj, convinced me I had good reason to come." Vinlon looked past Brutez, wondering, *Where's Gernthol? She must be near.*

Brutez released his arm. "What do you think of the fortress?"

The fortress? Vinlon wasn't thinking of the fortress, but now that he did, he wondered why Brutez was proud. A river and an ocean protected Pultanik. This place didn't even have a moat.

"I can't race equines around mine."

Brutez swept a hand toward the open gate. "Come inside."

The clanlord introduced his family.

Vinlon reciprocated. "You know my son, Hoj. He's foresworn marriage and children, so Jaspich is my heir." He indicated the tall, lean young man with him.

A white rectangle with a Herkyim blooddrop on it hung from the battlement over the gate. Vinlon passed under the portcullis, and *there she was*! He saw the pink-gowned woman of his search. Her back was turned to him as she walked away, trailing the long red hair he remembered, although graying, and she had the same lithe form. Then she was gone, disappeared among some tents.

His attention was brought back by a reunion of Hojyimt, as Nelber and Kulm came to Hoj. The three men wearing pink and black robes thumped the backs of one another.

Brutez commanded the man Vinlon wanted dead, "Prepare the old stronghold to accommodate the Warnekt."

"Yes, Clanlord," said the man, and he left.

"My wedlock relations, the Feldramt are close," Brutez told Vinlon. "I'll take you to them for brew and a hot meal. My men will watch your mounts and carts."

Vinlon wanted to listen to Hoj and Nelber talking, so he told Jaspich to lead the group going with Brutez, and that he would follow soon. Then he remembered he had something for Brutez in his pocket.

"You forgot this when you left Pultanik." He handed over a blooddrop pennant, with a smirk.

Brutez smirked, and took the pennant. Vinlon left him with Jaspich, introducing their families to one another, and joined Kulm listening to Hoj and Nelber.

"Hoj, you missed the great spectacle," said Nelber.

"I've seen plenty of races."

"Not that. Clanlord Brutez killed his wedlock father, Sir Grebnar the Bold."

Vinlon doubted what he heard. "Why?"

"Sir Grebnar challenged Brutez to single combat to determine who becomes Lord of the Snarshyimt. Brutez slew him outside this gate before the whole assembly."

As much as Vinlon regretted missing equines race, he would have liked to have seen one of the men who besieged Pultanik seven years ago kill the other. "Lord of the Snarshyimt. What does that mean?"

"The Jatneryimt and the leaders of the clans and tribes here declared fealty to him, all but Boewin and Mosik."

"The Lord of the Snarshyimt must be basking in his great victory." *No wonder Brutez is overly proud of his fortress,* Vinlon thought.

"He's not," said Nelber. "He didn't want to kill his wedlock father."

Vinlon didn't understand why not. His memory of slaying his wedlock father seven years ago remained gratifying.

Kevyar   Taubueth

"Talk to Tribemaster Warnek about caring for your son at Fenzdiwerp."

Jankwel had that stern expression that made Kevyar cringe. Their relationship improved after their son's birth. That day Kevyar stopped resenting his arranged marriage, and she responded by showing him more affection. He stopped seeing other women. Two years later, after Brutez's wife, Beksel, told her some things, Jankwel began to enjoy their marital relations.

Jorgis had urged Kevyar to tell her Thoiren wasn't his firstborn son. Jankwel wasn't surprised he had a mistress in Fenzdiwerp, but she didn't expect he had another son. She forgave him after time and long talks with Jorgis.

"You must care for your son in Fenzdiwerp," she reminded him more times than necessary, an annoying habit that didn't change.

Tribemaster Warnek's arrival at Taubueth gave him the chance. Jorgis had reminded him of his responsibility, once long ago. Kevyar understood his half brother's sentiment. Chief Thoiren had taken responsibility for Jorgis, his son born out of wedlock.

Jankwel sent Kevyar away to a council with a kiss, not a perfunctory peck, but a passioned meeting of the lips, promising more action for him that night. Hoj called for the council to meet in the Druogoinyim camp because the pink woman, Gernthol, refused to leave her tent after the Warnekt came.

The tent was full when Kevyar arrived, but a stool remained for him to sit. Chief Hamunth, Lord Chieftain Feldram, Lord Chrevram, and Mosik waited with Gernthol and her man with one thumb, Grapnef. All five Hojyimt were present, each wearing his ubiquitous pink and black robe—Adam, Nelber, Kulm, Jorgis, and of course, Hoj.

Kevyar knew one of the three Jatneryimt there, Puutnam, who once traveled to the island town now called Pinkulda.

Puutnam told him who the two others were. "Fidezz and Varnzper are married to Lady Beksel's cousins."

The council started, and Kevyar considered who *wasn't* there. Tribelord Boewin went home with his warriors immediately after Brutez killed Sir Grebnar, without declaring fealty. Tribemaster Warnek's absence was explained by his rift with Hoj's mother, Lady Gernthol, *but where was Brutez?*

Hoj spoke, "My father asked a pertinent question. You declared fealty to Clanlord Brutez as Lord of the Snarshyimt, but what does that mean?"

Kevyar knew what it should mean and stood to talk before anyone else did. "What else can it mean except he's our king?" He knew from his dream of the giant red tree with blood-drops changing to concave-sided triangles that Herkyim kings would rule before Swenikyim kings did.

"I didn't mean that," said Hamunth. "How do we benefit bowing to a king?"

"The Yarsishyimt have one," said Chrevram. "He resolves conflict. Lord Chieftain Feldram, a king could have settled your dispute with Tribelord Boewin."

Feldram flapped his arms as he talked. "I loaned the man warriors, and he *kept* them. Only now, years later, Mosik tells me the ones Boewin claimed were killed had actually switched sides."

"We need a king to deal with men like him, who slices a daughter's face on her wedding day," said Chrevram.

"A king maintains peace," said Kevyar. "Brutez proved he does that."

"My tribe never again need suffer the devastation wrought eight years ago," said Feldram. He looked at the three Jatneryimt. "Your Sir Grebnar the Bold had honor, but Matkulk was a brute. I have the limp, and my son the burn, to show for it."

"We could have caught Matkulk sooner with more help," said Puutnam. "A king could bring the entire force of a kingdom against a troublemaker."

"A king would deliver justice," said Feldram.

"Brutez brings justice," said Kevyar. "He executed my father's murderer, although he was his own brother. Chief Hamunth, he gave you justice, too."

"He gave me the loins of the men who violated my daughter," said Hamunth. He crossed his arms. "I'm hearing convincing arguments for bowing to a king as worthy as Brutez, but the title passes to his descendants. How do we know we're not putting ourselves under the rule of a future tyrant?"

"The Yarsishyim lords retain sovereignty over their domains under their king," said Chrevram. "Their lands are called lordsteads. In return for a crown, Brutez must bestow each of us irrefutable and hereditary dominion over our lordsteads."

"We Jatneryimt give homage to Brutez the same as his Herkyim warriors do," said Puutnam. "Our lands have become part of his domain."

Kevyar sought consensus. "What about the rest of us? Are we agreed? We offer Clanlord Brutez a crown in return for irrefutable and hereditary lordship."

Feldram and Chrevram were quick to agree, and Hamunth did after a moment's thought. Mosik was ambivalent, muttering something about getting help.

The Druogoinyim woman, Gernthol, who hadn't spoken, did now. "We Druogoint don't submit, nor do we declare fealty."

"Your man declared fealty over Sir Grebnar's body," said Kevyar.

"He wasn't supposed to." Gernthol smacked Grapnef's chest.

Grapnef asked, "What was I supposed to do? Everybody else with the fancy swords did."

Hoj spoke for the first time since starting the council. "What Grapnef was supposed to do is irrelevant. I'm Warlord of the Druogoint. I declare our fealty."

Gernthol's face turned red, some shade between the colors of her pink gown and the red of her hair. "Hoj, I'm the leader of the Druogoint." She clenched her fists.

"In my name," said Hoj. "Let's discuss this later, Mother."

"Let's talk now."

Hoj shrugged. "I'll renounce my leadership of the tribe if Toush declares fealty to Brutez as his sovereign king. He'll be granted irrefutable and hereditary dominion over

Druogoinyim lands."

Gernthol unclenched her fists and tossed long strands of hair over her shoulders. A smile formed below her beaklike nose. "That's acceptable if I'm named regent."

The council ended with a discussion about presenting the proposal to Brutez.

Kevyar asked Hoj afterward where to find his father, Vinlon.

"He stays in our camp." Hoj put a hand on Kevyar's shoulder. "You accomplished my council's purpose, Chief. It will be remembered for all time."

"I had my reason," said Kevyar. *His descendants would be kings.*

He went to the old stronghold, which was filled with Warnekyim tents. The day wasn't so hot after a morning with rain and continued cloudiness. Kevyar found Tribemaster Warnek within his tent.

Warnek didn't welcome him. "Chief Kevyar, you once mocked my daughter."

Kevyar thought back to his one previous meeting with him on the raft at Fenzdiwerp, not recalling what he said about his daughter. He could believe it wasn't kind, but the tribemaster could sure sustain a grudge. "I regret that. I came to discuss a different regret."

Vinlon leaned forward with a tankard of brew. "You have my rapt attention."

Kevyar supposed he had been drinking brew all day, at least since lunch. "A woman at Fenzdiwerp has a son."

"Let me guess, *your* son."

"I haven't seen him for six years. He should be coming of age."

"Does your wife know this?"

"I told her."

"A forgiving woman. I wish mine was," said Vinlon, drinking more brew.

"I ask you, Tribemaster, to see the boy and his mother

the next time you visit Fenzdiwerp. They live in a house I bought for them in the upper town where the streamer dumps into the river. I'll give you gold for them, but don't let them squander it."

Vinlon waved his hand without the tankard, as if swatting a fly. "Keep your gold. If the boy can be a warrior, I'll have him trained, or if he has the aptitude to become a forger, he'll become Master Banshim's apprentice. I'll find a future for him."

"You have my gratitude, Tribemaster."

"You can thank me by telling me what happened at Hoj's council."

"We're offering Clanlord Brutez a crown."

"A Snarshyim kingdom." Vinlon tapped his tankard. "That will be fearsome."

Hoj   Taubueth

Hoj peeked into his father's tent. "Father, I have a surprise."

"A good or bad one," said Vinlon.

"The best." Hoj stepped aside for his sister to enter, remaining outside with her young sons.

"Thigrel!"

"Father, Hoj insisted I see you. He told me you tried to save Uncle Toush."

"Thigrel!"

Hoj entered the tent with his nephews. His father held Thigrel in a tight embrace, and she wrapped her arms around him.

"Thigrel!"

Hoj spoke, "Father, do you want to meet your grandsons?"

Vinlon let go of the daughter he hadn't seen for eighteen years. His face streamed with tears. He beckoned to the older boy, "Come, Toush."

Hoj gave his first nephew a reassuring squeeze on the shoulder and urged him forward. The boy accepted an embrace from his grandfather.

Vinlon released Toush. "Did you ever tell me the other one's name?"

Hoj hadn't, waiting for the right time, and this was it. He told his nephew of less than five years, born before he left for Moeleenz, to tell his grandfather his name.

"My name is Vinlon!"

The tribemaster broke into gut-wrenching laughter. "Your grandmother couldn't have liked that!"

"I convinced Thigrel to name him that," said Hoj. "I derived great pleasure from Mother's reaction."

"Come, Vinlon, you deserve the biggest embrace," said the boy's grandfather.

While Vinlon embraced his young namesake, Thigrel asked, "Father, why did you kill Grandfather?"

Vinlon's smile disappeared. The tribemaster released his second grandson. "He insulted me, and he insulted you."

"I don't understand, Father, but Hoj taught me I must forgive, and so I do."

The time for the coronation was upon them, so Thigrel left with her sons.

Vinlon asked his son, "Hoj, aren't you going with them?"

"No, I'm renouncing leadership of the Druogoint. Toush will be Lord of Ranjin."

"Then come with me. Brutez has assigned the Warnekt a choice spot."

Vinlon changed into better clothes, all black. His tunic had loose sleeves with slits in the fabric. The jerkin and trousers were leather. Hoj wasn't concerned with his attire, wearing the same as usual: pink and black robes.

They joined the other Warnekt outside their tents within the old stronghold.

"Hoj is coming with us," Vinlon told Jaspich.

Jaspich convinced the tribemaster to limit their number of

pennants. "Too many would be pretentious." He carried one black ribbon.

Dekloes and Leenarth had two more. The Warnekt avoided much of the crowd flowing into Taubueth's great hall through the main doors outside the old stronghold by climbing into the back of it on stairs from behind the ancient old citadel. They entered the hall on the opposite end from the main doors, overlooking the main floor from a balcony at that end, and stood, having nowhere to sit.

Vinlon was awed by the gigantic stone arches buttressing the side walls and supporting the massive stone roof. "I haven't seen arches this size since Richee. How are the cursed Herkt able to construct bigger ones than my builders?"

Hoj had no answer and watched Snarshyim people from all over the land fill the vast hall. Each clan and tribe entered with modest displays of banners, making Hoj glad Jaspich convinced Vinlon to bring only three of his.

Jatneryim warriors, with a smatter of green and black banners in their ranks, packed an entire side, both the main floor and the side balcony. Maroon patches with dual flaps identified Mosik's mountain clansmen filling the high balcony over the main doors. The opposite side from the Jatneryimt belonged to five tribes—the Swenikt, the Hamuntht, the Feldramt, the Chrevramt, and the Druogoint. The mingled banners, including cobalt blue concaved triangles, amber forked tongues, dual brown triangles, purple notched rectangles, and pink trapezoids, meant the people stood by families rather than tribes, for more families than ever were formed from intertribal marriages.

A flourish of pink caught Hoj's attention, and he watched his mother take a spot not far inside the distant main door. His father couldn't stop watching her.

Large gaps in the walls between the buttressing arches filled the hall with ample light. The place wasn't designed to be heated in winter. Hoj couldn't imagine it being cold. Filled with a standing throng, the hall was stifling hot. The noise of hundreds of chattering people, coming from the main floor and balconies all around, sounded like a mighty wind.

A Herkyim banner, the blooddrop on a white rectangle, appeared at the entrance, hanging from a rod between two standard bearers. They carried it down the center aisle. The windy noise of voices in the hall calmed to a murmur and became silent.

Two lines of warriors followed. The sound of twelve pairs of feet marching in each line echoed from the stone floor. Each man brandished an ancient broadsword, bejeweled and golden-hilted. The swordsmen spaced themselves at even intervals along both sides of the aisle, raising their blades over the path between their lines.

Brutez walked through. He must have visited a Druogoinyim wardrobe because his trousers and tunic were fine-spun, the color of burnt brown leaves in autumn. His red-trimmed leather jerkin was maroon, and his boots were shiny black. A white cape draped over his back.

Beksel followed, wearing a long-sleeved gown, feathered with petals in myriad shades of red. Hoj heard it was fashioned from her wedding dress, still fitting after seven years and three children. The offspring came with her, two boys walking by her side, and a small girl carried by Nazzel. The loyal bodyguard, Larboelm, carried an iron blooddrop standard with the lead group. The old man, Zamtoth, was carried in a chair. The rest of the Herkt followed, none with banners. They stood, filling the aisle after Brutez and his immediate family passed through.

The bearers took the white-fielded blooddrop banner behind a padded bench at the inner end, taking it out from Hoj's view in the balcony. The man about to be crowned king stood with his back to the seat, facing the assembly. A large blooddrop was embroidered on back his white cape. Larboelm stood beside the seat, holding the iron blooddrop. Zamtoth's chair was set to one side. Beksel and the children sat in chairs on the other side, and Brutez sat on his bench. The twenty-four bearers of the Imperial Swords of Power lowered their long blades.

Chief Kevyar came from the side of the five tribes with a Swenikyim pennant. He placed the cobalt blue concaved triangle at Brutez's feet and knelt, bowing his head.

After a moment he raised his head and shouted. His words echoed from the high stone arch roof. "I declare fealty to you, Brutez, my sovereign lord and king!"

Brutez called, "Rise Lord Swenik."

Kevyar did.

Brutez stood, stooping to retrieve Kevyar's pennant. He presented the pennant to Kevyar with a declaration. "Your domain shall be the Lordstead of Swansh, an inheritance to be passed to your rightful heirs."

Kevyar returned to the assembly with his pennant, and Brutez resumed his seat.

Chief Hamunth brought his amber forked-tongue pennant. "I declare fealty to you, Brutez, my sovereign lord and king!"

"Rise Lord Hamunth. Your domain shall be the Lordstead of Pietong, an inheritance to be passed to your rightful heirs."

After Lord Chieftain Feldram declared fealty with his dual brown triangles, Brutez bestowed him his title. "Rise Lord Feldram. Your domain shall be the Lordstead of Kradig, an inheritance to be passed to your rightful heirs."

The next oath involved a purple notched rectangle.

"Rise Lord Chrevram. Your domain shall be the Lordstead of Biepazz, an inheritance to be passed to your rightful heirs."

The pink-clad Gernthol pushed through the crowd from the back of the assembly with Toush, a boy seven years of age carrying a pink trapezoid banner. Vinlon straightened his stance next to Hoj, watching the woman come closer. She helped her grandson remember the words of his oath.

"I declare fealty to you, Brutez, my sovereign lord and king!"

Brutez told the boy, "Rise Lord Druogoin. Your domain shall be the Lordstead of Ranjin, an inheritance to be passed to your rightful heirs. I appoint you, Lady Gernthol, regent over the Lordstead of Ranjin until Lord Druogoin comes of age."

The warriors with Jatneryim green and black banners, twelve in all, placed their standards before Brutez. One was Puutnam, speaking for the group. "We warriors of the Green and Black Citadels declare fealty to you, Lord Herk, Brutez our sovereign king."

The twelve returned to their places, leaving the banners behind. Then Mosik came from the high balcony over the entrance with his maroon banner. He stood facing Brutez seated on the bench, holding his banner on its pole before his face.

"Lord Herk, my banner has two flaps, one for my clan and the other for the clan Matkulk was born into, which you helped me subdue. I'll declare fealty to you as my sovereign lord and king when my banner has six flaps, after you help me subdue the four other mountain clans."

Brutez remained sitting. "Agreed. Then you shall be Lord Mosik and your lordstead the lands of the mountain clans. I invite you to enjoy my hospitality until returning to your lands."

When Mosik turned to depart, Hoj nudged his father. "Our turn."

Vinlon took Jaspich's black-ribbon pennant and followed Hoj down a stairs to the main floor. The assembly remained silent watching them. The four other Hojyimt joined them before Brutez, standing behind in a row of pink and black robes.

Brutez spoke from his seated position. "Tribemaster Warnek. Do you intend to declare fealty? You would be Lord Warnek, and your domain the Lordstead of Pultanik."

Hoj had no inkling how his father would answer.

Vinlon spoke, "Lord Herk, I'll declare fealty if you grant my request."

"Speak it."

Vinlon pointed with outstretched arm to the large warrior standing beside Brutez with the iron blooddrop standard. "I want *that* man put to death!"

Hundreds of chattering voices shattered the silence of the

assembly. Larboelm betrayed no expression, unflinching in his stance.

Brutez raised a hand, and his voice boomed through the hall. "Silence!"

When quiet was restored, he asked Vinlon, "Why do you ask for this man's life?"

"You gave justice to Chief Kevyar by slaying your brother. I want justice for this man killing my wife's brother."

"Larboelm, how do you respond?"

"I killed Tribemaster Warnek's wedlock brother, Toush the son of Warlord Druogoin, by order of Clanlord Vulrath of the Herkt."

Brutez fixed his eyes on Vinlon. "This man is loyal and true. He won't be put to death."

"Tribemaster Warnek," a woman's voice called from the back of the assembly. All looked to the woman dressed in pink. "Will you declare fealty to the king?"

A path parted in the crowd between Gernthol and Vinlon. Hoj's parents faced one another, a hall's length apart. Vinlon's gray eyes froze in cold fury. Gernthol returned the piercing stare, hands on her narrow hips. Everyone waited.

Vinlon turned to face Brutez, yelling, "I won't!"

Brutez again shouted the assembly to silence.

"Tribemaster Warnek, I invite you to enjoy my hospitality until returning to your lands. I wish for the peace we've known between us the past seven years to continue. If you stay out of my kingdom, my lords and I will stay out of your lands."

"Agreed."

Vinlon returned with his long black pennant up the stairs to the other Warnekt in the balcony, and all of them vacated the hall.

When they were gone, Hoj spoke to the seated man before him. "Rise, King Brutez."

The king stood.

Hoj declared, "Governments are established by the one sovereign God. King Brutez, you answer to him, the Lord of

Creation."

Brutez bowed. A crown for his head would be fashioned later.

"Hail to you Lord Herk and King Brutez," Hoj proclaimed. "Your domains shall be the Lordstead of Taubueth and the Kingdom of the Snarshyimt, inheritances to be passed to your rightful heirs."

Hoj turned around to face the whole assembly that packed the main floor and three of the four balconies in the great hall of Taubueth. He shouted, "Hail King Brutez, Lord of the Snarshyimt!"

The response was deafening. "Hail King Brutez, Lord of the Snarshyimt!"

BRUTEZ   **TAUBUETH**

King Brutez listened to his firstborn son read from a child's version of God's words that his mother wrote for him. The queen sat by the boy across the table in their quarters, ready to assist with any word he had trouble reading.

"After God made the animals, he made the first man and woman, Adam and Eve. All he made was very good. Then God rested."

The king resumed reading a small scroll with excerpts about the Yarsishyim kings Wikston had translated for him from a longer one in the Yarsishyim language. He tapped a spot in the scroll. "Beksel, it says here each lord sends some of his people to live with the king. It's called the royal court."

Prince Brutez paused from reading about the Garden of Eden.

"You have that now, the resident envoys and their families," said Beksel.

Brutez smiled. He knew more about being a king than he thought.

A knock brought him to the chamber's outer door, the way to the stairs going up to the outbuilding of herbs and remedies. The visitors were an unlikely couple, Lord Hamunth and Aunt Yeemzal.

"The chief," she said.

"Lord Hamunth," he said.

"Lord Hamunth." Yeemzal breathed deep before saying the rest. "The Lord of Pietong and I desire to be married."

Brutez didn't know what to do except embrace her and congratulate Hamunth. Beksel came for her round of embraces.

"We need somebody to say my father's part," said Yeemzal. "The old lord chieftain is long gone, so we're thinking who better than our sovereign lord and king?"

Brutez remembered the terrible night in the next room where he told her Shemjib was dead, and now he would be giving her to her next husband.

"None better, Aunt Yeemzal. When is this marriage taking place?"

"Before lunch in the hall upstairs."

"Both of our tribes are bringing food for the meal afterward," said Hamunth.

"I'll provide brew," said Brutez.

Their families convened in the donjon's main hall. Hamunth had a fresh-shaved head and face. He wore a straw-yellow tunic similar to the color of Larzil's hair, with a tan stagskin jerkin and similar trousers.

He spoke his first portion of the words. "It is not good for a man to be alone."

Brutez held Yeemzal's hand. Her gown mixed the Feldramyim and Herkyim colors, brown and red, and was lashed to pinch her waist as narrow as any maiden. The neckline plunged so far Brutez had never before seen so much of her breasts.

The king spoke his part. "You will have a helper suitable for you."

He released his aunt's hand, and she joined hands with

Hamunth.

The bridegroom took a scroll from Adam to read the rest of his words, rather than trying to remember them. "This is bone of my bones, and flesh of my flesh. She shall be called Woman, because she was taken out of Man. For this reason a man shall leave his father and his mother, and be joined to his wife; and we shall become one flesh."

Hamunth rolled the scroll closed. "One flesh at least twice a year," he said with a laugh.

Yeemzal had her second husband and a brood of stepchildren, and finally, Hamunth had his first wife.

Brutez spoke the first words to the newlywed couple so only they could hear. "Aunt Yeemzal, you once offered me your chambers for the night, and all I did was sleep. I offer you the same chambers for tonight."

Yeemzal and Hamunth looked at one another and said together, "We're not sleeping."

Epilogue

One hundred thirty-two years after the coronation of Brutez as King of the Snarshyimt, Hojyim scholars devised the modern calendar. That year was declared the one thousandth year of recorded history, based on the known Iriack writings at the time.

During the thirty-four years King Brutez ruled from Taubueth, the boundary of the kingdom reached the northern sea. Chrevram Wikston conquered Neshim, helped by his Yarsishyim relations, and captured Tribelord Boewin, whom he executed. He declared fealty to King Brutez at Taubueth, receiving from the king the title as the first Lord Wikston, Lord of Langech. Mosik declared fealty to the king after Brutez helped him subdue the other mountain clans. Expanding his rule westward to the end of the Swanshyim Forest, King Brutez subdued peoples not speaking the Snarshyim language, so the kingdom became an empire.

Tribemaster Vinlon of the Warnek never submitted to the crown at Taubueth to the end of his long life after the death of King Brutez. His longtime heir Jaspich became tribemaster and declared fealty to King Brutez the Second, so the Lordstead of Pultanik finally was added to the Snarshyim Empire. Brutez the Second pushed the imperial border westward to Moeleenzyim lands.

When Brutez the Second died in Recorded Year 933, Brutez the Third, the grandson of the founder of the First Herk Dynasty, acceded to the imperial throne. The Moeleenzyim tribes, united under a common sky blue rectangular banner, joined the Snarshyim Empire the same year by proclamation, so all the Snarshyim clans and tribes were ruled by the king at Taubueth. The Queen Grandmother Beksel lived to see the fulfillment of her husband's vision. The empire spanned a distance of five hundred horizons, lasting for 862 more years, and from its ashes rose the modern Snarshyim nation, a great nation for the rest of history.

Characters

Female names end with "l."

Herkt ⋂⋃⋎⊓
(Taubueth ⊓⋃σ∞⊃⊂ **)**

    Brutez, young warrior
    Heptor, younger brother of Brutez
    Zamtoth, father of Brutez and Heptor
    Zamtoth, slain oldest brother of Brutez
    Makstim, slain older brother of Brutez
    Hartezz, slain older brother of Brutez
    Shemjib, younger brother of Zamtoth
    Yeemzal, wife of Shemjib, sister of Lord Chieftain Feldram
    Rankeb, friend of Heptor
    Konrash, brother of Rankeb, friend of Heptor
    Nazzel, consort of Heptor
    Vel, woman from the ridge
    Vikth, half brother of Vel
    Zzuz, brother of Vel
    Jonerch, friend of Brutez
    Gordib, friend of Brutez
    Clanlord Vulrath
    Klinteg, nephew of Vulrath
    Larboelm, bodyguard of Vulrath
    Fenchrous, Blue River warrior

Jatneryimt ⊂⊥⊃ᴎ⋃⊃ᴦ0⋃ᴍ
(Doenesh ᴦᴏᴎ⋃⋃ a.k.a. Green Citadel)
(Mapvin ᴦ⊥⊃σ⋃ᴎ a.k.a. Black Citadel)
    Sir Grebnar the Bold
    Sir Rendif, Lord of the Jatneryimt
    Sejel, wife of Grebnar, sister of Rendif
    Chakstim, slain son of Grebnar and Sejel
    Rendif, slain son of Grebnar and Sejel
    Beksel, daughter of Grebnar and Sejel
    Puutnam, second cousin of Beksel
    Tersol, cousin of Sejel
    Matkulk, Lord of Mapvin
    Tharkwip, slain best friend of Grebnar
    Fidezz, wedlock son of Sir Rendif
    Varnzper, wedlock son of Sir Rendif
    Shrigen, bodyguard of Sir Grebnar the Bold
    Waenkth, bodyguard of Sir Grebnar the Bold

Warnekt ⋃⊥⊃ᴎ⋃ᴛ⊐
(Pultanik ⊃ω⊃⊐⊥ᴎ⋃ᴛ)
(Habergenefinanch ᴎ⊥σ⋃⊃ω⋃ᴎ⋃ᴄ⋃ᴎ⊥ᴦ0)
(Fenzdiwerp ⊂⋃ᴛᴄᴦ⋃⋃ᴎ⊃)
(Doesim Falls)
    Tribemaster Vinlon
    Radzig, subordinate and friend of Vinlon
    Yazdil, wife of Radzig
    Jaspich, son of Radzig and Yazdil

Banshim, master forger
Zzinel, daughter of Banshim
Leenarth, master archer
Dekloes, subordinate of Tribemaster Vinlon
Darjil, woman from Doesim Falls
Tetharng, father of Darjil
Spear, a male feline
Birdbane, a female feline

Swenikt ⌒ᴜᴜᴜꞋᴜ⋎⊓
(Pinkulda ⊃ᴜꞋ⋎ᴜ⊃ꞋᴜЈ**)**

Chief Thoiren
Befdaul, wife of Thoiren
Kevyar, son of Thoiren and Befdaul
Jankwel, wife of Kevyar
Davlek, was married to now-deceased daughter of Thoiren and Befdaul
Zuedon, father of Jankwel
Jorgis, son of Thoiren and a Chizdekyim woman, betrothed to Hamunth Larzil
Pokyer, servant of Jorgis

Hamuntht ⋂ЈᴦᴡꞋ⊃⊂⊓
(Pietong ⊃Ω⊓ᴜꞋꞋ**)**
(Chizdek ⊃ᴜ⊂Ꞌᴜ⋎**)**

Chief Hamunth
Larzil, daughter of Chief Hamunth and a Chizdekyim woman, betrothed to Swenik Jorgis

428 FEALTY TO THE KING

Buerosh, son of Chief Hamunth
Fidrek, son of Chief Hamunth
Adam, Chizdekyim bodyguard of Chief Hamunth
Enoch, Chizdekyim bodyguard of Chief Hamunth

Druogoint ᒣᑐᎬᏌᏒᎵᒣ
(Ranjin ᑐᒐᒍᏕᏌᏒ)

Warlord Druogoin

Gernthol, daughter of Warlord Druogoin, estranged wife of Warnek Vinlon, "Pink Lady"

Hoj, son of Gernthol and estranged son of Warnek Vinlon

Thigrel, daughter of Gernthol and estranged daughter of Warnek Vinlon

Nelber, subordinate of Warlord Druogoin

Kulm, son of Nelber

Pershnig, Gernthol's paramour

Grapnef, subordinate of Warlord Druogoin

Feldramt ᏟᏌᎠᎵᑐᒐᒣ
(Kradig ᎢᑐᒐᎴᏌᏕ)
(Agratuna ᒐᏕᑐᒐᎴᏬᎵᒐ)

Lord Chieftain Feldram

Majdel, wife of Lord Chieftain Feldram, daughter of Herk Zamtoth

Sangern, son of Lord Chieftain Feldram and Majdel

Chrenlon, son of Lord Chieftain Feldram and Majdel

Tarberg, subordinate of Lord Chieftain Feldram

Chrevramt ⟨script⟩
(Biepazz ⟨script⟩)
Lord Chrevram, cousin of Tribelord Boewin
Lady Chrevram, wife of Lord Chrevram
Wikston, son of Lord and Lady Chrevram
Zabfrul, daughter of Lord and Lady Chrevram
Steebnaf, subordinate of Lord Chrevram

Boewint ⟨script⟩
(Langech ⟨script⟩)
(Neshim ⟨script⟩)
Tribelord Boewin, cousin of Lord Chrevram
Lady Boewin, wife of Tribelord Boewin

Mountain Clan
Mosik, clan leader

Snarshyim ⌐∩⌐⌐┌┌o∪⌐ Language Primer

The written Snarshyim language is phonetic. All words are spelled exactly as they sound. The language has twenty-two consonant (framing) sounds and fifteen vowel (connecting) sounds, all represented by their own symbol in the Snarshyim alphabet.

The twenty-two lowercase consonants are listed below in Snarshyim and English. Uppercase Snarshyim symbols are formed by adding ⌐ to the front of the lowercase symbols. For instance, ⌐∩ is "G." Uppercase symbols are used only to start sentences. Proper nouns use all lowercase symbols, such as in Snarshyim's spelling of itself above.

Some Snarshyim symbols can be combined to form a blended symbol. For instance, ⌐⌐ is "br." For blends where the two portions of the symbol don't connect, a connector is added. For instance, ⌐∪ is "sw." For another example, note how the "sn" and "rsh" are connected in Snarshyim's spelling of itself above.

    σ b
    ᴅ ch (as in *church*, so "chr" is used for "tr" sounds as in *tree*)
    ɾ d
    ⊂ f
    ѕ g
    ɴ h
    ꭓ j
    ⊤ k (used for hard "c" sounds as in *cat*)
    Ɔ l
    ⌐ m
    ⋎ n
    Ɔ p
    Ɔ r

◡ s (used for soft "c" sounds as in *cell*)

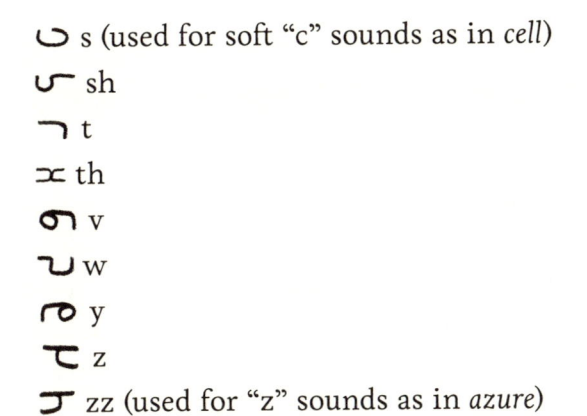

ʊ̄ sh

┐ t

⌶ th

ʕ v

ᴗ̄ w

ɾ̊ y

ʧ z

ʒ zz (used for "z" sounds as in *azure*)

The Snarshyim language has no consonants for "c," "q," and "x." The "c" sound uses "k" or "s" as previously noted, the "q" sound uses "k" ("kw" is used for "qu" sounds as in *queen*), and the "x" sound uses "eks."

The fifteen lowercase vowels are translated into English as follows:

⌣ a (same as in *bat*)

⌊ ae (same as in *bait*)

⌣̄ au (same as in *bought*)

ᴗ e (same as in *bet*)

₀ ee (same as in *beat*)

ᴜ i (same as in *bit*)

ᴖ ie (same as in *bite*)

⌣ o (same as in *cot*)

○ oe (same as in *boat*)

⊋ oi (same as in *boy*)

⊂ ou (same as in *bout*)

ɰ u (same as in *putt*)

∞ ue (same as in *fuel*)

ᴗ uo (same as in *boot*)

ᴗ̊ uu (same as in *put*)

Few Snarshyim words start or end with a vowel. Ones that do usually are taken from other languages. In the rare case of an uppercase vowel, the same ⌣ is added to the front of the lowercase vowel. For "A," "AU," "E," "EE," and "OU" where the two portions of the uppercase vowel don't connect, a connector is added. For instance, ⌣‿ is "A."

Snarshyim words rarely use consecutive vowels such as in *lion*. The ones that do usually are taken from other languages, and native Snarshyim speakers have difficulty pronouncing them.

The plural forms of Snarshyim nouns end with "t," no exceptions, therefore no Snarshyim singular nouns end with "t." No Snarshyim nouns end with "d" because Snarshyim verb infinitives end with "d." Names taken from other languages ending with "t" or "d" are changed to end with another framing sound, usually "sh" or "th."

The "–yim" suffix is the equivalent of "–ish" or "–ite," so *Herkyim* is equivalent to *Herkish*, and *Jatneryim* is equivalent to *Jatnerite*.

The Snarshyim language combines words into longer words such as in German. Nouns and adjectives are ordered from general to specific, and so *fenz*, which means *town*, precedes *diwerp*, which means *farming*, a specific type of town, and together *Fenzdiwerp* means *Farming Town* or *Farmington*.

In the same manner, names are ordered from general to specific, so family names precede given names as in Korean and other Oriental languages. So the clanlord's name is *Herk Brutez*, and the tribemaster's name is *Warnek Vinlon*.

Glossary

Backhorn—Goat-like animal

Barn fowl—Chicken-like bird

Birthcordspot—Belly button

Birthmarksign—Scabby lump everyone is born with on the skin over the heart

Bovine—Animal like cattle or oxen

Bushtail—Squirrel-like rodent

Canine—Dog-like animal

Cubit—Distance from the tip of the forefinger to the elbow, about eighteen inches

Darkwing—Bat-like mammal

Deep Winter—Shortest day of the year or thereabout

Equine—Horse-like animal

Feline—Cat-like animal

Firerock—Rare translucent rock that retains light and glows

Flatsnout—Pig-like animal (flatsnout strips are bacon)

High Summer—Longest day of the year or thereabout

Hoof Ring—Horseshoe

Horizon—Distance to the horizon from eye-level over flat terrain, about 3 miles or 10,000 cubits

Longear—Rabbit-like animal

Lupine—Wolf-like animal

Marshbill—Duck-like bird

Moonstar—Luminous point of light next to the moon, brighter than any star or planet

Skimmer—Canoe

Starch Root—Potato-like food

Streamer—Urination trough

Ursine—Bear-like animal

Vinefruit—Grapes

Vulpine—Fox-like animal

Webspinster—Spider-like insect

Wedgewing—Goose-like bird

Wedlock Brother—Brother-in-law

Wedlock Daughter—Daughter-in-law

Wedlock Father—Father-in-law

Wedlock Mother—Mother-in-law

Wedlock Sister—Sister-in-law

Wedlock Son—Son-in-law

Woolstock—Sheep-like animals

The opening chapter from the next novel

BASED ON THE HISTORY OF THE MODERN SNARSHYIM NATION
FOREBODING... RECORDED YEAR 1996

Flower Bombs

*Makeland 11th Budding In
(Tuesday, April 1st)*

SENCH ZUEDON   **TAUZZREEN**

A distant rumble, coming closer, preceded any sighting of the treads. The ground trembled underfoot, and water rippled in Mayor Sench Zuedon's cup. A crowd stood three to five rows deep along both sides of Tauzzreen Avenue, a thoroughfare of the city with the same name. These men and women were supposed to be on holiday, and the children had no school. They all were wearing light coats, and some wore hats on this crisp early spring day.

    The mayor stood on a temporary wooden platform outside the city offices with other local dignitaries and their families. He shielded his eyes from the bright glare of sunlight, and considered the azure dome overhead, unblemished by clouds. "This could have been a fine Founding Day with this nice weather."

His wife, Larzil, swept a long fluff of blond hair from her face and leaned on his shoulder. "We've had warmer ones."

And worse, Zuedon thought. *Last year we had snow.* Founding Day, the eleventh day after New Year, could have any weather. At least no wind stirred this year's crisp air.

His brother, Bronlan, flanked his other side. "This day would have been plenty good for the parade."

The usual Founding Day parade of fire trucks, fancy coaches, street performers, bands, and civic groups walking behind banners was pre-empted. The avenue's four lanes were devoid of traffic, and no coaches filled any of the parallel parking spaces lining the curbs. The rumble of the imposter parade approached, becoming a louder metallic clatter.

Bronlan pointed. "Here they come."

The lead treads appeared coming around a quarter turn in Tauzzreen Avenue by a great hill less than a horizon westward. The steep slope provided a backdrop of needled trees. More rows of the fearsome war machines followed three-wide across the avenue, sprouting the big barrels of their main armaments, and bristling with repeaters. Their tracks tore the pavement to pieces.

"Curses, we just resurfaced this street," said Zuedon.

His business associate, Sidlim Jonerch, leaned forward from behind. "This is an outrage, Zuedon. The army could have paraded these treads without unloading them from their trucks."

"The chancellor is overplaying his power." Zuedon had hoped so, although it was not Chancellor Robintz Vinlon, but the men using him. "He doesn't realize the effect of a government invading its own city."

My city, Zuedon mused, a city of his own making. Today Tauzzreen would be celebrating the seventeenth year since its founding, if it wasn't being put under martial law. Its original name was Fenzsench (*Senchtown*) before Larzil convinced him that was pretentious, and so he renamed it after the river flowing through it.

"They're not shy about displaying the colors," said Bronlan.

Each tread flew the Snarshyim national flag from its communication antenna. The flag had a cobalt blue background with a stylized rendition of a great red bird rising from a fire. The bird's head was a concave-sided triangle between outstretched wings, with tapered streamers for feathers.

A man stood stiff-backed in the hatch of the lead row's middle tread, holding onto hand bars by his hips. As the armored formation clattered closer, passing through the nearest intersection of a cross street to Tauzzreen Avenue, the details of his dress uniform became visible. It had a geometric pattern of black leather and gray woolstock with red trim and battle ribbons in a plethora of color across his chest. Pips on his hat and shoulders indicated his rank.

Sidlim nudged Zuedon. "General Warnedeker? I thought he was a larger man."

Zuedon never had met Warnedeker, but his government moles kept him informed. The chancellor's advisors considered him to be the only general with the audacity to occupy a domestic city.

"He's less than four cubits," said Zuedon. The clattering of tracks churning up the pavement, and the roar of engines, had become so loud he had to shout. "No taller than you, Jonerch."

A deeper droning sound seemed to oscillate from the shaking ground, but increasing in pitch and volume, the noise came overhead. Bronlan pointed to fighter aircraft coming up the valley over the Tauzzreen River, several squadrons flying in wedge formations. The shrill whine of high-spun engines and propellers overwhelmed the cacophony of the treads.

Zuedon gazed upward to dozens of silver aircraft passing overhead with barely enough altitude to clear the tallest buildings of central Tauzzreen. The formations continued northward on way, he supposed, to buzz his mansions on the lakeshore.

"An outrage!" Sidlim shouted after the fighters became

distant enough for him to be heard. "Those are your Tornadoes, Bronlan!"

Zuedon expected no less, that the military would use the aircraft constructed by his brother's company in the show of force. "They're trying to provoke us."

"What are we going to do, Zuedon?"

"Not what they want. We're not doing anything."

Warnedeker Vikth — Tauzzreen

Cursed Air Command! Warnedeker Vikth refused to look up. If he commanded the squadrons, he would have left them on the ground. Last year the general had opposed separating the air attack and defense forces from army command. Bad enough the navy commanded itself, and more irksome, since the coming of platform ships, the sea force maintained its own air units, and his son was a flyer in one.

Warnedeker didn't approve of unloading the treads from the trucks either. Why the provocation? Chancellor Robintz seemed to want the locals to fight back. The general's duty was to obey, even when orders from his civilian superiors made no sense. Warnedeker recognized his role of protecting the freedom of the Snarshyim people. The Kwatarthyimt and the Noldeesyimt lived in countries with military governments, and those were repressive regimes.

Not that Sench Zuedon shouldn't be put in his place, Warnedeker considered. Sench, the world's richest man, had built Tauzzreen to be his personal empire. Such a man wasn't to be trusted.

The general kept his chin up, surveying the scene of a passive populace standing in ranks on both sides. The young city was impressive, only seventeen years since its founding. The main avenue was a marketplace of thriving businesses, and more buildings were under construction, including a tall one with twenty-five levels. Warnedeker knew from his briefing how the city had its own police and firefighting forces, a school system, and even a college and a university. Its hospital already was considered one of the best. The city also had an express road.

Tauzzreen had become an economic epicenter. The best workers with the brightest minds were relocating there from all over the Snarshyim nation at a rate of a thousand every month. The population soon would surpass a hundred thousand, making Tauzzreen the tenth largest city in the country.

As the city's growth exploded, so did Sench's wealth, and his people adored him while sharing the prosperity. *A dangerous man, and not to be trusted.* Warnedeker understood his government's rationale for its crackdown.

The general spoke into a mouthpiece by the hatch, ordering his tread commander to stop in front of the reviewing stand. He resisted an urge to have the turret turned so its size thirty-six barrel was aimed at Sench and his entourage. The situation already had become too provocative, and children were on the stand.

Sench had nine offspring. *He has too much of everything,* Warnedeker thought, spotting three blond girls of the same age who must be his triplets. Their blond mother, a pleasing woman to look at, was standing by her husband. Warnedeker wondered how she kept herself trim after so much birthing, although with typical Sench efficiency, she produced nine babies in seven gestations.

The general climbed off the tread. He didn't wait for his aides, and ascended the platform to meet Sench Zuedon.

Zuedon removed a knitted band from his ears that made his mass of sandy hair stand upright like a sheaf of grain. He raised his hands, palms open, and smiled. "General Warnedeker, welcome to my city."

My city, he says, Warnedeker pondered. He returned the open-handed greeting. The Snarshyimt, a sensible people, didn't spread illness by touching one another in their salutations.

"My wife, Larzil," Sench introduced.

Sench Larzil's green eyes were as captivating as actual emeralds.

Zuedon identified the other personages on the platform, but Warnedeker knew them from his briefing. Sench Bronlan was Zuedon's older brother. Sidlim Jonerch was second to Zuedon in administering his conglomerate of companies and holdings. The entire Rodents Club, the city's prominent civic group, seemed to be present with the notable exception of Zuedon's best friend, Speendom Chak.

"General, we offer our cooperation," said Zuedon.

"What if I ask you to surrender your firearms?"

"We'll give you whatever you find."

Warnedeker realized he hadn't seen any civilian with a firearm since entering Tauzzreen. None of the Rodents members were visibly armed, nor was anyone in the crowd along the avenue, not even the police. "We won't look."

Zuedon nodded in mutual understanding. Tauzzreen probably was the most armed city in the Snarshyim nation, if not the world, but Warnedeker wouldn't make firearms a concern if he didn't see them.

Sidlim Jonerch wasn't so cordial. He stepped between Zuedon and Warnedeker. "By what authority do you occupy a sovereign city, General?"

"I personally received the order from the chancellor when I met with him in his office."

"He has no authority to deploy troops against citizens within the borders of the Snarshyim nation."

"He does when there's insurrection."

"Insurrection!" Sidlim's face turned blood red, and veins pulsed on his balding head.

Zuedon coaxed his colleague to step aside. "General, I'm not aware of any insurrection."

"You threatened to secede from Swansh."

"Why is the national government concerned because we want to join another sovereign state? Don't you exist to serve the Snarshyim states?"

"We do, and the governor of Swansh appealed to the chancellor."

Zuedon snorted. "Governor No Fun. He ramrodded the law banning flower bombs."

Of course Tauzzreen's dispute with the state government involved more serious matters than flower bombs. Warnedeker knew taxation, and a city with more armaments than some countries, were the real issues. The general smiled. "I'm a fun person. I like flower bombs as much as anyone. Do you have a stockpile for Founding Day?"

"The biggest ever, our way of telling Swansh where to cram its law."

Warnedeker kept smiling. "Mayor Sench, your flower bombs shouldn't be wasted." He would see Tauzzreen celebrating its occupation.

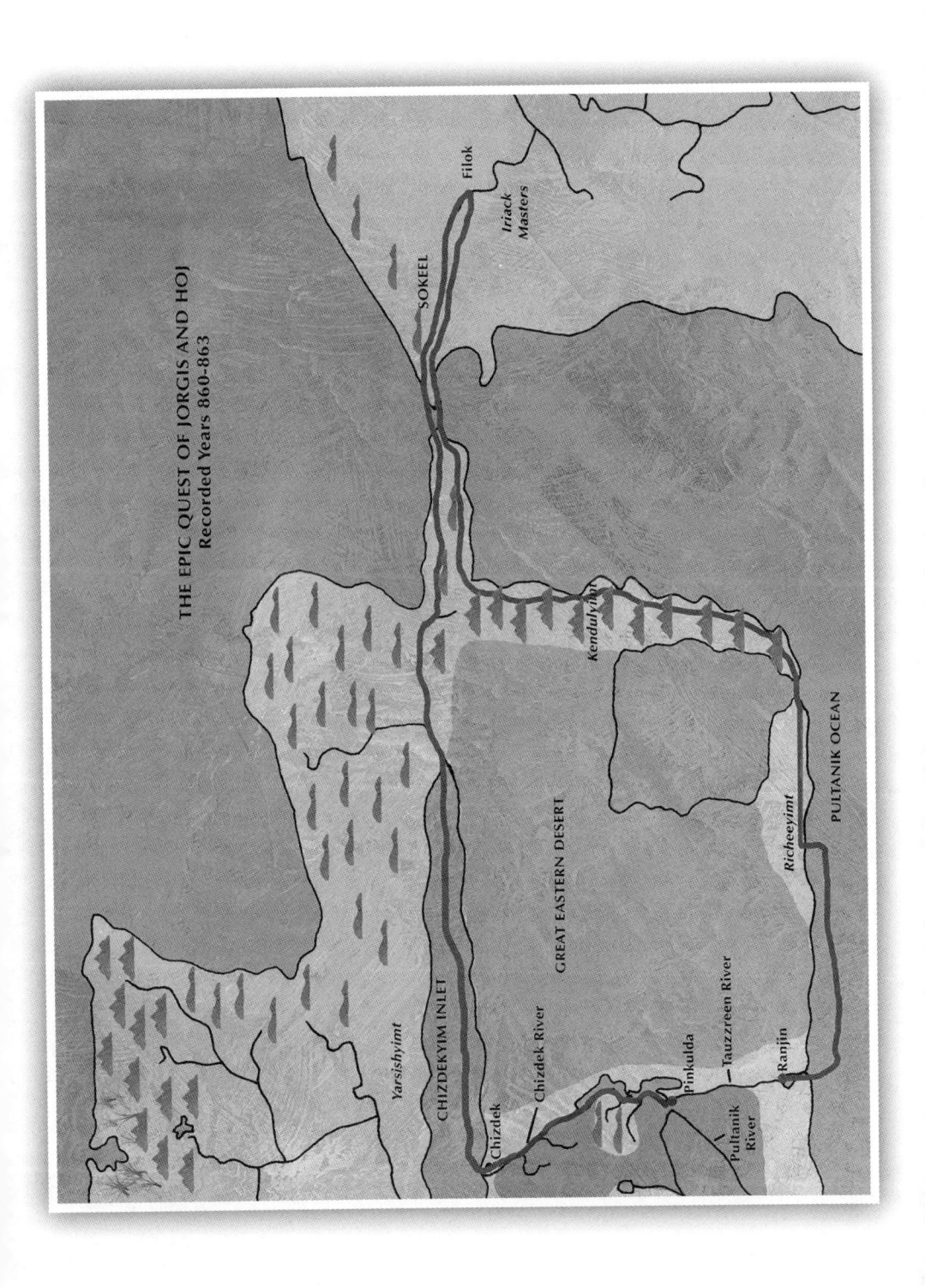

THE EPIC QUEST OF JORGIS AND HOJ
Recorded Years 860-863